Alpha of Her Dreams
A Paranormal Shifter Romance
Vera Foxx

Foxx Fantasy Publishing

First paperback edition: November 2022

Publisher: **Foxx Fantasy Publishing LLC**

Editing by: Cissell Ink

Dedication

To all those who strive to make their dreams into reality.

Contents

Dear Reader

Attention: This book contains content for ages 18+. Werewolves, sex, blood, possessive alphas and a crazy princess are included. There is a dominance and submissive relationship between the two main characters. All consensual.

This book is part of a series but can be read as a stand-alone. You are given enough information to include yourself in the entire story. If you would like to read more about these famous couples, check out the rest of the series at the back of the book.

Enjoy!

Chapter One

Evelyn

Sharp thumps jolted the lanky girl from her sleep. Evelyn sighed loudly, wiping droplets from her brow. She grabbed the smooth bark of the sissiel fern tree. Bark so smooth, it felt like velvet to the touch. Gripping her legs around the thickness of the limb, she listened carefully to the continuous thumping of a nearby ax. Her interest was piqued, her back straightening as she listened. Swaying in the breeze, her frayed and tattered pale pink dress was covered in holes, dirt, and grime.

This tree held many memories for her, too many to count and almost too many to remember. She had grown with this tree; it was planted shortly after the war that her parents had helped win ten years before.

Her parents planted a tree in honor of each child they brought into the world, and they thought this tree would be an excellent reminder of their daughter, who'd lived her first month of life through a war that forever changed the realm. The sissiel fern tree was not like any other tree in Bergarian; it was soft on the outside while most trees were rough and difficult to penetrate. It was so soft; one could easily fall asleep on the wide limbs that extended far into the forest. It reminded her of her mother's gentle demeanor, but the inside of this tree held the strength of her father.

The leaves and vines that hung down from its branches would soothe any troubles the young girl had. The pixies who lived in the tree fluttered down and left soft caresses that danced across the girl's olive skin. Too many times had the girl come to this exact tree to sleep, to get away from her worries.

The thumping continued. The girl shook the sleep from her eye and crawled down from the high branches. Once at the last branch, she jumped, landing perfectly on the balls of her feet. Her dress that had once danced across the marbled floors of the palace now sat halfway up her calf, dirt decorating the fine lace that once threaded around the perfectly tailored dress.

Her hair was a mess, leaves still hidden beneath the layers of curl. She stepped toward the continuous thumping. This was her place, just on the outskirts of the palace grounds. Not even the guards could find her. Her ability to cloak herself came from her alpha abilities; quick thinking aided her.

Deeper into the forest, she strolled confidently, the dried leaves crinkling under her feet until she came to a small clearing, free of any trees. The light sources' rays filtered through the leaves that hung over the clearing. The free-spirited girl paused and watched a woodsman taking his ax and hacking log after log. Staying behind the tree, she watched in awe as he continued. Sweat dripped from his body, soaking his tunic wholly.

He wasn't yet a man, far younger than that, but older than her. His chest was broad, and his muscles rippled with each strike of the log. She knew he was handsome and would be the perfect mate for a woman ever so willing to take in this woodsman, but the thought of him having his arms around another she-wolf gave her an unsettled feeling.

"I know someone is there," he called out, wiping his brow. He threw the ax down, and it struck the stump he used as a platform for his chopping.

"Come on out, I don't bite." The girl scoffed because she very well knew that everyone in this realm could bite, but she came out anyway, standing tall with her shoulders held back.

Her father told her never to show fear, never to let her guard down, but for a brief moment, she did, staring at the strength of this young adult.

"What's a little girl like you doing out here? Shouldn't you have a keeper?" he asked, finally turning. His face was bare of any beard or stubble, and he'd combed his dark sandy locks back with his fingers. The girl scoffed, crossing her arms.

"I'm not some little girl," she spat out. "I'm a warrior, and I don't need any keeper," she growled back at him. The woodsman only chuckled, sitting down on the stump. His linen pants wrinkled beneath him as he bent down to grab his water skin. "I'm serious," she said. "I can beat you up with one arm tied behind my back."

And she very well could; she had pinned warriors that were almost the size of this woodsman. Her father had trained her young, and she was agile and quick like her mother.

"Is that so?" He splashed water over his face, undeterred by her remarks. "No ordinary child would dare come this deep into the woods and not be scared. I guess I'll have to take your word for it."

The woodsman slung his bag over his chest, turning away from her. Evelyn pranced softly in the crunching leaves and jumped over the stump, landing on the woodsman's back. Together, they tumbled onto the ground. He landed with a thud, and Evelyn hid a giggle. She stood up, putting her fists on her hips, proud of her work.

"Hey now!" The woodsman scurried to his feet. "I wasn't ready." He brushed debris from his clothing. The girl smirked, crossing her arms.

"First rule of a warrior is never to let your guard down, and you, woodsman, and you did just that." She wiggled her finger. "Just because you see me as a little girl doesn't mean I'm not ferocious."

"By the way you dress, you do look like some sort of feral," he muttered just loud enough for her to hear.

The girl crossed her arms, ready to howl for her father to come to find this woodsman cutting down his trees until a purple rabbit hopped by from the bushes. Her head tilted until she gently pinched her arm, looking for pain and finding none.

Just a dream.

Yet, she'd found no one else in her dreams like this before. Not unless it was a dream that repeated her day and, in those dreams, she could not change them. "What's your name?" She found herself wanting...wanting to know why this young man was here in her dreams. This was supposed to be her haven. A place where her grandmother couldn't tell her what to do, when to do it, how to eat and dress, how to act. This was her space, and now the young woodsman dared to impinge on her space.

The young woodsman cocked an eyebrow, standing at his full height. He was much taller than her, but that was to be expected because he was almost full grown.

"Why should I give you that?" He crossed his arms. "A name is a powerful thing."

Evelyn shuffled her feet, unable to come up with a reply. She had never been rendered speechless before. People usually gave into her demands, or she at least found an argument to get her way—with her parents anyway, who saw that their daughter was too smart for her own good.

"How is a name powerful?" she asked. "What makes a name so special?"

The woodsman lowered himself to her height, raising an eyebrow. "Because if a demon or a witch has your name, then they can cast spells on you. How am I to know in this dream you are not one of those beings?"

The girl gasped. "You know this is a dream?"

The woodsman nodded, standing up to full height. "Never let your guard down, little girl."

She rolled her eyes at the advice she'd just given him.

"I don't believe you are a demon, but one can't be too careful, not since..."

"The war," she muttered, putting her hands behind her back. The woodsman nodded, grabbing the ax, and turned to the forest.

The girl couldn't understand how he knew this was just a dream. It was *her* dream. She couldn't very well invite others into her dreams. That sounded downright silly. Then again, she was becoming more powerful by the day, and who knew what she would be able to do with her dreaming abilities?

"But you know I'm not a demon." She jumped up beside him. The longing in her voice beckoned him to slow his pace. "I don't hold any evil." She looked up at him. "I'm just a Dream Wanderer."

The woodsman stopped, looking down at her. "I haven't heard of such a thing, little girl."

Evelyn blew out a frustrated breath. About to give her name, she closed her lips tight, scratching her head. He said a name was powerful. Maybe he was one of these demons or warlocks he'd just spoken of.

"You can call me Little Warrior, but not little girl," she snarled. "I'm going to be like my father." She hooked her thump into her chest.

"Strongest of them all, best in battle. Anyway..." she trailed off. Pulling up the torn sleeve of her dress, she showed off the muscle that she'd been building. She was so proud when those muscles showed through, her father had even thrown her a tea party with all her stuffed animals.

The woodsman looked at her thoughtfully, like a piece of a puzzle he couldn't understand.

"A Dream Wanderer is someone who has control of their dreams. I can make anything happen, but you, I can't figure out why you are here. I didn't wish you here," she muttered. "A Dream Wanderer can mold things, create that they want. Sometimes I can even see into the future if I will it hard enough. I'm still learning to control it." She gazed back through the trees like she could see the tree that had started it all.

Evelyn believed that the tree has bestowed magical powers upon her. That it gave her a gift that had downright scared her in the beginning—flashes of the past, of things she had never seen. She couldn't understand the nightmares that haunted her dreams until her mother calmly explained those terrifying images. She could not bend the images to make them softer or more beautiful. They were all in the past, and the past could not be changed.

The woodsman's eyes softened. Evelyn tried to put up the walls she created to appear so strong, but he was seeing right through them. He threw his ax at a nearby tree, and it planted firmly in place into the bark. "You can call me,"—he rubbed his chin in thought—"Guard. Because that is what I strive to be. Someone who protects the things that are the most precious and important." The little warrior smiled, seeing that the stern face he'd worn earlier had faded. He wasn't holding himself away from her any longer. He was leaning towards her, facing her like she was worth listening to. Not dismissing her like she was nothing.

"So, we can be friends, then?" She stuck out her hand. The little warrior didn't have many friends. She was too rough for the girls, and the boys feared her and her father. Not to mention the warriors, she was a ferocious pup in a dress.

"Will you visit some more in my dreams?" The little warrior stood, her hand right in front of him, ready for him to take. His face hardened, and for a split moment, Evelyn thought that he would refuse the gesture. Disappointment filled her.

"You said you did not will me here?" the Guard asked.

The girl shook her head, disappointment flooding her. "I'm not sure how you got here." The little warrior shrugged her shoulders. "But I do wish for you to come back. I'd like to know who you are and what you mean to me. I mean, no one has visited me here before."

"I'm not sure how you got into my dreams," the Guard muttered to himself.

The more the girl stared, the more she came to realize that he didn't believe she was a Dream Wanderer.

"If the gods planted me here, had me see you, then maybe I will see you again." The guard held out his hand to shake. The frown that marked her face rose to a gentle smile, and their hands met.

If only her grandmother could see her now, giving a smile so endearing it would make princes across the realm melt.

Small tickling warmth radiated into their palms, but they dared not let go. They had made a pact to see each other again, even if she couldn't control the man that stood in her dreams.

The girl's shoulder shook, her arm pulling and pushing against the Guard's. He looked down in question until she shrugged her shoulders. "Someone is waking me. I must go," she said, pulling away. The Guard looked at her longingly, like he wasn't ready for her to vanish, but before another word was said, someone whispered "Evelyn" in her ears.

⁂

"Evelyn." The whisper became louder until my eyes batted open to see my mother sitting on the bed. I hummed, sitting up and pushing away my tangled hair.

"Having one of your dreams again?" my mother asked softly, rising from the bed. She glided across the floor, her tea-length dress swaying, and pulled away the thick curtains with her gentle fingers. The light sources shone through the floor-to-ceiling windows overlooking the Cerulean Moon Kingdom.

"Yeah, I did," I muttered, swinging my legs over the bed.

"A dream from the past? Or did you create a new one?" Mom poured me a glass of water from the nightstand.

"Of the past." I looked inside my cup. "And it was my favorite one."

Chapter Two

Evelyn

"Late, late, late," I muttered, trying to put on the obnoxious heels grandmother made me wear. The castle halls were long, and time was always short, especially when lessons started at eight.

Who in their right mind wants to get up that early to read a book? Play the piano? Anything that uses your brain?

Now, physical labor, fighting and sparring? That was something I could get behind. Rolling in the dirt, climbing trees, sparring with the royal soldiers, even if they were complete wussies about fighting with a princess. Rolling my eyes, I rounded the corner, bumping into one of the royal guards.

Thumping into his chest with my hardened head, I caught myself before falling on my ass; luckily for me, his stance never wavered. "Late again, princess?" Joshua raised an eyebrow. His cleanly shaven face, buzzed haircut, and thick bushy eyebrows didn't deter me from staring at the monstrosity, as I hopped on one foot to put on the other heel.

"I'm not late," I scoffed. "Everyone else is ridiculously early." I waved as I ran down the carpeted hallway. The thick walls of the palace were constructed mostly with stone. Some hallways didn't have the enormous bay windows that the outer hallways of the palace had. Candles and torches had been the raging commodity around here until mom took over. She at least had some sense in that regard, wanting to use more magic to light the darker hallways.

Mom hated the dark. She loved the bright light of the Golden Light Kingdom, and she was slowly redecorating. So slow, it had been almost eighteen years to the day.

Now, small white orbs filled the torches and flickered on and off as people came and went, saving the castle enough money to fund more free food markets for those that needed it. If only grandmother could see it that way, she was still stuck in the past—always complaining that everything was fine before.

Grandmother wasn't one for change, and Pop wasn't going to fight her unless he had to. He was the calm one of the relationship, but he could be a complete push-over at times.

I hopped one more time, making sure the heel of my foot sat firmly in the shoe, and pushed open the door to the dungeon-like classroom. No windows, just four walls of lightly colored stone filled with posters of kingdoms, earth, and the gods. All eyes sat on me as I brushed my hair back, gracefully swinging it into the breeze I created with my fast movement and slid across the room to my front and center seat.

Take that, grandma. See how graceful I can be?

"Are you finished with your theatrics, Evelyn?" My grandmother, Eden, the former queen of the Cerulean Moon Kingdom, tightened her jaw and folded her hands against her overly extravagant dress. Her platinum blonde hair was braided to perfection, not a single piece out of place, and curved around her shoulder, laying over her breast.

Mikel, her son, snickered beside me, nudging me with his elbow. It was almost comical, in a human aspect, to have an uncle that was only three months younger than you, but in the supernatural world, that was just the norm. We were more like brother and sister but completely opposite in personalities. Thank the gods he didn't inherit his mother's stuck-up attitude and knew how to let loose a little.

"Evelyn, you are two minutes late." She pulled out her pocket watch from the bodice of her dress. "How many times do I need to remind you that being punctual is—"

"...the most important task that a princess should have. It is the pivotal movement in negotiations with other countries and most of all, shows a sign of respect for those around you," I finished her quote with my nose stuck in the air. Grandmother's eye twitched, and Melody, my sister—sitting behind me—tapped my shoulder.

"She isn't in the mood, Evie. I suggest you lay off today." Melody retreated behind me, her nose back in some other book she liked to read. Melody and I had a fine relationship, but we were almost too different. She preferred the quiet life, head behind a book. I, on the other hand, was always ready to jump into a new adventure.

"Sorry, grandmother." I cleared my throat. "My lateness is inexcusable." My grandmother's stance softened, her finger tangling with the pull-down string of the map of Bergarian. She revealed the title of today's lesson. My uncles, Ian, Hutton, and Rigg, all groaned from the back of the room when the title appeared.

"The Dark War," my grandmother began. "Reshaped the land that you now see today. Not only was the land dark and barren, but an entire kingdom was lost." I withheld a groan. It wasn't that The Dark War was unimportant, but the lingering effects still breathed darkness when I dreamed.

When I was eight years old, I had nightmares—the entire land of Bergarian, cracking down the middle and fire erupting from the pits of the Underworld. Three dark demon shadows oppressed the land, killing helpless wolves, fae, and other beings. I would wake up screaming in the night, remembering the sword that struck Queen Melina of the Golden Light Kingdom. My father lay lifeless before my mother as she clutched at him for dear life.

I had almost lost my mother that day as she gave her complete power over to him—pulling the dark sludge from his soul and snatching him from the Grim Reaper's hands. That night had been unbearable. I stayed awake for days at a time, daring not to close my eyes for fear my parents would never wake up. My dreams were so real, so vivid that I thought they were real events.

I had seen the entire war when I was a child. The bloodshed, the cries, the death. I didn't need to hear about it during lessons, and I didn't need to have my grandmother tell me how I was born amid our kingdom's turmoil. I felt guilty enough being born in such a time, my mom worrying about me while I had been taken away to the earth realm to keep me safe.

I had witnessed the war over and over in my head until my mother put a stop to it when she realized what I was dreaming. When I explained to her what I saw, horror etched onto her face while I explained I couldn't fall asleep again because I worried she would not be there when I woke. It terrified her. Mom and dad were the only ones that knew of my vivid dreams of the past, and after doing extensive research, realized that I had the makings of becoming a Dream Wanderer.

Once mom had diagnosed me, she grabbed every book she could get her hands on, making sure that no one, not even the witches or her own mother knew about my gift. She said having this gift can sometimes be both a blessing and a curse, and she was sure someone would try to exploit my dreams. Mom loved her own mother dearly, but knew if my grandmother caught wind of it, she would stress expanding and growing the gift.

Mom explained my gift would grow in time, and with the books about Dream Wandering, I had learned to control what I dreamed. The past was left behind, and the nightmares were now long gone. Now, my dreams only lived in the present.

A place where the mysterious guard began showing himself. Now I was addicted to sleep, almost not wanting to wake.

"Are you still listening?" My grandmother slammed the ruler down on my desk. I coughed, acting as if the tickle in my throat was keeping me from speaking. "Then can you answer my question?" She raised an eyebrow.

Shit.

I glanced at Mikel, who shrugged his shoulders. He was as lost as I was. The man kept his face straight and his shoulder back. He looked more princely than all of us. He could be too serious at times. "*Virion,*" Melody linked me. "*And you owe me your dessert tonight.*" She retreated from the mind-link.

"Virion," I spoke out loud. Grandmother eyed me suspiciously until she returned to the map, pulling it down again. "*Thanks, Melody,*" I linked back. I could hear the rustling of the wild curls she had yet to tame over the fabric of her dress as she shook her head.

"That's right, Virion was the sorcerer necromancer that held three demon spirits in his body..." Grandmother droned on again.

I sighed, half listening, so I didn't have to give up another one of my desserts. My fingers tapped on the desk, my back slumping in the seat until the two hours of history finished. My uncles and Melody began to clear their desks, and I stood up, taking the one notebook and quill I'd brought with me.

"Evelyn, a word?" My grandmother took the spectacles off, not that they did anything remotely for her vision—just an extra magnification on smaller texts. Melody looked back as she headed out the door, nodding her head to let me know she would wait.

"Evelyn," Grandmother said demeaningly.

"Evie," I stated, crossing my arms. "I like to be called Evie and you know it." Grandmother sighed, rubbing her temples.

"Out of all the children here, you are the only one that gives me this much trouble," she said. "You have too much of your father in you."

I cocked my hip, laying my hand on top of it. "Is that a bad thing, then?" I countered. "That I have more of my father's spirit than my mother's."

"No, no." She waved her hands. "I'm not saying it's a bad thing, but at least you can show some respect toward me and your family. You take no pride in your work, and you throw it around like it is a joke." She laid her hand over her desk. "You are to rule this country one day, Evelyn, and you need to take responsibility. You will be eighteen in two weeks!" She held out two fingers.

"Your mother was just twenty-one years old when she took the throne and had hardly any schooling. She could have been greater if I had just taught her for a few years. Imagine what you could do with this kingdom with all the knowledge you could be learning instead of rolling around in the mud with a bunch of dogs," she spat out.

My head ticked in anger.

"Evelyn." My grandmother backed away. Her eyes widened, grabbing the ruler she had clutched in her hand. "Evelyn, I'm sorry." She continued to back away. My red claws lengthened and scratched across the dark-stained desk. My eyes glowed. My wolf Cinder shone her red eyes brightly.

"What did you say about my mother?" I kicked my heels to the side of the room. They landed with a thud on the wall.

"Those are Louboutin's!" Grandmother reached out like they were more precious.

"And about the royal guards who allow me to train with them every day? The guards that protect you? You call them dogs?" Cinder growled, echoing into the room. "And you say I am disrespectful?" I heaved in a breath, my claws clicking against the wall as I slammed my hand on the other side of her head. As I scratched down the blackboard, she shuddered, holding her ruler close.

"I have listened to you, taken your lessons, your tests, and have done my best to contain my half-beast while you scold me in front of your children and my sister, but no more." I shook my head. My fangs had elongated, my jaw cracking. "You should have known by now that I will never live up to your expectations, but then you go and rag on my mother, your own daughter?" My wolf venom dripped onto the floor.

"No one will believe you, Evelyn." My grandmother trembled, shaking her head. "I was once queen. Your parents and the people would believe me over you. It was an accident anyway." She waved her hand in defiance. "I was speaking out of turn due to anger."

"But what is it that you say?" Cinder growled out again. "That when we speak in anger, that is usually when true feelings come to the surface?"

Grandmother shook in her shoes, her dress becoming wrinkled from the heat of my body as I pressed into her.

"This is where I draw the line." I pushed away, not regretting my outrage. Father would vouch for me, believe me over her. No doubt, my mother would be hurt if she found out her own mother thought she was less than the queen her mother wanted her to be.

All these years, I kept silent. Didn't expose my grandmother for what she really was. Normally, the bluntness of her gut-wrenching words gravitated toward me. How I was a failure. This was the first I'd heard my grandmother telling me her true feelings about my parents. The light of the kingdom, the heroes of Bergarian. No more would I listen to her ramblings on what a true queen should be like.

My only regret was having Melody on the other side of the door for this.

"Evelyn," she called out as I reached the door. My feet reverted to my human form, my claws retracting. I turned to see the fear still in her eyes, her hands shaking as she reached out.

"I'm sorry... I overstepped."

I scoffed at her words. "While I may not fit the mold of your version of a princess, I never speak ill of my family or the subjects that give their lives for their country." I shook my head in disgust. "After The Dark War, I thought you would understand that."

Melody stood at the door, holding her book to her chest. The sweet almost sixteen-year-old looked on at our grandmother with such disappointment. For years, she thought our grandmother was someone to look up to, with her knowledge of the kingdom and various facts about Bergarian. Melody wanted nothing more than to be like her.

Now, I had tainted that for my sister, and regret blossomed in my chest. "I'm sorry you saw that, Melody." I tilted her cheek away from the door. Melody sniffed, gripping her history book tighter.

"Melody." Grandmother stepped forward, her face going pale. "What did you hear? It isn't true," she pleaded.

"No, I'm glad I did," Melody whispered. "I see why you were so bull-headed all those years, Evie. You were trying to prove yourself, huh?"

I huffed, pulling my sister into my embrace. "Yeah, I guess I was. Now I won't worry about pleasing her anymore, because our lessons are over. Isn't that right, Grandmother?" Grandmother lifted her tear-filled eyes.

"For me as well." Melody gripped my hand. "We will attend to our own studies." With that, we both left my grandmother in the lesson room. A once imperial queen, now just a tutor to her own sons and no longer a teacher to the future of the Cerulean Moon Kingdom.

Chapter Three

Evelyn

"You don't think I was too harsh?" My arm was wrapped around Melody's. Her steady feet kept me grounded while my insides shook. No one just told off the once high ice-queen like that, not even me. I had kept my mouth shut for years about how she treated me. Even with the minor insults in class, she had said much harsher things to me.

In my younger years, I was lenient with my grandmother. I wasn't strong, still a pup that had yet to come into her wolf. She was supposed to be the country's monarch, a ruler that had reined far longer than any of her predecessors.

She was supposed to know better, to help teach me to become a better princess.

And I always failed.

Never good enough.

My grandmother had given me a fast-paced and upbeat musical piece for the grand piano that sat in the middle of the music room. I was alone with her, something I despised, but I'd earned extra practice on the foul keys because of my clumsiness.

"Sit up straight," she snapped. "I don't know why you fight me so much, Evelyn. I don't understand it. Your mother is busy trying to help rebuild the Kingdom of Vermillion with His Majesty Sebastian, yet you still try to interfere. Causing messes for her, making her work harder. Clara needs all the help she can get, and you are making her fail."

I never tried to interfere with my mother and how she ruled the country. My mother allowed me to assist. I had helped set up the mirror which she would use to communicate with the interim king, and mom was getting dressed with dad's help. Then grandmother walked into the room, which startled me, and I spilled my mother's tea all over the table.

My grandmother hated my clumsiness as much as she hated me.

I hissed, the hot tea scalding my fingertips. I was only nine and wasn't used to pain. "Oh, Evie, are you alright?" Mom stopped buttoning her dress, pulling my fingers to her lips. She kissed them gently, getting ready to heal me with her gift until her eye darted to the clearing of a throat at the doorway.

"Evelyn spilled your tea. Let me take her so you can conduct your meeting," my grandmother said sweetly as she put her hands on my shoulders. I stiffened, knowing precisely what she was doing. *Taking me away to be punished.*

My mother knelt on the floor. My grandmother cleared her throat again as if to scold her own daughter until dad emerged from the shadows. It was insanely sweet since he always looked after mom and me. The twitch in his eye toward grandmother almost made me giggle.

Dad wasn't overly fond of Grandmother, and I knew exactly why. She was overbearing.

A silent conversation floated between dad and grandmother. She stepped away, bowing her head. "I'm sure Evelyn would like to do something else, rather than sit in on the meeting," she crooned. "Maybe we can go get some chocolates from the kitchen."

Dad eyed her warily, but his vision line returned to mom. She had dark circles under her eyes, and her cheeks were sunken. Her bright, cheery attitude had been missing for weeks, and the last thing I wanted to do to my mom was to give her more stress.

The Vermillion Kingdom still had its problems, and she'd taken it upon herself to help her friend. Sebastian was considered the rich uncle that liked to spoil us.

"I'll go," I said confidently. "I'm sorry I messed up your table." Looking guilty, I took a rag off the tea cart and went to clean it.

"Oh, Evie, it was an accident." Mom pulled me to her, petting my hair. "If you want to stay you can, you can see Sebastian and Christine. You haven't seen them in a while."

I could, but then that would give even more ammunition for Grandmother, and she was hell-bent on punishing me. I wouldn't come between my mom and her mother. I mean, she called her own mom "mother," and I must call her Grandmother. Indeed, there was a strained relationship. Dad didn't look too pleased with her still.

"I'm alright, I'll go. Next time." I kissed her cheek.

Dad leaned down, picking me up and setting me on his hip. "Sparring later, little warrior princess?" He cocked an eyebrow. Grandmother rolled her eyes, not liking that a princess of my supposed caliber was fighting amongst the guards.

"Can't wait, Dad!" I kissed his cheek, then he set me down and that was when *she* led me to the music room.

Now I sat with burned fingers and sore knuckles from yesterday's sparring, only to feel the air rush by me as the ruler slapped the leather bench.

"Again, Evelyn. With graceful strokes, learning this instrument will give you more elegant movements in our daily life."

I played the piece repeatedly until my body slumped in exhaustion. I could play the music with my eyes closed, but that didn't deter my evil grandmother. I sniffled, but I didn't cry. I never cried. And I would never cry in front of *her*.

"I suppose that will do." She leaned over my shoulder. It took all my strength not to sneer at her. One day, I wouldn't be the tiny little pup that cowered in front of her. One day, I would show her who was really in charge. If my mother weren't so frail this morning, I would have given Grandmother a piece of my mind.

Keep her on her toes.

"You know, if you want to rule this kingdom, you best act the part, Evelyn. Even your mother knows when to be graceful." My heart pounded in my chest, the notes on the page blurring in my vision. Her sickly sweet voice, one that so many of her loyal subjects still listened to, rattled me down to my toes. "The goddess paired your father with my daughter, that I won't question. It saddens me to see that you would inherit some of his"—she smacked her lips together—"some of his, not so finer qualities."

As dad would say, "that dumb bitch."

I growled, my hand pushing the music sheets to the floor. "You don't speak of my dad that way!" A howl erupted inside my mind—the first time I ever heard my wolf. She may not be ready to break the mold of my body, but she was there, coaxing me to be stronger.

Grandmother stepped back, her hand touching her chest. "Did you just growl?" She cocked an eyebrow. "Don't think that won't stop me from trying to teach you the ways of your bloodline, Evelyn."

"Evie," I huffed. "I like the name Evie and try all you like, but I'll make it hard for you." I stood, stepping in front of her. She took a step back, a hint of fear laced between her wolf and mine. My eyes flashed the anger of my wolf feeling disrespected. Hell, even the harsh words about my father had her seething.

"Cinder," the wolf whispered to me. *"I'm here now, and you will not be alone."* I sighed heavily; my back turned to my grandmother. I would no longer be alone, feeling the brunt of her comments. I had my wolf. She would help me protect my family.

"If you stress out Mom, I'll give you something to worry about, Grandmother," I warned. Her eyebrows knitted in confusion. "Because now." I felt my hands, the blisters on my bruised knuckles from this morning's hot tea had healed. "I have my wolf inside me and if you push Mom, make her or make Melody feel less than..." I chuckled darkly, making my grandmother stepped away.

Yeah, I did inherit my father's darkness.

"She may come out to bite you."

The urge to protect my family rose inside me. Sure, I was young—nine years old to hear your wolf—but any pup's wolf would surface early if it felt threatened. Except for dad, whose wolf came to him at eight years old and forced him to shift early. That was because my father's wolf, Torin, was strong and fierce. Cinder had a gentle but protective side to her that helped us balance each other just enough to protect my mother.

Keeping my grandmother on her toes had been deliberate all these years—keeping her away from mom, keeping her away from my father, who might very well kill her if she dared criticize my mom. Yes, keeping things to myself was for the best, she wouldn't hurt me. Physically, anyway.

"Of course, you were not harsh," Melody scolded. I raised my hand to my chest, rubbing the aching feeling. I wrapped around Melody, and she stiffened, listening to my heart. She had just come into her wolf a year ago. Her senses grew stronger every day. "Your heart, why does its rhythm beat differently?"

My knees buckled, and I fell to the floor. I grunted, rubbing my chest harder until Cinder came to my aide.

"You've bottled things up long enough," Cinder cooed. Her chestnut fur blew in my mind. *"Now, the dreams you tried to hide are returning to haunt you."* I gritted my teeth, my mind flashing images of my grandmother scolding me. I would rather take a punch to the gut instead of dealing with my problems.

"You may be strong physically," Cinder scolded me. *"But your mind is defeated."* I huffed another breath, Melody screaming for the guards to fetch mom and dad. She rubbed my back. My mind repeatedly flashed back to the piano scene—the ruler hitting the bench, the rhythmic notes invading my ears...

The day I took up my family's burdens.

"Come quick!" Melody pulled my hand to her chest, and my mom ran to my side in the ballet slippers she liked to wear. Grandmother hated those flats; she hated how mom wouldn't dress more like the queen she wanted her to be. Always wearing the tea length sun dresses she loved, always a dusting of flour on her cheeks when she baked dessert each night.

Stupid bitch.

Fuck, now she'll hassle mom now that I told her off.

I groaned, Cinder pawing at me to chill the fuck out. "Stop," I whined to Cinder, unable to speak to her. My mind was foggy, more memories coming through the floodgates. Memories that had become dreams, dreams that I could feel with every ounce of me.

"What happened?" my dad barked. He picked me up, cradling me to his chest.

"Is it a dream, Evie?" Mom's voice shook. Melody gave her a questioning look before my body shuttered.

"Yes," I whispered.

"Bad dreams, warrior princess?"

I smiled slightly at dad's pet name.

"Reliving painful memories," Cinder's voice spoke through me. "She's held onto them too long."

My father's arms tensed around me, squeezing me tighter into his chest.

"Let's get her to her room." Mother stood, her hand on my forehead as they took me down the hall. Melody spouted questions, mom answering them to the best of her ability without giving away the truth. I chuckled to myself. Mom didn't realize how brilliant Melody really was.

Sure, Melody was quiet, kept to herself, but her brain never stopped. She stopped, letting my parents take me to my room. Melody's feet pattered across the floor, no doubt running to the library to find something to help.

"Have the nanny put the twins down," Mom spoke to one of the guards. Dimitri and Dax were little demons on paws at just three years old. They only slept when mom rocked them to sleep.

Good luck, nanny. I wish you well.

Dad laid me on the bed, while mom grabbed a wet cloth, wiping my face. I had sweat pouring from my head, my mind trying to fight off the terrible memories that flooded through me. "Let it run its course," mom whispered harshly. "The more you fight it, the more you will suffer. You know this."

Dad only grunted, ordering the palace physicians to be brought in to give me a sedative. I'd be damned if I willed myself to sleep, to watch all the painful memories filter through like a film from a movie. I didn't need to see all the cruelties grandmother subjected me to, didn't need to relive them all.

"She's been holding back from you," Cinder spoke to my mother.

Mom's hand paused, her fingers brushing my cheek. "What has she been holding back, Cinder?" Mom's eyes watered, and the dam nearly broke inside me.

"Keeping secrets, protecting you and the family," was all that Cinder said before my eyes fluttered as the smell of drifting incense filled my lungs.

Chapter Four

Kit

I had just closed my eyes. I was only going to rest them while the rest of my team sparred against one another until the winners were ready to challenge me. Holding the highest rank in my class had its perks but waiting around for someone to spar against could put me in a foul mood. I was a mover, a doer, and right now I was doing nothing.

When I opened my eyes next, I had been transported to the haven that my Dream Wanderer placed me in. I shook my head, rubbing my hand down my face, realizing that I had not, in fact, closed my eyes but drifted off to sleep entirely. Being one that was always on alert, I was sure my classmates would jeer at me later.

Uptight was the perfect description of my personality. I wasn't playful. I hated social events and spent most of my time in the gym, sparring, or reading war tactics—concentrating on the future and the dreams I had for it.

I was going to be a Royal Guard—not just any guard, but the queen's personal guard. I had decided it at just six years old when Queen Clara had shown special interest in me. It was either her own intuition or the gods putting me in front of her, but she chose to see me when no one else did.

I was a runt, the child that was afraid of everything. Until Queen Clara had shown me that there was more to me than just an empty shell. I could be a warrior as long as I believed in myself. And without the queen's constant praise and my determination to realize my potential, I never would have been accepted here at the academy.

Queen Clara had pulled strings; I was sure of it. That didn't bother me in the slightest because I was going to prove myself to her and all the pups that saw me as less than. I hardened myself against friendships. I put my focus on repaying Queen Clara with her kindness. I would also show her mate that I was worthy enough to protect the royal family.

I stood up, my body clad in just leathers and an open white tunic. Not sure if My Little Warrior purposefully put me in something so immaculate on purpose, or if it was her own subconscious. Dusting away the dried leaves, I walked to her magical tree, as she called it.

It had been mid-day when I closed my eyes, and meeting her during the daylight hours was odd. Something wasn't right if she pulled me into her dream during the daylight. It meant she was sleeping, too. My Little Warrior didn't sleep. She had told me many times she never napped, too busy sparring with her father's men, dealing with her awful grandmother, and protecting her family from her grandmother's wickedness.

We had yet to divulge anything personal that would expose our names, family, and ranks. Even though I had shortly figured out she was no demon but the angel that had fallen into my heart without mercy.

How she broke my tough exterior, I'll never know.

By this time, she would have sought me out, barely letting my eyes open. She would barrel through the forest, letting the tight leather pants, her corset top, and her long hair—flowing wild and free—catch on the branches. Her smile was contagious. And as she grew into the beautiful woman she was always destined to be, I wasn't sure I was ever going to let her go.

A tiny, lanky thing. A little girl full of bite and sass that pierced her way into my bitter heart. At sixteen when I met her, I tried to shy away from her, but she continued to bring me back. Whether it was intentional, I wasn't sure. She taught me to smile and to break free while she had become more grounded, confident, and secure.

I smirked, walking through the forest, my bare feet leading me to the tree where she always appeared. Her foot dangled from the large branch, the vines and leaves keeping the rest of her body hidden. "Little Warrior?" I called out. Her foot continued to dangle, waving in the breeze.

Putting my hands on my hips, I huffed in annoyance. If she was playing some sort of game, I wasn't in the mood. I still had daylight hours back in reality and much to do still. Could she not be more reasonable and wait until this evening? "Warrior!" I called again until I climbed the low-lying branches.

As I climbed, she came into view. Her body lay on the thick, broad branch like it was a double bed. The softness of the bark and the tenderness of the wood would make a fine bed for those that preferred to stay in the wilderness.

I tsked, climbing over her, and sat at her feet. She had never been asleep when I encountered her before. Usually, she was the one playing a trick to wake me. Now she lay here in strange clothes that were not her norm. An oversized white linen shirt, one that covered her just enough around her hips and thighs. A tight bodice around the middle, keeping her hourglass figure. The long sleeves were ruffled, and her shoulders were bare.

She was ethereally beautiful. The calmness she radiated when she slept was new and welcome. Once she had become seventeen, the attraction I had for her grew strong. My wolf even stirred inside me, which was odd for a beast like him. With My Warrior's birthday in a few weeks, she would be eighteen, and my heart sunk at the thought. She would be old enough to find her mate.

My heart throbbed to know this. It shouldn't, but it did. She was my dream girl, and I was just the same boy that she looked up to like a mentor or friend. "Little Warrior." I touched her bare shoulder. Her eyebrows were furrowed, her lips gently twitching.

Could it be possible to have a dream within a dream? Sitting back on my haunches, I took the time to memorize every line that adorned her body. The pinkness of her cheeks, the curve of her body, and the golden glow of her skin.

Gods, she was beautiful. Why was it just now I was realizing how much she had ensnared me?

When she turned seventeen, I felt it and I swore she might have too. The aching in my heart, the burning inside me to hold her close and keep her here in the safeness of my arms haunted my mind while I was awake. Could there be a way to stay within this dream forever?

I had hidden away from all mating parties at Alabaster Academy once I came of age. The drive to find a mate never came. I didn't want to put myself out there to find her because I had been so happy in the dreams with this Little Warrior, who was not so little anymore.

Her eyes twitched, a stray lash falling on her cheek. Taking my finger, I gently brushed it away.

Her hair curled around her neck, drawing my eye to it. What would I do if she came to me with a bite of claiming on her neck? That she had found her mate, the one she was supposed to be with? My hand grabbed hers, and it automatically intertwined with mine. I couldn't feel the spark; I had prayed to the goddess that this Dream Wanderer may be mine. That one day, the fire would fly up my arm, and I could honestly know she was my destined.

My Warrior stirred, her back arching to stretch. Dropping my hand, I sat back, raising a knee to let my arm rest. Her blue eyes fluttered open and a smile that reached her ears had my heart banging in my chest.

"Hello, my Grumpy Guard," her voice was low, raspy. Like she woke from a long slumber,

Ignoring her terrible nickname for me, I leaned in close. "Are you alright?" I hovered over her, grabbing her hand. She glanced at my hand over hers and a pink tint brushed her cheeks.

"It's been a rough few days," she muttered, not moving her hand. "I didn't think I would see you," she said sadly. Her smile was for me, to keep me from worrying, but I knew better.

My Warrior hid her emotions on the inside. She could be a hard one to read, and that was why I kept the feelings I had for her hidden. Divulging to each other about finding our mates never became an option, and it was done purposefully on my part. My Warrior didn't bring it up either, even the day when I turned eighteen.

Did she worry about me finding my mate like I worried about her?

"Is it about your grandmother?" I growled in my chest. Too many times had My Warrior come to me in anger. Sparring against each other had been a great release for us. She was truly an educated warrior, and very well could be an Alpha based on the way she fought. Her training and experience matched my own, and it filled me with great pride she was a capable partner to spar with.

"Yes," she groaned, throwing her hands up in the air. She sat crossed-legged, her dress barely covering the front of her body.

Eyes up at her face, man.

"I told her off," she grunted, crossing her arms.

"About bloody time!" I barked out. "How long have you put up with her? I've been telling you for years to do it."

"But my family..." she whispered.

"Warrior." I pulled her hands toward me, cupping them in mine. "If your parents are as strong as you, which I'm pretty sure they are." I eyed her playfully. "Then they could have handled themselves all along. I bet they will be furious at you for keeping this secret from them." I let go of her hands, she frowned "Your mother and father seem like a strong, capable wolves," I whispered.

"They are strong physically, but my dad can be a bit of a hothead and my mom is just so tender with her emotions. I wanted to protect them," she whispered. "I know their relationship is strained, and I didn't need to be the fuel on the fire for more arguments. Keeping my grandmother's attention on me rather than my sister or parents was a better option."

I sighed, leaning back on a branch. "But they are your parents, and from what you've told me about them, they sound like they love you. They are going to be devastated you kept this from them. You've suffered all these years, and I had to comfort you every night," I said dramatically, putting the back of my hand on my forehead. "It was utterly exhausting."

"Hey!" she slapped my chest playfully. "You enjoyed talking to me almost every night, at least that is what you told me. You weren't lying, were you?" Her playfulness faded, worry falling across her face.

What are these emotions she is displaying? Is she that worried I would be bothered? Quite the opposite.

"I would never lie to you, Little Warrior. You've been the best thing that has happened to my dreams." I smiled. "You've made me a better wolf, and I think you've changed too." I wiggled my eyebrows. "I mean, look at you now, wearing a dress that doesn't have a speck of dirt, and your hair looks like it has actually seen a comb."

"Oh my gods!" She ripped her hands away, grabbing her hair. "I was never that bad!" she protested.

"You certainly were! Do you not remember our first meeting? A pink dress, torn around the bottom, dirt on the frills, and leaves in your hair?

You were a feral child that needed someone to look after you." I laughed. "And for some reason, the gods put us together for me to ground you."

"They did not," she huffed.

"And"—I added—"To help me pull my head out of my rear to see that life wasn't just about training." My Little Warrior's lashes fluttered at me. "You are the only wolf that can make me laugh, make me feel more at ease. You should take the compliment with pride." Taking my finger, I pulled up her chin, directing her eyes to mine. "Hey, I'm so damn proud of you." She grinned an authentic smile that showed off those beautiful fangs. "And I'm glad your wolf decided that enough was enough." I leaned away from her.

"Yeah, well, you should have seen my grandmother. I scared the shit out of her. Her wolf was shaking. Not that the poor thing sees the light of day." She rolled her eyes. "Honestly, I think the last time she shifted was when she had to protect her son when she was pregnant and that was…" She counted on her fingers. "Oh, seventeen years ago." She laughed.

My Little Warrior barely gave me clues to who she was, where she lived, or why she had to act so prim and proper. My guess her family was high in social status if she was taking etiquette lessons with her grandmother bossing her around.

And who ever heard of a wolf not letting their animal out to play?

I never dug deeper, and she never divulged much else except for the need to know, and maybe that was good because if I did figure out who she was…I would find her in the waking world.

Chapter Five

Evelyn

Could he be any more handsome?

Trying not to swoon in front of this wolf was becoming more difficult with each passing dream. He always said the right things, looked the part, and was muscular as hell. His normal attire was nothing but soft terry cloth shorts and a bare chest, but this was certainly a welcome surprise seeing him in leathers and a tunic.

It gave the whole romance feel. Like one of those romantic novels that I swore to everyone that knew me that I would never read. Erotic love stories had become my best friend, and the loose stone under my bed would reveal I stashed too many of my forbidden novels inside.

The Guard looked like he could be on the cover of one. The dirty blonde hair and those pretty chocolate eyes had me touching myself every morning when I left him.

"You alright?" He waved his hand in front of my face. I blushed, hiding my face, and hoping his wolf couldn't hear my thumping heart. Luckily, all of our senses were dulled in this dream world, otherwise he would smell the arousal leaking from me.

"Yeah, just thinking about what happened. I can't believe I'm seeing you here, since I'm pretty sure I fell asleep during the day."

Right, Evie, you just "fell asleep." More like your parents drugged you to take care of your problems before you squeal on your grandmother.

Gods help me.

"What did happen, I need all the dirty details." My Guard flung his cheek bone length hair back, shaking it so perfectly it looked like glitter shined in his hair when the light struck it. I giggled like a little schoolgirl watching that smirk rise on his face.

The once broody, uncomfortable and unsure of himself sixteen-year-old was certainly gone. Now his bright personality shown, and I wondered if he was only like this here. He still had his moments, just like the face he was giving me now as I sat here, looking at him like a god.

"Well?" He arched his brow. "Come on, Little Warrior, I need all of it. Every detail you can give me. I need to know you're safe now. Safe from the insufferable woman you dared let harm you." He shook his head.

"She never touched me," I interjected.

My Guard growled, his white fangs lengthening. "If you were mine, Little Warrior..." His eyebrows raised, clearing his throat. "If your mate knew about this, he'd make sure you didn't do something so reckless. Hiding the pain you suffered for all these years wasn't the smartest thing you've ever done."

My eyes widened, watching him stand. Could he possibly have meant what he said, *if I was his?* Too many times I thought I could be, that maybe he was my mate, but not once had he shown any emotion when he touched me. Sure, we sparred, fought, and learned from each other, but not once had he told me he felt the fire between our skin.

He wouldn't hide that from me, would he?

A fire erupted in my stomach. Maybe, just maybe when I turned eighteen, the goddess would bless me. I'd know that he was mine because I had never wanted a man so badly in all my life.

My Guard cleared his throat again, sitting across from me. The wind had settled, and the fireflies began to light beneath the branches as we sat. His finger shook shamefully at me as I composed myself, keeping the excitement in my stomach.

Just maybe.

Two weeks, just two weeks, and I'll be eighteen.

"From the beginning," He rubbed the stubble on his face. "From the beginning, tell me what happened," he commanded.

Sometimes he could just be so bossy.

From start to finish, from being late, from the snide comments and trying to embarrass me in front of my fellow classmates, his face remained calm. Then when I approached the delicate topic of what she called the 'warriors,' since I couldn't give away that I had guards, I paused, my throat going dry.

"Don't skip, Little Warrior," he growled.

"I resent the 'little' part." I smiled, looking everywhere but him. My heart fluttered, feeling his fingers grace my jawline, pulling me back to his gaze.

"Don't change the subject, and I'll call you My Little Warrior all I want. It's penance for dragging me in here night after night." He tried to hide his smile, keeping his face stern with the ever-stoic guard that I'm sure showed no emotion when he left this world.

"Fine, but you won't be happy with what she said." I gulped. "She said I was wasting my time training when I should prepare to take over the family business. That I..." I gritted my teeth at the venomous words. Balling my fist in anger, I spat it out. "That I should stop rolling around with the dogs!"

The surrounding life that buzzed with funny creatures great and small, paused. The wind that would continue to bring fresh air and traces of the light sources across our bodies stilled. Dust particles that would float by and the insects in the trees even calmed themselves as we all sat in utter silence.

My Guard didn't move. His gorgeous features lay frozen in time. The air in his chest didn't rise. Feeling the panic, my hand slid across the velvet bark of the tree, overlapping the hand he used to steady himself. He closed his eyes, taking a deep breath.

"Then what else?" he muttered.

I explained the rest of the story until the point where I passed out so helplessly on the floor. He rolled his head back. Once my dad hears about this, I would be seeing a completely different reaction. It was refreshing not having to see a male beast-out mode so thoroughly he could only be calmed by my mother's touch.

"Are you okay?" I whispered. "I was so angry too, it was all–"

"You did well," My Guard muttered. "You handled it much better than I would have, actually." My eyes widened. Surely not. Between us, I was the irrational one. I could say things without thinking and put my foot in my mouth. My Guard was cool, calm, collected, and tactful.

"I don't think that's true–"

"It is," he interrupted again. "A comment like that would have had my wolf seething. You did well, Warrior." He grabbed my hand.

Today had been the most we had touched each other, and I wasn't complaining. It was nice to feel the warmth of his hand and, just maybe, he was being calmed by my touch. Because just maybe I was his mate.

"You kept your head on your shoulders. You may be blood related, but that doesn't mean she can do or say whatever she wants because of her status. Don't expect the wolves around her to take kindly to what she said either."

This I knew for certain. Anyone calling any werewolf a dog was the ultimate insult. In no way, shape, or form were we anything like the four-legged canines the humans kept as pets. If only My Guard knew how big of a deal this was. Just a normal wolf saying it...yeah sure, it was bad.

But my grandmother was the former queen. The damn queen of the Cerulean Moon Kingdom.

Shit, if word got out...

"Hey, what's wrong?" He pulled me closer to him as the blood drained from my face.

"Do you think my parents will tell everyone what she said?" I muttered. "I mean, she's family. I still care about her, but it's just... gods this is hard to say." I rubbed my forehead. "It's so hard not being able to tell you everything!" I banged on my leg.

His hand pushed a curl away from my forehead. "Yeah, it does suck, doesn't it? I'm still not convinced you aren't a demon in disguise though," he teased.

"What!?" I snapped at him.

"Yeah, you could be trying to steal my heart or something. Get it nice, fat, and plump with friendship and love and then, smack! You gobble me up once I tell you, my name." He kept his face still with no emotion until we both laughed.

My arms at my sides, I leaned back on the branch behind me. "I can never read you. One minute you're all serious, and the next you're making jokes. I bet you are the life of the party with your friends."

My Guard brushed off a vine that had wrapped around his arm. "Nah, Little Warrior. I don't have that many friends. Close ones anyway."

"Just me then?" I fluttered my lashes, cupping my cheek with my hand. "I'm so honored to be a part of your inner circle."

"You know you are the only real friend I need, Warrior."

My heart thumped in my chest. He really didn't understand how hard I was falling. "Same goes for me, Guard." I mock saluted.

"Brat."

"Mr. Cranky Pants," I snipped playfully. Jumping from the tree, I heard a yell of opposition as I began to run. The dress I wore barely covered my back end, but when you were running from your best friend, all was fair in the spoils of the chase.

I continued to laugh, my hair catching on the branches. Of course, he would be right about my damn hair; he was right about everything. The heavy panting of his wolf came from behind me. My wolf yipped in my head to shift, but we very well knew not to do that.

My wolf was far too easy to spot, and my half-beast form even more so. Cinder had her chocolate fur, but the white markings of her paws were too like my mom's and those were too well known. I raced barefoot until the heavy breathing of My Guard's wolf stopped. The surroundings turned hazy, and the muffled sounds of a voice called me.

"Evie, wake up, Princess." His deep voice had me closing my eyes and shutting another dream away. My father stared down at me.

"Hi, Dad."

"Fuck, princess, you scared me." He reached down, pulling me up into his embrace. For a beast of a man covered in tatts, piercings, and now gauges that pulled on his earlobes, you wouldn't think he would give a shit about his kids.

But he most certainly did. His children.

Pulling away, he gave me a scowl that would have other wolves shaking in their fur. His eyebrows pointed downward, his breath heaved, and his tone of voice deepened. "What were you thinking holding back on repressed memories and dreams?"

I sheepishly shrugged my shoulders, only for dad to wipe a hand down his face.

"Why is it so annoying you don't get scared of me? I'm your father. I have to instill some sort of fear."

I snickered, patting his hand. "Kinda hard to get scared of the big bad wolf when he used to have play tea parties with a five-year-old while wearing a tutu."

He groaned, leaning back in the chair. "Your mom was going to make me adult tea later. Didn't have a choice."

I cocked my head to the side, not really wanting to know that code word.

A feminine throat clearing caught my attention. I peered to my right, seeing my mother glare at me from the pillow beside me. She propped her head up on her hand, and her finger tapped my nose. "You're in trouble," she sang.

Oh hell, if mom said you were in trouble, you were on her list. I had only been on her list one time and that was when I ran off after my dream with the Guard to find the magical tree from my dream. I got no dessert for a month, and dad almost gave the first platoon of guards in charge of keeping the family safe an aneurysm.

Poor guys.

"Mom," I tried to soothe, but that squint in her eye told me not to even push.

"Evie, you need to spit it out. What has been troubling you, and why have you been repressing dreams?"

I groaned, flopping back on the bed.

There was just so much.

"Evelyn!" Mom scolded and father growled.

Using My Guard's lessons on reading the room and when to expel information, I tried to reason with myself about the best plan. Dad looked tired, mom looked worse for wear, and I could see Melody peeking around the door trying to listen in. I rubbed my face with my hand, feeling the sweat building.

"Can I at least wake up first? Eat something? I promise to tell you everything, but I need more time to process what I re-lived." It wasn't a lie. I had seen things I had forgotten and tried to forget what grandmother said and did. No matter how many years between those moments with her, they would haunt me for the rest of my living days.

Mother sighed heavily, nodding her head. "I suppose we should give you some time to process." Dad groaned, his back leaning back in the chair. "Your father needs some taking care of, so we will leave you be until tonight in the office." Her angry scowl fleeted away. "You've slept for three days, Evie. You had us worried sick." Mom's voice softened.

Three days?

And why is it that the only thing that really stood out from my dreams was My Guard? Sure, the memory dreams were terrible, but it all looked like fogged glass compared to seeing the crystal-clear view of his face. His handsome, stern face. *My* Mr. Grouchy Pants.

Smiling dreamily, remembering how angry and concerned he appeared for my well-being, my tension left my body. *He cared.* My Guard could certainly render me speechless. And who knew if he was even real? Maybe my mind created this wolf and for all I know, he didn't even exist.

I frowned, saddened at the thought. Surely someone so handsome, so kind, yet stern in so many ways would be hard to create for my minuscule mind.

"Hello?" Melody's voice sang as she waved her hand in front of my face. "I have never seen so many emotions cross your face in such a short period, Sister," she stared at me in concern. "I'm not sure why I never saw it before, but obviously you like being in a dream-like state the way you daydream all the time."

I snorted, waving my hand in the air. "Where's Mom and Dad?" I glanced around the room. Taking a large whiff, I covered my nose in disgust. Damn those alpha senses.

"Yeah, they couldn't even make it to their room. They are doing it in the linen closet just outside." Melody grinned, hooking her thumb in the direction of the door.

Melody and I had wondered why Mom and Dad could be seen walking out of random linen closets throughout the palace. It wasn't until we both got our periods at the same time what it all made sense. The birds and the bees were a traumatic tale given to us by Mom.

As if it couldn't get any worse, she told us that once we found our mates, we could use these closets any time we wanted. All of them had been remodeled with soundproof padding between the walls shortly after they moved to the palace.

It was then we realized how truly horny our parents were if they couldn't even make it to their bedroom.

"Gods, that's so disgusting." I pinched my nose, and Melody shook her head. Melody had learned how to turn off her nose, but one of her other senses would be heightened. I'd rather smell than hear what our parents were doing, but she handled it well.

"Why didn't anyone tell me about your gift?" Melody shrugged her shoulders. "I would have kept it a secret. I'm guessing that is what you guys were trying to do, anyway." Melody leaned back in her chair, crossing her arms. She had her bifocals clipped to her dress. She dressed like Mom and even had Mom's seamstress tailor her dresses to match. Melody had a curvier figure than all of us. Her wolf was thick with a curvaceous body. Melody was actually very fast in her wolf form, only because she didn't like to fight like the rest of us.

"We didn't want any slip-ups. You know how Grandmother is. If she found out I had a gift, she would make me practice and force me to develop it before I was ready. Her own gift didn't emerge until she was four or five hundred. Could you imagine how she would jump at the chance to evolve it? I didn't want that, and neither did Mom and Dad. They were protecting me." I shuffled in the bed.

"I understand that, but damn it, Evie, you've done a lot on your own. I was too blind to see Grandmother's ability to make you miserable. I was just too fascinated by the history, the studies—"

I laid a finger on my sister's lips. "Hush now, or you'll pop a blood vessel somewhere." Melody snorted, probably trying to come up with some reply that it wasn't possible for our kind to do anything of the sort. "I knew you looked up to Grandmother and some of the wisdom she had." I rolled my eyes. "I only wanted you to hold on to your childhood a little longer."

"I'm not much of a child anymore, you know." She stood from her seat. "In fact, I am pretty sure I can beat you on any test."

"And I could kick your ass on any sparring day," I quipped.

She hummed in agreement, leaning over the bed to hug me. "I'm glad you're okay, but now I want in. It's someone else's turn to take care of you."

The morning had fled, and the light sources hid behind the rich forest behind the palace. My stomach was in tangles, and my fingers bled from pulling at the cuticles. This was it, the big revelation of why I kept secrets from my family. I couldn't handle constant reminders of my grandmother verbally abusing me for all those years because I continued to live it.

I just prayed Mom had sated Dad enough, so he didn't go completely ballistic. When Torin got pissed, my wolf would get riled up and we would both force shift. Having two half-beasts would fill the private study pretty quickly, and knocking over one of mom's flower arrangements was not something we wanted to trifle with.

Oh, but if it was chocolate silk pie, Dad's favorite, the Underworld would definitely open up again if those fell to the floor. Mom would have to make two or three at a time to keep up with his appetite.

I feet walked bare footed down the carpet to my doom. The once, crimson-colored carpet when we first moved into the palace, was now decorated with a royal blue with beautiful cream swirls in the long corridor to the study, had me smiling. Mom had thrown such a fuss with Grandmother when she said the red rugs were fine and that they'd been there for centuries and would last a couple more.

Red was a color my mom despised after being kidnapped by the former king of Vamparia—Mom couldn't stomach anything red. No red roses of any kind for miles, and the red tapestries and carpeting had all been replaced. It was dad who'd put his foot down about it, upset that his mate would cringe walking into every hallway.

Another reason why Grandmother had such a problem with dad. He was Mom's sounding board.

The ceiling to floor door was cracked, voices filtering out. One voice was there that I was hoping wouldn't be. It would take me twice as long to gracefully explain why I held back my memories.

Grandmother sat eloquently in a purple, floor-length ball gown. Her hair was done up to the perfect bun, with ringlets framing her face. Pop, my grandfather, had his arm wrapped around her, staring at her adoringly. My nausea grew tenfold, my stomach twitching with nervousness at the idea of what Pop might say.

"Evie." Mom walked over to me. I towered over her as she led me to the couch. She had me sit between Dad and her. It was the perfect view to see my grandmother's reactions. At first, I thought she would be nervous as I walked in—showing my wolf in front of her had shaken her the other day—but now she was cool and detached.

She sipped from her teacup, setting it gracefully on the glass table in front of her. "Well, what is it we are talking about?"

My father scowled, his large arm sliding around me and my mother. "We never invited you, not sure why you are here," he ruffed. "This is a family affair."

"And am I not family?" she asked, offended. "I want to look after the wellbeing of my granddaughter and if she passed out right after being in my care, I need to know why."

"I didn't pass out," I pointed out. "They gave me a sedative to calm me down." Grandmother eyed me warily. I swore her wolf showed submissiveness, but my grandmother showed no fear. "If she wants to stay, that's fine," I stated. "Makes things easier on my part."

Her eyes slightly widened, as she gripped Pop's thigh.

Rip it off like a bandage.

Melody erupted into the room, shutting the door, and stood in front of the overly decorated wood. "Come sit." Mom patted the seat next to her. Melody shook her head, understanding what I was about to do. She was keeping the exit blocked, so Grandmother couldn't storm out like she commonly would when she was losing a fight.

"I don't like this," Dad growled. "Not one bit. Are you two girls hiding something?"

Grandmother and Pop paled, probably feeling Torin bubble to the surface.

"There's no more hiding, dad. I'm here to tell you everything."

Mom's questioning stare between me and my grandmother became anger. "What is going on? Evie? Mother?" The stare down between mother and daughter didn't falter until I stood up, putting my back to the ornate desk filled with parchments and scrolls. Taking a deep breath and feeling the heated stare of my grandmother, I glared back.

"Didn't think I'd have the balls to do this, huh?" I crossed my arms. "Didn't think I would actually go through with it, or did you come here to intimidate me, huh?"

"Language," Grandmother scolded.

"Evie?" Mom pleaded. "What is going on!?"

"Mom, dad, I'll tell you." I smirked.

"I've had enough, Evie. Stop this nonsense." Grandmother slammed her hand on the armchair. "Your attitude has always been terrible, and I was redirecting you to be the proper ruler of this country."

Dad growled, his claws raking across the arm of the sofa.

Yep, mom was going to be pissed about that.

Dad's growl resounded from the glass table, the pies shaking in their tins.

"Mom, Dad, Grandmother thinks that you and Father can't rule the country properly and said she was going to mold me into what a true queen should be. I purposefully dealt with her so the relationship between you and her wouldn't be strained. Once I realized what I had to do to protect you, Cinder came to me. I kept Grandmother away from you and Dad so she wouldn't hurt you both with her venomous words."

Mom's mouth dropped and Father's yellow eyes glared, his growl growing stronger.

"That was why you gained your wolf so early! Because you were under duress!? Mother!?" Mom's face turned red, her breath ragged with heat. "This is when you received your gift as well?" she snapped, standing to her feet. "Your wolf, your gift, you obtained them early because of this woman?!" Mom yelled and pointed at Grandmother like she was just another commoner and not her birth mother.

Grandmother didn't flinch, her back straight as a board. Pop took his arm away from her, his eyes filling with sadness. "Eden, please tell me this isn't true?"

"I am doing what Evelyn needs. A firm hand, an ideal none of you have done for her." Her head turned to her mate. "She is to be ruler one day. I'm teaching her everything she needs to know that I failed to instill in our daughter. Evelyn needs to grow up, stop playing around in the dirt and running off with the guards to spar," she raised her voice. Pop slummed in his seat, his hand running through his hair.

"Would you like to tell everyone what you called the guards, the warriors, those who pledge to protect you and this country, dearest Grandmother?" Grandmother's eyes narrowed. My father's skin shifted into the rugged black fur. Mom wasn't much better. Her arms were full of red fur, her white paws emerging.

"I don't know what you are talking about," she snapped quietly, looking away.

Stepping forward in my white tunic dress and large belt that highlighted my toned stomach, I looked down at her. The picture perfect, former queen now ready to fall. The words leaving me would forever change how the people of this nation would see her.

"Are you sure you want to do this?" she whispered. The hint of shame in her voice made me swallow, but she needed to learn. Learn that she couldn't talk to her daughter nor her granddaughters and grandsons the way she did. Who knows what sort of damage her own sons had faced through the years while I suffered in silence?

Did they suffer too? Was I too worried about myself?

My body trembled inside, thinking of my poor uncles.

"Grandmother said that I played and trained amongst the dogs."

Chapter Six

Kit

"The hell!?" I jumped up from the shade beneath the tree. The training grounds were filled with wolves that wished to become more than just mediocre warriors. They wanted more. More training, a stronger wolf.

I had seen far too many wolves come and go. The training was rigorous, especially in the beginning, to weed out the weak. The ones whose families sent their sons and daughters to get them into shape, they left within the first year. Little did their families know, you couldn't force your wolf to emerge. They had to want, crave for the honor..

My wolf was one of the weakest when I arrived, then Luna Clara put in a good word for me. My desire and drive to be the best and the strongest won many battles, and now I was the strongest of the lot.

Shouts and howls boomed as I stood up. Drenched head to toe, my classmates jeered and pointed as I stood. My wolf, Riddick, huffing in annoyance, shook our head to rid the water from our hair.

"Alright, that's enough," Volke shouted. He was an old Alpha by four hundred years. He spent most of his days at the Alabaster Academy and in the evenings, retreated to the Blue Waters pack with his mate, where most of the retired Alphas and Lunas lived. "If we have Kit falling asleep, then I must be workin' ya too hard. How about we end early?" He waved at my classmates to leave, but my two annoyingly attached roommates stood beside me.

"I don't get my turn then?" I slung my hair again, getting Clint and Leland wet.

"Hey, man!" They brushed it off and slapped their hands on my back. "You should be happy you don't have to spar today. Don't want to mess up your mug too much for the mixer tonight." I rolled my eyes, Volke throwing me a towel as we walked to the dormitories.

"You know I don't go to those things," Kit complained. "I don't need any of that partying right now." They rolled their eyes while we all walked in silence back to the dormitories.

Two dormitories, four stories high and covered in vines and bushes, blended into the surroundings so well, one would never find them if you just glanced over the area. Even flying from up above, the dragons had trouble spotting them. One dormitory held those that were still going through schooling up to the age of seventeen. The other held those who had completed the rigorous education and who were now concentrating on strengthening their wolves.

Only the top caliber of wolves received the invitation to receive the advanced training. Just the top ten percent of each class would graduate into the advanced training, which included battle strategies, pack laws, and rules. I had made it, and I was damn proud.

Clint and Leland led me through the dirt path until Volke threw his voice our way. "Kit? A word before you go hide in your burrow?"

I snorted, turning back and waving my roommates on.

"You're planning on attending the mixer tonight, aren't you?" Instead of the typical chastising, he softened his face. Volke's soft face was odd. My wolf growled, not understanding his angle.

"You're twenty-three and you have yet to attend. Don't you want to find your mate?" I huffed not looking him in the eye. "Kit, to gain a stronger wolf, you must merge your soul with your mate, not that that should be the only reason you find him or her."

I sighed heavily, running my hand through my hair. "It isn't that I don't want to find her. It's just that I've got other things on my mind. Got to better myself before I'm worthy of such a gift," I lied.

Volke tilted his head in thought, studying me. Nothing could get past Volke. He could tell you if you snuck an extra dessert, stayed up too late, or were shamelessly spying on the topless sirens sunbathing on the beach over the weekend.

"Don't believe you." He pouted . "You are expected to be there tonight." He pointed at me. "That's an order, warrior. If you want to achieve advancement to the King and Queen's Royal Guard, you will obey it." Volke nodded his head to dismiss me. I bowed, crossing my arm over my chest, and stepped away.

Perfect guards never argued, they took orders.

When I stepped into my room, Riddick had his hackles up, his claws pawing at me. He had no desire to see a bunch of heated females looking for mates. We all knew what that led to. Disappointment and a promise of a companionship for the night. We wanted our Warrior, to sleep and be with her. My wolf had become fond of her, and hell, I had too.

"Somebody's in trouble," Leland sang. Clint threw a pillow at me, which I caught without turning around. "And now he's a grump," Leland added, coming out of the washroom. "Listen, Kit. You gotta loosen up. Have some fun with us tonight. Even if you don't meet your mate, there are plenty of ladies to dance with. It's all about this uniform." He pulled one leg through the white pant leg. The red sash wrapped around the waistline contrasted deeply with the white tailored outfit.

"I think he's worried about failure," Clint added. "He's worried about failing since he excels in everything. And not finding his mate at the first mixer would just devastate the poor boy."

I rolled my eyes, ignoring the jokes. "Your wishes are coming true. I'm going tonight." I grabbed a clean towel and threw it over my shoulder. The business of the room, the shuffling, the throwing of clothes, and shaving one's face stopped as they watched my back retreat.

"No shit." Leland smiled. "Finally, coming out with us instead of getting your beauty sleep. We'll show you a great time!" He slapped my back as I recoiled into the bathroom.

Pure torture.

Music from Earth, Bergarian, and Atlantis thrummed through the speakers. It wasn't often the school allowed technology for pleasure, but this was an *event*. Strobing lights drew light pixies from the surrounding forests who came to gawk at the mating event.

Whisps rounded the tables, their blue lights guiding shifters, fae, and sirens to their intendeds. I steered away from them. Not that it would help if my mate was here. I would be sought out and pulled into her direction either by smell or the little blue annoyances.

Sweaty bodies rubbed against each other, arousal weighing heavily in the musky air. Not to mention the enormous amounts of alcohol. The substance sloshed from side to side as another punch bowl rolled in on a serving cart. The gargantuan fountains of wine and our mock recipe for ambrosia had hordes of supernaturals gathering for another glass. I shook my head, watching in pity of the poor souls too depressed to hold back from the poison.

All mating age wolves from the academy attended, along with other shifters, fae, elves, and sirens joining in on the fun. Sirens would have to swim great distances to make such an event, but it was worth it all to find your mate.

I prayed to the goddess I wouldn't find her tonight—too guilty with my thoughts drifting to My Warrior. She would shine at an event like this. If she wore a dress anything like what she had just a few hours before, all the warriors would be after her.

Her long flowing hair, her smile as she pranced around the tables, sampling each food from the different corners of Bergarian. Then again, she was most likely a noble. Maybe she already knew the fare of the land.

She would start attending events such as this soon. Men from all races would dare to approach her, touch her, smell her to find out if she belonged to them.

My hand gripped the shot glass, shattering it on the table where I sat. She-wolves stared at me in confusion, moving their group away from me.

"Dude, lighten up." Clint plopped down beside me. "You really don't know how to have fun, do you?" I grunted, wiping my hands free from the pebbles of glass.

"Or are you just grumpy that you didn't find her tonight?" Leland asked, sitting beside me.

"I didn't want to find her tonight." A fae came round the table offering me another shot. Taking it, I waved her over for two more until those were gone as well.

"Shit, you can put that shit away." Clint laughed. "Remind me not to get in a drinking game with him." He pointed to Leland.

"I bet he would be a hilarious drunk," Leland commented. "Let's see how far he can go. Kit, you in? Obviously, you don't care about appearances right now, and we haven't found our mates yet either." He wiggled his eyebrows. Shrugging my shoulders, they both hooted for a large tray of werewine, ambrosia, and the sort.

An hour and a half later, I had drunk far too much and my friends not enough. The hope they would pass out was a terrible thought because drinking only made them more talkative.

"And then, this she-wolf asked me if they not only worked on getting our wolves bigger but our junk as well! You know, be a real alpha male!" he said mockingly. He laughed, patting me on the back. I chuckled, sipping down my last shot. "But I told her the truth though—that I was already too massive for them to work on my dick and that it would end up dragging in the dirt in my wolf form."

That did it.

I rolled my head back in laughter, my roommates laughing along with me. As the laughter died, I glanced at my watch and saw it was nearly two in the morning. The party had long since died, but those who were miserable at not finding their mates had stayed at the tables to drink away their sorrow.

Mind drifting back to My Little Warrior, I wonder if she was waiting in our dream oasis. Stepping back from the table, I leaned until Clint caught me and sat me back down.

"Easy man, wait until the wine wears off a bit before you start walking." He laughed.

"I need to get back, need to go to sleep." I faked yawning. I tried to stand again, but Leland pushed my shoulders back down.

"Nah man, rules of the party. Wolf's gotta heal ya. Give it twenty minutes," he said. I growled, not wanting to wait any longer. Maybe I could sleep here? The table seemed steady enough.

"Dude, what is it with you and sleep?" Clint mentioned casually. "You've been a stickler for bedtimes since you turned sixteen. Are you going through a ten-year growth spurt?

I lifted my lips in a smile, leaning back in my chair. It could be the alcohol talking, but for once, I wanted to open up with the roommates I had spent the past fifteen years with. They were the only ones that put up with my *sorry stoic ass*. A nickname I was often called by a certain sparring warrior. Wouldn't My Little Warrior want to see me opening up to others, anyway?

"Mr. Grouchy Pants," I could hear her say in the back of my mind. *"Live a little."*

"Have you ever..."—I began, catching the attention of the table—"thought that your dreams were better than reality?" I paused, waiting to see if my friends listened. They sat, peering at their drinks, then back to me. "That there are some days you don't want to wake up because the person you see inside your dream is far greater than anything you could ever see in the real world. The world you both create and mold to what you wanted becomes your heaven. Your dreams become more real, and your waking world becomes your nightmare, all because this one person has captured your heart and you never want to let them go?"

The table sat in silence. The few others that sat idly grabbed their drinks to walk away with blank looks on their faces. I sounded crazy. I knew I did, and the werewine wasn't helping, but it felt so much better to get it off my chest.

"Are you depressed?" Clint put his hand on my arm. "Do we need to get you to see someone? You aren't suicidal, are you? You can't hurt yourself, man, think of your future mate."

I stared at him in confusion until Leland agreed.

"He's right." He nodded frantically. "Here we can get you to the doctor, he can help you sort out these feelings."

I shook my head and pushed their hands away. "I'm not depressed or suicidal!" I sobered. "I'm just asking if any of your dreams were better than reality. Obviously, you don't have those same dreams," I muttered, drinking down a glass of water.

"Only the ones that produce wet dreams." Clint smirked.

"Ew man, don't need to hear about that," Leland snorted. "Wait! Do you think a demon has gotten into your mind? Like an incubus or succubus? You didn't tell them your name, did you?"

I sighed heavily, standing from the table. If she was a succubus, she had played the longest game of torture with me. "Forget I said anything," I snapped. "I'm feeling much better. I'm heading to bed. Don't get in any trouble."

Chapter Seven

Evelyn

"**G**randmother said I played and trained amongst the dogs."

That statement didn't just echo through the room but the entire realm. My father paused, his eyes burning with fury at the disrespectful word the former queen had called her army, her protection. The same army that put their lives on the line every day to protect not just the royal family but the entire kingdom.

The same warriors who many of had lost their parents, grandparents, cousins, sisters, and brothers to an evil so profound we thought all could have been lost just eighteen years prior. My parents stood in shock. Mom's mouth hung open and tears filled her eyes. Her tiny hands drifted over her mouth as a small cry left her lips.

Pop stood slowly, leaving my grandmother on the couch while he studied her with judgmental eyes. "Eden," Pop whispered, his head swaying, and stepped away. "I cannot believe you would stoop so low." His voice broke. Pop was a king with heart, no doubt Mom had gained his personality. It often made me wonder who should have been the true ruler all along.

Grandmother was born into the royal line. Pop found her at just the age of eighteen during their first mating ball.

He was a warrior just out of training and had come to the ball hoping to find his mate. Not only did he find a mate but also became the future ruler of the Cerulean Moon Kingdom.

"You certainly cannot believe this absurdity," Grandmother scoffed. "Are you not going to ask my side of the story?" Pop shook his head, his hand shooting through his hair. What was going on inside his head had to be a mess, and I was glad he blocked us all from feeling his emotions.

"Eden, not once has Evelyn misled us. Even as a child she was always truthful. I can hear her heart beating just fine. Her emotions are there, the grief, the suffering. Look what you've done," he whispered earnestly. Grandmother broke her stare from me, now watching her daughter gradually sit on the couch.

"Mother, I thought we were doing better. You were finally letting me rule and not hindering me. But now I find out you were just trying to indoctrinate my own daughter for your own selfish reasons?" A tear ran down my mom's cheek. Dad's silence had been deafening, his chest rising and falling with the beat of mom's heart.

A rich growl convulsed the room. Books fell from the shelves, scrolls dropped to the floor, and Torin took over his body. Bones cracking, father's clothes fell from his body until Torin stood at just over seven feet. Dad's half-beast had his hind legs bumping into the couches, side tables, and vases. Grandmother sat back in her seat, her eyes enlarging, body trembling as she pushed herself further into it.

Dad had done a beautiful job not shifting in the palace for many years. It was a rule mom had to enforce as they slowly redecorated the castle. Cinder reacted to his form, feeling the threat of how upset our parents were. I shook my head, trying to calm her, but her eyes glowed, her protectiveness shining through to protect our mother, who was doing her best to keep from sobbing.

Fuck, this was hard.

"Language, Evie," mom spoke through the link.

"She hurt you, hurt dad, I think cursing is allowed," I replied.

"Your father, you are just like him." She shook her head, rubbing her temples.

"Play with the dogs?" Torin growled, venom leaking from his fangs. "Those *warriors* serve you day in and day out without question and you call them *dogs?*" he snapped.

"Eden, this is inexcusable," Pop interjected. "It's treason to even reference that any werewolf would be considered a dog, and you have spoken it about your own subjects," he shouted.

Grandmother's head reared back at Pop's outburst. Pop was more reserved and let Grandmother walk all over him. He would do anything for her. He loved her with every fiber of his being. Somehow, he spoiled her and gave her everything she wanted. Now, she treated manipulated others to get what she wanted.

"All these years?" Mom peered at me with tears on her lashes. "My sweet Evie, I wish you would have told me," she whispered. "That she pushed you, hurt you. I thought everything was fine."

"I didn't want you to hurt, Mom. Having a relationship with your mother was important. You didn't grow up with her, giving you some happy times with her seemed important. Cinder thought differently, and I thought I could handle her." I lowered my shoulders in defeat. "I kept most of the repeating memory dreams away, the ones that would hurt me further, but a few days ago it was just too much. Cinder wouldn't hold them back for me any longer and said I needed to face it." I peered at my grandmother, who continued to keep Pop in her sight.

Pop shook his head, not coming to her rescue.

Mom seized onto dad with her tiny hands around his clawed pinky finger. "Kane, will you just hold me?" she begged. I gulped, watching to see dad's reaction. He was seething, wanting to murder his mother-in-law for hurting two of the women he loved. Dad's other hand balled into a fist so tightly blood dripped on mom's cream-colored rug.

That was going to be a bitch to get out.

"She will be punished." Dad pulled mom into his arms, cradling her against his chest. He towered over everyone in the room, leaving an ominous shadow over the couch where grandmother sat. Mom wasn't weak, not as weak as she led on at this moment. She was doing it for dad. Dad felt like he was in control of his mate, keeping her safe from her own mother because he unfortunately couldn't hit a woman, let alone a former queen.

Cinder growled again when Grandmother shot her eyes back at me. "This is your fault," she whispered. "You see how you ruined this family?"

Well, someone has balls.

Cinder forced the shift. Like father, like daughter. My bones splintered, ripping through the tunic dress, and my chestnut fur ran down my skin. Instead of going into our wolf form, we resumed our battle stance of our half-beast like father had. Two legs, long arms, and claws were ready to attack. Cinder lurched forward, hands on either side of our grandmother's head as she leaned back. The heat of my breath caused her hair to frizz, the pins that kept her perfectly groomed hair falling out of place.

No one in the room interfered, no one dared to step in front of her to save her as Cinder ripped fabric beside her head. "It's not," I snapped. This woman had done enough, and to blatantly accuse and blame me for this family falling apart was on her shoulders. As much as I had shown her I wasn't perturbed by her words, it cut me to the core.

Part of me felt it was true.

"You ruined it yourself," I snapped.

Dad wrapped an arm around my shoulder, mom still in his arms. Mom had her hands firmly on his chest, keeping her fingers brushing the small patches of skin where his scars laid from the war. It was right in the middle of his chest. A firm reminder of what he'd sacrificed.

Dad and I continued to breathe heavily, while Pop leaned up against the door next to Melody. She had her arms around his waist, face buried in his chest.

"We do this diplomatically," Mom said with steel. "With my mother being a former queen, we at least owe her that."

Backing away, we stood back on our hind legs. Mom was tenderly set on the ground, but her arm was still around dad's forearm. Mom glared, standing firm while grandmother caught her breath.

"Melody," Mom called coolly. "What is the punishment for treason against one's own kind?" Grandmother scoffed, standing from her sitting position. She pushed down her now wrinkled dress, moving her hand to push her hair behind her ears.

"You have to be joking," she said snobbishly. "That is an old law, and no one ever uses it anymore, Clarabelle. You can't be serious." Mom's brow furrowed.

Oh, she's in for it now.

Don't piss off mom.

Mom growled, letting go of dad's arm and latching on to grandmother's wrist. A bright light glowed as their skins touched, and grandmother fell to her knees. I snorted, watching grandmother experience the pain that mom collected from those she heals. Taking that pain and pushing it into someone else's body had become a weapon she used in battle. Now she used it on her own family.

Mom obviously hadn't emptied out her reserves in a while because grandmother screamed as her knees hit the floor, and she tried to push mom away. Mom pulled her hand back quickly, and guards ran into the room. Spears and claws came out as they watched the former queen fall to the floor.

Melody and I stared down at our grandmother who had once stood tall, feeling that she was better than everyone else. Now she laid on the ground, gasping for breath as her wolf healed her.

"Unacceptable, Clara," Grandmother braced herself with both hands on the floor to push up. Rubbing her wrist across her mouth, she scoffed. "You can't do anything to me. I am former royalty. I helped build this kingdom back after my father destroyed it, and I won't see it fall."

Dad snarled as the eyes of the guards expanded in disbelief. "Leave us," he snapped. They all shut the door, more guards arriving but obeying dad's command. Joshua, my favorite guard, eyed me warily, and I only shot him a quick thanks before he shut the doors.

"I've never been more serious in my life, Eden," Mom said coldly. Dad's claw pulled mom close. "Melody?" she commanded.

Melody cleared her throat, stepping away from Pop. "The old law states death."

Pop stood silent. Mom frowned, but dad looked pretty happy.

"You cannot do this!" Grandmother shouted. "I cannot believe this, if I had raised you..."

"But you didn't, did you, Eden," Mom scolded.

"I am your mother," she wagged her finger.

"Is she wanting to get shocked again?" I linked dad.

"Knew she was a cold-hearted witch," he sneered. *"I'm just glad your mother has found her voice."* Dad looked longingly at her, eyes full of love. Mom didn't share the same sentiment right now. She was too busy being pissed off.

"I will not, because no mother of mine would treat me or my children the way you have treated us, your wolves, your kingdom. You are lucky that I adore father so much or I would have had you hung in the streets, read out your wrongs, and removed your name from the history of this kingdom," she said coolly.

"Dad," I linked. *"I didn't know mom could get this mad."*

"Me either. It's hot as hell," he replied. I rolled my eyes, seeing that dad's half-beast was getting ready to sport a boner.

"Dad, stop, Your daughters are in the room."

"It's natural. Your mate will do the same unless something's wrong with him."

"Guards!" Mom shouted. The enormous crowd of guards filtered into the room. Pop pulled Melody away, holding onto her tight as they entered.

"As ruling queen, I am having you arrest Eden, former Queen of the Cerulean Moon Kingdom, on the acts of treason against your own kind, referring to them as dogs." Guards with questioning looks now stared at Grandmother in disgust. "You hold no respect for your fellow wolves, your family, or your own mate." Mom's eyes drifted to Pop, who remained silent. He nodded, begging for mom to continue.

"Details of your punishment will be determined. You will now be escorted to the nobles' dungeon cell and await further punishment. Guards, remove her."

Holy hell.

Chapter Eight

Evelyn

Grandmother glared at the guards. Her body slinked away from the doorway and further into the room. "You can't do this, Clarabelle. This isn't right, and you know it." Mom rubbed her temples. Dad took his colossal form and sat on the tiny-to-him sofa and pulled mom into his lap. Torin, the beast of the room, growled, causing the guards to panic.

"Arrest her, you heard your queen," Torin spat before dad could get a word in. Five guards approached, Joshua standing in front of Pop as if to guard him against his own mate. "Clara, stop this," Grandmother panicked. "We can talk about this."

Mom shook her head, which was firmly braced against Torin's neck. Mom had had it. She had held on so long. Her heart was undoubtedly more tender than mine would ever be, but that was what was so great about my parents. They were complete opposites that balanced each other in the purest way.

Grandmother didn't go quietly. She kicked and screamed until they grabbed hold of her, wrapping ropes of silver laced with wolfsbane around her. Enough to keep her from shifting, but not enough to harm her. She screeched, causing Pop to wince, but he dared not look her way. Grandmother screamed for him and begged for him to come help, but Pop continued to comfort Melody, who sobbed in his arms.

"You've made your bed, Eden," Pop finally said as they dragged her out the door. "You've hurt our daughter and your granddaughter. That is something I will have a hard time forgiving." Grandmother's eyes softened, and the screams ceased. Her body slumped into the guards' arms as they dragged her away.

Melody shut the doors behind them as they left, and the tension in the room subsided. The room felt lighter. We breathed easier, and the thrumming of hearts beating inside chests slowed. Mom sat up on dad's lap and my wolf, Cinder, relaxed enough to allow us to shift back into our human selves.

It was a slow, agonizing shift. I felt every crack, every bone snapping. I whimpered, feeling the pain but also welcoming it. It was a coming home sort of pain, not just feeling the guilt eat at me in my heart but also in the bones and skin that transformed me back into the body that failed to protect the family.

Dad stood, still in his beast form, picking up the torn black tunic he originally wore and wrapping it around my body. I began to tie the shreds together, trying to weave them appropriately to cover my privates. I was sure I looked like a warrior princess now. My hair was a mess, my breasts and private parts were covered just enough so I didn't have to feel embarrassed to be naked. Not that it mattered. I was a warrior, and warriors don't worry about such trivial things as nudity.

But dad did. He hated the idea of mom or any of his daughters being naked in front of anyone. He was always ready with a shirt to cover as we trained. His protectiveness didn't suffocate me but made me feel cared for in his own barbaric way.

Once dad was satisfied I was covered, he shifted as well. He opted to stay naked, sitting on the sofa with a pillow covering his privates. That didn't stop mom from crawling over and sitting in his lap, running her fingers through his hair to calm him.

Would My Guard be like that? Need that much comfort to calm him? The previous dream I had with him, he took my hand in his and breathed easier when we touched. I couldn't be sure. It could just be the friendly touch, but I secretly hoped it was me that had the same effect.

Pop sighed, pulling Melody with him, and led her to the sofa. He picked up the now broken tea set from the floor and set it on the cracked table. "Don't make your decision about your mother based on my account. What she has done is inexcusable, and I feel it is my fault."

"It's not," mom replied quickly. "She has control of her own actions, and you can't blame yourself for your mate's wrongdoings." Mom gulped, her hands wringing around each other.

"Mom, I'm sorry for keeping it from you. Once she said things about the warriors, the guards, I didn't think I could hold it in anymore. Cinder was done with helping me. She was ready to just let it all out."

Mom nodded. "I'm still upset you didn't come to me, Evie. For most of your childhood, you had to worry about her, and for that, I will forever blame myself for not paying attention," she explained. I opened my mouth to protest, but she held up her hand to stop me. "I guess I need to blame your father, too. You inherited his fierceness to protect this family and those closest to him. It's only natural for you to want to do that." Mom smiled.

"Hey, I was good the past hour," he grumbled. "I didn't hit her or do anything you would be mad about, and yet you blame me about the fucking exceptional genetics our children inherited." Mom giggled, patting his chest.

"Oh, Alpha, I'm just playing with you." Mom placed a chaste kiss on his lips. "Dad?" Mom called for Pop, who was still looking longingly at the door. "I have an idea on how to deal with mom, but I want your opinion. If you say no, I understand, and we can figure something else out."

Pop shook his head, his hand rubbing up and down his beard. "Clara, she needs a firm hand to bring her back to reality. To remind her who she was when we first mated. I can't give her that, but you can. You have Kane by your side, and even though you don't want to see it, you have some of your mother's stubbornness in you. Use that to your advantage."

Mom bit her lip. She and Dad had a silent conversation while I sat beside Pop. My head resting on his shoulder.

Pop was the sweetest guy I knew, probably the softest king to date. Maybe that was why grandmother thought she had to be strong for both of them, but then got carried away. Her father, my great-grandfather, was a real asshole. He wanted power and ultimately started the shifter wars over a thousand years ago. Somehow, Grandma was able to overthrow him. It wasn't a story well known within the family because grandmother didn't want to go into details of what happened. Just that, she overpowered him during the war, found Pop, and together they put a stop to all the fighting.

"I'm sorry I didn't tell you either, Pop," I muttered.

He only petted my head, rocking me back and forth. "I understand why you didn't, and I'm not angry at all, Princess. You are strong. I'm glad you got that from your dad. He's a magnificent wolf."

Dad frowned as he heard that, his eyes softening while mom cleared her throat. "Dad, I've come to a decision, but I want your opinion." She licked her lips. "I wish to banish Mother." Melody gasped, gripping Pop's hand. As much as Melody knew how wrong Grandmother was, she still looked up to her. "Now hear me out. It will be for a trial period. Mother will be banished to Earth and spend time with the shifter snow leopards in the Siberian mountains. They are a very rural, snow-covered community. She will remain there for a period of ten years, working with them as part of their pack and getting her hands dirty. This will help her reconnect with her wolf..." She paused. "I feel like if she forced herself to shift, become better acquainted with Amula, that she would listen to her."

I'd never even seen Amula, Grandmother's wolf. I thought maybe she hid herself away within Grandmother's body and didn't want to appear again.

"She's suppressed her, and I want her to have to rely on Amula while she's—"

"Almost freezing to death?" I added unapologetically. Mom bit her lip, nodding.

"Living there, she will have to rely on her wolf for warmth and comfort. I also want to have Taliyah cast a glamor spell so no one will realize who she is. That way, no extra help or aid will come to her."

Pop only stared at mother, and after a few minutes of silence, he agreed. "It is a wonderful idea, Clara. Innovative, clever, creative. I do ask one thing of you, however." He ran his hand over his face. "That I accompany her. She may be the one guilty, but my love and my bond to her are too strong to stay away."

"I figured as much," Mom said. "Even though I don't want to see you go." Mom let go of dad, walking past the broken glass of the table, and pulled Pop into a tender embrace.

I don't think I had ever seen my grandmother hug my mom. I could very well have missed it, but Grandmother's royal and queenly appearance wouldn't allow her to put such emotions on display. How she ended up with Pop was a mystery, but hopefully, this banishment would serve to better her, to reconnect her with the wolf she seemed to have lost.

Two weeks had passed. Grandmother was taken care of far more swiftly than other criminals of the land. Being royal had perks, I suppose. Melody helped mom with the proper documents since it had been many, many moons since anyone of royal status had been punished.

Everything was done by the books, except for one thing that was considered punishment. Mom decided not to hold a public humiliation, the Reading of Sins, as many called it. Despite the wrongs she had committed, it didn't completely overshadow what she had done for her country. She brought it freedom, a new age when she took over after her father, and Mom wanted to preserve and recognize Grandmother's legacy.

. Guards were sworn to secrecy about the specific details of the former queen's treason. Mom let the kingdom talk, not correcting or agreeing with any of the gossip.

Sorceress and former queen Taliyah and her mate Jasper arrived yesterday to cast the glamor spell. Grandmother's beautiful appearance was now that of an average-looking wolf. She had remained quiet during the entire ordeal as she stood in the throne room, her head held low. Pop stood beside her, taking on the same glamor spell, but even with his below average looks, he still looked handsome to me.

Pop smiled, pulling Grandmother's hand to his lips, and kissed it. It was the first time that they had seen or touched each other in nearly two weeks. Both of their faces had faded, grey settling in their cheeks, but once they touched, the small glow in their cheeks returned.

Pop was right, he couldn't stay away from her.

All of my uncles, Mikal, Ian, Hutton, and Rigg, stood with their hands behind their backs. They had said their goodbyes to their mother earlier in the week. Mikal was taking it the hardest, only because he now felt like he needed to watch his younger brothers, even if they were all just a year apart in age.

Mikal couldn't understand why his mother was being taken to Earth for banishment. At first, he blamed me for overreacting, but once Pop explained what she said about the guards, he apologized to me profusely.

Mom told her brothers they would still receive the best education, even stating that they could take control of what they wanted to learn. Mikal was too worried about his younger brothers to declare what he wanted in his education, only that he wanted his younger brothers taken care of. Ultimately, they decided to spend a year in each kingdom of Bergarian—a year in Vermillion, Golden Light Kingdom, and even Atlantis.

It still didn't make me feel any better that my uncles would be away. Mikal reassured me they would be fine and looked forward to some freedom. Maybe we were both suffering and too scared to say anything.

I felt I had broken our family. Now we would be spread apart between realms because I couldn't hold in Cinder.

Cinder growled, hating my guilt. She reassured me this was how it was supposed to be. The churning in my gut from last night's events didn't help me either. I held back a sob, trying to listen to the formalities.

"You will have three guards traveling with you to Earth. A sorceress will wait on the other side of the portal to transport you to Siberia," Mom stated as she sat on the throne. Dad settled in Torin's body. The two-legged beast was still on edge with Mom staying awake for nights on end, worried she was making the wrong decision. Torin, being in his form, helped calm him, even if this wasn't just a battle between the physical, just the mental. He felt control in this state.

"Once they see you are there and settled with the pride, they will return. Kane and I will visit you in five years and see your progress. You will take the full time of ten years. Good behavior will not bring you home any faster," Mom stated.

Pop had already conveyed his goodbyes to all of us. This meeting in the throne room was a formality to let the rest of the Wolf Court see that Grandmother had been given her orders and that they would be followed.

Pop gave me a wink. Melody laced her fingers with mine as we watched the guards escort them away.

"The spell will fade in exactly ten years," Taliyah spoke. "If they are on Earth, it still won't matter. It will fade and the shifters will see who they really are."

Mom hummed, hugging Taliyah. "I appreciate you doing this. I know you like to stay away."

Taliyah and Jasper were banished from the Vermillion throne after the war. The Vermillion Parliament wanted a full-blooded vampire to take the throne, and Taliyah's mixed witch and vampire genes from her biological father's affair made them uneasy. Then having Jasper as a mate that supposedly wanted to take my mom for himself in the beginning stirred even more trouble. Now they waited for Cassius to take the throne in five years' time while Sebastian and Christine ruled as interim royalty to help rebuild Vermillion back to its former glory. Of course, Taliyah had a hand in all the decisions. Sebastian took Taliyah's suggestions seriously because he thought she should have continued to rule.

Taliyah saved the entirety of Vermillion, and the Parliament was too set in their ways to see it. They wanted a full-blood vampire royal. As long as Taliyah and Jasper's son was a full-blooded vampire and not a werewolf or witch, he would take the throne at twenty-five. Which he was, thank the gods. The parliament made it very clear they wanted a vampire and wouldn't settle for anything less for their "beloved kingdom."

Cassius was seven months younger than me, but he looked much older, more dignified and refined than I. He had shoulder length, jet black hair, permanent fangs that peeked through his lips, but who knew what he looked like from his nose upward. He wore a dark mask that covered most of his face. What little skin it did show, such as his chiseled jaw and slender neck, was beautiful. His height along with his dark clothing and mysterious aura gave him the appeal of a sexy demon summoned from the Underworld.

And freakishly mysterious.

"How are you, Cassius?" I stepped forward, curtsying. I wasn't a complete idiot. I knew when I had to be royal and polite. Even if he looked like a cold-hearted prince, I would not be completely rude.

Cassius bowed stiffly, one arm over his waist and the other behind his back. His dark bluntly cut, shoulder length hair fell in front of his face. "Splendid. And how are you, Princess Evelyn?" I snorted, not princess like, I swear Cassius' lip twitched.

"Just Evie, you know that *Prince Cassius,*" I mocked. "Are you staying for the mating ball tomorrow?" I gritted my teeth.

"Yes, mother is adamant that I attend each mating ball until I find her." He sighed. "She just doesn't understand my mission right now, and it is not the time for my mate to come into the picture." Cassis stood straight, looking at me.

"She's trying to help. My mom is making me go, too," I muttered, keeping my voice low so my parents didn't hear while Mom signed the last few documents for Grandmother's departure.

Cassius tilted his head, his gloved hand extending to pick up my hand that dangled by my dress. "And you do not wish to find your mate yet, either?"

I shook my head, shame filling me. My birthday was yesterday, and it was taking everything inside me to keep from breaking down into tears. Again.

Because the one wolf I wanted wasn't meant to be mine.

Chapter Nine

Kit

My Little Warrior kept a tight lip about her birthday fast approaching. Each day, well night, she told me how much trouble her grandmother was in. That the family was devastated learning the trials and hardships My Warrior had gone through, along with her grandmother's blasphemous words against her own kind. Her grandmother was banished by the head Alpha. Little Warrior wasn't completely certain when her grandmother would return. The guilt ate her up and all I could do was pull her into me, sitting back on the soft bark of the tree while we watched the crazy animals she came up with do various tricks to make me laugh.

She comforted me more than I comforted her, or maybe my presence was enough for her and her wolf to be calm. We stayed like this for days, hardly speaking. It was an unspoken rule we wouldn't talk about our future mates, the details of our lives, or who we really were. Yet, we knew everything about each other.

She thought I may have forgotten, or maybe she just kept it to herself, but tonight was the night she turned eighteen. If My Warrior felt anything toward me and her touch runs up my arm and doesn't feel the spark, the bond, it will kill her. I knew I was going to die all over again, knowing that we were not made for one another.

Yet I didn't have the heart to tell her she wasn't my mate. Keeping it hidden all those years may have been selfish, but she was young then, and I didn't have strong romantic feelings toward her. Each passing birthday, the older she became, those feelings grew. I should have stopped them, I should have reminded myself that she wasn't mine, but my wolf was too attuned to her. Then she turned seventeen, and my heart grew even more fond of her.

Hell, I loved her, and I wanted her to love me too.

I couldn't feel the sparks as I held her these past few weeks, and now she was going to know. She had been reserved this week. I chalked it up to the mess with her grandmother, but maybe it was more anxiety about what this dream might bring. She was going to be terribly disappointed if she truly had feelings for me.

Maybe this was all just a terrible dream. A dream that had lasted for nearly eight years with no signs of letting up. She could be a succubus for all I knew. But would a succubus be as sweet as her?

Shaking my head, I walked up to the same tree I'd guided myself to for two weeks. She didn't come down, waiting for me to climb up and find her. Was she afraid? Had she already found her mate? I growled in frustration. I didn't want anyone to have her; I wanted her, and my wolf felt the same.

"Warrior?" I called out. I was dressed in the same leather pants and white open front tunic from days past. We hadn't worn sparring clothes for days, and she'd even worn the same white colored loose tunic dress. It suited her, hell even the leather sparring pants did. She always looked beautiful. My stomach in knots, I called out to her again, readying myself to climb until I heard a whisper of her voice.

"I'm here," she called from behind the tree.

"What are you doing back there?" I chuckled, getting ready to round the tree. "Why are you hiding from me?"

She sighed heavily until I saw her hand hold the bark. "Just worried about what you might think."

I placed my hands on my hips, tilting my head in confusion. "Since when do you care what people think, Warrior? Last I recall, you snorted like a boar when I told you that pixie joke involving a bottle of love potion and a dragonfly." She giggled. "Ah, there she is. Now why don't you come around from that tree and let me see what you are so worried about? You know I'd never judge you."

"Promise?" she whispered. This wasn't My Warrior. My Warrior was confident, bold, and could be downright scary in the sparring ring.

"Warrior, present yourself. You are riling me up," I said sternly. Her breath heaved and her bare foot hit the grass at the base of the tree. She wasn't wearing her casual tunic dress, leather pants or even loose t-shirt and shorts. Those were long gone, and this Warrior became someone else.

One hand traced the large base of the tree trunk, her body walking alongside it. Her blue eyes looked up at me with trepidation. Her lips were rosy red, and deep lash paint coated her eyelashes. Her hair was curled to perfection, and her red dress hugged her body at the waist and trailed around her hips, stopping at mid-thigh. The deep V-neck caused me to stiffen, and not just my body.

I had grown hard, and hell, I had never grown a damn erection in our magical realm, but I had one now. Her teeth bit down on her lip as she came closer. It felt like an eternity as her bare feet tickled over the grass until she reached me.

"So?" her voice was low and sultry as she strode toward me. "What do you think?"

I gulped. "It's red."

"I'm glad your mother taught your colors well." She smiled softly. Pulling up her fingers, she picked at them absentmindedly, glancing at her nails and then at me.

Red.

It was the Bergarian mating color. Seas of reds had filtered in the mixer just weeks ago, and it almost made me sick. I remembered how Queen Clara hated the color, but even she wouldn't change a thousand year old tradition. Red was the mating color in almost every culture of this realm. Red to lure in your mate, to draw you in.

"Take a breath, Guard." Evelyn's hand went to touch my bare chest, but I stepped away. The pained look in her eyes had my chest tightening. Looking away, she brushed her hand to her thigh.

Damn it.

"Listen, I didn't mean…"

She backed away, shaking her head.

"No, you are absolutely stunning. I mean gods, you're gorgeous." I stepped forward, still not touching her.

"Then why did you back away?" The once confident woman broke, and I was breaking her further. She did think of me as something more. It wasn't just a one-sided attraction, and now I had to let her down, gently.

"There is something I need to tell you, and there is no easy way of saying this."

Evelyn's hands balled into fists. "You are going to reject me?"

My mouth hung open, the wind picking up around us. The vines touching our bodies gave small swats of pain from the small leaves on bare skin. The sky darkened, and light sources retreated.

"Gods, no! I would never do that to you, Warrior. I care about you too much to ever do such a dreadful thing."

Her eyes filled with tears, her face softening. "Then what is it? Would you rather have me in the old clothes?" She blinked, her brown corset and black leathers now covering her body.

"I'll take whatever you can give me, your friendship, companionship, your love," I begged. "Because I don't want to give you up, and I have been selfish over the years not telling you, but then I was afraid you wouldn't speak to me again. That I would never see you."

My Warrior's eyebrows furrowed in confusion. "What do you mean? I don't understand?"

"Touch me, Warrior."

With desperation in her eyes, she grabbed my hand. She stilled. My Warrior hit my hand and shook it a few more times, just to see if the spark would come to life. If I wasn't so damn sad about her finding out we weren't mates, I would have laughed. She pulled my hand to her neck, and she had me lay my fingers across her mark.

"I don't understand," she sniffed. "I really thought—"

"That I was yours?" I tilted my head, lifting her chin up to look at me. She was crying, and she never cried. "You dressed like this for me?" I smiled, puffing out my chest.

"I thought we were. I'm an idiot." She shook her head and tried to pull away. Pulling her back into my embrace, I held her close. My lips touched her forehead. She stiffened for a moment but then relaxed, putting her arms around me.

"When I turned eighteen, I really hoped you were mine, Warrior."

I laid my cheek on her forehead. "But I couldn't be sure, didn't want to say anything because maybe you just needed to come of age too, but now—"

"Now you know." Her voice turned firm. Stepping out of my arms, she turned her head. "We aren't made for each other, and now I'm embarrassed."

"Now, hold on a minute," I wagged my finger at her. "I think you could still be my mate. This is a strange dream world. We can hardly smell each other; we don't have the peak senses here. There is still hope." My voice cracked. "I didn't know you felt the same..."

My Warrior wiped her cheek with her hand. "Yeah, well, now you know." She sniffed. "And we aren't mates. You're dreaming."

"I think you are the one dreaming, Warrior." Her eyes widened, her breath catching. "And you are the one that brought me here. You're a

Dream Wanderer. You said you weren't bringing me here, that you weren't enchanting me to be in your presence. Now, is that true?"

She stuttered, catching her breath. "Of course it's true. I don't know how you are here. Ever since my dreams came, you have been here." I reached for her, pulling her in by the waist. Her body plastered against mine.

"We will not worry about this tonight," I brushed her hair away from her face.

"We aren't?" she questioned.

Shaking my head, I cupped my hand to her cheek. "Tonight is your birthday. I think we should spend it celebrating, don't you?"

My Warrior sighed. "How can I celebrate when—"

I put a finger to her lips. "You let me worry about it." The expression in her eyes let me know she didn't agree, but I ignored it. "Now, how about you get back in that red dress? I was rather fond of it." I smirked. She snorted, making me laugh as her eyes closed and the gorgeous dress fell back on her body. Her hair tumbled down to beautiful tresses of curls, and her eyes were soft and warm.

"Gorgeous," I whispered, pulling one of her hands to the side with one hand, while my other wrapped around her waist. "Now, I think you are owed a special dance on your birthday, are you not?" I raised an eyebrow.

It was a rite of passage, a woman choosing a man to dance with on her birthday if she didn't find her mate. Males, of course, were given no such of tradition, but hell, it was a beautiful sight to see a woman choose someone she thought to be second best to her mate. With her grandmother being sent away, My Warrior declined to have a party for herself, but there was a mixer later she was required to attend by order of her mother.

One I hoped she would not attend.

"I thought I was to choose who I danced with," she countered, swaying as we listened to the crickets and birds of the mysterious dream.

"Yeah, well, I figured I would be your first choice anyway," I said cockily. She giggled while I pulled her closer, having her head rest just under my neck.

We swayed to the quietness of the forest. The dream surrounding us was its own song. Our breathing matched, hell, I swore I thought our hearts thrummed rhythmically with each other as I held her close.

My Warrior lifted her head, after what felt like hours holding her close to me. "We can't do this; we can't become so attached to each other. It isn't fair to our mates," she whispered. "You deserve your soul mate, Guard. You deserve the soul that was intended to you by the goddess." She pulled away, but I pulled her back into my arms.

"I still think we could be mates," I said firmly. "You need to stop thinking so hard. Give me your name so I can find you. I'll hunt you down and pull you into my arms, and then you can have me in the waking world."

My Warrior played with my open tunic, feeling the strings that lay untied with her fingers. "I can't do that." A tear fell down her face.

"And why the hell not?" I snapped. My wolf flashed his eyes, but My Warrior's stance did not falter.

"Because what would happen if we met, and we weren't truly mates," she whispered. "Then we would be more broken than we are now." She sniffed. "A couple of silly wolves that fell in love that weren't supposed to."

Silence came between us until I grasped her upper arms, squeezing me tightly. "Then I will take you as mine," I said with conviction. "Because without a shadow of a doubt, I want you as my mate, Warrior. Give me your name," I pleaded. "Let me find you, take you, make you my mate and my soulmate." She shook her head.

"My mother and father told me how amazing finding a mate can be. The instant attraction, the love, the passion between them." She looked away. "I've promised my father I would find my mate, my true mate. If he found out I took one that wasn't gifted to me from the goddess, he would have your head, and I can't have that happen."

"I will fight for you. Anything that stands in my way, I'm willing to do what it takes. Please, your name," I pleaded again.

"I'm saving you for your mate, I'm doing this because I care about you, Guard. Someone out there is better and once you see her, she'll make you forget all about me," she sobbed. The black paint fell from her face, her red lips stained by the dark colors of her tears. "I couldn't live with myself if you found her while you were with me, if we had to break things off to be with her."

"I would never!" I roared. "I would never leave you. You are my mate, Warrior. A name now," I commanded. My orders within the Alabaster Academy were stronger than any other, wolves bowed before me but not this wolf. She held her back straight, pushing her hair over her back.

Who the hell was she?

"No, Guard." Her voice strengthened. "You will thank me one day, that I made you wait to find your true mate."

"I will never," I growled. My lips curled in disgust. "You're it for me. I'm going to find you." The dream sequence was waning, details of the dream fading into nothing but a blur.

"Don't leave yet," I begged her. "Not yet. Let me find you. Now that I know your feelings, there has to be more."

"If the goddess wants us to find each other in reality, then it will happen," she replied somberly.

But I wanted her now. I wanted to feel the beat of her heart, her skin touching mine. I pulled her close, the fading of the dream coming in swiftly. Her blue eyes bore into me, my hand cupping her cheek. There was no fear, only her soul shattering into a million pieces.

"I'll see you in the next dream. We will discuss this further." Her weak smile wobbled, not giving me an answer. Without thinking, I crashed my lips into hers. My body pulling her close to me as I massaged her lips. The warmth of her lips parted, inviting me to sneak my tongue into her mouth. Letting me in, I rubbed my tongue across hers. Moaning into the kiss, she wrapped her arms around my shoulders. Feeling contentment, my wolf howled for joy as she kept her body close, not fighting for dominance and taking what I gave her.

My hand gripped the back of her head, pulling her head back so I could kiss down her neck. As soon as I got to the nape of her neck, my lips twitched, feeling her body melt into me. Her marking spot was right there, just a kiss there was all I wanted. Before my lips descended, my eyes flew open, and I saw nothing but the white walls of the room I shared with my roommates.

Chapter Ten

Evelyn

"You wanted to see me?" Taliyah interrupted Cassius's and my conversation. He bowed to his mother and walked over to be with his father. Mom and Dad looked over in curiosity, but their attention was diverted away as Jasper and Cassius impeded their vision.

"I need your help," I whispered.

Taliyah studied me, her deep red eyes widening in confusion. Using her telepathic powers, she read the thoughts that sang loudly in my mind.

"I need help blocking my dreams."

Her eyes widened. *"Why would you want to do such a thing?"* she asked as she led me out of the throne room. Her arm touched me, and she breathed out a sigh. *"You're a Dream Wanderer?"*

It was no secret that Taliyah was a strong sorceress. She was powerful and had grown even more so during her self-exile to the northern part of the Cerulean Moon Kingdom. With a touch, she could know what I was, and if she probed deeper within my thoughts, she could discover what I was thinking.

"No one knows about this gift except your immediate family?" she asked.

"That's right. And mom doesn't know that I'm asking you to do this. I know it's unhealthy to block a power, but I really need this right now. Even if it is just for a while," I pleaded.

Taliyah murmured to herself, tapping her lips. "I might have something. You have to be sure you want to block your dreams because once you take this elixir, it will block all of your night dreams for at least six months," she warned. "Dream Wanderers thrive on their dreams. It's part of who you are. It's a gift, Evelyn, and I really wish you wouldn't use this. Dreams can give you warnings and advice and fill you with hope. It's a gift many would want to have."

I pursed my lips, heeding her warning. "What are the side effects?"

"I don't know. Dream Wanderers are rare—there have been only a few supernaturals to study. I would want to stay in contact with you if you took it. I'm strongly advising against it, however," she said sternly. "Why would you want to block such a gift? Are you having trouble controlling it?"

"Something like that," I muttered. "Someone is visiting me in the dream that I don't want to visit any longer and I don't know how to keep them away."

Taliyah grew pensive, pulling at the dark navy dress she wore. "Are they bothering you? Is that why you don't want to dream? Is it causing nightmares instead? If someone is hurting you in a dream, Evelyn, then I can perform an exorcism."

I shook my head violently. "No, no, they aren't hurting me."

"I can read your mind without asking," Taliyah warned. "I can't let one of my best friend's daughters be hurt."

"I swear I'm not being hurt, not physically. I just don't want to see this person anymore. Please don't read my mind, it's embarrassing," I pleaded.

Taliyah's face softened, her arm reaching out to pull me into a hug. "I would never. I'm just worried about you. You are nothing but a stone wall on the outside, Evelyn, you always have been. On the inside, I think you are just as soft as your mother." I sniffed, holding her close. "If you really want to do this, meet me outside of my room before the mating ball tonight. I'll give you the elixir."

After hours of preparation for my first Mating Ball, I stood outside of Taliyah's door. I skimmed up and down the hallways to make sure my younger brothers weren't sneaking up behind me. They loved to play a good game of hide and seek and somehow, I always became their favorite prey.

I cleared my throat, my hand rising to knock on the light-colored door only to have it open with Jasper smiling. "Evie, come on in. Taliyah is waiting for you."

I beamed, stepping inside. Their living area was large, fit for a visiting king or queen, which it should be rightfully so for the couple, yet they had to live in a humble cabin. Due to the Vermillion parliament hating that Taliyah was not a full-blooded vampire. Sebastian and Christine took their places now until Cassius was of age to retake the throne.

Jasper cut wood, hunted, mended fences, and did anything outdoors. Taliyah practiced her sorcery, mostly creating healing agents for those that lived a more secluded life in the northern area of the kingdom. It was a small happy life, and really, they seemed happier every year that passed. The only dark cloud looming over them was that their son would come to the throne, and they wouldn't be able to follow him.

"Come on in." Taliyah was putting her curled hair up into a bun. Her navy-blue dress, filled with silver and gold diamonds, trickled to the floor. Mom had it made especially for Taliyah because she would neither create nor wear such a thing in the middle of the forest.

Laying the brush down on the ivory table, she picked up a purple bottle with gold rope around it. It would be concealed in the pocket of my dress. She sighed, standing, and came toward me. "I worked on it this afternoon, fresh ingredients so the potency will make it last."

Cassius stepped out of an adjoining bedroom, moving closer. His black tux and the deep red underside of his cape gave me shivers as he strode forward. A silver crown sat on his head and his hand reached out to grasp mine, giving it a chaste kiss.

"It is certainly too bad you aren't mates," Jasper commented. "It would have made it easier for the kingdoms to get along better."

Taliyah shoved Jasper playfully. "Are you kidding? They are too much alike in trying to protect their families. They would be torn apart with distance trying to maintain both kingdoms." Jasper shrugged, kissing Taliyah on the forehead.

My lips tingled, remembering how the Guard kissed me before the dream had faded away. It was my first kiss, my first dream kiss, anyway. I wanted the fire, the sparks, the fireworks to engulf me from my mate, but there was no doubt of the attraction that we shared. Now that was all going to end, because if I saw him again, I knew he would try to find out my name, who I was, and how to find me.

What was I to do then? Let him find me? Take me even if I wasn't his true mate? Dad would destroy him, even if I told dad I loved him. My family was too adamant about finding mates and keeping the tradition of the Moon Goddess finding the best one for you. I couldn't disappoint my family further.

I'd already pulled the family apart once. I would not do it again. If that meant sacrificing my happiness, I would. Besides, My Guard deserved the best, and the best was his mate. No matter what ridiculousness he had floating in his head that we could be together.

We were just a dream.

But a wonderful dream.

"I don't keep secrets between families," Taliyah stepped closer to me. "Your mother and father know you are here."

"T-they do?"

"Yes, and before you take this, they would like to speak with you. They are putting their trust in you to do that."

I bit my lip as I took the bottle.

"I don't know what is going on. Maybe you're trying to get rid of the memory dreams that your power sends you, but they are there for a reason. This person who keeps showing up has to mean something to you in your reality."

That was what I once thought, that's what I thought My Guard was there for. To show me he was my mate, but even in a dream, he wasn't mine. "I know, but I still would like to take it."

Taliyah sighed, leading me to the door. "They will meet you in the receiving room above the ballroom." She patted my shoulders. "Just remember, it lasts for six months, and I want to check in with you frequently to see how you are doing. For any side effects."

I silently nodded. "Can I get more when the six months run out?" I asked hopefully.

Taliyah clasped her hands together. "Let's see what happens, shall we?" There was no promise in her voice. It was the same voice my mother used when she said, "maybe" I could go out and play in the rain. It usually meant no, but that small sliver of hope made me keep going about my day. And I would hold on to that sliver of hope as long as it kept me away from the guard of my dreams.

Mom sat on father's lap. Her eyes drifting. The twins, Dax and Dimitri, had been giving mom a run for her money, wanting nothing more than to cuddle up in her arms whenever they were near. Along with dealing with Grandma, Pop, and her brothers, she was beyond exhausted. Now she had to deal with me, the daughter that wanted to rid herself of her powers for a short period to heal.

Mom, being the sounding board of the family, explained she wasn't angry that I would ask Tayliah for an elixir to help. Mom was upset that I wouldn't speak to her first. Putting more stress on mom wasn't what I wanted, so of course I kept a secret. And another large one.

"I'm sorry you didn't have a larger birthday celebration, Evelyn," mom yawned. I shook my head, throwing my hand out awkwardly.

"Seriously, mom, I'm not into that kind of stuff. The Mating Ball is enough of a party. The palace didn't need two parties back-to-back." Dad huffed in agreement. He hated the mating balls as much as doing royal kingly stuff.

"At least there is cake!" Melody chimed in. Her love for sweets was going to hurt her wolf one day. I laughed, watching her eye the dessert table below. Sweets and hot cocoa, that's all that girl would live off.

"Do you think he's here?" I heard mom whisper to dad.

"Possibly. What do you think, Princess? Think your mate is out there?" Dad held mom close again, kissing her cheek as he gazed across the ballroom.

It was a sea of women in red gowns and men in tuxes. It was undoubtedly a formal affair when any dance was held in the palace, and the ocean of red-clothed women waited for their mates. I swallowed heavily, whispering to myself. "I certainly hope not."

Mother frowned, leaving dad behind. Peering down at her, I couldn't believe how much taller I really was than her. Almost by a head and a half. She was stunning, a tiny thing as dad would love to mutter under his breath. I had always been jealous of how small she was, because she was the woman I had looked up to, based my standard of beauty upon.

It didn't matter to me that most werewolf women were tall and muscular. She was different, and that strengthened her. Melody wasn't far behind in my mother's looks, she had the same shorter stature, except she'd been gifted with stunning curves.

Why was I having these terrible feelings? I never worried about looks with My Guard. He always made me feel comfortable in my own skin. Even when I was young, going through the terrible awkward stages of finding myself and my wolf, I was the prettiest little girl he had ever seen. Of course, I turned up my nose at the compliment, even telling him to keep his cooties away from me.

My Guard thought me just fine. He called me gorgeous and said he wanted to find me. He wanted me more than he wanted his own mate, but what if she came along one day? A mate bond was stronger than anything imaginable, a force to be reckoned with. He wanted to give that up for me?

I bit my cheek, wincing at the sharp fang inserting into the soft skin.

"Evie," mom said. "Are you wanting to hide your dreams because of your grandmother and the memories, or is it something more?"

I sighed heavily, watching shifter after shifter finding their mates below.

"It's more, mom, but I don't want to talk about it. I promise that it has nothing to do with you or the family. It's about me, sorting through some issues I have." I took a breath. "I'm just trying to learn who I am is all."

Mom wrapped her arms around my waist, and I returned the affection. *Please let that be a good enough answer.*

"Evie, there is no rush. If you do not wish to find your mate tonight, you don't have to. The goddess works in mysterious ways, and he will be presented to you when it's time, alright? Know that I'm here, and do not keep things that worry you from me. I'm your mother, I want to listen, not have you bottle it up inside. You are so like your father. He hides it until he explodes or almost kills some poor wolf." She smiled.

"I wouldn't mind a bit of sparring right now." I chuckled.

"That's my princess." Dad patted my head. "Now, it is a tradition that the princess has to participate in at least one dance if their mate is not present. If you don't want to, you don't have to." Dad tried to smile, but it was crooked and uncomfortable.

"Don't want me to dance, Dad?"

"Not really," he growled. "I'd rather break their arms rather than have any wolf touch you."

Oh, little do you know.

"What about a friend? Someone we both trust?" I asked. "You know, for the sake of appearances of the princess' first Mating Ball dance. The kingdom still thinks I'm too much of a tomboy to show up in a dress. I need to shock them a bit."

"Like who?" Dad growled. My eyes shot to Cassius, but his mother shook her head and giggled. Cassius may have a mask on his face, but his neck turned deep red. I giggled until I saw Joshua standing in the corner in his resting position.

"Joshua?" I called. The family guard sauntered toward us, the large buzzed-cut brute bowed stiffly and put his arms to the side. "Will you give me my first dance?" I waved my hand nervously.

For the first time, I saw all of Joshua's teeth. They were bright white, and his eyes lit up with amusement. "I would love to, Princess—"

"Evie," I interrupted. Joshua held out his arm and father pushed him back by his neck and into the nearby wall. The music in the ballroom stopped, all eyes now on the observation floor of the dance floor.

"Kane!" Mom shouted at him, but she let him go.

"Touch her anywhere other than where you are supposed to, and you will end up as ogre bait," Dad spat out.

Chapter Eleven

Kit

"**G**et up, Kit." Leland shook me. "Are you sick or something? Why isn't he up?" He poked me again, and I gripped his hand tightly, hearing the crunch of bone. "The hell, dude!? You broke my finger!" He jolted back, holding his hand to his chest.

"Gods, never touch Kit. He hates it when people touch him. Plus, you ruined his beauty sleep, he fucking hates that!" Clint slapped the back of Leland's head.

"He's usually up by now. I've never had to wake him," Leland complained. "But we are gonna be late for breakfast if he doesn't get up now."

I blew out a breath, blinking my eyes repeatedly, and jolted out of bed. The light sources had already peered through the window, and the room was warming from their rays. "It's late?" I muttered. "But..."

"You alright, man?" Leland asked, and I growled. Clint stepped back.

"I didn't dream," I panicked. I pushed myself away from the room. Rubbing my face in my hands, I lost it. There had only been a few times since I've met My Warrior that we didn't visit each other's dreams. Those days, I was forewarned because she was having sleepovers with either her sister or distant cousins and sleep was not to be had during those sorts of things.

I had no warning this time and the last time we spoke, she was devastated and broken. She didn't want to see me anymore. She was inconsolable. Repeated that I wasn't hers, and she dared to tell me not to find her.

She can't keep me away, not with the feelings I had for her. Any sort of spark of want all began with her, and I couldn't just let her go. My need for her had grown tenfold since that night she came of age.

Letting out a breath, I leaned my hands on the bathroom sink. Maybe it was a fluke. Perhaps she couldn't sleep because she was worried about us both.

Everything would be alright, it had to be. Tonight, I will be in a calmer state. I wasn't expecting so much emotion to come from her. She was tough as nails—didn't let things get under her skin—but this obviously hit a spot softer than I ever could have imagined. She kept her feelings hidden from me well, even though I couldn't figure out she wanted me until it was too late.

The red dress, the hair, the makeup. It wasn't her, but she dressed that way because she thought I would find it beautiful. She was beautiful all on her own, but I loved her how she was. Wild and free, a woman that didn't give a shit what other people thought.

She was the mate for me. The goddess couldn't be cruel to allow us to develop such powerful feelings without it meaning something.

I flinched at knocking on the bathroom door.

"You alright, man?" Clint asked. "You don't seem yourself."

I shook my head, letting out a heated breath. "Yeah, yeah, I'm fine."

My Warrior wouldn't give up so easily. She was a fighter. She couldn't keep me away. She couldn't control my presence in her dreams. Tonight, tonight I will be ready. I'll create a plan to earn her name. To meet, just to see if the flares fly when we finally touch each other. Surely, she would give me that, but even then, if the sparks didn't come, I don't know if I could let her go.

Evelyn

Three weeks had passed with no signs of any dreams. I slept in the blackness and woke with nothing but a hollow hole in my heart. Part of me was missing, and the twist in my gut grew by the day. I had become a walking zombie, taking uncalculating steps through the palace by day and to spar with the guards in the evenings. Then at night, I lay awake because I had nothing else to look forward to.

It wasn't only my dreams taken from me, but my ambitions, too. I had no desire to do more, to better myself. My life had turned into a hollow shell. Not even sparring with dad excited me, and I was spiraling out of control.

My mom took notice of my personality change but took it as my guilt about holding emotions about Grandmother and the family, which was partly true. My uncles had already left for the Golden Light Kingdom to spend time there, and Pop was obviously gone with Grandmother.

It was lonely, and the palace was not as loud and cheerful as it once was, at least not in my eyes.

"How are Wesley and Charlotte?" I asked dad.

I was passing by my parents' study, and for once, they weren't hiding in a closet somewhere. Dad still wasn't over me dancing with Joshua at the Mating Ball which was a complete disaster. They evidently don't teach the graduates from the Alabaster Academy to dance because he had two left feet. Every time he stepped on one of my shoes, I let out a squeak, and my father would growl harshly into the ballroom. It echoed so loud that it had everyone trembling.

Yeah, having My Guard come find me would have been a disaster.

"Their daughter is still missing. She would have been fifteen years old today," Mom said sadly.

Ember was Charlotte and Wesley's first daughter, three years younger than me. Somehow, she'd been abducted from her bedroom in the middle of a stormy night and had never been seen or heard from again. To this day, wolves hunted for her, and million-dollar rewards had even been sent out amongst the humans so they would use every resource they had to find her.

Charlotte, who I saw as the fun aunt, was devastated. She felt it was her fault she couldn't protect her children. She was one of the top security tech developers in the human world. In spite of that, their daughter had been taken from inside their house. No smells, no alarm tricks, not a single footprint to be seen.

"Evie, is that you?" Mom stood from the desk. Dad kept his hand on her lower back as I entered. "Why aren't you sleeping, hun? Ever since the ball, you haven't... oh wait." She paused, putting her fingers to her swollen lips.

Gods can they not keep their mouths off each for longer than five minutes?

"Is it a side-effect of the elixir? You can't sleep now?" Mom rushed over to comfort me, but I shook my head.

"No, other things are keeping me awake," I lied. Father raised an eyebrow but said nothing. "I dream nothing," I said honestly. "Just black, it's been different."

Mom slumped her shoulders. "I don't like it. You aren't the same Evie. I won't allow you to drink it again."

"But mom, I'm really fine—"

"No," she snapped. "I am touching your hand right now and feel the pain inside you. You will not take it again, and that's final. We can work out your problems together but putting that harmful magic inside you will only hurt you later."

Slumping my shoulders, I nodded.

"How are Dante and Hunter?" I asked. They were Ember's younger siblings. The youngest, Stephen, was only a few months old when she was taken and wouldn't remember her.

"They miss her." Mom allowed me to change the subject. "There is a new pack forming just outside the Night Crawler territory, and they want to train with Wesley and, in exchange, try to find Ember. The new alpha is actually your father's cousin, Ebony."

"Is there any way we can help Wesley and Charlotte? Any resources we can share?" I asked.

Mom shook her head, going back behind the desk. "Our power doesn't extend as far in the Earth realm, unfortunately. They have Cyrene there with her coven, doing everything they can. They even tried to contact Hades for help, but he hasn't responded."

"That's a shame." I gritted my teeth. "Especially with all Charlotte had done for him, getting rid of that nasty demon years ago." My finger traced mom's desk, while father sat behind mom, kissing her cheek. Dad was quiet, and so in love, it almost made me sick, especially since I didn't have anyone like that.

Not that I wanted my mate right now. I was too much of a mess, too much of an emotional train wreck. I still wanted My Guard, and he was probably furious with me. Maybe we would meet again when the spell wore off, but who knew, he may have already found his mate and wouldn't need me anymore.

My heart withered at the thought of that notion.

Laid out on mom's desk was the map of Earth. It was larger than our world, but not very interesting. Sure, there were fascinating places but none I wanted to visit. My home was here, but maybe a visit would be nice one day.

I could use a change of scenery and something useful to do to distract me.

"Mom?" I raised an eyebrow, my finger touching the circling around the territory of the Black Claw pack on the map of Earth. Its territory was large, the largest in North America. Wesley has doubled its size in the past twenty years alone. "I would like to give aid to Charlotte and Wesley. I want to go help them find their daughter."

Dad balled his fist and hit the desk, knocking over mom's lemonade. "Absolutely not." He growled. "You can't leave this palace and go off to Earth. You've never been, it's too dangerous. You can't shift when you want, and you have to hide yourself," he spat out. "I forbid it."

I stuck my hands on my hips. He wanted a fight? I'd give him one. I haven't had a good ruffling of feathers in quite a while.

"I'm the best warrior you've got besides yourself. Are you telling me I can't take care of myself?"

Father grunted, pulling mom closer. "You can't go," he huffed.

"Dad," I whined. "I'm an adult! If I am to rule one day, I need to have vast experience. Having another Alpha out there will help. I can even take Melody!" I said excitedly. "She has always wanted to visit Earth. Now that she isn't bound by books and homework all the time, she can watch out for me. You know, so I don't do something stupid."

Mom made a face. "That didn't help your argument," she giggled. "We don't think you would do anything stupid, and in fact, I think it's a good idea." Mom studied dad who disagreed with her.

A vein bulged around his temple, and his fur sprouted on his arms. "No," he growled again. "I won't put a realm between my daughter and me again."

I pouted, something I wouldn't have normally done, but it was time to present it.

Dad raises both of his eyebrows. "The fuck is that?" He chuckled.

"A pout?" I muttered, still sticking out my lip.

"Looks like a snake bit you on the mouth. Put that away."

"What kind of snake would make my lip swollen like that?" I asked. "Didn't think males had venom in their cocks."

"What?!" he roared, shaking the room. "Who the fuck touched you?! I will kill them!"

I smiled brightly, my cheeks hurting with laughter while I fell on the couch. Mom was snorting, her hand hitting the desk.

"Dad, I'm kidding. I've never seen or touched one." I dried my tears with my fingers.

"Everything alright?" Melody appeared in the doorway, wiping away the sleep from her eyes. She had on fuzzy shorts, long socks, and her hair was a tangled mess.

"Want to go to the earth realm with me and help Charlotte and Wesley for a while?" I asked, and Melody beamed.

"Would I ever! I'll go pack!" Melody turned to leave the room.

"Wait!" Dad growled again, causing us to still in our tracks.

"There will be rules, many rules you will abide by." He wagged his finger at me. "And you will take at least one royal guard with you."

"So, you are going to let us go?" Melody clapped her hands silently beside the door. Melody had the whole innocent vibe going on, she pouted her lip and dad crumbled.

Not fucking fair.

Mom nudged him with his elbow. "Come on, they are old enough. Plus, Sorceress Cyrene will be there," she chided.

He ran his hand through his hair. "I just worry, their security has been breached before, and I..."

"You don't trust them?" Mom gasped.

Dad shook his head. "No, I can't imagine what they are going through. If I lost any of my women, even the boys, I don't know what I would do. Even seeing Evie now, how she walks the hallways like a ghost, it upsets me. You aren't my Evie anymore. Just a ghost of who you used to be." Dad hung his head, his nose going to mom's shoulder.

"Aw, Dad." I jumped into his arms. Dad wasn't good at expressing his emotions, hell, even speaking, but when he did, everyone listened. "I'm alright. Just figuring some things out."

Like, you not killing the man I love that isn't my mate.

"Pleeeeease, Daddy?" Melody pouted again.

"Alright, fine," he grumbled.

"Hey, how come her pout works on you?" I pointed.

Melody pranced around the room. "Because I'm the favorite."

"Are not!" I argued, jumping from Dad's arms. "I'm the fighter. He likes me more." I puffed out my chest.

"And I'm the cute one." She put her finger to her lips, giving me a wink, and dashed out the door.

"It's on," I growled, running to chase after her.

Chapter Twelve

Kit

"He's looking a bit roguish. Do you think he looks roguish?" Clint said from the sidelines. He wasn't making his comments subtle, and it had the entire sparring ring staring at him in disbelief. The wolf that stood in front of me was Callahan—a stuck-up Earth warrior that had come here to earn his wolf an Alpha title. He wanted his own pack, or to take some other Alpha's place on Earth. That wasn't the way things worked in Bergarian, but it sure did on earth.

Callahan snarled, his lip curling with disgust. For some reason or another, he had pinned me as one of those weaker warriors, but I was anything but. Keeping to myself away from others' gazes, out of the limelight, wasn't a matter of fear or weakness. I came here to pay Queen Clara back, to show her I was worthy to be her guard. And hell, today was the day I would prove myself to them all.

"He has certainly become darker, no doubt about that," Leland agreed. The sand beneath my bare feet shifted, I lunged forward to capture Callahan by the ankles. It was a risky move, going for the feet, a move not very common amongst the bigger warriors. It took him by surprise, landing him on his back.

"Like, his hair has grown darker, can't you see?" Clint waved his hand out in front of him, assessing me like I was a prize beef cow ready to be sold. "And his eyes, boy, his eyes have gone a few shades darker too. Do you think he has perhaps gone rogue?" He feigned horror.

"Would you shut up!" Callahan snarled, using his claws to rip at my shoulder to release himself from my grip. My shoulder twisted, gathering a greater grip of his upper arms, pulling them backwards and pinning his chest to the ground. The ring, instead of cheering and jeering, all fell silent. The pixies flying by even stopped to watch as I felt my fur rippling down my bare back.

"It's because of those dreams," Leland whispered. The crowd had their gazes pinned on the fight. I could hear the whispers of my classmates placing bets on who would really win. Many betting coin but even the poor ones were betting off their desserts, eager to get in on the action.

"I would find having a dreamless night rather refreshing, but not that one. I've never seen such a worn-out rug in all my life," Clint replied.

They were lucky they were my roommates, otherwise I would stop the fight to rip out their throats. But they were worried. I wasn't the same wolf I was a month ago. All dreams had stopped, and my life had become meaningless. I had forgotten my ambitions, my desire to become a royal guard.

My heart had been crushed to pieces, and I couldn't decide how to take it. So, I turned to the one thing I knew how to do, and that was fighting. A true guard doesn't talk about their feelings or show emotion; they are there to protect.

Callahan yelled a battle cry. His darker skin met my tan skin, and I twisted my body until my elbow struck his back, throwing him to the sand face first. My teeth elongated, my mouth salivating as I pushed his head

away and laid my teeth on his neck. The bell rang at the opposite side of
the ring, announcing my win.

My wolf, Riddick, shook our body, letting out a tremendous howl. My
roommates jumped the fence, slapping my back with congratulations and
cheers. Students shouted praise until the thick hair on my back sprung
forth. The deep sandy blonde morphed into a deeper color, more rich,
vibrant and easily hidden in the shadows. My eyes closed, feeling a power
rise buried inside me.

Volke, racing into the ring, stood in front of me. "Back away," he pushed
my roommates away until my knees hit the sand. Body shaking, skin
pulling away, I growled in displeasure at this fresh pain.

We howled, not sure of physical pain or the mental we had kept hidden
away, but it was riveting to feel the heat of the light sources on our fur. The
howl finished. I rose in a defensive stance. I felt stronger, more powerful.
But with all this power, there was nothing I could do to bring back my
dreams and the woman I had longed for.

I panted, feeling the stares of those around me. Their silence didn't
bother me. It was welcome as I set my paw forward to feel the texture of
the sand. It was more defined. I could feel the individual grains beneath
my paw. I breathed in deep, smelling the air. At first, I concentrated on the
surrounding air, then extended it, reaching beyond the ring, beyond the
confinement holds of the training center and that was when I smelled a
comforting scent.

Queen Clara.

"Go slow," Volke spoke calmly.

My breathing evened; my vision came back to the wolf in front of me.
His smile grew wide, eyes twinkling with anticipation. My back arched, my
paws stretched, and we pushed our body back into our human form.

Volke crossed his arm and bowed to me. I stood, confused, but did the
same to him. He shook his head, extending his hand for me to take. Shaking

it and pulling me closer, he patted me on the back. "Congratulations, Alpha, you've exceeded expectations."

I stilled, my wolf howling inside me. We did it; we made it.

"I've been wondering what was eating you up. Your attitude had changed, and you were hard to get along with. Maybe your wolf was gearing up for his next level of transformation." He chuckled. "But gods, you did it, and at just twenty-four, well done." He patted my shoulder. "Queen Clara will be proud. She is on her way as we speak. Go clean up, and King Kane will make the announcement." Another hit to the back.

I coughed in surprise, and my roommates gathered around me.

"Holy hell, you kicked his ass." Clint threw my shorts at me. Pulling them on, I heard Callahan and his goons swearing at my friends.

Letting out a breath, I ran my hand through my hair. I had made myself an Alpha and achieved my dream, but I didn't have the person I wanted to share it with. She wasn't here and refused to see me. Sure, my roommates cared about me, but I would not celebrate my achievements with them. They didn't know me on a deeper level, like my Warrior did. She knew my fears, my desire to become the best wolf I could be, and the dark secrets of inadequacy that none of my roommates and my friends knew.

Leland leaned in and whispered, "And you shifted to an Alpha. That is fucking amazing! Did you see Callahan's friends? They have been here fifteen years, and they still have yet to reach Alpha status. Your wolf was pissed! What is your secret?"

"Is it those dreamless nights? Taking some sort of drug to help you sleep so hard?" Clint leaned in the other ear. "Or are you getting some tail on the side?" Clint took his finger and stuck it through the hole his other two fingers formed. Leland laughed, pushing Clint away from me as I walked out of the ring.

"Back to stoic Kit," Clint grumbled. "I swear he is about as fun as a stick in a turd pile."

"And I enjoy playing with sticks, but not when they're in a turd pile," Leland added.

I shook my head, not getting them at all.

"Kit!" Queen Clara ran from the vast green field that held the lake beside the Academy. It was the last fresh water source until you reached the beaches. There had been many parties along that lake once the mixers were over with. Nothing but a giant orgy and sand up your ass.

"Your Majesty." I bowed, but the Queen's delicate hands touched either side of my face to pull me up.

"None of that." She waved her hand. "You know not to address me like that. Now stand up and let me see you!"

"Don't look at him too hard." Kane strode up beside her.

I didn't think it was possible, but the King continued to grow by the year. He had to be almost seven feet tall—nothing but muscles, tattoos, and piercings. I didn't think he had anything left to pierce when I was younger, but somehow, he managed to do it.

Queen Clara playfully hit his chest, her dress flowing around her as the hem kissed her calves. "Looks like you're an Alpha now," Kane said without emotion. "Just recent?" He raised an eyebrow.

Volke grasped me by the shoulder, bowing before the royal family. "Just before you arrived, I imagine he is tired."

I stood straight. Even with no uniform, I was going to display my training. I was ready to become a guard, but part of me held back. My wolf continued to whimper night after night after we fell asleep, wondering if our Warrior was avoiding us, hurt, or possibly found her mate. The not-knowing was killing me, and the only reason I'd shifted was that my wolf wanted to find her, make sure she was alright.

"Kit, you can show emotion, you know?" Clara joked, walking back with us to the academy. She took three steps to her mate's one, but that didn't deter the excitement she exuded. She was always the cheerful, crazy she-wolf that tamed the beast, so he did not scare us all.

Once we were seated, Volke grabbed me a drink and nodded to relieve himself so Clara and Kane could speak with me. Once a quarter, they would visit and see how I was doing and progressing. Each time, Clara praised how well I was doing, and Kane would just nod in approval.

"So, what's going on, Kit?" Clara's voice now went from cheerful to concerned. I shook my head, chuckling and putting the water on the table.

"I'm great, I'm an Alpha now." I scratched my arm. "It's what I've wanted, so I could better serve you and your mate. I hope you will still consider me a qualified applicant to be your guard."

Clara smiled tenderly, but the darkness that loomed over me told her I wasn't giving her the full truth. "What is it now, Kit? I know you; something is bothering you. You have circles under your eyes, your wolf is a mess, pacing around your mind like it's searching for something. What are you searching for? Is it your mate?"

My wolf lowered his ears. No doubt Clara could see my wolf doing so. The Royals had more powers amongst the shifters than we all realized. The Royals themselves had secrets their people did not know.

"I'm not ready to find my mate," I half lied. Kane raised a brow, and my leg jumped up and down. "I'm," I paused. I wasn't sure what to say. My friends laughed at me when I told them I had a girl haunt my dream for years. They called me crazy for a long time and still to this day, wondered if I needed to just wank one-off.

"It's crazy, it's nothing." I took a swig of my water.

Clara shook her head, narrowing her eyes. Waving her finger in front of me, she tsked. "You listen here, Kit. I would like to think you and I are close..." And gods, we were. Weekly letters on my training, what peace treaties she was conducting, and her travels. Everything except her children and her parents. She kept them to herself. Most of the kingdom wondered if their children even existed because they were hidden away. Only the Crimson Shadows pack, and the palace guards saw royal children and the previous king and queen regularly.

I'm sure she left out a lot about her life, but it was nice to get a letter from the Queen herself. Many were jealous and thought I was just a stuck-up snob.

I had worked hard for her ever since the day she helped me find myself. She had protected me when she was at her weakest, and now I was going to protect her when I was at my strongest.

"If you laugh, it's alright. You may think I'm crazy too," I muttered.

Clara scowled. "I would never. I take things seriously, Kit." She touched my hand, and Kane growled. I took no offense and smirked at the big king. He wouldn't hurt me and for some strange reason, I wasn't all that scared of him.

"I've been having dreams for a long time." I gulped. Clara backed away, leaning back into her mate's arms. "For the longest time, I thought it was a demon child trying to trick me into telling her my name so she could take over my body." I smiled.

"Night after night, she visited me. We grew up together. She was ten, I was sixteen. She doesn't know this, but she came into my dreams at a time in my life when I was questioning even continuing the program. It was tough. I was still the smallest in my class, but she looked up at me like I was the king of Bergarian. No offense." I chuckled at Kane. He only grunted.

"When I turned eighteen, I hoped she could be my mate. I was sadly disappointed when I touched her hand. I felt no sparks, even if my stomach fluttered around her. I swear I had no romantic feelings for her at such a young age, but somehow, I knew in my gut she was going to grow up and be exactly what I needed. She was the light that helped me through, and I felt like she could be more when she was older."

Clara stared up at Kane. They appeared to be having a silent conversation. I was sure I'd lose my position as the guard, and my breath shuddered.

"When she turned seventeen, I developed romantic feelings for her, and they only grew as the year went on. She just had her eighteenth birthday and now...now I swear I'm in love with this woman that has haunted my dreams." I gripped my fists together. "But she didn't feel it either. She felt nothing and the look of disappointment on her face broke me." I rubbed my chest.

Clara grabbed Kane's leg. Warmth spread through her eyes like she was going to cry for me. The sweetest Queen of all Bergarian had a heart of gold.

"I told her I'd find her, make sure that we weren't mates, but we had to meet. Feelings this strong shouldn't keep us apart, right? We met in a dream; senses can be dulled there. So, I told her I would find her, but she wouldn't give me a name, said it was stupid to do that since we weren't mates, and it would make it harder for us to let go." I growled. "She was starting to wake up, our dream was fading, and I told her we would talk the next night, but that night never came."

Tears streaked down Clara's cheeks. Kane pulled her into his lap, wiping them away with the pads of his thumbs. "The next night she did not come, nor the next," I muttered. "This past month has been hell. The only good that came out of it was my wolf reached where we wanted to be in strength, but now I have no one to share it with that matters...except the two of you," I added quickly.

Clara giggled, wiping away her tears. "Kit, that sounds so hard. Do you think she is real? This girl?"

I nodded frantically. "She is, I know she is. She calls herself a Dream Wanderer, and the only thing she can't figure out is how I always end up in her dreams. She must have figured out how to get rid of me because I haven't seen her since."

Clara stiffened, holding deep breaths. "A Dream Wanderer?" Her head tilted to the side. "Those are...quite rare."

I nodded, my leg shaking.

"I don't know if it is a demon messing with my emotions, but I feel something for her, and all I can call her is a Little Warrior because she still won't give me her name."

"Have you given her yours?" She leaned forward.

I shook my head until I rested it on my hands, leaning on my legs. "I didn't have time. The dream faded. It usually means one of us woke up."

Clara blew out a breath. Kane continued to hold her close as she thought. "Kit, I want to try something." She held out her hands, and I laid mine in hers. Clara studied them as the light grew from her palms, moving my hands in unique positions as she stared. She hummed and pulled away.

"I have something important to tell you."

Chapter Thirteen

Kit

Staring at my queen incredulously, I rubbed my hand down my face. Kane shifted in his seat, mumbling under his breath. Something about growing some balls and taking what I wanted. Of course, he would say something like that, not taking into account the feelings of this woman that haunted me. Besides, I wasn't sure if she was my mate. I couldn't steal her away if she didn't truly want it.

"I think you need to lighten up," Clara stated. She beamed at me like she had solved all my problems with that one statement.

I nodded, sitting back in my seat and taking a sip of my drink. "Right, I'll do that," I said with all seriousness. She only laughed, shaking her head.

"No, I am serious. Your time has been spent all these years getting your Alpha status, and look what you have done? You made it! You've hit your goal with the help of this dream girl." Clara raised her finger in quotations. "She has disappeared from your life when you needed it, it riled you up and made your wolf fierce, a silent storm that broke the mold of just 'being,' and then you actually used the power deep inside you," she explained. "She came into your life when you needed it. She left when you needed it. Am

I saying she's gone forever?" She shrugged her shoulders, looking at her mate.

"I don't think so. In fact, I think this is the time for you to learn to live without her. You've relied on her for so long. Your mind is constantly on her. Now you must learn to stand on your own two feet. Maybe she is doing just the same."

I flinched, the words hitting me harder than a pixie flying into a tree at full force. Could I have reached Alpha status with her? I was strong, damn strong, but having her with me, did it hold me back as well, not quite tipping me over the edge where I needed to go to accept the wolf that I was destined to be?

"For example." Clara wiggled on Kane's lap. He groaned, holding her hips still. "Kane was strong before I met him and while I was with him, it made him stronger, too. However, Torin, he didn't break through any sort of mold, the best he could be, the final tipping point of his transformation was when I was taken from him."

Kane frowned, gripping her tightly.

"What I'm saying is the gods have a purpose. The fates even more so. Do you believe this woman is your mate?" Clara tipped her head in amusement.

"More than anything," I said with conviction.

"Then you will see her again," she said with absolute certainty. "The goddess doesn't mess around with mate stuff, and you know this. A bond is a wonderful gift and these dreams you had were with reason and purpose. This woman isn't there right now because you both need to grow. Learn how to live without each other. When you finally meet your mate, you will be stronger than ever."

"This woman is my mate," I grumbled. Kane's lip twitched in amusement, his stern face softening. "And I don't want to let her go, not yet."

"Good," Clara smiled. "Because if you feel this strongly about her, even without any of the physical signs such as touch but feel it within your heart." She leaned over, touching my chest. Kane growled but did nothing as her hand glowed on my chest. "Then she must be your destined one, don't you think?"

Letting out a shuddering breath, I did the only thing I could do, which was to agree.

"And Kit?" Clara sat back on Kane's lap. He took her hand and rubbed it on his chest to get rid of my smell. I playfully rolled my eyes while Kane gazed intently at me. "Ah, there is part of the playfulness I'm talking about! Loosen up!" I gave her a half smile, and she settled back. "I'm loving this new, darker hair. Did it come out when your wolf emerged to Alpha status?"

"It's normal. It happens with some wolves," Kane interrupted. "It means that Kit's wolf is growing stronger. The darker his hair becomes, the stronger he will be. This is unfortunately a sign that you were not born an Alpha. Other Alphas will wish to fight with you, trying to deter your wolf from becoming stronger. They will see you as a threat, having an Alpha with no pack." Kane rubbed his rough chin. "In fact, I think I have a mission for you and your wolf. It'll make you better, if that is what you wish?" He raised a brow.

"A-anything!" I said excitedly. "I'll do what it takes to be the best for you and Clara."

Kane grunted in approval. "Good, then this is what will happen, pup."

Leland and Clint pushed their faces against the window, breathing heavily while Kane explained my mission. It would be a two-year-long affair, traveling around to the different shifter packs of Bergarian. It would be like the tour I had done on Earth years ago, where we learned the various fighting techniques of Earth. This time, we would spend a considerable amount of time in not only packs and prides but also the Vermillion and Golden Light Kingdoms as well. If we were lucky, we could travel near the Orc territory. The hordes have been practicing with the new orclings. The race had found their mates soon after the war, a promise that was given to them by the Moon Goddess for helping us win. They still called her a Moon Fairy, however.

"Are they alright?" Clara tried not to stare out the window. The heated breath from their noses fogged up the glass. Kane's growling, grumbling, and profanities became louder, and it wouldn't be long before he attacked.

"Guys, cut it out," I yelled. Standing up, Kane stood with me, and they all bolted from the window. If Kane knew the real reason they were there, they would be nothing but ogre food. They had a crush on the little queen, like most of the young wolves. She was everything a wolf could want, and it didn't help that the aura she exuded was nothing but calm and serenity.

"I suppose I'll have to meet them one day." She laughed. "Maybe then they'll get over whatever it is."

"You will not meet them," Kane snapped. "Unless their cocks are tied up with their mates. No unmated males are allowed near you."

Clara cleared her throat, nodding to me.

"Except Kit, he's the only exception," Kane said.

I chuckled, and Clara smiled again. "We will talk to your trainers. I'm sure they will want to send a group to travel with you, but this trek is for you, Kit."

Kane nodded. "You are to fight with all the Alphas, with the understanding you won't take their pack or prides. Volke will attend and make sure the fights are clean."

"I know you can do it," Clara said. "I still expect letters weekly, and I want to know your progress. You'll come back with quite a colorful spread of metals to show off to your mate." She glowed.

"Not unless I meet her out there." I nodded to the window. "I'll be traveling all over. Maybe she will be waiting for me."

Clara just nodded, hands wringing in her lap. "Of course, but don't get disappointed if you don't find her. She's out there, you know that for sure. And who knows, your dreams of her may come back too!" Kane growled, nudging her. Laughing awkwardly, they both stood to leave.

Evelyn

Watching from afar, I saw myself crawling across the limb. Covered in mud, my hair pulled into a tight French braid, my leathers coming just below the knee. The ties that bound the braids tightly together swung with the wind. They were the only part of my body that was moving, and I saw myself mutter a prayer to the gods that the limb wouldn't moan in dissatisfaction with the weight I sat upon it.

The day was clouded; raindrops dripping through the leaves of the tree. My smile widened as My Guard came into view. I caught my breath at his usual attire—leathers and his bare chest. How did I not notice how damn attractive he was, even as young as I was, I'll never know?

His face bore no marks of facial hair. He was cleanly shaven, and his hair was cut in the popular Bergarian style of longer on the top, with the sides shaved close to the scalp. I licked my lips, watching as he called for me. "Little Warrior, where are you? I know you're around here." His jaw clenched. That brief twitch in his eye was as funny as the first time I had pounced him in surprise.

My eyes rolled, my hand gripping the bark of the tree. If only little me knew how much he hated the eye roll and would soon feel that wrath later in our meetings. My little self's smile widened as My Guard came closer, his hands on his hips, looking at his surroundings except for up into the trees.

Wolves hated climbing trees, so it was to my advantage if he thought I would stay close to the ground. I leapt from the tree, screaming a battle cry of my ancestors. I winced, watching my little body land on My Guard as we both fell with a thump.

I snorted, laughing to myself as the Guard groaned and flipped me over onto the muddy ground. The steady rain I created made a nice mud pit, and we were covered head to toe. My little-self laughed, and My Guard began tugging at my arms and legs.

"Are you hurt?" he growled at me. Obviously, he was annoyed, but the twitch of his lips had me coo at the beast from afar. "You are so reckless; you could have hurt yourself! What were you thinking?" he scolded.

I shrugged, laughing more. "You should have seen your face! It was all, 'ahhh, help me. I'm a defenseless little puppy.'" I waved my hands around. "The female beastly wolf jumped out of a tree and made me pee my pants!" My Guard growled but tickled me as I screamed. I wouldn't scream for mercy. A daughter of the greatest beast of Bergarian would never do such a thing. I took it until he tired of my screams of laughter.

"You shouldn't do that." He finally stopped. "I've never seen a girl such as you who likes to play in the mud and climb trees. Could you not like to play tea parties and talk to stuffed toys?"

My giggling stopped and my bright face turned sour. "Who says I have to be all prim and proper?" I shouted. "If you don't like who I am, then I can just leave you be, and you can go wander around alone." I huffed, standing in the mud. "Everyone expects me to be some China doll, but I'm not and I never will be. I'm a warrior," I shouted.

I bit my lip as I watched from afar. My knees quaked, and I finally rested in the small patch of grass as I continued.

Where did my fire go the past month?

My Guard stood up smiling. "And there she is, the confident Little Warrior I knew you were." He rubbed my head with his muddy palm, chuckling. "I was wondering when you would show your true self again."

"Huh?" My tiny form stared up at him.

"For a few days, you have been nothing but a timid thing. Not laughing, talking, or playing tricks. What happened to you, Warrior?" He knelt in the mud, holding out his hand. My body fidgeted, wiping away the mud from my cheek.

"Grandmother scolded me, saying I'd never find a mate because I acted like a boy," I whimpered. "So, I tried to be good, but with the mud and you wandering around, it gave me an idea and I couldn't pass it up." Little me slapped her hands to the side of her body. Mud flew and landed right in My Guard's face.

"Well." He wiped the mud from his face. "I hope you learned your lesson that your grandmother is wrong," he said sternly. "Because what you've done is catch your prey and not just any prey, but a wolf that is more experienced than you by many years. And now my ego has been hurt." Taking the mud he wiped from his face, he dabbed it on my nose.

"And that's a good thing?" I tilted my head.

"A good thing? You kept yourself hidden not just from sight, but from smell. I had no clue where you were! I'm one of the best trackers. I'm hurt now, Warrior." He laid his hand on his chest, feigning as if he were truly wounded. "I'll have to go back to practice my tracking skills because a little girl eluded me."

"Hey!" I stomped. "Not a little girl. I'm fucking twelve!"

"A little girl with a potty mouth." He smiled.

"Dad said I can." I pointed to myself. "Cause I'm his daughter, and I shouldn't take shit from no one."

My Guard laughed. "Then why didn't you remember it when your grandmother told you that you wouldn't find a mate?" He cocked an eyebrow. Leading me over to the cool spring, he threw water in his face, and I did the same, washing away the mud from our bodies.

"Because..." my voice faded. "Maybe she's right. Maybe my mate wouldn't want someone that likes to fight, spar, play tracking games, and beat the shit out of people. Maybe, they would want someone that was more like my mom. Everyone loves her and I do, too. It's just, I'm not like that. I like to run free," I said sadly. Tears came to my eyes, remembering how hard this night was for me.

That was the first time I ever felt I wouldn't be enough for my mate, because my grandmother said I acted too much like a warrior. I had a terrible mouth, no respect for my grandmother, and I couldn't keep any friends. Sure, the kids my age knew how to fight, but I was vicious. My dad already had me training with the royal guards, and I could take down most of them at my young age.

Of course, none of the girls or even boys would play with me. My sister and uncles were my only friends, besides My Guard.

"Hey," My Guard tilted my chin up so I could see him. His face was clean, his dirty blonde hair wet from removing the mud. Part of me felt an inch of regret getting his pretty face dirty, but my twelve-year-old self didn't seem to care. I looked up at him like he was the world, the person I would want to be.

He was respectful, serious at times, and day by day, he came more and more out of his shell. He was something to behold underneath—not the marble statue and emotionless guard I used to think he was.

"Your mate will love you fiercely just the way you are. You want to know how I know?"

"How?" I asked with passion. "How do you know he will still want me?"

"Because the goddess doesn't make mistakes. The goddess pairs two together because their souls match perfectly. In fact, your mate will most likely like your fire and use it to his advantage when he chases you down to make you his." My face blushed, looking away from him. "He would like the challenge of trying to tame you, but never let him. You stay as ferocious and wild as you are." My Guard kissed the back of my hand, an endearment he did the first time I came clean about my grandmother and how much she hurt me.

"Ew," I rubbed the back of my hand against my hip. He barked out his laughter and pushed me playfully into the stream.

Chapter Fourteen

Evelyn

"Yoo-hoo!" A hand waved in front of my face, until I grabbed the wrist of the attacker and pulled them around, securing them in a headlock.

"It's me, you big dork," Melody coughed, gasping.

I let her go as she slid off the chair. "Fuck, you scared me," I growled.

"What the heck?" Melody rubbed her neck. "I've been talking to you for the past ten minutes, and you were staring out that window like the Goddess herself was doing a reenactment of creating werewolves."

I scoffed, rattling my head. "Sorry, I got lost in my head there." I tried to suppress the grimace. The daydreams had become more frequent since we set out on our journey to the Black Claw pack, clear across the country and far away from the portal that led back to Bergarian. We stayed at the palace for a mere week to prepare for the long journey, taking with us three guards, including Joshua, who had been extremely close lately.

Any sight of trouble, meaning if I didn't get my bottled water within a certain amount of time, and he was yelling at some servant or other to hurry. I didn't appreciate the extra treatment, but then again, they all were on alert. Two princesses traveling across the realms, then clear across the country, was a big deal.

Not that we were advertising our arrival. On the contrary, we kept it a secret. We took our time crossing the portal. Making it a site seeing trip and saying hello to the alpha whose pack guards the random stone arch in the middle of a forest. We said our goodbyes so we could arrive at the private airport, which was still two hours away. Mind you, we still flew in style. Alpha Wesley wouldn't have it any other way with his friends' daughters coming in—especially when we told him we were here to help search.

"Evie!" Melody moaned in irritation.

"What?" I shrugged, looking back over the wing of the plane. Her face eased, grabbing my hand.

"Are you okay? It's like...when you escape inside your head, it's getting harder for you to come out of it," she confided. "What was going on when you were just staring out the window, ignoring me?"

I bit my lip, pulling on the long braid that mom had done just hours before. For as long as I'd been able it, I kept secrets. No one paid particularly close attention when I hid Grandmother's abuse over the years, but now I had watchful eyes on me at all times. As much as they are trying to help, it was making things worse, stressing me so I couldn't figure out things on my own.

"You know I'm not dreaming, right?"

Melody nodded. She understood the elixir's properties, and let's say she was not happy with Taliyah after she read about what I took. The side-effects were far greater than the sorceress expected on a Dream Wanderer and, with Melody's skill set in the library, she let our parents know I was in for a ride.

"I'm daydreaming," I whispered.

Melody nudged me to continue as she stared around the small plane and made sure the guards were paying attention to their game. The roar of the engine had drowned out our whispers, so we figured we were safe.

"I dream while I am awake. I re-dream dreams I've already had. Watch myself from afar. When I sit and clear my mind, it sucks me inside my head. Watching the past and being unable to change it. Not just things that have happened in the past in reality but dreams I have dreamed before."

Melody brought out her notebook, ready to take notes, but my hand stilled her. She sighed, putting it away. I didn't want to be the science project. I wanted to be her sister. Just letting me be, letting her listen. It was what I owed her and my family after keeping my feelings hidden for years.

"What are the dreams about? It says Dream Wanderers dream of the past because dreams are important, they have meaning," Melody pressed. "So, what was it about?"

A faint smile brushed my lips. "There was a wolfling." I chuckled.

Melody turned her face in surprise, her hand slapping my thighs. "Oh, tell! Please, please!"

I pushed her away playfully, putting my finger to my lips. "Shh, you will wake the others," I chastised, looking back. Joshua looked up, giving me a wink.

Ew.

Melody's bright green eyes blinked rapidly, waiting for me to explain. For the first time, I told someone about my mystery Guard. How he appeared to me, gave me lessons; and I gave him better social skills, since he was a big grump. I concluded my story, leaving out the heartbreak of him not being my mate.

Of course, Melody, being too smart for her own good, widened her eyes in realization. "You fell for the Guard, didn't you, Evie?"

I sniffed, nodding.

"That is why you asked for the elixir after your birthday. He isn't your mate either, is he?"

I shook my head, my lip quivering.

"Evie—" Melody sat on my lap as mom would to dad. "You poor thing. That's why you wanted to get rid of your dreams. Not just Grandmother?" Melody wrapped her arms around me as I held her.

"I only wanted it because of him. I couldn't bear that he wasn't mine. I couldn't see him anymore with these feelings." I sniffed, gripping my chest.

"You know things happen for a reason, right?"

I rolled my eyes. "You sound like mom."

"The elixir will wear off in time, Evie. What are you going to do then? How will you face him?"

"You are not making me feel better," I growled. "Get off me." I playfully shoved her.

She giggled, sitting back in her seat. "Gods, did you kiss him!?" she squeaked.

I shook my head, and my braid hit me in the face.

"Liaaaar!" she squealed again. "You do that squeak thing when you lie." Melody shook her finger. "You also get all antsy with your fingers. You are tapping them over and over on your thigh. Oh gods! You kissed him!"

"Technically, he kissed me," I whispered.

Melody's jaw dropped, her hands gripping the armrests. Waiting for the judgment, I held my breath. We had been told, well, strongly advised by mom that our mate will love us whether we had experience or not. Dad, on the other hand, said he would chop off any balls that came near us and no one was to touch his daughters. So, we both had stayed away from boys. Not that anyone wanted the wild child, but a book worm...maybe. I've read plenty of naughty books where the bad boys hook up with the book nerds.

"What was it like?" her eyes twinkled with anticipation. "Was it everything you ever dreamed?" Her hands clasped together dreamily.

"Yes." I felt out of my element talking about this. Blood rushed to my cheeks as I remembered warm lips touching me, traveling down to the nape of my neck. My fingers trailed down to my marking spot, and Melody snapped her fingers in front of me.

"Was there tongue?" she asked greedily.

"Melody!"

"What? I need dirty details!"

"I'm not telling you all that, you perv. I'll lend you some of my shifter erotica novels, and you can get an idea what a kiss is like." I threw the airline blanket on her.

"I already read those. Mom has some exceptional ones, too." She wiggled her eyebrows.

"You went into my room!?" I hissed. "You little shit, I'm gonna—"

"Ladies and gentlemen, please take your seats and fasten your seatbelts. We are beginning our descent," the overhead speaker announced.

"I'm saved!" Melody waved her hands in the air before buckling her seatbelt.

Rolling my eyes, I gazed back to the window, watching the cities of concrete, steel, and paved streets. It was so cold, so human. A flicker of fear ran through me, not being able to see the trees and the foliage of the forest until the private airport that Wesley had installed in his territory came into view. I sighed in relief, seeing the tall trees and imagining them scratching the private jet's underbelly as we flew over.

"Have you buckled up, your highnesses?" Joshua glanced over to Melody, his hand resting on the back of my chair until his eyes lingered on me. I was dressed in earth clothing, a black shirt with my dark wash jeans. It was definitely not the most comfortable thing to wear. My twat was cut up the middle and my usual soft leather pants were strongly missed.

"Thanks, Joshua. We got it." I buckled my seat belt. His gaze lingered on my covered breasts and left.

"I don't like that," Melody growled. "Since you had that dance with him, he has been watching you more closely. He dares not get near you around dad, but now that he's with us, I'm wondering what he'll do." Melody grabbed her notebook and began to doodle.

"Like to see him try to do anything." I glanced out the window. The wheels now skidding across the pavement. "I'll castrate him with one claw." Melody chuckled, knowing that was exactly what I would do to him.

We stepped out of the plane, the engines still whirring as we descended from the open doorway that doubled as stairs. I would never get used to flying in a machine such as this. It didn't look like it was meant for the air, but then again, a giant lizard didn't either.

Our guards stood at the bottom, their hands over their chests in a sign of respect. I frowned as I stepped onto the black asphalt. "You aren't to cause a scene, soldiers. Crossing your arms like that is going to create unwanted attention."

Joshua, the highest ranked, stepped forward. "I asked them to. It's a sign of respect, Your Highness, and you deserve it."

"Boy, he's laying it on thick," Melody mind-linked me. *"Might as well butter your butt and let him lick it."*

"You are such a perv," I replied.

"I don't like him," Cinder spoke. *"He has a motive."*

"And that being?" I raised an eyebrow.

"To get into these gods-forsaken tight jeans that are giving you a muffin top."

"Cinder," I growled. *"We do not have a muffin top."*

"Why couldn't you wear a dress like Melody? We could run better in it." Cinder curled up inside my head.

"You mean you would rather us look like a proper princess?" I chided.

"Hell no, just so we can have the freedom to run as fast as we want in human form. Not that ripping these clothes off right now for a shift doesn't sound too bad, either." I sighed, pinching the bridge of my nose.

"Joshua, no more of these poses. The Black Claw pack knows who we are. We are family here, and I don't expect anyone to give us formalities. Don't go bossing people around," I commanded. The other guards, Mason and Basim, stood down, leaning their necks to the side in submission. I growled again. Joshua sank to his knees.

This asshat.

"Stand up," I growled warningly as cars approach.

"Your highness... I..."

I turned and walked away from him, joining Melody. Together, we skipped toward the entourage of wolves. The black SUV's parked, the rear passenger door opening, and an alpha female stepped out. She wore black leather pants, combat boots, and had a killer black corset top.

"Hey, she's got leather pants on," I muttered.

"They aren't vegan leather made by the elves; they're made from cow. I bet she's hot under those things. Her junk is probably all stinky." Melody held her nose. I didn't care if they weren't comfortable. She looked like a total badass. "That's Ebony. Dad's cousin. I swear Raine and her were switched at birth."

Melody wasn't kidding. She had tattoos and piercings galore, and she also had the family resting bitch face. Dad was more resting beast face, but bitch would work for her. Her eyebrows were pierced on one side, as was her nose on the other side. Tattoos of wolves, tribal patterns, and skulls of snakes and dragons covered her arms.

I want a tattoo.

"I think I found my new best friend," I murmured to Melody.

"I resent that." She playfully elbowed me.

Ebony approached her gate not like an alpha male, but with the grace of a powerful female alpha. The aura she emitted was powerful, and dare I say, it might match mine?

"Sorry, Alpha Wesley couldn't be here," Ebony said sternly. She surveyed the area, watching anything and everything but us. "Luna Charlotte was having trouble from last night's storm." Ebony's eyes softened briefly before she was back to her emotionless wall.

"It's great to meet you." I held out my hand. She looked down at it and blew a bubble from the gum she was chewing.

She's so cool.

She doesn't give a shit about anybody.

"And I'm Melody. You look just like dad, it's so crazy! I bet you get that all the time."

"Yes," Ebony drawled. "I do." She cocked her head. "But I'm nothing like your father, I won't coddle you while you are working with us, so know that."

If I wasn't trying to act calm and collected, I would've bounced on the balls of my feet.

"I hope so. I need to get my ass kicked." I smiled. Not that it was really going to happen, but I'd let her think what she wanted.

"Oh, I plan on kicking your ass," Ebony said darkly.

My excitement dwindled as she stepped forward. She was much darker than I was prepared for. Dad had a little light in him, but then I realized it was mom that gave him that.

"Because no pretty little princess-warrior-wannabe is going to get in my way while I train my pack and help look for the missing pup. I'm here on business, not babysitting."

"Um, hello? Sorry..." Melody waved for Ebony's attention. She didn't give it as she continued to stare me down. I gave it right back.

"But she's eighteen, so she isn't a pup and not really a teenager wolfling either. She's an adult," Melody argued.

Ebony popped a bubble in my face. Her leather stretched over her chest muscles from heavy breathing. "Right," she drawled. Feeling the guards approaching behind me, I glared, sending them back ten paces.

"You stay or I'll send you home. King orders or not," I linked them. Joshua scowled but stayed behind.

Maybe he is trainable.

"My tigress!" A male, obviously an omega, strode up to Ebony with no fear. He was muscular, but his skin was light, and his build was not that of a warrior. He had bright gold eyes and silver hair he tossed when his glowing eyes fluttered at Ebony.

Ebony blew out a breath, her face softening as she turned. "Easton, I told you to wait in the car," Ebony grumbled, but the amusement on her face brightened her gruff voice.

"I know, tigress, but you were taking too long. I was worried." Easton grabbed her around the waist. He was the same height as Ebony. Wrapping his brawny arm around her, he kissed her on her neck.

"Oh! You must be the princesses!" He beamed. "I'm so excited you ladies are here. I made sure you both got the better rooms in the pack house. I even picked out the flowers and put mini fridges in your rooms. The warriors around here are fierce when it comes to food, and there are never any leftovers!" he whined. He continued speaking, his voice changing octaves the more excited he got. Ebony stood quietly, her hand brushing his hair as he continued his antics.

"*He reminds me of mom,*" Melody said through the link. "*I feel like I am in an alternate universe. I mean, he even has the same style as mom,*" Melody pointed out. He had on a light blue shirt with khaki pants, and his hand continually petted Ebony's arm as if to calm her. It worked. She didn't look like she had a stick up her ass anymore.

"And yeah, so you ladies should have everything," he concluded. "I'm helping Luna Charlotte for a few days. You may not see her." He lowered his head. "It really is awful. Those storms mess her up so bad, but she won't accept help from anyone. I just kind of took over. I hope she doesn't mind."

"Easton?" Melody stepped closer. Ebony growled, but Melody paid no mind. Melody was an alpha and although she might hate fighting, she was strategic, however. She would outwit anyone in a fight. "I'm sure Charlotte is loving what you're doing, and I'm really excited to get to know you." She beamed. "Maybe we can get away so these two can hurry and fight out the alpha stuff and be friends," Melody giggled.

Easton glared at Ebony who shrugged her shoulders. "Tigress, you need to be nice," he chastised. "Just because Evelyn is here doesn't mean you get to act like a butt to get a rise out of her." Easton turned, grabbing my hand. "You do not know how excited she has been to have you ladies here, especially with someone with strength near hers so she can get a good workout. Everyone is just so weak compared to her. It gets downright depressing when she has to hold back all the time. She kept saying Evelyn this and Evelyn that, can't wait to show her these sick moves!" Easton laughed.

"Easton," Ebony growled. He only snorted, pulling her in for a kiss.

"She's nothing but a kitten, I tell her, but she won't let me call her that in public. Now, come on, I've got roasts cooking for dinner, and we need to get back or the other omegas are going to freak if I don't have the dough rising for the croissants in time." Easton pulled Ebony, whose lip twitched, and followed her mate to the car.

"Like I said," Melody said out loud. "Like an alternate dimension version."

Chapter Fifteen

Kit

"This is a bad idea." I stared at myself in the mirror. I had on a traditional outfit of just dark linen pants and a tan tunic with black embroidered leaves. My hair was a mess. I ran my fingers through it way too often. My two dumb friends stared back at me from the full-length mirror, looking like idiots. Our large tent, although primitive looking from the outside, was furnished extravagantly on the inside. Mirrors, chests of clothing, and cots that could be mistaken for a soft twin bed were lined up along one side of the fabric.

"You look great!" Clint slapped my back. I stumbled forward, growling at the sudden push. "You need to lighten up. I'm glad you agreed to go on a date. Rather shocked, really."

Clara had sent many letters over the months, asking about my travels. It had been three months to the day since I last saw her when she demanded I "lighten up" and have some fun. She was excited that I was travelin and to see the different areas of Bergarian and challenge Alphas to fight to make my wolf even stronger.

Riddick had become a force to be reckoned with and much more powerful than I had ever thought I would be. My mind constantly drifted to My Warrior as I begged the gods to bring her back to me. No woman could ever compare to her, and going on this date was bound to be a disaster. If my queen had not commanded me to go on at least one, I wouldn't be going at all.

"Gah, you look like you're on your way to the River Styx." Leland scowled as he pulled a black sash to tighten his linens. "You got a date with the hottest panther shifter in the pride, and you act like you gotta make out with the devil."

She very well could be. Neari's stares made me uncomfortable. Now I knew how a woman felt when a male tried to stake his claim on someone that wasn't his.

I couldn't be so sure of the innocence of this date. Neari had a fire in her deeper than they realized. Sure, she looked like a kitten, but she was strong, the pride's Alpha's daughter to be exact. She was no woman to be messed with and had yet to go on a date to find her mate since she came of age four years ago. Somehow, I caught her interest, and now I had to play nice for the rest of the evening.

"As long as we are back before the moon is high, I'll be cordial," I grunted, tying the strings of my tunic.

"You promised the queen you would have fun. Come on." Leland rolled his shoulders, then sprayed musk on his neck. "Shifters don't have to be celibate before they meet their mate, you know. It depends on personal preferences. I mean, the king supposedly banged every woman within a fifty-mile radius until one day he couldn't control his wolf anymore."

"But then he became celibate for fifty some years before he met his mate," Clint added.

"Maybe he was being punished for touching things that weren't his," Leland said quietly. The tent went silent, the wolves occupying the other cots scowled.

"You have no filter," I snapped at Leland. "He deeply regrets what he did. Why do you think I would want to touch another woman? A woman has already been decided for my soul, the perfect match. Why would I want another? What would you think if your mate had been with another?"

Frustration surged in Leland, growling low at me. It only confirmed my suspicions. He didn't want anyone to touch what was his. Why did we hold such a double standard for the males and females of our species?

"I get what you mean." Clint stepped in front of Leland. "You know that we all have different needs as shifters. We are sexual creatures. We need release at some point."

"Your hand can accomplish your desires, Clint." My eyes narrowed. "Hell, go look at the mating parchments and books you have studied so much, can you not use your imagination?"

Clint blushed, stepping away. "You are so blunt." Clint chuckled. "Maybe I don't have that great of an imagination."

"Or dreams to help sate our desires," Leland added as he threw gel in his hair.

There had been too many nights I had to retreat to a private area of the forest to take care of myself. The kiss we shared, even though it was spur of the moment, still stung my lips when I woke each morning. The softness and the underlying desire pooled in my gut when I thought of her—her olive skin, the curve of her neck, the marking spot that I wanted to take. My cock grew hard at the thought of taking her and ravaging her, and each night, I waited with lust in my cock and love in my heart, hoping she would return.

It was only hours ago when I had found a cave for privacy. My hand stroked my dick long and hard, imagining it was my sweet Warrior. Her plump breasts, the insatiable curve of her ass. I wanted nothing more than to run my hand up and down my cock before I went on this date.

"Easy there," Clint joked, opening the flap of the tent. "We got to get a move on to meet the ladies. No spilling seed in anyone's cunt. This is just practice for our mates." Leland nodded to Clint in understanding.

My friends may have talked a big game, but neither had buried themselves in anyone else's body. May it be a man or woman. They had told me the pleasure of oral sex, but even then, I felt like I was betraying the one I cared most about. Books upon books had been delivered to our tents from Volke, who seemed to think I was, in fact, a eunuch because I had never once looked at any other woman in this reality.

Leland and Clint had set up this group date for us. Clara thought it would be wise if I spent time with the other sex, even though my heart was taken. I scowled, wondering why she would want me to even think about touching another woman, but now I believed it was in order for me to become more comfortable with myself.

I had spent too many years buried in work and devotion to the cause of becoming the guard her family deserved that I'd never found myself. I was a guard; that was all. But I wasn't a lover; nor was I am great communicator, and doing this would help me open up.

Or so she thinks.

The only person I wanted to open up to was My Warrior.

"Alright, ready?" Leland straightened his pants. His tunic was already wrinkled from pulling on it.

Maybe I wasn't really helping myself, but my friends had become comfortable with themselves. I pulled Leland by the shoulders, having him face me. Straightening his tunic and ruffling his hair, I gently patted his cheek. "You're fine soldier, now loosen up." I smirked, and he gasped like a girl.

"He told me to loosen up. Can you believe that?" He darted his eyes to Clint, who was too busy checking out his date. All three of the women were tall. My friend's eyes bulged out of their head at the barely there clothing inspired by the heat of the jungle climate. Brown leathers, heavily decorated necklaces, and bracelets. Their hair was done in tiny locs with beads encompassing them. Their ears were heavily adorned with earrings, and their skin was as dark as the night.

They were gorgeous women, but the Alpha's daughter stuck out the most. She wore the skimpiest clothing—with only enough leather to cover her breasts and private areas. Her body was muscular and smooth, and the brightest smile embellished her face.

"Alpha Kit, a pleasure," she purred. "I'm Neari and these are my friends Kala and Telah." She waved her hands at her friends. Leland and Clint's eyes bugged out.

Gods.

"Pleasure to meet you, Neari." I stepped forward, bowing, and kissed her hand. It felt awkward. There was no spark of desire like I had for My Warrior, but the way Neari's eyes lit up, I knew I was going to be in trouble. She had expectations, but those expectations, I was not willing to handle.

"Maybe we should negotiate before we head out on this date." I stood up straighter. "Let each other know of the other's expectations."

Clint stared at me in disbelief. "This isn't some kind of negotiation," he whispered. "It's a date. You go with the flow."

Neari tilted her head in amusement. "What sort of negotiations?" She smiled seductively. Her purring grew louder, and Riddick growled inside my chest.

"Such as, I am here to gain experience of interacting with a female. To understand what I can do to help my mate in the future. I'm not here to explore my sexual desires."

Neari frowned, but it was quickly hidden by a gentle laugh. "We will see." She stepped forward, putting her arm into the crook of mine. "Contracts can be negotiable, but I understand your concern. You wish to save yourself," she whispered in my ear.

I stood firm and unwavering.

"Don't worry, I won't bite you," she giggled, waving at her friends to continue down the worn path.

"This is fucking terrible," Riddick groaned inside me. *"Can we just leave? It's hot and sticky. They can have their jungle. I'm so ready to move to the next camp tomorrow."*

"You and me both," I replied.

The tropical climate was not comfortable for a wolf. Our blood ran hot and the animals in this area of Bergarian were not what I expected. Snakes of unusually large proportions and massive fish with colossal jaws that stayed close to the shoreline to capture any animal that attempted to drink the cooler waters.

"What do you think of this little paradise?" Neari steered me to the back of their pride's central area. The pride had one large territory with several settlements spread throughout. They lived naturally, living off the land, bartering with other shifters and tribes. Some homes were lavish, built of stone and brick, while others had huts with smoke trailing above them. It was all according to preference.

No one starved, Clara made sure of that, but the queen couldn't see everything, and you could very much see the social caste system here was intact. Omegas were the food deliverers and the cleaners—the bottom caste. Many looked unhappy and wore clothes that were nothing but rags.

Neari, along with her friends, wore the finer things. The omegas and warriors were divided, not aiding each other in any of the chores. I gripped my fists. This wasn't what Clara would want for shifters. They were to be equal but different in the same way.

"Do you not care about your omegas?" I asked quietly. "They look barely clothed."

Neari scoffed, waving her head. "They love living here. They get their own food and huts. What more could they want?"

"Sleep. They look like they need sleep," I said sternly. "Do they ever have days off?"

Neari looked at me in confusion. "They earn their keep, just as the warriors and my father do. They do the menial work while we protect them," she said softly. "We give them plenty, and they are to return the favor by serving us." Neari continued to steer me away from the group. Leland and Clint had stolen kisses from the girls earlier, but their dates had ended.

My Warrior had already branded my lips, and I was not planning on tarnishing them until Neari had me pinned to the tree with her claws. Her face leaned forward, lips pushing into mine. I grunted, taking her by the shoulders and pushing her off.

"The hell do you think you are doing?" I snarled.

Neari, placing her hand on her chest, feigned innocence.

"I was just giving you what you wanted, Kit. Your body knows that it needs a release. Why not with me? I don't just choose anyone; you should be honored."

I spat at the ground, showing my distaste. "You don't get to assume anything. From the beginning, you knew my declaration that this was nothing but practice for our mates. I did not plan to do anything with you but give you a good time, get to know you, and help my friends." I paced back and forth, my body seething with anger.

"Come on, you need to lighten up." She rolled her eyes, crossing her arms.

The switch in my head flipped. "I've heard enough of people telling me to lighten up!" I growled, pushing her back into the opposite tree.

The sparkle in her eye turned to lust, her hand lowering to touch me between my thighs. Before she could, I stepped away.

"You are so brazen to think that I want you when I have a perfectly suitable mate out there," I yelled at her. "This was a mistake, Neari. There is no doubt about that. I don't need you; I don't need my friends or anyone else telling me to 'lighten up.'" I spat. "I will be right as rain when I get my hands on my mate, and that is all that matters." I turned away, and Neari growled.

"You are such a prude," she calmly stated, shifting her attitude quickly. My eyebrow raised as I continued to step back.

"You walk around here, all high and mighty, because you are so close with Queen Clara. Everyone sees how you work that to your advantage." She picked at her fingers. "In fact, everyone thinks she gave you some sort of spell to strengthen you, that you didn't really even earn your Alpha status on your own."

I tightened my fists, Riddick growling inside me to rip her apart. It would be so easy. Sure, she was an alpha, but she had nothing compared us. We had more years of training.

"I was just trying to help you, let them see you didn't have to be so stuck up, that you can make mistakes, and you can learn to enjoy life. Because what mate is going to want you if you act like a stick is up your ass all the time? Will she really want a wolf that doesn't know how to please her? I was granting you a favor, allowing you to practice on me."

What. The. Fuck.

"I won't argue with you, you aren't worth it," I murmured. Trading arguments with a panther shifter was foolish. If she didn't see the problem with their antiquated way of handling omegas, then she wouldn't understand the simplicity of wanting to keep my cock for my mate.

Returning to camp, I headed to my tent, where my roommates talked animatedly.

"I only kissed her," Clint threw his hands up. "Touched nothing else. I just wanted to make sure I could kiss right, I swear."

"I don't care what you do!" I snapped. "It's your decision, your life. Now I want you both to stay out of mine!" I yelled. Pulling off my tunic and shoes, I ran out of the tent into the forest. I needed to shift. I needed to get away from the entire pride. Her smell was on my lips, tainting the lips that were only meant for my mate.

I snarled, shifting into my wolf.

Running across the thick underbrush, I howled as I circled the territory. It wasn't overly large, but it was big enough to give me the run I desired. The foul taste of her lips, the dirty, disgusting thoughts that must have crossed her mind. I was a gentleman, or so I thought, and she had read far too much into it. I stated my piece in the beginning, and she blatantly ignored it.

Leaving tomorrow would be for the best. But not before I took care of the pride's barbaric caste system by challenging the alpha who'd raised such a spoiled, asinine daughter. This was the one pride I had decided not to seek a fight with. Volke thought it odd, but their training methods were different, and I thought it would be unfair.

Now that I saw that the Alpha and his daughter were blinded by their greed and sense of entitlement, my duty was to rectify it and to implement the King and Queen's vision for all the Cerulean Moon Kingdom—equality, fairness, and protection for the weak.

Chapter Sixteen

Kit

Once I returned to the tent, Neari's friends sat on the cot, twiddling their thumbs. Gold chains hung around their necks, clinking with their elegant movements. Clint and Leland stood. Both of their gazes hit mine with such intensity it nearly made me stumble back. These weren't my two jovial friends. They were emerging alphas, and the room was smothering.

"She fucking kissed you without consent?" Clint snapped. "You were saving that for..."

I held up my hand to stop him. The women seemed unsure about whether to stay or go, but Clint and Leland put their hands on the women's shoulders.

"They came to speak to us about Neari's resentment about being reject- ed," Clint spat out. "Even though she very well knew your intentions."

"No one says no to Neari," Kala said, fumbling with her necklace. "And I mean no one. I can't believe she let you walk away."

"I'm stronger than her. Woman or not. I'll defend myself," I stated. "And the way your Alpha runs things here doesn't coincide with the King and

Queen's order. Everyone in the kingdom is to be equal and share the load, but obviously your omegas get the last pick of rations, clothing, and the rest. It's counter to the ways of the land."

"What ways?" Telah asked. "We have always been like this, even before the war. Was there some sort of declaration?"

"Fuck," I whispered, studying my friends. Clint only nodded to me then ran off, probably to find Volke. He was our professor, our trainer, and even though I was an Alpha now, I still sought him out for guidance. No doubt he would be pissed at what we had seen. He had been hiding in his tent with his mate, someone he rarely got to spend time with back at the academy. They both kept to themselves during our days of rest here, only coming out to make sure we weren't creating havoc.

Strutting in, still buckling his pants, he scowled. "I thought you weren't challenging this pride, Kit. Thought I would have some time off for a few days."

"I have decided to challenge the Alpha, but I want stipulations if I win," I said forcefully.

Volke raised a brow. "What for?"

"That they eliminate the caste system. They are to act as equals and treat their omegas with respect," I spat out. The women who sat near Clint and Leland all nodded.

"We've seen the Alpha abuse some omegas. We thought this was the way things were in the shifter kingdom. If we had known, we would have done something about it. We just try to stay out of the way, not get in trouble," Kala murmured.

Volke growled, heaving out a breath. "A caste system? Fuck. I should have noticed!" He growled, looking for something to hit.

"Wasn't your fault, Alpha, Sir. This was your time with your mate. We believe they have been hiding a lot of it, but when we took the girls on dates, we noticed much more than we should have," Leland added.

"As much as I want to see the bastard suffer, this is far deeper than anything we can do, Kit. To overthrow an Alpha, even if you are an Alpha yourself, will be difficult. He's a large panther—been Alpha for years." Volke's voice tightened. "Has anyone challenged him?" He directed his gaze toward the girls, and they both shook their heads.

"No one would dare," Telah replied.

My fist tightened. This was a task that had to be done. We had been here four days. Today alone was enough evidence for my classmates to see that there was something wrong. The rags for clothing... The pitiful look on the smaller children's faces... It was enough to rip me up inside.

I should have gone out more, spoke with the pride. Instead, I holed up in my tent, feeling sorry for myself and not living.

"I'm challenging. For the right of the pack," I said sternly. "And I want the King and Queen to be aware of this and find someone to take over the pride. I'm still not done training; I just want to make sure the omegas are taken care of."

Volke let out a sigh. "If you lose, Kit, you lose. He could very well kill you."

"Then I die trying. These omegas deserve a better life. If no one will stand up for them, then it's down to me. I'll have the Alpha's title and change the way things work around here."

A faint smile rose on his lips. "You're a magnificent wolf, Kit." Volke put his hand on my shoulder. "I am but a bystander, but I still worry about your safety. This was just to be a small visit, and you have managed to get a fight out of it." He grinned.

"One that will count the most, Alpha," I bowed my head.

Volke chuckled. "No, son, you don't call me Alpha anymore. We are equals, in fact, you may beat this old wolf one day. Not that I would try to take you on." He winked. "I'll have the King and Queen notified." Volke stepped out of the tent, his hand gripping the wooden pole. "And Kit?" My eyes met his. "Be careful."

The next morning, I stood in the middle of the encampment of panther shifters. The omegas stood on one side of the camp while warriors stood with the Alpha on the other. His mate, who was much smaller than he was, stood behind him with her fingers interlaced with his. She was an omega too, but the guards protecting her would let no one see what she looked like.

"You are challenging me?" Alpha Rahili asked. "Not only that, but you dare to kiss my daughter without permission?" He growled. The panthers on both sides of the clearing hissed, their fur rippling on their bodies.

Yells of protests came from Volke, Clint, and Leland.

"That couldn't be farther from the truth! She kissed me, and I rejected her. My body is for my mate only. Maybe you should teach her manners so she doesn't try to take what is not hers!" I yelled across the bonfire.

Fangs fell from his mouth, the loincloth he wore grew tighter as his body tried to shift. "What are the terms of the challenge?" he spat out. "I'd rather kill you now than argue with a puny pup."

"Kick his ass, Kit!" Clint yelled from behind me.

I shook my head at his words of encouragement, but that only stirred the Alpha panther further. "You give me the pack. You don't take care of your omegas. They are treated as slaves when the King and Queen sent out declarations of the equality. You were supposed to be the enforcer of those laws—proper meals and sharing the work. Your warriors train for three hours a day, yet your omegas work from dawn until dusk. You walk around with jewels around your neck, yet your omegas can barely cover their bodies. Your time is over, Rahili!" I yelled.

His growl echoed through the silence. "If I win, you die. No one challenges me and gets away with it. I will kill you slowly and rip you piece by piece," he panted. I smiled, loving the reaction of this foul creature. "And don't call me by my name, you worthless wolf!"

I snorted, pulling off my clothes.

"He won't fight fair," Kala stepped beside me, taking my clothes. "He will cheat, throw dust in your face. You can't let him win," she pleaded.

The fear in her eyes fueled my fire to win. Not that I was going to let him win. "There is nothing to worry about, Kala. You shouldn't be over here. Stand back so you don't get hurt."

Kala nodded, but instead of going to where her caste gathered, she stood with the omegas. Their eyes widened until a few of them engulfed her in hugs. Telah ran over to join them. Slowly more and more panthers, tired of Rahili's oppression, chose the side of the omegas.

I smiled, watching the pride coming together on its own, even without the help of their alpha. All they needed was a push, someone to step up for them.

A scream stretched across the encampment. Rahili threw my body to the ground and ripped long claw marks across my chest. Before the next blow could land, I shifted, my body rippling with black fur, and bared my teeth.

Rahili climbed the tree, his claws scratching the bark, and knocked branches down. I howled, watching the bastard run and hide. Shouts from my friends and the omegas for me back away only stirred more excitement. Riddick came forth, taking control as the panther leapt from the tree onto me.

Darting forward as Rahili watched in irritation, I turned my back and clawed the overgrown pussy cat's face when he landed. Roaring with anger, he snapped to grab my paw with his fangs. I let him take the paw and pulled out my signature move, that few could manage or understand. I popped the joint that connected my femur to my hip, giving me ample movement to bury my face underneath Rahili's neck. My leg popped into place as he tried to shake away, but it only helped to tighten my grip. Riddick pulled the tendons on my leg, pulling it back into place far faster than Rahili's panther could handle. I tried to shake away from Rahili's claws, to catch a better grip, releasing only slightly when Rahili's windpipe came closer.

My signature move, the one I had never taught to any other wolf besides My Warrior, could bring any beast to the ground. Not that this panther was too much to handle. I wasn't finished, too angry for the omegas that had suffered under his paw.

The fight was ending, his power fading. He may have been large in human form, but his panther was weak. Too proud to train with his warriors, he thought himself too high and mighty to be seen with those that protected him. I could end it all right here, crush his windpipe. My anger seeped through to Riddick, who tightened our hold.

His mate stepped away from the warriors, her screams deafening as I bit harder, hearing the crunch of his trachea.

"Please stop, please!" she screamed, grabbing her neck. "He yields, he will yield!"

Seeing the desperation in her eyes, I let go, but not before pushing the panther's face into the dirt. My claw hovered over his eye, threatening to take it out.

"Does Alpha Rahili yield?" Volke stepped from the crowd. The warriors of the pack stood silent, watching their Alpha lay nearly slain on the ground.

"He yields," his mate cried. "He says he yields."

"Confirmation?" Volke gazed to the warriors, who all bowed their head.

"He yields." One spoke, and that was when I shifted back to my human form.

"Thank you for bringing this to Their Majesties' attention," Preston, the Ambassador of the southern region kingdom said. "They will be most pleased with your findings, Alpha Kit, and the rewards will be great."

"I don't need a reward," I said stiffly. "Just knowing that the omegas are taken care of, and a new, proper Alpha will take over the pride will suffice." Looking over at Neari, I could see her hatred for me only doubling, but she wasn't my problem anymore. Since she was not Acting Alpha, she would not need to be punished, but looked after by the soldiers from the palace as they reconstructed the pride.

"There are three panther shifters at the Alabaster Academy. They are younger than you, but we have trained them in the ways our Majesties would want. In a few years, they will fight and figure out who will take over. Until then, I will remain here to help reconstruct," he said dutifully.

Neari turned away from me, clenching her fists. My friends pulled me up on their shoulders. We hardly had time to celebrate. After my win, Rahili lost his title and was demoted to warrior. He would be sent to the palace. No doubt Clara would have a field day dealing with that one.

His mate, Sasha, was indeed an omega. Her mate didn't treat her the way he should. The luna of the pride had ashy undertones to her skin, her face gaunt and withered. Her eyes were hollow, no longer filled with life. But despite all that, she was the most beautiful panther shifter of the tribe. Questions of whether she was his true mate were brought to light because the mark on her shoulder was pale—a sign of a forced or untrue mating. Queen Clara would have to decide what would happen to this luna.

"I say cheers all around for Kit!" Leland roared.

My classmates howled except for the few that would always cause trouble, including Callahan. Leland flipped him the bird when we heard Callahan complaining he was going to challenge the Alpha and it was his idea.

My friends led me back to the encampment and drank themselves stupid. The entire area was now filled with palace soldiers, so we could rest at ease until we departed the next day. Between fighting, the diplomatic policies to follow after defeating this unlawful alpha, we spent the entire day waiting. Preston had to prepare documents for me to sign, to relinquish my power over the Pride and give it to someone that would be better suited for the rebuilding and redecorating its members. Once the documents were completed, we were granted leave so we could move to our next destination.

"Have a drink!" Clint shoved a bottle at me.

I took a swig and passed it down, not in the mood to get drunk. I was still running on adrenaline and needed more time to myself. I watched as my classmates laughed, some even coming to sit with me and chat. They had taken the time to get to know me, and not see me as the loner, the unapproachable. Which regrettably, I used to be, but not anymore. I now considered many of them my friends.

Standing up and dusting my pants off, I headed to my tent. They were all still celebrating, many beckoning me to return, but they understood how I was. I was more reserved than them. It wasn't because of who they were or how I thought of them. It was who I was. I had become comfortable with that. My trust, my walls only crumbled for one woman. The woman who still had yet to visit me in my dreams in too long.

Pulling my tunic from my body, I set down yet more pieces of metal—one for Bravery and one for Protection of the Weak—that meant nothing to me. That last one I would be sure to wear proudly on the front of the lapel of my uniform.

I laid my head back and closed my eyes as I listened to the cheers from my traveling pack. I prayed to the gods once more that I would see her face and see the smile I had longed to behold. As my body relaxed, I felt myself drift away into a sea of nothingness until my eyes opened again to see long legs, curly auburn hair, and olive skin running toward me.

Chapter Seventeen

Evelyn

"It isn't fair. How do you keep beating me? No one *ever* beats me!" *Besides dad, anyway.* I huffed, laying on my back where I'd been mercilessly thrown. My Guard leaned over me, his hands on his knees, watching me intently.

"You just don't have the right moves, I guess?" he shrugged, putting his hands in his pockets and walking away.

"Now, you wait just a minute!" I wagged my finger, following him. "Let's go again, come on, I'm going to figure it out." I got into a defensive stance, my knees crouched. With hands in front of me wiggling my fingers in anticipation, I wait until he turns to me, a smirk spread across his face.

That devilishly handsome smirk.

"You won't figure it out. None of my other competitors have. What makes you think you will?" He raised an eyebrow in mockery.

"What? Just because I'm younger than you? That I'm a girl?" My face scrunched in anger.

"Hey, no, I did not mean it like that. It has nothing to do with you being a girl," he said sternly.

Great, now he sees me as a girl.

"I don't know what kind of training you've had, but it is nothing like where I'm from. I'm going to figure it out, and when I do, I'll use it against you. Somehow you have greater flexibility, and I'm determined to figure out how."

"Flexibility, huh? You think that is why I have the upper hand?" My Guard strode toward me, more like sauntering.

At sixteen years old, I knew he was devilishly handsome, but he was hands-off. He was six years older, and I was nothing but a kid to him. It didn't help that all I wanted to do was spar, climb trees, and run everywhere I went. His mate would most likely be a prim and proper girl that was scared to get her feet wet.

He kind of deserves that. A girl to dote on and take care of. I wasn't that type of girl, I mean, woman. I can take care of myself, take care of others.

"Yeah, flexibility. You are twisting your body at some odd angle." I moved my arms awkwardly while he laughed. "I'm going to figure it out. I've almost got it. Come on, give us a go, one more time," I said, raising my finger for emphasis. I playfully growled, and he eventually submitted. His muscles rippled under the skin, and a sheen of sweat glistened in the sun.

Thank gods he wasn't wearing a tunic.

Wait, what was I doing again?

He shifted, his wolf emerging. Keeping my human form since my wolf's fur was too unique to show him without giving away who I was, I grabbed him around his torso so I could wrestle him to the ground. I pulled his leg, and it stretched as I thought it would. So instead of continuing, I grabbed his shoulder, stretching it further from the source. He howled and my grin widened as I put him on his back, my body pushing into his chest.

"Ah ha! You little cheat, you're dislocating your shoulder!" I screamed triumphantly. It popped back into place, and his body shifted back into his human form. It was a quick win since my hypothesis proved correct. He stared up at me, huffing.

"You figured it out." He wiped his forehead. "And it isn't cheating. There is no rule that states that. Besides, all is fair when fighting an enemy. And you best not tell anyone my move!"

Yes, command me some more.

"Who would I tell? I may use it myself if I get in a sticky situation," I boasted. "I'll be unstoppable now. I'll have all the power." I glanced at my hands as if seeing them for the first time.

My Guard's lip twitched, trying not to laugh.

"Stealing signature moves will not make you unstoppable. I was thrown off that you figured it out," he grumbled.

"Well, there is a weakness to it, as you can tell." I pointed to his shoulder. "When your arm is out of the socket, it leaves you vulnerable and gives you a soft spot right here." I pointed to his back. "What if there were two rogues you were trying to fight with? If they figured it out, they could rip the entire leg off. We can't have a tripod for a wolf now, can we?" I snorted.

"No one has figured it out yet," he retorted.

"I did. The poor, defenseless little warrior," I crooned. "It's only a matter of time until someone else figures it out."

"Touché." He rolled his eyes and stood. "Guess I'll have to work on that." My Guard put his hands on his hips. "So does this mean you're going to use it during our sparring lessons now?"

"Who said I was taking lessons anymore?" I bragged. "I just beat the master. I think we are on a level playing field now. Or actually." I tapped my lips. "Pretty sure I'm the master because I've been fighting you in human form all along. If I had let my wolf out, I would have kicked your ass a long time ago."

My Guard pursed his lips.

"Isn't that right?" I pinched his cheeks until he grabbed my wrist. Pulling me around, he threw me over his shoulder, and I hit the ground on my back. The wind was knocked out of me. I swung one of my legs beneath him and knocked him off his feet. We both landed with a thud, our heads now laying parallel with each other.

His blonde hair had grown darker over the years. I wasn't sure if it was because he didn't get out in the sun, or if it was some genetic thing. Many young boys had blonde hair when they were younger that turned a beautiful deep brown as they aged. But the dark highlights that framed his face, including the stubble on his cheeks, were much darker than brunette.

"You are something else," he choked on the air escaping from his lungs.

"I know," I giggled, watching him rub his ass.

Not that I was looking.

"But do you really?" he asked in all seriousness. "Do you know you are 'something else'?"

I frowned, not understanding his meaning. Did he mean "something else" in a good or bad way? My thoughts ran to my grandmother, she would think I was, certainly, "something else." She would shake her head, scold me, and tell me I was going to be a "lost cause."

"I don't think I understand what you mean," I replied, looking into the deep blue sky filled with puffy pink clouds shaped like rabbits, dragons, and unicorns.

Unicorns were so cool, why couldn't they be real?

When they get mad, they could go stab, stab, stab to their opponent, and no one would care because they were *unicorns.*

"I mean it, Warrior. I've seen men and women fight, and none of them are as stubborn as you. You're smart and cunning and don't see failure as an option. It's a hard attribute to find in anyone, especially with the burdens you carry. Yet with your grandmother you stay quiet, festering on the inside. Sometimes I think I have you figured out, then you surprise me."

I turned my head to look at his gorgeous face. "Yeah, well, that's my specialty. Keep everyone on their toes. It's better that way, so—"

"You don't let anyone in." He finished my sentence. "I don't open up to anyone either, Warrior, and look what you've done to me. Talking about my feelings and shit."

"Oh, the Guard just cursed. I am rubbing off on you." I giggled.

"You most certainly are." My Guard grabbed my hand, squeezing it tight as we watched the clouds go by.

"Evie!" A thump to the forehead had me shaking away the daydream. "These daydreams are getting ridiculous. That is the third one today!" Melody huffed in annoyance, sitting back down at the cafeteria table. She scribbled in her notebook as I popped another Skittle into my mouth.

"Why don't we have Skittles back home?" I popped another one into my mouth. "These little bursts of flavor are fantastic. Maybe mom will have some imported to Bergarian?" I said excitedly.

Melody shook her head, continuing to write. "No, we keep as much of Earth out of Bergarian as we can. We don't need colorful wrappers covering the land." She snorted. "All that pollution around here, it's amazing supernaturals want to live on earth at all."

"But if it was a favorite chocolate bar, then you would totally beg mom," I added.

"That's different. Chocolate is delicious, those rainbow crap balls are disgusting." She stuck up her nose in disgust. "Now, what was the dream about this time?"

I wiggled my eyebrows at her. "Wouldn't you like to know?"

"So, something plain and simple, right?" she huffed and unwrapped a chocolate bar. "Because it was a past dream, I'm guessing he wouldn't touch you when you were underage."

"Yeah, too noble for that." I laughed. "Or that he didn't think I was his mate then either," I whispered.

Easton, who'd become close friends with Melody, slapped his hands on the table, breathing heavily, and growled. Today, he wore a pale pink shirt. His white hair was combed back. The gel had been plastered on thick, his bedhead had not been under control lately.

Ebony and I had spared every single day for over five months. Neither one of us would yield to the other, no one losing or winning. It was my fault. I was holding back because I looked up to Ebony. She was a great and powerful wolf, but my royal genes combined with my dad's genetics made me unstoppable. I didn't want to ruin Ebony's winning streak, but I didn't want to lose either. Dad said I was never to lose and not to give pity to a warrior just because of their ego.

So, I have just stretched the fight into a stalemate.

"You have to stop this," Easton panted. "I can only handle so much sex in one day, and getting my ass paddled to relieve her stress is giving me blisters on my butt!"

I coughed a purple skittle onto the table. It skipped down the wood and bounced into one of the warriors's drinks. He eyed me carefully, then took a sip and crunched on the tiny ball of sugar.

Ew.

"Excuse me?" I choked again.

"You heard him," Melody said, unaffected. "She's a domme, he's the sub." She nonchalantly waved her pen to Easton. "If we weren't cousins with Ebony, I'd ask to watch," she whispered.

"Good gods, Melody!" Where did my sister come from? I thought she was just a bookworm. Apparently, she really had been reading nothing but erotica.

"Yes, and my poor butt." He rubbed it. "She's spanked my ass over and over. I don't think I can take much more," he whined. "You have to beat her, give her some pain. Not that I am complaining about mine." He blushed bright pink. "It's just that she's trying to punish herself, and she thinks she needs to take care of me to overcompensate for herself. It isn't healthy," he breathed.

I groaned, putting my head on the table. "But she hates me. She growls at me all the time, if I beat her, she'll hate me more," I whined.

In the months we'd been here, there had been many missions to the upper east coast to find Wesley and Charlotte's daughter, and they'd been disasters. Ebony had yelled at me and scolded me for the littlest things. The worst part was, I idolized her. She was so freaking cool, the tats, the earrings. I looked up to her. She was the epitome of dad rolled into a female package. Something I wanted to be. Yet she hated me.

"She doesn't hate you." Easton rolled his eyes. "Ebony adores you."

"Huh, I kind of get a different vibe." I raised my feet, putting them on the table. "Ebony is a freaking goddess to me, but she looks at me like I'm the dirt between her tatted toes. You haven't seen us work together, Easton." Melody nodded in agreement.

Easton sighed, sitting down at the table. He winced, leaning his butt cheek to one side.

Wow, guess he really got paddled.

"Listen, I tell you this from the bottom of my heart. But you need to kick her biscuits, slather some jam on them, and take a bite. Make her remember you took her down. She's more pissed you're holding back and not handing her ass to her on a platter."

"You guys and biscuits and asses, I swear. Both of you are too much like mom, it scares me," I snapped. Melody laughed, and Easton shook his head.

"If I'm anything like Her Majesty, I'll take it as a compliment. Now, speaking of biscuits, I've got some in the oven." He left the table without another word, and Melody's attention shifted back to me.

"You and Easton seem close." I popped another skittle in my mouth. "Not surprising since he is mom from another dimension. Never heard of a male getting swatted at before."

Melody snorted. "Because you are an uncultured swine when it comes to the practices of BDSM. I'll give you some books."

"Nah, I'm fine. I'd rather figure out what my mate wants from me first." I smiled sadly.

Not a day went by that I didn't think of My Guard, and it was only getting worse. The elixir was slowly seeping out of my body, but that didn't deter the daydreams. Some days, I could hardly function. My eyes would glaze over in a fog, leaving reality behind.

It was getting hard to concentrate, hard to focus on the task at hand, but the magic had nearly left my body. Then I could see him.

What would I say to him? Would he still be there when I returned to the dream world? Would he even want to speak with me again?

What if...he'd found his mate? A surge of jealousy ran through me. He said he wanted me back then. That he would find me. The one thing I knew for sure was that I could not let him find me in the real world. Dad would have his balls because I would do unexplainable things to My Guard if we finally met. I wanted him to take me, love me, touch me, and my self-control would fade away in his presence.

What did he feel like in the real world? The dream world could feel numb at times. We didn't feel the full brunt of the hits we would take while we sparred. In reality, is he truly that warm? Would his glorious scent amplify if I stood beside him? Gods, if I met him, I wouldn't be able to control myself, and he wasn't even my mate.

Shame coursed through me. I wanted to save myself for my mate, but the emotion I felt for My Guard was unbridled.

The pack house door slammed open. The lightning filtered around the silhouette of Ebony's wolf form. The thunder rattled the chandelier hanging from the ceiling. The flickering of lights gave an ominous feel to the room. Rain pelted down into the dirt, then sprayed onto the rug of the cafeteria beneath her feet. A heaving, agitated, raging wolf stood in the doorway. It was as black as Torin, and the red glowing eyes stared at me with fury.

Ebony.

Was it noon already? I leaned my head back, ready to face yet another sparring match that would last for hours with no winner. Easton whistled from the kitchen door, drawing my attention, and pointed to his eyes and then to mine.

Oh, right? I have to kick her ass today.

I stood, the three guards—Joshua, Mason, and Basim—that had become our shadows followed. I grabbed my bag full of pee-colored, nasty-ass shit skittles and handed them to Basim. "Here, want some yellow skittles?"

He stuttered, his eyes widening, and held out his hand for the bag. "For me?"

"Yup, all for you." I patted his shoulder and walked past them.

"She gave me my favorite flavor skittles," he whispered. I rolled my eyes. Who in their right mind would like yellow skittles? Oh yeah, Basim would. He thought everything was sunshine and rainbows. Shrugging, I almost smiled at the craziness he was. Even if they were the bodyguards that followed us around, they'd grown on me with their crazy antics.

Another growl rippled across the cafeteria.

"I'm comin'! Keep your twat in your fur!" I shouted.

Melody groaned, taking her notebook with us.

"You watching today, sis?"

She shook her head. Melody hated violence, but every few weeks she would watch a good spar.

"Nah, I'm heading to visit Cyrene to talk to her about your issue and watch them try to summon Hades for the twentieth time."

"Don't go summoning any demons. I don't have time to deal with that shit right now."

Melody shook her head, heading in the opposite direction.

"It's just a contacting spell to see if he can help with the ward that appears to be broken." Melody sighed.

Once upon a time, Hades had cast a ward over the entire Black Claw pack. It was for the help of returning a demon to the Underworld that he had created and could no longer track. Hard to believe that Charlotte, a timid Luna, was the one to take down the demon who had tormented her for years. Once she had her wolf, though, anything was possible.

In return, Hades put a ward on the entire pack. No evil entities could get in, while humans were forced to turn around and walk away with the ward. Until one night, something broke through. Stealing their daughter from under their noses.

"I'm just going to see if they have everything in place and they say the incantation correctly. You can never be too careful when trying to summon the King of the Underworld."

"I don't envy you there," I called out. "Just try not to get sucked down into a blazing pit of fire, will ya?" I snorted, walking away. That's just what I needed—more complications. And there were few things more complicated than visiting the Underworld.

Chapter Eighteen

Evelyn

I stepped into the rain, and my clothes instantly became soggy. The sparring ring wasn't far from the cafeteria. The training grounds were located purposefully close by Alpha Wesley because he knew how hungry his warriors could get.

The first day Ebony and I sparred, her pack and Wesley's pack all watched the show. As the weeks and months progressed and with no clear winner each day, the crowd thinned, which pissed Ebony off.

Despite her "I don't give a shit" attitude, she wanted the pack she was forming to know that she was a bad ass. Maybe that was why I hadn't completely beaten her, I didn't want her pack to feel like their alpha was less than. Then again, I had royal blood running through my veins, as well as the same genes she had. Inevitably, I would be stronger, but she wanted to prove that she could hold her own.

And she had. Every day when the clock struck noon, she dragged me out to the training field—rain, shine, or snow—and we fought for hours until Wesley called it off. Now that it was raining and storming with lightening in the distance, he wouldn't be here to be our voice of reason. Charlotte had huddled herself as well as her children into their small plantation home.

Their daughter had been taken during a storm similar to this. Charlotte hated the storms because they made her feel weak and unable to protect her children. Now she questioned her ability to help Wesley take care of the pack. No one blamed her or accused her of not doing her job. She put a lot of the pressure on herself.

Today was the day, though. Because of Easton's request, I would be sure to finish today's fight, even if it meant severing the relationship with Ebony. I wanted to be her friend, but after this, I knew she wouldn't be.

Ebony, who was already in her wolf form, scratched at the ground, growling. I slowly took off my clothes and shifted. I had been fighting in my wolf form, not wanting to take advantage of my half-beast form because I found it unfair to fight against another wolf unless I was truly in danger. As my auburn hair filled in, Ebony howled, the steam billowing from her mouth. Her eyes blazed with fury, and my hackles rose.

"Right? We ready for the fight today?" Joshua took it upon himself and raised his arm. The crowd grew thicker despite the rain. Many came in their wolves, watching or pacing as they gathered round us. Snapping my teeth together, Joshua lowered his hand, and I leapt from my position and barreled into Ebony.

She whimpered as I pushed her to the ground. Her jaws snapped at my ankles as I backed away. Snarling, shaking her head, she ran forward. She wanted to lock her teeth into my neck, but I turned my body, using my hind legs to kick her in the side of her torso. She grunted, falling to the ground.

I snorted, the steam rising from my nostrils. Suddenly, her front paws swept the ground, throwing mud and rock into my eye. I snorted, shaking my head until I felt her pounce, rolling us into the mud. Snarling, I latched my teeth on to whatever I could. My teeth scraped together as we pulled at her skin and fur, causing her to howl.

Ebony bit my hind leg, causing me to let go of my grip. She growled deeply. The ground shook, and the wolves around us fell to the ground. Cinder, pissed as hell that we'd let Ebony get a cheap shot, surged forward. We dislocated our leg joint at the hip. It caused Ebony's maw to jerk open in surprise and we turned our body at a better angle for attack.

Ebony let go, confused by our swiftness and agility. Cinder barreled into her once more, knocking Ebony to her back. The mud and the dirt caked in our fur made it difficult for me to see where her shoulder and neck began. Going with instinct and using the light of the lightning glowing around us, I sank my teeth into her neck. Not enough to kill her, but enough to force her into submission.

She leaned her neck to the side, giving me ample room to crush her if I wanted. It was a sign of submission, and the dance we had played with each other the past months had finally ended.

"That's it!" Joshua strode into the arena, waving his hands. The wolves on the sidelines watched intently as I backed away from Ebony. She continued to lie in the mud, letting the rain pelt down onto her fur, washing away the blood from her wounds. My leg had already healed, as I shifted to my human skin. Basim and Mason held out a blanket to cover me and held an umbrella over my head.

As Ebony turned back into her skin, Easton ran from the house. He held out her own blanket and towel as he helped her wrap up.

"Do you yield Alpha Ebony to Her Highness, Princess Evelyn?" I rolled my eyes at Joshua. He was getting on my last nerve, and some days, I wanted to kick his ass.

Ebony held the blanket tight around her body, Easton rubbing her back softly, kissing her dirty cheek. For once, after a fight, I felt shy. Not once had I cared about kicking anyone's ass, but this felt different. I respected Ebony. She was older, wiser, and her taste in clothing was pretty kick ass.

"Yes, I yield." Ebony strode over, holding out her hand for me to take. Grasping her forearm, we shook. Our fight had been concluded. Wolves howled in the background, the guards and Easton shouting in praise that it was over. From the house where Wesley and Charlotte stood, the front porch light flickered on and off. I smiled, watching her children wave.

"Took you long enough, didn't it?" Ebony raised her pierced eyebrow.

"What do you mean?" I asked sheepishly.

"You know what I mean, pup. You could have kicked my ass the first day but didn't. That's why I've been pissed at you all these months. Waiting for your sorry ass to get the balls to finally take the title of what has always been yours. It has been annoying," she growled. "What finally made you give in?"

Easton stood behind her, shaking his head with his widened eyes.

"Figured enough was enough," I told her. Her stern face didn't change and my face paled. "Right, so Easton said you were beating his ass so much he was getting blisters, so I had to step in."

Ebony's face hardened and Easton backed away with the umbrella. "So, you did it for my mate, not for me or for yourself?" she asked calmly.

I sighed, scratching the back of my neck. "No, I did it for myself, too. I knew I could beat you, but I wanted you to like me, so I just, you know, drew it out a little," I confessed.

"And what did you learn from it?"

I tightened my blanket around me. "That I should kick people's ass the first time, so I don't cause more problems?" I phrased it as a question.

Ebony cracked a smile, the piercing from her tongue rolling on her lips. She nodded, accepting my answer. "Guess I'll take that."

"Wait, wait, wait," I held out my hands, almost losing the blanket surrounding me. "Just like that? You aren't pissed at me anymore? Going to actually talk to me instead of bossing me around and being a prick?"

Ebony threw her head back and laughed.

"I think you broke her," Easton whispered. The crowd was dissipating, going back to their houses as the rain came down harder. Ebony continued to laugh, and I backed away.

"Let me know when she's done laughing, and maybe we can hang out later." I turned to leave, but Ebony stopped me.

"Hold up." She wiped away a tear. It very well could have been a mock tear, but with the rain, I would never know. "Your dad told me to do this to you, so don't get too pissed," she said. "Family or not, your father wants to know if you can handle beating down anyone or anything, despite who they are. You and your dad spar all the time. You will kick your sister's ass no problem. But when it comes to someone you look up to, which he knew you would look up to me..." She patted herself on the shoulder. "He wanted to know if you would have the balls to do it. Your damn grandmother did a number on you. He wanted to make sure you don't take shit from anyone. Even from me."

I hung my mouth open in disbelief.

"Easy there, don't have to go all shocked on me," she laughed. "Now, go get cleaned up. We are going into town to celebrate."

A few hours later, we pulled up to a bar just outside a major city. Bricks were falling off the building. The roof was just about done in and the men going in and out of the bar looked worse for wear.

"A princess shouldn't be going into a place like this," Joshua muttered under his breath.

"No one asked you," I snapped. "Ebony, Easton, Melody, and you guys are here. Pretty sure we can handle a bunch of humans."

Joshua tapped his fingers on the steering wheel of the SUV, not enjoying his chastising.

"Come on, lighten up." I grabbed his shoulder. "This isn't Bergarian where we have to worry about a bunch of magical entities. This is a human bar. We are here to play some pool and have a couple of beers."

"You aren't even twenty-one yet," Melody rolled her eyes. "Humans won't give you any."

Ebony cleared her throat, her hand reaching to the handle on the door. "This isn't a human bar; this is a supernatural one. There's a glamor spell on it. It's safe. Now come on." She pushed the door open, and we all went to the front door to be greeted by another werewolf.

He looked us up and down, and his eyes widened, taking in our aura. Three alpha werewolves and three high-ranking guards were enough for anyone to take a second look. "Gods, this is stifling." He backed away. Even if his human form was large, he knew better that to mess with the three alphas.

"Just here for a drink, Duncan." Ebony patted his shoulder. Easton growled, pulling Ebony's hand away from him. "These are my friends. We aren't here to cause trouble." Duncan nodded, opening the door to the rundown bar that had miraculously turned into a black light lit room. Lights bounced across the walls and over a few couples on the dancefloor. To the right, most of the patrons filled a large bar.

"Thank gods, they'll have some of the strong shit," Basim replied, leading us to the bar.

"You aren't drinking," Joshua muttered. "We are on duty until we go home."

I scowled, looking over at Joshua. "You guys can rotate. Go ahead, Basim. You and Mason can drink while Joshua stays sober. Next time we go out, Joshua gets to drink."

"Don't think that's a good idea." Joshua tried to hover, puffing out his chest. We were almost the same height, so his puffy man boob chest didn't bother me.

"Are you questioning my authority, Joshua?" I growled. Those close to us stood still, Joshua's face paling.

"Y-your father requested we take care of you," he stuttered. "I must know you are safe, Your Highness, it would be detrimental to my life and to my heart if anything happened to you."

I sighed, running my hand down my face. Maybe I was being a bit bitchy.

"As much as I appreciate it, please rest assured nothing bad is going to happen. Dad will not hurt you. Melody and Easton are staying sober and you, Basim, and Mason need a break." Basim and Mason's eyes lit up.

"I care about you guys. You protect me and my sister and put us first. Now I want you guys to have some fun. The only reason I'm drinking is because I kicked some ass." Ebony slid a bottle of werewine and a small rectangular package down the bar. I snatched the glass before it could fall to the floor. "How bad could tonight go, anyway?" Shrugging my shoulders, I chugged the bottle.

After drinking the entire bottle, I opened the thin package wrapped in newspaper. I pulled out a pair of steel-colored brass knuckles. Ebony sat on Easton's lap, tipping the neck of the bottle of her beverage toward me.

"For when you want to play dirty," she winked.

The evening was beginning to get out of hand. Not that I didn't expect it to with a bunch of werewolves drinking.

Basim and Mason sang karaoke. Who knew that they would be into animated cartoons and their theme songs? I swear this specific skill set that they had gained needed to be put to good use. Maybe they could do some kid birthday parties? I laughed, listening to them singing the male and female voices to *A Whole New World* while I sat at the small table close to the stage. Ebony was making out with Easton. Her ass was in his lap as he rubbed his face on her breasts.

"I wonder if Ebony has her tits pierced?" I asked Melody. She had been talking to a vampire that sat nearby, no doubt asking how the species was doing on earth. Vampire laws still filtered over into the earth realm, not allowing forced feedings and such, but you never knew if they followed it or not. Vermillion was still coming back after many centuries of being poor and mismanaged, and enforcers on earth were few and far between.

"I'm sorry, what?" Melody asked as she wrote in her notebook again.

"How many of those books have you been through? You write everything?" I chugged my fourth bottle. I felt buzzed, and I wasn't planning on stopping anytime soon.

"Because I'm trying to fill up the library with new information. Everything is dated and there needs to be someone to keep records for this new generation."

I hummed, not paying attention.

Joshua stayed close to the bar, watching. More like watching me. I wiggled at the uncomfortable stare but shook it off. I'd known him since I was young, and we'd become close. I considered him a friend. Since the dance we shared at the ball, he had been acting differently. Luckily, he had made no moves that would warrant me kicking his ass.

I drank down my eighth bottle, Ebony and Easton finally joined us. Basim and Mason's tune was wavering, and the bar had shut down the karaoke machine.

Thank the gods.

"So Ebony, important question." I burped silently, and Melody scowled. "Do you have your tits pierced?"

Ebony laughed, and Easton reached up to pinch her nipple. "Of course she does. She even has her clit pierced." Easton reached between her thighs and cupped her pussy. The surrounding crowd paused, looking at her.

"And it feels so fucking good when he sticks his dick in," Ebony purred. "I'm begging for him to pierce his dick, but that's just not his thing." Ebony pulled on Easton's pants looking inside. "It's still big and mouthwatering, though." Easton's face turned six different shades of red, then he buried it in her breasts.

"I think I came a little," Melody whispered, and the table erupted into laughter.

"What about tattoos?" I asked Easton. "Would you ever get one?"

Easton bobbed his head back and forth. "Maybe something with 'property of Ebony.'" He smiled, looking at her as if she carried the moon. "But really, not my thing either. I enjoy seeing my mate covered in art, though. It's beautiful."

I hummed, taking another drink.

"What about you?" Ebony nodded her head at me. "Would you like to get one?"

I bit my lip, smiling. I wanted a tattoo so bad I couldn't stand it. Dad had never said no, but he hadn't said yes either. I was eighteen now, and he couldn't really say anything, could he?

"I want one," I declared. "In fact, I want one tonight." I dropped the beer on the table. "Know a place?"

"You're drunk." Melody pulled on my arm. "Sit down before you embarrass yourself."

"Oh, like how you announced you got wet thinking about Easton's dick being pierced?" I snorted.

Melody shook her head, turning red. "No, I like the idea of one being pierced, not that...not...with...Easton." She looked away. Ebony held her hand over her mouth, trying not to laugh. It was the most carefree I'd seen her in all the time I'd known her.

"They do tattoos in the back." Easton nodded to the back of the bar. "I mean, you could go get one. They do a good job. Ebony got one on her ass last week. It's a cute little emoji unicorn." Easton beamed.

"I fucking love unicorns!" I yelled at her.

"Me too!" she yelled back. The sway in our steps caused us to stumble, but we quickly caught our footing and headed to the back.

Our entourage followed, bringing more werewine as I picked out my first tattoo.

Stumbling back into the pack house, I giggled too loudly and fell to the floor. Melody picked me up, shooing the guards away so they wouldn't touch me. "I'll get her to bed," she snapped. "Don't want dad to find out you went into her room."

"Shit, you're right," Mason whispered. "I can't get killed, not yet. I haven't found my mate yet."

"I wish I was your mate," Basim replied. "We would have so much fun," he slapped his back.

"We would have fun. We can sing duets at the bar all the time, work together. It would be the shit!" They both high-fived each other. Joshua groaned, pushing them inside.

"Both of you, quiet or I will make you sleep outside," he hissed. Mason sniffled like his feelings were hurt.

"Aww." I stepped out of Melody's embrace and went to Mason. "Are you sad?" I patted his cheeks adoringly.

"Joshua is mean," he complained, pointing at him. Joshua folded his arms, scowling at him.

I leaned in, whispering in Mason's ear, "If it makes you feel better. I'll give you my dessert after lunch tomorrow. Then you will have two"—I held out three fingers—"desserts. That work?"

Mason beamed, nodding his head. "You are the best!" He hugged me while we both giggled quietly. "See, she likes me, too. She shared her cookies with me, and skittles with you." He pointed to Basim. "And nothing for him." He pointed to Joshua, who was now stomping up the stairs.

I snorted. It echoed through the hallway. Melody sighed and pulled me up the stairs. "Good night, guys!" I tried to whisper, but it came out as a yell. Melody slapped her hand over my mouth and led me into my room. Shoving me on the bed, I screamed, "weeeee," and plopped on the bed.

"Go to sleep, you crazy pup." Melody shook her head, covering me with the blankets. "You are something else." She kissed my forehead and turned off the bedside lamp.

I hummed contentedly, now feeling extremely tired as my head rubbed the fluffy pillow.

Tapping her fingers on the door frame, she paused to turn back. "Evie?" I hummed, keeping my eyes closed. "What did you get tattooed on your hip? You let everyone stay for your sternum tattoo but made everyone leave for the hip one. What is it?"

I hummed, pretending like I hadn't heard her. Her demands became distant memories, her voice fading along with the noise of the crickets outside until I slipped into a dream for the first time in many, many months.

Chapter Nineteen

Kit

"Guard!"

I blinked, rubbing the sleep from my eyes. I must have drunk too much because I swore I felt like I was back in the dream world that I'd missed so much. And her voice, her voice was there, coming from her crazy forest with white barked trees and blue-green leaves.

"Guard!"

I heard her cry again; this time, I turned my head, and I saw those shapely olive-toned legs coming closer. It couldn't be, could it? Shaking my head, I moved into a crouched position to stand, but the force of her exuberant talk knocked me over.

"Guard! You are here! I'm so thrilled!" Her arms went around my neck. My body jolted as I continued to try and rise to a half-sitting position. I happily wrapped my arms around her waist.

"Is this real?" I murmured, feeling the heat of her back on my hand. I tried to push her back, but she only gripped me tighter.

"Of course, it's real!" She squealed too loud for my ear. I winced, my wolf whimpering at the noise. My Warrior rambled, spouting off nonsense

I couldn't understand. "I mean, it's a dream, so it isn't real, but it's as real as it's going to be for our sort of real," she rambled. My Warrior's grip grew tighter, causing me to cough, and she pulled away.

"I'm so glad the elixir wore off. I've missed you so much!" She cupped my cheeks and squeezed them together, causing my lips to pout. "I'm so sorry I pushed you away, but I couldn't see you after finding out you weren't my mate. It hurt my heart too much, and I was such a coward, and I didn't want to hurt you, or have my dad hurt you. I mean seriously, he's a big bad wolf, and I'm scared he would crush you even though you are insanely strong, and so capable and shit..."

I blinked, putting my finger over her lips to stop her. She opened her mouth and sucked my finger between her lips.

Holy. Hell.

Pulling it out, she pouted and hugged me again. "I'm so glad you're here, that you're back! Happy to have you again in my dreams where you belong!"

"Easy there," I pushed her away. Her smile beamed brightly, and I couldn't help but smile back at her and pull her back into a hug. "I've missed you too." I rubbed my hand up and down her back. She straddled me, her legs on either side of my thighs. A black leather skirt rode up her hips. It was a miniature skirt, and it wasn't the typical soft leather of Bergarian, either. It reminded me of Earth. Not to mention the black t-shirt that held a picture with a mouth and tongue hanging out of it.

With the million questions I had for her, the only one that escaped my lips was, "Where are you? Are you on Earth?"

She flinched.

"I won't come find you," I soothed. "This is just...not your usual attire."

My Warrior nodded, picking at her nails.

"I had to get away to keep my mind off you," she whispered. "I'm staying with my family's close friends and learning how they spar on Earth."

Her breath fanned my face, and then I realized something was very off about her. She smelled of werewine. "Have you been drinking?" I snapped. What the hell was she thinking? My drive to protect her had grown strong. The thrill of finding her and keeping her grew by the minute.

In the dark hours of the night, I worried I could be wrong, that she would actually find her real mate and I would never see her again. I deserved all the answers I could get; and hell, she was going to give them to me.

"Maaaaaybe." She winked. "I kicked an Alpha's ass today, so we all went to celebrate at a bar."

"A bar?!" I growled. "Those aren't safe! What were you thinking?"

"I didn't dance with anyone." She put her hands on her hips. "Is that why you're so mad? Because you're jealous? After all this time not seeing each other, you are going into a jealous fit?" She huffed, crossing her arms. Her breasts heaved upward. They sat right in front of me, and it was all I could do not to lean into them.

Sighing, I ran my hand through my hair. "No, I've missed you, Sugar. You do not know how much I've missed you. I worried you might have found your mate, even though I still think you are mine."

She blushed, looking away with a small smile. "Sugar, huh? She replied.

I nodded. "I worried about you every day. It has been so lonely, a piece of me missing. Every night I waited for you."

"Aw, you are so sweet." She patted my chest. "I am sorry, I'm sorry I was away." The sparkle of excitement dimmed. Her body curving in upon itself.

"Hey, none of that." I tilted up her chin. "Tell me what happened. How were you able to keep me away? I was so angry; you just don't know." I tightened my fists.

She grabbed one and kissed the back of my hand.

Fuck.

"I knew of a sorceress. She gave me an elixir to keep my dreams away. She wasn't sure what would happen since I was a Dream Wanderer and let me just tell you my daydreams have sucked!"

"Daydreams?" I held onto her tighter.

"Yeah, daydreams. I would sit, minding my own business, and my head would clear and my eyes would fog over." My Warrior used her fingers to brush her eyes downward and opened them again dramatically. "And then I would relive every dream we had together." She smiled sadly. "They were great to relive again, but I couldn't talk to you. I just had to watch."

I gripped her tighter, kissing her forehead.

"Damn, you're so sweet. I should have never drunk that stuff."

"And you never will again. Do you understand me?" I commanded. "You tell me before you do anything like that. You didn't just hurt yourself, but me as well." I gripped her tight.

"I didn't mean to. I don't think we are mates. I didn't want to prolong the pain," she whined.

"It was more painful not seeing you, Sugar. My dreams have been dark without my angel to light the way," I said with conviction.

"You are so cheesy." She beamed. "I really like that." Our faces drew closer together until she hiccupped.

"Oh sorry." She covered her mouth. "I got carried away with my friends."

"No more drinking. It isn't good for your wolf. Especially when you are training to be some beastly warrior. You can't let your guard down, not for one minute."

"It was just one night; I won't do it anymore." She waved her hand dismissively. "I just wanted to let go. The dreams were bothering me, not being able to talk to you, and I just wanted to let loose. Oh!" She jumped, landing straight on my cock.

"Fuck, easy."

"Oh sorry, did I hit Little Guard?"

She looked down between her legs. She wore bright red cotton under-wear that peeked out of her skirt.

I groaned, trying not to look. "It isn't a little guard!"

"Oh sorry, big, massive, enormous, mighty beast!" She threw her hands in the air, losing her balance as we crashed back into the purple moss below us. Tiny sparks of light flew as we landed, and she giggled furiously.

"Yeah, no more drinking," I muttered. I pulled her off my lap before I touched her too much and my cock stirred to life. My future mate looked up at me with her big, crystal blue eyes.

"But anyway." She ignored me. "I got this outstanding tattoo. Wanna see?"

Before I could tell her to wait, she pulled up her shirt, showing off a beautiful red lacy bra. Beneath it, on her sternum, was a tattoo of the crescent moon with vines and trees decorating underneath her breasts.

Mighty Zeus.

Her smile widened. My eyes were glued to the smoothness of her skin and the delicate patterns of ink that crossed it.

"It's great, huh? Didn't even hurt! Here." She grabbed my hand and had me touch underneath her breast.

Gods.

"It's already healed! Amazing, huh?"

"Yes," I said breathlessly. "Amazing." My cock, which was already hard, was going to explode. Before I went to sleep each night, I was going to have to take care of it if I wanted to give her pleasure.

"I also got another one. Want to see?" She began to pull down her skirt, and I grabbed her hand before she could go any lower.

"You're still drunk. Let's wait on that one until you're thinking clearly."

And for my cock to calm down.

Shrugging, she put her shirt down and scooted onto my lap. No longer surprised at her brazen actions, I welcomed it and wrapped my arms around her. These were the moments I cherished and missed the most—the times where I just held her at the base of the tree, and we basked in each other's presence.

I didn't care too much for company, but then again, she was the only company that I needed.

"You aren't too mad at me?" she asked. My mate picked at her nails, pulling at the skin until I pulled her hand away before she could hurt herself.

"Where did my confident wolf go?" I asked her incredulously. Shrugging, she sat on her knees to keep her skirt covering her delectable thighs. Pushing my erection away, she shifted, and a whimper left her lips at my long pause.

"I am not mad at you, Sugar. I'm just disappointed you didn't talk to me first. I was being a controlling bastard before you left, and I scared you."

"You didn't scare me," she muttered. "I scared myself because all my life I have been taught to wait for my mate and—"

"I stole a kiss from you," I interrupted.

She took a deep breath in and nodded. "Not that I didn't mind," she added hastily. "But the more I've thought about it, it was a dream kiss, not a reality kiss." She side-eyed me, looking for a reaction.

"I suppose you are right." I smirked. "Does that mean you'll let me kiss you again?" I asked hopefully.

Her breath caught, her head turning toward me. "You mean, you still want to?" Her breaths were shallow, her heart racing through her chest.

"More than anything." I brushed her wild hair from her face. "Just because you stayed away from me all these months doesn't mean I don't want you. No, it means I want you more. It only solidified what I really wanted. And that's you, Little Warrior."

"Not little," she replied in a whisper.

"You will always be My Little Warrior, whether you think you are big or not. To me, you will always be my fragile little dream mate and nothing else." I paused, waiting for a reaction. I knew I could be forceful, downright commanding. But with my new Alpha status, I couldn't deny to myself what I felt, what I wanted. She wanted it to. She just needed more convincing.

"But only in the dream?" she asked. "We can only act like mates in the dream. I can't reject my mate. It isn't how things are done, it is what the goddess wants, it's what I want. It is what you should want." She put her hand to her chest.

"You will have your mate, Sugar." I tilted her head up to me. *And I will be your mate.* "But here, inside this dream, you are mine as I am yours. When you find your mate, when we cross that path, we will figure it out."

"I would have to go to him," she said sadly. "It wouldn't be fair to him."

"*She's ours,*" Riddick yelled inside my mind. "*She will always be ours, in the dream world and on the outside. We must find her to prove it to her.*"

"*We will find her, my friend. But first, we must convince her we will always be hers in here. Claim her in her dreams, before we claim her in reality,*" I replied. "*Have her fall so deeply in love with us, she would want to reject the mate in the real world to have us.*"

"*I say just take her,*" Riddick growled. "*She is ours anyway.*"

"*That is where you and I differ. I am the patient one while you are a wolf of action. Don't you see she has more growing up to do? To find her feelings? To find herself? Her grandmother took too much away from her. She fears she will make the wrong move, not trusting herself. Afraid of hurting others.*"

"*Still want to bone her,*" Riddick growled.

I chuckled, My Warrior tilting her head in confusion. "Fine. What happens in the dream world, stays. It is all but a dream, yes?" She bit her lip, and I leaned forward. Her plump lip dragged away from her teeth. "I need an answer from you. Are you willing to let go? Let me be a part of your dream world. For us to be happy? Truly happy?"

"I-I want that." She blushed. "I'm just scared."

"My Warrior? Scared? Has the Underworld frozen over?" I playfully looked around, grabbing my chest in feigned shock.

"I can't love you," she said seriously. "I can't love you in the real world, not until—"

"But you can love me here? Can't you? Because I know I love you," I said sternly. "And if you can only love me here," I put her hand on my chest. "Then I'll take whatever I can get from you."

"Guard," she sniffed. I pulled her into my embrace, her arms reaching around my neck. "I just don't want to get hurt."

"And you won't," I snapped.

Because damnit, you will be mine in our dreams and in reality.

Chapter Twenty

Evelyn

My Guard had me straddle him, his arms wrapped around my back and his hands soothingly holding me tight. I sighed blissfully.

I couldn't believe he was here.

Had I really forgotten that six months had passed? Surely not. I had thought of him every day. I wasn't even sure if it had been a full six months, but with me being an Alpha, I'm sure my body purged the elixir faster than what Taliyah's estimate.

My mind was becoming less fuzzy. The realization that I was here with him and not in a stupid daydream came at me like a slap in the face. My mind went over how I raced to him, how happy, how carefree. I bit my cheek, looking around the dream world that I had missed so much.

Then it hit me again.

I just showed him my boobs.

I paled, my arms going slack, and his chuckle roared through me.

"You just sobered up, didn't you?" He continued laughing.

I buried my nose in his shoulder. "Oh gods, what have I done?"

He threw his head back and howled, pushing me away, but I kept my head lowered, not wanting to show him the blush on my face. That was when the linen in his pants moved, and his friend popped up.

Damnit, where the hell can I look!?

"Easy there." He didn't call out, his massive erection prodding my thigh, but he certainly moved my chin so he could look straight at me. "I've been thinking about them since you turned eighteen, so getting a glimpse of them was the perfect apology for leaving me all these months." I bit my lip, not at the compliment of him wanting to stare at my breasts, but for the fact that *I left him.*

"I'm so sorry," I whispered. "I don't know what I was thinking, I really didn't." I shook my head.

"Hey now, we have already talked about this, and I'm not mad. You had to grow on your own, find yourself. Look at you now?" He waved his hand over my outfit. "You are on Earth. You've never been, have you?"

I shook my head. "A few times, before I met you. We have friends we are close with. One of their children got pup-napped. They've been hunting for her for years and now that I'm old enough, my parents allowed me to come over to help search for her."

"Oh Sugar, I'm sorry."

I nodded. "She's three years younger than me. She was super sweet, a little obsessed over Hades though. She was digging the whole 'King of the Underworld,' vibe." I laughed nervously.

"That's kind of disturbing," My Guard muttered.

"She is really smart, just like her mom. Anyway." I picked at my nails. "I came over here to help find her. I've been on several missions. We're planning to go west and check out the big cities over there and see if we can find her."

"That's noble of you, Warrior. As always, you are being selfless." His finger traced my cheekbone.

"Except when I took the elixir. That was pretty selfish, wasn't it?" I whispered.

"Warrior, you were looking out for yourself, and I went insane at the thought of you not wanting to meet me. To agree for me to take you. You need not to worry any longer. I will respect your wishes. Can't promise anything if I meet you in reality though." He winked.

I snorted, snuggling up to him once more.

This was so damn nice. No wonder mom and dad cuddled all the time. Wonder what it would be like to do the "closet" things with My Guard.

Wait, nope, can't think about that.

"What have you been doing since I've been gone?" I sighed as he leaned back into the moss. The soft, sponge like material spread out under the beautiful white lights, and the trees above us covered us in the shade.

Pixies flew around us, staring, giggling, and flying back into the trees. How I'd missed this place. It was a world of calm—an escape from the real world. It brought me peace and time to relax and not feel the obligations of the world. If My Guard wasn't with me, however, this place would be so lonely.

He really completed the dream.

"You were gone for a month, and I was restless," he said sternly. "I was a real ogre to everyone. They were worried about me." He squeezed me tight.

"I'm so—"

"Nope." He rolled over and placed a kiss on my lips. He pulled back, his eyes wide with the realization of what he'd done. My hands trailed up his tunic, pulling him closer until our lips met again. The warmth of his mouth, his large hands encompassing the back of my neck to deepen the kiss, turned me to putty into his arms. His other hand came around, pulling my lower back closer to his body.

I sighed blissfully as he pulled away. "Open your mouth," he ordered. Parting my lips, he descended again, his tongue reaching for mine. My arms slipped around his neck, my fingers threading through his hair.

His tongue massaged my mouth, the kiss becoming heated. His hands wandered around my back and into my hair until he pulled on it lightly. Moaning, my legs wrapped around him, and his cock pushed deeper into my leg.

"Guard," I squeezed his shoulders, and he backed away while we both panted.

Holy Hera.

"Don't say sorry," he gulped. "Or I'll have to silence you again," he whispered into my mouth.

"Maybe I should say sorry more often," I teased, running my fingers through his hair.

His eyes twinkled, and his wolf showed himself. It wasn't the same eyes I was used to seeing. These were a deep gold. Seeing him for what he was, he was the same Guard, but parts of his features had changed. Studying him, I pulled a lock of his bangs away from his face.

"Did.... Did you dye your hair?" I asked.

"You are just now noticing? How much did you drink?" He rubbed his nose against me.

"Sorry, I was too busy staring at your body." I giggled.

"Fair enough, it is pretty good looking, right?" He pulled up his tunic, showing off an extensive plane of sculptured abs and an Adonis belt. "All for you." He wiggled his eyebrows.

Goddess.

"Speechless, Sugar?"

I could only nod, reaching toward him, but he pulled his tunic down to hide his body. "Maybe later, we have catching up to do."

My face turned red yet again as he rolled over. We faced each other, but our hands continued to play with each other's fingers.

I am in some deep shit.

There was no way I would want to give this up if my mate came along. This was just a dream, just a place where I met the wolf that had comforted me through years when I needed it. He was more than that. He was my friend who'd turned into a romantic interest.

A romantic interest you have already fallen in love with.

"Anyway," I drawled. "What did you do to your hair? Not that I don't love it, it's just different." I played with his hair again, and he sighed, closing his eyes. His wolf purred, egging me to continue. I laughed, running my fingers through his hair some more.

"You are going to put me to sleep," he muttered.

"Don't think you can fall asleep in a dream." I paused. "Huh, I wonder if you can. We can do anything in a dream, but does that mean you wake up in the real world?"

"Shhhh." He waved his finger around until he landed it on my lips. "No thinking too much."

I laughed, pulling my hand away until he grabbed it and put it back on his head.

"Pet me and I'll tell you," he muttered.

Shaking my head, I continued to pet through his hair. His eyes opened, showing me those pretty gold eyes again. Staring at him closely and concentrating, I felt it. Within the dream, my senses might be dulled, but if I concentrated, it was there.

"You... you are an Alpha?" I screeched. His eyes opened wider, hearing my scream of excitement. "You made your wolf an Alpha!? That's so rare! How did you do it?!"

"Sugar, you act like it's so hard. I'm amazingly talented, that's why," he said cockily, rolling on his back.

"What? You dork, it's super hard. How did it happen? Did you kill someone while you shifted or something?" My eyes widened, wondering what emotional state set him off, set his wolf off for him to lose control. And then it hit me.

His eyes softened, and he grabbed my hand. "It was you not being with me, Little Warrior. I was so angry, so out of sorts. Had doubts about you not being mine—"

"But I'm not—"

"Hush," he growled. "You are mine. You just don't know it yet."

I nodded, holding his hand.

"Anyway, my wolf was pissed and stressed. We just let loose while I was fighting another wolf. I didn't kill him, unfortunately. But it was enough for me to grow. As much as I hated you being away from me, I'm not sure if I would have grown if you hadn't taken the elixir. You ground me, make me sane, but the bit of craziness helped me form into a better wolf. And as for my hair?" He ran his fingers through it. "It gets darker the stronger I get."

"You aren't just saying that, are you?" I raised an eyebrow. "That it was good for us to be apart?"

"I wouldn't bullshit you, Sugar. You know I don't say stuff I don't mean."

That was utterly true. I remembered when I first sparred with him at eleven, and he told me my form sucked. Even though I was strong, My Guard taught me the importance of an excellent form and how to anticipate the enemy's moves before an attack. It helped me later in life. I'm far faster, stronger, and more powerful because of his teachings, even with my dad giving me help along the way. Sometimes dad could be too doting on his daughters.

"We needed some time apart; I see that now." He put his hand behind his head. "But it was torture every day, not knowing if you'd really found someone else." He sighed.

"Me too," I whispered. "I thought you'd found your mate, and I didn't know what I was going to do if I came back here, and you were gone. Or, if you were here and would always be here despite you having a mate." Tears formed in my eyes. "That is what I worry about most—us finding someone else in reality but in the dreams we are here."

"And what if that happens?" He rolled on his stomach to face me. "We are in a dream. It's not technically cheating."

"But I would feel like I am betraying you when I was with someone else. And the thought of some other she-wolf touching you pisses me off," I growled.

"The feeling is mutual." He pulled my head closer to his. "That is why I know we are mates. A pull this strong in the dream world has to mean something. Me being here with you means something."

"If you say so," I whispered, not wanting to argue. Not here, not now. I wanted to savor every bit of time I had with him. If that meant forgetting my mate in the real world and just enjoying the now, so be it. My body and my heart wanted him. For now, I just wanted to be happy and live here.

"Hey." I sat up. "If we are going to pretend that we are mates—"

"We are mates," he growled.

Oh, so possessive.

"Right, we are." I eyed him, giving him a wink. "Then we should have a house, huh?"

"We are going to play house now? I thought we were over that stage when you were ten."

I scoffed at him, standing up. "Oh Guard, you said we're mates in here." I pointed at the ground. "And mates have houses to live in, right? Or do you expect me to make out with you on the moss all the time?"

He smirked, patting the ground next to him. "No one else is in here." He stood up, wrapping his arms around my waist. I tried to push away, but his grip grew tighter. He leaned forward, brushing his lips around my ear. "And I won't just be kissing you, you know?" His tongue licked my neck. "I plan on doing devilish things to this body, but if you feel more comfortable doing it inside a cottage, I won't be picky." His wolf purred, nuzzling into my neck.

My legs weakened as he chuckled darkly, hand wrapping around my waist. He kissed down my neck, his hand tracing the waistband of my leather skirt.

"Guard?"

He hummed, his hot breath trailing down my neck and onto the skin of my chest. "What do you need, Sugar?"

"I-I-I, what?" How was I to tell him what I needed? And when did he become so talkative and sure of himself? He acted like he'd done this before. "Have you, done anything, like this?"

His head backed away. Cold air replaced the heat of his body. "Never," he growled. "You are the only woman I've ever wanted to touch. Why would you ask such a thing?" His face was furious, and I backed away. "Warrior, wait," he pulled me back. "I'm sorry. My wolf is frantic. He wants you as much as I do, and I need you."

"I n-need you too. I'm just nervous. I've read stuff too...like some books and stuff but...you don't act nervous." My voice shook.

"Because I have planned out what I wanted to do to you for many months," he said darkly. "Every kiss, every touch and exactly what I'm going to say to you while you fall apart in my arms. How I am going to part your lower pink, puffy lips, how my tongue will lap up your juices while you scream for mercy."

My lips parted in surprise.

"I'm going to own you in this dream. I'm going to make you mine and soon, all you are going to want is to have me and only me."

"But—"

"I've done my research, I've done my studies on a woman's anatomy, and I know I am more than capable of making you happy in all ways. Not just in body, but in heart as well."

Fuck.

Chapter Twenty One

Evelyn

With a skip in my step, I trotted down the pack house grand staircase. Humming, I reached the cafeteria with the hordes of warriors and pups running up and down the buffet line. Sunday was the one day I could sleep in, and I took advantage of it, even if that meant that I might miss breakfast.

Humming, I piled my plate high with all the fixings—pancakes, sausage, bacon, fruit, and oatmeal. Cinder purred in my head, rolling on her back as I poured the home-made maple syrup on top. I would have continued to skip down the rows of tables and chairs but with the enormous amount of food, along with two large glasses of chocolate milk—all in memory of my mother's favorite drink to give us as children in the morning—I needed to move more carefully. I sat down gingerly at the table, gently placing my plate in front of me, and moved the silverware to its correct spot. With my milk to my top right and my napkin on my lap, I took a deep breath and let out a delighted sigh as I began eating.

The first fork-full of eggs melted in my mouth, my stomach growling for more. The table had gone silent as I sat in my little world in my head.

A week had already passed with My Guard invading my dreams. Each night, we spoke of everything we'd missed; I even got to hear about his two friends, which he used to regard as Roommate A and Roommate B. But now, since our time apart, he had opened up to them, and they had become more than roommates, but friends in a time of need. So now we had Friend A and Friend B.

I snorted to myself, finishing the eggs and moving onto the pancakes.

We had put the finishing touches on our cottage. It really was like playing house. Our dream now created the way we wanted. The tree that I had grown so fond of, the one that sat out in the forest outside the palace, was still in its rightful place. It only seemed fair since that was where I woke up in the dream.

Never moving it and keeping it as the only constant in the dream seemed like an easy decision. Now what lay underneath the tree was something to behold. Our cottage was a home away from reality where no one could disturb us. Not that anyone could see us in our dreams, but it was that extra layer of protection that I liked.

It was tucked away underneath the dangling vines, with brown siding to match the surrounding forest. A plank swing hung from the branches not too far away, the vines twirled with flowers and deep blue-green leaves wrapped around the ropes. The cottage had deep purple and green and moss-colored roof with wildflowers sprouting over it. The doorway was secured with a door constructed from the toughest wood I could think of from Bergarian. The windows were paned, and white lace curtains decorated the inside.

It reminded me of the homes near the Crimson Shadows's pack house—well hidden in the forest, becoming one with nature and not taking away from it. On the inside was a different story. I decorated the walls with white shiplap with its clean simplicity that I had seen in Charlotte and Wesley's home. Mostly it was plain in color, just natural whites, creams, and tans. It gave it a clean, cloud-like feel, and it should feel that way because the white wrought iron bed looked like the gods slept there.

A large, white fluffy comforter covered the bed. Extra white furs, pillows and an abundance of tulle hung from the ceiling. The open windows made the tulle dance on a constant breeze as shadows drifted across the light tan wooden floorboards.

Unfortunately, we had yet to use the bed. Just heavy kissing on the love seat that sat at the base of the bed. It was like getting to know him all over again, but in a different light. For so many years, he saw me as the young girl learning from him. It wasn't until recently had My Guard bloomed new lustful feelings for me. I on the other hand, always saw him as handsome. He was exactly the kind of person I would want for as a mate. But now that our feelings were out in the open, there was an air of new shyness—a new way to look at things when you cared for someone so deeply.

Maybe that was why he hadn't taken a step further, he wanted to get to know me all over again.

Or maybe I should make a move?

I'd rather spar for forty-eight hours straight than make the first move. I was too damn terrified. What if I messed up? Maybe he wanted to make the first move. His words were so confident when we first met, but now he was faltering in his actions. I mean, he hadn't even touched my boobs yet.

"That's it." A fork slammed on the table. I jolted, slinging my head back until I met my sister's eyes.

"What?!" I squeaked. Tweedle Dee, Tweedle Dumb and Dumber stared at Melody with open mouths. I snorted again, giggling to myself remembering what My Guard thought of the names I'd given my "friends." Joshua, of course, was Dumber because he could be a bit dense.

My Guard laughed so hard, I thought I'd broken him.

"Why are you so happy?" Melody cocked her head in confusion. "Everyone is worried about you—"

"People are always worried." I waved my hand dismissively. "If it's not one thing, it's another. The best thing is not to worry about it," I said matter-of-factly. I stabbed into my pancakes, dripping with syrup. I moaned, "Gods, these are so good." Licking the fork extra-long to make sure I got all the sugary goodness, I stabbed at another piece.

Joshua cleared his throat, looking back down at his plate. He continued to clear it, shifting around in his seat. I eyed my sister in confusion. She shrugged, and I continued eating.

"What's got you all happy? Not that it isn't a good thing, it's just. You skip and you're humming. It's just different."

Yeah, it was different. A warrior does not hum.

"Maybe she has a boy toy," Tweedle Dee, AKA, Basim said without missing a beat. Tweedle Dumb smacked him upside the head.

"Evie doesn't leave her room at night, you idiot. She thinks she needs all this 'beauty sleep.'" Mason air quoted.

I rolled my eyes as they argued with each other. While my attitude had been improving, theirs weren't. Maybe they needed to get laid. Hell, I know I needed to with all the heavy make out sessions. And not once had he grabbed my boob...

"Evie!" Melody sighed exasperatedly. "These daydreams are getting annoying," she whispered, taking a sip of her hot cocoa.

"I have had no daydreams in a week." I wiggled my eyebrows, and she spat out her hot cocoa all over Joshua. He roared, swiping at his eyes, and stood up from the table. The room went silent once they noticed the brown drink covering his white muscle t-shirt.

I snorted, trying not to laugh, and hid my amusement with my arm.

"Oh, Joshua, I'm so sorry!" Melody went to stand up and grab a napkin, but he shook his head.

"It's alright, Your Highness," he grumbled. "I'll go change." Joshua left, his grouchy vibe finally disappearing with him, and the room burst into a fit of laughter.

Yeah, nobody was a fan of grumpy Joshua.

Maybe he needed to get laid, too.

"You need to spill," Melody mind-linked me, fully aware that our other guards were sitting with us. Even with a mind-link she was blatantly obvious when she linked. Melody liked to stare, waiting for a reaction from whatever she'd said. She could read people's emotions so well just by looking at their faces.

"Like I said, for a week I have had no daydreams," I said.

"Aaaaand." She licked her lips, sighing and resting her head on her hand.

"He was there, and he was happy to see me." I blushed. *"And relieved."* Cinder rolled on her back, wagging her tail. Cinder was in love with our Guard too. It was going to make it so much harder later once we found our mates.

"Did you kiss?" Melody swooned.

"Yes, kissing, lots of kissing." I giggled. Basim and Mason eyed me suspiciously as I cleared my throat.

"What about your mate?" Melody asked, concerned. *"Didn't you want to wait for your mate? What are you going to do? Have you even thought about it?"*

Had I even thought about it? Ha, she insults me.

"Of course I've thought about it." I pushed the fruit around on my plate. *"We both did. He still seems to think I am his mate, but there are no sparks on my skin, Mel. None of that amazing shock you get when you touch someone that I've heard so much about. I'm not sure if it is lust or just my heart falling in love with him without a bond. You know, like most humans do with each other."* I popped a grape into my mouth. *"We both realized it's just a dream, it isn't real. Our physical bodies aren't really acting, just... just our dream bodies I guess."*

Melody grew thoughtful, nodding her head. *"Logically, it makes sense,"* she replied. *"I just don't want to see you get hurt if he really isn't your mate. I couldn't stand to see your heart broken. It's already been broken by a family member that was supposed to look out for your interests and now..."*

I cleared my throat, interrupting her. *"I know Mel, I know. I'll be fine. I have it under control."*

Yeah, I had no control. I was in far too deep.

"Well, we know when we are not wanted," Mason said, nudging Basim. "We can go sit somewhere else." I sat up straighter, pulling Mason back down in his seat.

"I'm sorry, we were just talking girl stuff. Didn't think you would want to hear about that."

"Maybe we do," Basim jumped into the conversation. "We are tired of being left out. We are just the guards, not even your friends." He sulked.

That was a punch in the gut.

"Guys, I see you as way more than just our guards," I said.

Melody nodded. "You both have been amazing. We love having you around. You make us laugh! There are some things we can't share all the time though." Melody sipped more of her hot cocoa. "Girl stuff is girl stuff." She winked at Mason, who blushed.

What the hell was that? I raised a brow at Melody, who shrugged her shoulders. *"I need dirty deets on that later,"* I linked her. She smirked, sipping her cocoa.

"Is it about a wolf seeking your affections? You know your father wouldn't have that," Basim replied with a growl. "We need to keep you pure for your mate. It was your father's orders."

I narrowed my eyes at Basim. "My dad is not in charge of my love life," I snapped. "He is protective of me, but this body and the decisions I have made to save myself for my mate is my own. No wolf has touched it, and none will until I find my mate. How dare you think otherwise?" I growled.

Alright, chill out, woman.

Basim and Mason shuddered back, baring their necks.

"Evie!" Melody scowled. "You stop that. They are our friends. They are looking out for you." Her eyes softened.

"Really," Basim said. "We are just looking out for you, not just as your guards, but as your friends. It's not like we would go tattle to your parents, you're right, it is your body. We just don't want some wolf trying to touch you after you have declared you were saving yourself for your mate. Just trying to help." He sighed.

Mason lowered his head, studying his plate. Melody frowned, watching him closely until he perked his head up as Basim jabbed him in the gut.

"I never thought once that our princess would succumb to some wolf other than her mate," Basim added. "She has too good of a head on her shoulders. She would want to please her mate, wait for him. That is what her Majesty has taught her. It is what I have strived to do as well." He puffed out his chest.

"Say that to the pornos under your mattress," Mason snorted.

"I can look but not touch!" he snarled back.

"Easy guys," Melody tried to calm them.

My appetite was ruined. Now the guilt weighed heavy. Was I cheating on my mate? Was I taking things too far by kissing, creating another world with another wolf that wasn't destined to be mine? Was I emotionally cheating on him?

My mood soured, and I pushed my food away.

"Evie?" Melody watched as I stood up from the table.

"I'm going for a run." I stepped away from the table. Basim and Mason stood to follow, but I snarled, looking back at them.

"You stay. I'll be in the territory. I want to be alone. Disobey that order and I'll see to it your royal guard status is revoked."

"Evie!" Melody went to stand again but before I could hear her say another word, I stomped out the door and into the cold snow.

The blanket of white was a far cry from the snow in Bergarian. It was pure white instead of the opal-colored snowflakes that I had come to love when I visited the dragon tribes in the mountains. I didn't strip my off clothes, Cinder had taking over and ripped them to shreds. She was ready to feel the cold snow between the tendrils of fur. My bones broke slowly, still getting used to our half-beast form. My face elongated, fangs descending, and my body grew until I stood seven feet tall, with auburn and red highlighted fur trailing down my back. I howled. The entire pack froze, distracted from their daily activities.

Wesley and Charlotte stood on the path leading to the pack house steps, Dante, Hunter and Stephen staring on in awe as I took two enormous steps toward the forest. No doubt I would be asked why I had shifted into my half-beast; it wasn't often that I did because it scared the pups, and I hated them looking at me in fear.

My heated breath surrounded my maw until it faded away with the wind as I pushed forward. Running through the trees, jumping over streams, I howled again as my thick padded feet crunched into the snow.

Fury, pain, and confusion ran through me as I swiped my claw through the thick bark of the pine trees. My mind reeled with guilt, but my desire to feel happiness in the depths of my dreams was so strong. Too strong to fight, I was powerless to leave the Guard that had invaded my dreams from the very beginning of my gift. There was no elixir or spell that could keep me away from him. My body was too strong to keep spells away for long. Either my day or night dreams. He would be there. Waiting for me to succumb to the dire love he said he had for me.

If I could just let go, forget that there was a mate in the real world waiting for me somewhere, I could be so much happier. So much freer to fulfill the happiness inside me.

"Are you happy?" I asked My Guard who sat at the edge of the sparring ring. At fifteen years old, I found him to be someone to look up to. His determination, his worry-free attitude... But there was something dark inside him. He hid himself from the real world. I didn't like that he had isolated himself from everyone else. I wanted to know more about who he was, what his purpose was for being inside my dreams night after night.

My Guard huffed, throwing down the weighted iron he had used to work his muscles. He smirked as he approached me. He had a twinkle in his eye, leaning on the ring where I sat. Gods, he was handsome, it caused me to catch my breath.

"Because you look grumpy all the time, you need to lighten up," I added.

"You aren't the first wolf to tell me that," he replied. "In fact, if I had a silver coin for every—"

"Well, maybe you should then," I snapped. "Because it sounds like people are trying to help you out, but you refuse it. They would stop if you would get that vine out of your ass."

His lips twitched. "You have got quite a mouth for a little warrior, you know?"

"Dad says it doesn't matter what language I use, as long as my actions show integrity. Do your actions show integrity, or are you just an ass to everyone?"

His face grew stern. "I'm not a butt to you," he argued back, quirking an eyebrow.

"No? Never would have guessed." I smiled, pushing him in the shoulder. My Guard laughed, rubbing the sweat from his forehead. "See, that smile is gorgeous. I'm sure you could attract more friends with a face like that."

"Warrior, you are the only wolf I smile for."

Chapter Twenty Two

Kit

A week.

It had been a week since I'd returned to My Warrior's dreams, and I had yet to take it a step further. Part of the week we spent creating our own home away from reality. As dull as it sounded, it was rather fun watching her come up with ideas. She would close her eyes as if to picture it in her mind, and it would slowly manifest before us. All of it was created from nothing and turned into something solid and strong.

It was certainly a gift I was quite jealous of because in this world; I held nothing of value. I couldn't create anything to make her happy. Instead, I had to rely on her, which was an idea that would unsettle me in the real world. However, here I could just be, let her take control and watch her make magic.

During the week of creating our home away from home, my classmates, along with Volke and his mate, traveled to the southernmost part of the Bergarian lands. These lands were new and not heavily mapped. This territory held the land of the orcs, the newest species that had joined our land since the Dark War.

King Osirus had stumbled upon them when dealing with a hostage situation long ago and luckily for us, the orcs were willing to help with the war with the promise to remove the wall that separated our lands. The wall that kept the Forbidden Forest hidden away came down, and the orcs now roamed freely. Unfortunately, the ogres that also lived within their land were now scattered about the country. Some were friendly enough anyway, but others had become dangerous and would have to be disposed of.

"Does he always look like that?" I was torn from my thoughts as one orc, known as Sugha pointed straight at me. My friends had been talking non-stop to the infamous green beings of muscles. Their fascination with them had become downright annoying with the constant questions about their anatomy, fighting techniques, way of life. Orcs, we learned, were immune to magic, a trait that ultimately helped us gain the upper hand in the war.

"Yeah, he always looks like that," Clint said. "Like he's constipated."

I scoffed, shaking my head. "I do not," I retorted, walking forward. "And I'm not constipated either. I'm in perfectly good regulation according to my wolf."

Leland threw his head back, laughing, and I couldn't help but smile.

"Ah, he smiles from time to time. Usually about the mistress that visits his dreams." Clint nudged the large green bolder. Sugha didn't move, but a smirk crossed his face. The muscles of these beings were well defined, and they were large in stature, almost hitting eight feet tall. Their culture was vastly different from any other species of Bergarian that we had come to know, wearing hardly anything but leathers or loin cloths to cover their privates. The weapons they wore on their backs were either plain clubs or spiked clubs. Occasionally, we even saw one with an ax. They wore their scars like tattoos.

"He's a strange one, that one. Doesn't give as much emotion as you two do." Sugha nodded to Leland.

"We wear our emotion on our sleeve. Most wolves do, but Kit is hard to read. He's only just recently become more open to us, so don't pay him any mind if he doesn't speak too you much." Leland laughed.

Sugha grunted, pulling his club from his back. "Well, I wish to fight him then. I think we would have a fair fight."

My eyes widened. Orcs were indeed huge, and I'd heard of it taking three or four wolves to pull one down in a fight. A one-on-one fight with Sugha was a task I was not ready to undertake.

"Are you sure about that? Usually, you let us have two wolves at a time," Leland asked hesitantly. "Kit is strong, recently changing to an Alpha, but I think you might be too much."

"You wound me," I joked to Leland, pushing his shoulder. "I'm sure I can at least try to keep up."

Sugha banged on his chest as a child ran toward him and hugged his leg.

"Pa! Mama wants you! She said you are done fighting today!"

Sugha groaned, picking up the little orcling. The deeper green skin of Sugha and the boy in his arms was different. The orcling was lighter green, with smaller tusks protruding from the bottom jaw. His face was more rounded instead of sculpted, and the little fists he used to bang on his father's chest more delicate.

"Does she want me to stop fighting so I am to take care of you or her?" He wiggled his brows at Clint and Leland who snickered. "My mate is always begging for this." Sugha gripped his dick through the loin cloth and thrust his hips. "Never thought the day would come that I could bury myself into a mate. The Moon Fairy blessed the orcs for fighting in that war." Sugha put the child down. It ran away screaming for his mother in laughter.

"I'm just glad for the texts your kingdom provided us, otherwise I would have never known how to please her and convince her to be mine," he boasted. "Some of us had to tweak some things. Your species doesn't have as large of a cock and knot as we do."

Leland was drinking from his water skin when he spat it out all over Clint. "A knot!? On your dick?!" He spat, wiping away the water.

"Fucking gross, dude!" Clint wiped away the water from his face.

"Yes, it is how we claim our mates. Your species bites, we let our cocks do all the work," he grunted. "We brand their pussy, not their neck. Now, if you will excuse me, I must go brand her again." Sugha threw his head back in laughter as he stomped away from us.

"That...was something." I cleared my throat. The entire conversation was weird. Talking about an orc's cock was not on my list of things to do today. Instead, it was figuring out a way to make the first move with my mate.

I couldn't be all talk with My Warrior. I had to prove my talk with my actions, and I was failing miserably. Soon she would wonder if my words were truth if I didn't act upon them. While I rubbed the back of my neck, Leland and Clint stared at me with smirks on their faces.

"You wanna fuck your dream girl, huh?" Clint nodded, putting his hands on his hips. "You need some advice."

"First off, I don't want to fuck her," I growled.

They both chuckled as they walked with me back to our tent.

"Right dude, you wanna make loooove," Clint sang. "I getchu man." Leland shoved Clint who shoved Leland right back.

"Just forget it." I opened the flap of the tent. Many of my classmates had taken it upon themselves to get their own tents, including Callahan. He and his prick friends had decided that staying in a tent full of wolves and shifters that actually wanted to improve themselves by understanding the culture of the land was beneath them. They trained with each other, fighting tooth and nail, trying to gain stronger wolves.

"No, no." Clint rushed to me, putting his hands on my shoulders. "Really, what's up? You are confident about everything else. What is it that's giving you such a such a hard time? It's a dream? It shouldn't matter if you mess up because the next night you can just make up for it."

"It's real. You don't understand." I ran my hand through my hair. "This girl is real, like a real person walking around somewhere here or on Earth. She has a special gift that gives her the ability to have me in her dreams and…" I dare not tell them her gift. I didn't want to give her away. However, they had to understand the seriousness of it all.

"She's my mate," I spouted out.

Both of my friends' mouths stood agape as I shuffled around the room. I pulled out a new set of lounging clothes, and my friends looked at each other.

"Your mate?" Clint whispered. "Are you serious? You met your mate in a dream?"

"When do I ever joke?" I retorted.

"Sparks and everything?" Leland whispered. I shook my head, my fist pounding on the table in the room.

"No, senses are dulled in the dream. I swear she is, though. There is no other reason I would be this obsessed with her. I want her like I need water and air. She makes me feel alive, makes me a person who I am not here in reality. If I could just meet her and prove it to her, but she doesn't believe me. She thinks her mate is out there, but her feelings for me are just as strong. I know they are." I threw my shirt off and sat on the cot, my hands holding up my head as I leaned over my knees.

"We care about each other, on a deeper level. Now, we've both agreed to keep things in the dream," I muttered. "If she finds her mate in reality, she will go to him. But I know I'm hers," I growled. Forcing myself to stand, I looked into the full-length mirror. "She's mine, and no one will take her from me. I just need her to fall so in love with me she will reject any mate in reality. I want to win her over without a bond."

Clint and Leland stood quietly. An impressive feat for them.

I was grateful to have their full attention. "I just don't know how to make the first move in showing her physically that I want her."

Two smiles slowly rose on their lips.

Oh shit.

"So, when you are making out, have her lie down," Clint explained.

"Maybe we shouldn't do this, it's too weird," I tried to stand up, but Leland pushed me back down with a hand on my shoulder.

"No, dude, if she's your mate, you gotta do this, man. Get her to only crave your cock, and you're golden when you meet her. Now pay attention," Leland snapped. They both had grown utterly excited to explain the ways of mating—how to please and how to act dominant toward your mate.

Sure, I was dominant on the field, but like hell was I dominant to My Warrior. She was tough. I wasn't sure what line of Alpha she came from, even if it felt familiar. She had taken quite the precautions not to shift and show me her wolf because she said I would find out who she was and which Alpha line she hailed from. She was a sneaky wolf, but I was determined to find out who she was.

"Anyway, you need to follow your instincts. Remember, in chapter four of the Mating Manual? Follow your nose." He winked tapping his nose. "You were all about studying. I'm sure you get what I'm saying?"

I cleared my throat, loosening the invisible collar on my neck.

"No, you didn't get the little innuendo? Use your nose, man? The fragrance of the opposite sex!"

I cleared my throat again.

"You are making him uncomfortable," Leland snapped. He put his hand on my thigh, and I growled at his touch. "Sorry." He drew his hand away. "Anyway. Just go with her smell. If she's turned on, go for it. If you guys are making out, I'm sure you've smelled it before."

I gulped. I had smelled it. It was fucking intoxicating, and I wanted to bury my nose in it.

Oh, I see.

"Since you are so uncomfortable," Clint said, sounding disappointed. "Here are some manuals." He threw them on my cot. "I swear, no one takes this seriously. There are diagrams, scenarios, the whole nine yards. Queen Clara made sure every pack had one, and it was mass produced for those that wanted to stay pure for their mates. Now use it, you talk all high and mighty of the royals, now use the tools she gave to the entire kingdom. And know this." He pointed at me. "First time is going to be awkward as hell. Lucky for you, she's a virgin too."

I rolled my eyes at him. I shouldn't have said anything.

Leland and Clint stood and walked out. "We will leave you to your own devices," Clint said seriously.

"You are making this freaking weird," I muttered.

"Mating is natural. Just grow some balls and grab for what you want," Clint said seriously.

Those words echoed through my head as they left. I'd heard those same words from Kane when I sat in front of him and Clara before my departure.

Just take what I wanted, simple enough, right?

Chapter Twenty Three

Kit

Racing to the cottage, I caught the sweet and savory smell of baking. White puffs of smoke drifted from the small brick chimney, piquing my interest. Smiling, I could see the sweet face of My Warrior with her nose scrunched and her body concentrating on the task at hand. Sneaking up beside the window, I peered in to see her kneading dough. She had flour dusted across her nose, and her brow furrowed as she punched the dough.

I winced, knowing her mood must be sour, so I would forgo trying to scare her. "Knock, knock?" I opened the door to see her face instantly illuminate when I wandered in. I smiled back, having erotic thoughts about a future when I would come home from working at the palace to find my mate at home with a few pups, cooking over the stove, and her tired face brightening at the sight of me. It was a dream to see her in such a state, but then again, I never asked her if she ever wanted pups. She, of course, would want to fight in some capacity, and I had hoped to give that to her as well.

"Hi!" she said breathlessly, forgetting her flour-dusted hands and wrapping them around my neck. My lips met hers. The sweet, gentle kiss she established turned to a heated one while my hands wrapped around her trim waist. My erection grew, my need for her becoming overwhelming, but the nagging thought in the back of my mind of her scowling at bread dough pushed me away.

She whimpered, but I leaned in quickly to give her one more kiss to hush her complaints. Cupping her face, wiping the flour from her cheek with the pad of my thumb, I opened the can of worms. "What troubles you, Warrior? And since when do you bake?" I took in a deep breath, smelling the concoction of cinnamon, chocolate, and bananas. *Banana Bread.* How could I have not known my future mate could create such food?

Because you never asked her, asshole.

"While I grew up, the kitchen was a safe haven." She broke away from me, grabbing a plate of cookies. The small kitchen table was filled with pastries, cookies, pies—one that stood out the most was a chocolate silk. It was decorated with sweet cream and chocolate shavings. It was decorated so delicately, it reminded me of my years as a pup in the Ever-Green Pack back on Earth.

My family grew up in Ever-Green. A pack that specifically protected the portal to this world. I had several older brothers, all warriors at the time, but I was the runt. I was picked on maliciously, not just by my brothers, but by the other pack pups. It was a difficult time being five years old, being the youngest and definably not the strongest. I had retreated into myself and became a shy pup that feared everything until a certain waitress entered my life.

Queen Clara, then known as the random human that came to live on a plot of land her aunt had left her when she died, took me under her wing. She snuck me treats such as cookies and taught me the game of hide and seek, which improved my tracking skills. When her mate, Alpha Kane took her back to the pack house, she invited me into the kitchen and let me help make chocolate silk pies decorated like this.

I paused, looking at it longingly as My Warrior explained what all she had done before I came to our dream home. "How long have you been asleep?" I asked, taking a gander at all the sugary food. "You made all this here? You didn't create it with your mind?" I put my finger into the sweet cream and licked it, groaning at the taste.

"Yeah, I went to bed early. Really early." She blushed. "Kind of had a bad day, ran until my wolf could no longer pant properly and went to bed without supper." Her eyes cast downward, kneading the dough as if to kill it.

"Warrior, what happened?" I pushed back a lock of hair that had escaped her messy bun.

She shook her head to shake off the pain, but I knew better.

"Put the dough down," I commanded.

Her kneading fingers stopped, the dough plopping to the surface of the counter.

"Now look at me." Taking her sweet face and turning it toward me, I cupped her cheek. "Tell me everything."

She bit her lip, and my cock grew inside my linen pants. Luckily linens were large enough for my cock to grow comfortably and not strain against rough fabric.

"Did someone say something to upset you?" I asked.

"Something like that." She looked away, but my finger caught her chin to direct her eyes back to me.

"I need to know."

"And what would you do about it?" She leaned up against the counter. "Not like you can go beat them up. You don't know where I am, don't know who they are. I don't have to tell you anything," she snapped.

I growled and pulled her by her lower back, shoving my cock against her lower body. Gasping, she went to pull away, but that was when I smelled it—her arousal.

Fuck, it was gorgeous. A hint of cherry blossoms intertwined with champagne. "I am your mate," I growled. "I will do everything to help you feel better and if that means making you forget your problems here, then so be it."

She panted. Feeling her nipples push against her tunic made me smile internally. She wanted to forget her problems, and I was happy to give it to her until she gave me what I wanted. My fangs nipped at her earlobe. "Tell me what was said, Warrior."

"Nuh uh." She pressed her legs together, her ass leaning up against the counter. The worry that had littered my mind about how I would take our physical relationship to the next level dwindled as I smelled her lust. My knee nudged between her legs, parting them. My arms to each side, I pinned her against the counter. Flour coated her back, and she let out a squeak.

"Warrior, this isn't a game," I growled.

Oh, it was a game. A game of cat and mouse, and My Little Warrior wanted to be the submissive for once. Never thought I would see the day she'd yield, but her walls were crumbling, and it was my chance to strike.

"Why are you so upset, Sugar?" My voice went low, commanding, and she pushed out her chest.

"It was nothing. Really."

"Somehow, I don't believe that," I said, picking her up by her waist and setting her on the counter.

"The flour!" she squealed.

"Screw the flour," I latched on to her neck, sucking, nipping. She moaned, feeling my tiny love bites until I pulled away. Groaning, she grabbed my shoulders to put my lips back on her slender neck.

"I'll give you more, of this," I sucked on her neck again "if you give me something."

She panted, wrapping her legs around my waist.

"You want more, don't you?" She bit her lip, but I pulled it away from her fangs with my thumb. "From now on, that lip is mine. Don't abuse it."

"Gods," she whispered. "Fine, I'll tell you."

I kept my face stern, waiting as she sighed heavily.

"Just some friends. They were trying to figure out why I was so happy. They said I was skipping around like a pixie." She wrinkled her nose.

"A pixie, huh?" I chuckled. "What else?"

"One person said it was because I was getting laid. Another person said I would never cheat on my mate because I made a promise to wait for them." She glanced down into her lap. She turned her head and gasped at the sight of my cock straining against my pants.

"And why does that upset you?" I kissed down her neck to her collarbone. A marking spot was sensitive, so I did a dick move and kissed it. Her hips thrust closer to my cock, gyrating to get friction. I moaned, feeling the heat of her pussy against me.

"What else, Warrior?" One hand trailed down her neck, down to her collarbone, and hovered over her breast. "I know that isn't it."

"Please touch me," she whimpered, her hand covering the top of my hand and pushing it to her breast. "Please."

"Tell me the rest," I growled. "Or I won't give you anything." Her legs squeezed tighter around me. My self-restraint waned.

"It made me feel guilty," she panted. Her eyes half lidded; she pulled my tunic string to open it and feel my bare chest. My wolf howled inside me, enjoying the touch of our mate. The heat of her palms gave me chills as her hands travelled lower.

"Warrior," I growled again.

Stopping her movements, she blinked back unshed tears.

"Warrior," I breathed. "Please tell me."

"It made me feel like I was cheating on my mate," she cried. "What would I say to him if I'd ever kissed someone else or done something to someone else?!"

I pulled her into my embrace, kissing the top of her head. "Warrior," I cooed. "You aren't cheating on your mate. You are in a dream. We aren't really touching. Would you get mad at him if he had dreams of someone else?"

"You shouldn't ask a woman that," she mocked in anger. "Because women think it's cheating."

"Men don't. And it isn't like he is going to ask you if you made out with another wolf or shifter in a dream. How random would that be? Sugar, we aren't cheating on our mates."

You. Are. Mine.

"You really don't count it as cheating?" she sniffed.

"Using your vocabulary to get my point across, *fuck* no."

She smiled, burying her face in my chest.

"If it bothers you that much, we won't do anything."

My Warrior stilled.

"I don't want you upset; that's the last thing I want."

"Really?"

"Really. Even if I know you are my mate. If you wish for us to wait until we meet, then so be it."

My Warrior snorted. Instead of pushing me away, she pulled me into a kiss. The shock froze my hands until she pushed my hand to her breast.

"It is just a dream," she mumbled into my lips. "Maybe you aren't even real, and that saddens me the most."

"I am most certainly real," I purred. "If this isn't enough indication, I don't know what else to tell you."

I pushed my cock into her core. Gasping, her mouth parted enough for me to slide my tongue into her mouth. Wrapping my hands around her ass, her dress tunic rode up her thighs, and my hands caught her ass. The barely there underwear she wore forced a groan from my lips while she entangled her fingers in my hair.

"Fuck," I muttered into her lips. She smiled. I could feel her heart race faster with my body pressed against hers as I pushed her into the bed. The duvet was soft as I laid her there. She freed her hair from the hair tie binding it, and it spread across the mattress. My lips left her mouth, as I kissed down her neck.

"Gods you're beautiful," I muttered, kissing the top of her chest.

"Guard," she pulled my hand away from the mattress and pushed it to her breast. "You want to have these, don't you?"

I pawed at her tunic, untying the mess of strings.

"Yes, please. Touch me."

My head dipped as her breast sprang free from the delicate silk bra she wore. She didn't need support. Her breasts were perky. Her pink nipples hardened at my touch as my fingers pinched them softly.

"Gods!" She arched her back, forcing more of her breast into my mouth. My mouth took in the other nipple, sucking, nibbling, biting. Fuck, breasts were incredible. Now I knew what all the hype was about. They were soft, warm, comfortable as I squeezed the hell out of them.

Her fingers ran through my hair, pulling me closer to her chest. "Guard, more, more."

I let go of her nipple with a pop, her nipple standing tall. I pushed my cock into the mattress, trying to get friction. It was becoming too painful, but my mate needed more.

I sucked on the other nipple, and her hips bucked, her arousal filling my nose.

"More, I need more."

I hummed, biting and then licking the sting away from her breasts. I straddled her, taking off my shirt. Her eyes, half lidded, took in my body. I had never felt so nervous. I had been without a tunic many times in front of her, but this was painting me in a different light. A light that would push me to the fore as a mate and not that of the friend I'd been for all these years.

"Wow, I didn't think you could get sexier and here you are," she laughed. Sitting up, she ran her hands up my abs and to my chest. Her lips kissed the left side of my chest and then the other. My hand gripped the back of her head, pulling at her hair until she stared up at me.

"Gods that tongue, Warrior." Her tongue escaped her mouth, licking her lips.

"Your ass has always been my favorite, but I'm really enjoying these," she growled.

"Just wait until you see my cock," I said cockily. Her eyes widened, and my finger closed her lips. "Not yet, I want to savor you first."

Crawling away from her, I sat, my back propped against the headboard. She took her arms out of her tunic, letting it fall around her waist and leaving her pussy and ass covered.

A shame, but still too soon.

"Come here." I crooked a finger, having her straddle me. Her pussy hovered over my cock, until I pushed her lower, adjusting myself for what was to come. "I want you to move your pussy over my cock." My hands gripped hers, gently moving her. "Act like you're riding me. Move your body. Use me to make yourself feel good."

She blushed, her face bright red. "I, I don't think I can."

I smiled, watching, for the first of many times to come, her shyness rising. "Let me help you."

I guided her hips. Her pussy was hot, even through the layers of clothes. My cock reveled in the softness of her pussy. "Damn, you feel good." Her breasts bounced, my mouth finding her nipples as she slid her pussy up and down my stiff ridge.

"Guard," she moaned. Her pleasure rising, her body becoming more comfortable, she pushed herself onto my cock. "It's warm," she whispered to herself.

"It feels..." my hand reached around, pushing her panties up so I could palm her bare ass. "That's it, good job." I leaned my head back, watching her breasts heave. "Fuck, you feel good. I can't wait to sheath myself in you."

Her back arched, a sheen of sweat forming on her brow. Her lips parted and the sweetest moan left her. That was enough to push me over the edge. My cock throbbed, feeling the wetness of her pussy leaking into my pants. Groaning, my mouth descended back to her nipple, sucking hard to prolong her orgasm as she continued to ride me. I couldn't let my seed escape too soon and shorten the pleasure she was receiving.

Panting, I pulled her to my chest, laying down on the fluffy duvet. Petting her hair, the wet strands of dew made me smile. She never was one that went halfway on anything, that even meant grinding her sweet body on my cock.

"Wow," she breathed. "And that was just on the outside of our clothes," she whispered, kissing my chest.

Damnit.

"Can you imagine with just our skin?" I felt the faint smile on her lips, her teeth biting at her thumbnail. "You do not know how hot that was."

"I think I do," I said dryly.

Because I just messed the fuck out of my pants.

My Warrior was back in the small kitchen she created. The stove was covered in pans of pie filling, while the oven was filled with pastries. I sauntered over after taking a shower in the small bathroom. In the middle of cleaning herself up, she realized we were going to need something larger if we planned to explore our sexual side. So, she created a large tub and a massive shower.

For a fleeting moment, I felt she may not want to experience this side of our relationship. She had left me once before, leaving me for months on end worrying about her. She had given up taking that elixir and that fear she would do it again would always remain until she was officially mine. I was quickly mistaken when she came out of the bathroom wearing nothing but a red silk nightdress that came down to her mid-thigh. The small straps let me see the muscles in her shoulders and arms. Her slender and muscular body entranced me as she walked past. She giggled, and I pulled her wrist back around to face me.

"Are you tempting me, Sugar? Because you know, I will bite."

My Warrior hid her smile and shook her head. "I would never tempt you. Besides being a Guard and an Alpha, you should have excellent control of your cock, don't you think?" She fluttered her lashes.

"You very well know Alphas have a hard time staying away from their mates," I growled. "You are no different."

She frowned. "But you aren't—"

I silenced her with a kiss. "Whatever you say, Warrior. Now show me these desserts."

My Warrior pulled me over and sat down at the small pastry-filled table. She went to the cabinet and reached up high for a glass, and her dress rose to the curve of her ass. I bit my fist, watching as she slowly came down to the floor and winked at me.

She was going to get it.

Picking up a chocolate chip cookie, I took a bite. The flavor exploded in my mouth. I moaned, leaning back in my chair. This taste, there was a specific ingredient in it that made it stand out from all the other cookies I'd ever had. I had tasted this cookie before, but I wasn't sure where.

"Try the chocolate silk pie, it's my dad's favorite." She smiled, setting a piece on the table. "I went to sleep early so I could cook my worries away. Mom taught me that when you're upset, you should do service for someone else, it makes you feel better. And who better to service than you,"

Fuuuuuck.

My fork swiped the chocolate silk pie, and my eyes widened. I had tasted this pie before as well. I took a large bite and stared at My Warrior. She sat down with her plate of sugar and sighed.

"You said your mother taught you to cook?" I inquired.

"Yeah, she was actually a waitress a long time ago. She used to do a little bit of everything. Cooking, cleaning, but she really loved to make desserts. She taught my sister and I—" she paused putting her fork down. "Sorry, that was getting to be a little personal."

My mate didn't have to say any more, because I already knew exactly who she was.

Chapter Twenty-Four

Kit

*N*o damn way.

The realms couldn't possibly be that small.

I had filled my mouth with the homemade chocolate silk pie—the same pie recipe that I'd stuffed my face with when I was a child. How did I not know earlier? It was the same comfort food that her mother had given me to ease my worries, to help my anxiety at being the smallest of the pack. I had forgotten the taste all these years. Clara was far too busy to send a pie to a lowly warrior, but she wrote to me every week. I had missed this food and the nostalgia of a happier time when I had found myself and my purpose.

The pie was decorated just to her specifications. Large swirls of cream and dark chocolate shavings. Even the portion size, which was a quarter of the pie, was the same that Clara gave to everyone.

My Warrior hummed, taking in a bite with her fork. She wiggled in her seat, and my eyes widened. Clara had the same wiggle when she ate something delicious, and Kane would have to put his hand on her thigh to calm her. Reaching over, my hand shaking, I laid my hand on her leg. Her wiggles ceased, and she smiled, gulping down a slice.

Her slender neck and her heart-shaped face were a mirror image of her mother. Her dark auburn hair matching that of her aunt and those electric blue eyes of her father stood out in the darkest of nights. The pieces of the puzzle came together. She was the product of the king and queen, and it was only now I saw her for who she really was.

Evelyn was the eldest daughter of the royals. The children of Clara and Kain had no public portraits once they turned five. Clara wanted her children to have a hidden life in the palace instead of an overwhelming crowd of shifters hunting for their affections and friendship. She kept them grounded, despite their royal heritage, so they could make friends based on who they were as a person instead of their status.

Now that she was eighteen and expected to attend balls, more of Bergarian would recognize who she was and try to seek favor with her.

But gods, she was beautiful. The perfect mixture of her parents but of course, she had something more. She was far more than any woman that I had ever encountered—the first woman I'd found attractive, the match to my soul even without the bonding spark to confirm it.

"Everything okay?" She tilted her head in confusion.

My astonishment quickly morphed into a smile, not wanting to give away that I knew something. My Warrior was all too aware of my emotions, my actions and now that I knew who she was, it was going to be hard to hide it from her.

"Everything is fine." I squeezed her leg as I took another bite. She continued to eat, soft mewls of happiness stirring within her.

She was a damn princess.

Internally, I was losing it. I had treated her like any other warrior. I had sparred, wrestled, chastised. I was not remotely gentle when we fought with each other. She should have been kept precious, given her status.

"Wow, you're an idiot," Riddick rolled his eyes so far back I thought I saw the back of my brain. Internally, I groaned. When Riddick came to the surface to talk, it was usually to insult me. *"Her entire life she has been told how to act, how to be the perfect granddaughter of the former queen, and now you think she should be held up on a pedestal?"*

"I just wish I would have known. I would have—"

"What? Treated her like glass? You obviously know she isn't like that. Like her damn father, she's rough around the edges but sweet and savory in the middle, like her mother. Our Warrior is fucking strong."

That was true. She was strong. She could kick my ass any day. How could I not have seen it before? Gods, what the hell have I done?

"Stop panicking or she is going to figure out something is wrong with you." Riddick growled. *"This doesn't change our feelings about her; it doesn't change the fact that she is our mate. You have fallen for her without the bond, and we both know that our queen knows we are mates,"* he stated.

"What are you talking about?" As soon as I thought the words to Riddick, he turned a switch in my brain that led me back several years. For an odd reason, I had either turned it into a dream or a lost memory because the scene before me was more vivid than I ever could recall.

I was watching myself, holding a baby in my arms with Luna Clara staring at us both on a hospital bed. I rocked the baby in a gentle sway as the sweet baby girl's eyes closed. The clothing I wore was a gift from Luna Clara. A uniform made specifically for me during her mating ceremony. It was a suit intended for a future Royal guard made in my tiny size.

"I think we just found Evelyn's mate," I heard Clara speak to Kane through a mind link. He grunted, rubbing her shoulder as they both watched.

"It seems so."

The ripples of the dream faded, bringing me back to the present. *"That was why Clara wasn't worried about my dreams,"* I told Riddick. *"She's known all along that she was mine. She knew Evelyn had these dreams, that she was a Wanderer."*

"Now he gets it," Riddick feigned enthusiasm. "*Evelyn has always been ours. Back then, during our youth and soon to be when we are mated. Now let's go fucking find her and mark her!*" Riddick yipped in excitement.

My shoulders slumped. As much as I wanted to find her, demand for my queen to tell me where her daughter was, it wasn't right. Evelyn wasn't ready. She was still growing and at only eighteen, still so young. Evelyn would know we were mates once we met, but I needed her to love me, to want to have me without the bond. My Warrior had not given me her whole heart, worried I wasn't hers. In a sweet, innocent way, I wanted her to love me without it. To make our bond even stronger when we came together.

"*I don't like it,*" Riddick howled. "*Why not take what is ours now?*"

"*Because she has to find herself,*" I said sadly. "*Let her grow without her grandmother hovering. Stay away from the limelight of being a princess so she can become the warrior she wants to be. To stand up for herself, to be the wolf she will become. A queen.*"

Riddick sat on his hide legs, his head buried in his front paws. "*We've waited so long for her.*"

"*Not as long as others,*" I argued.

"*What if something happens? What if someone tries to claim her?*" he whimpered.

"*That would never happen.*" I chuckled. "*Evelyn is too hung up on finding her mate. We are fighting with ourselves on this one. An interesting outcome I would love to see.*" I smiled, watching Evelyn grab a spoon and dollop more cream on my plate.

"*She's gonna be pissed,*" he growled. "*Then she won't let us mate her right away.*"

"*Oh, she will,*" I countered. "*The strongest bond was forged between a dragon and a human who did not know they were mates. They fell in love before they bonded. Now they carry the weight of a new species over their heads. The gods have planned this, to have us meet and fall in love. To create a bond so strong nothing could break it."*

Riddick huffed in annoyance. *"But you know, it won't be the same,"* he argued suddenly. *"You know who our mate is, it wouldn't make the bond stronger. The dragon and human didn't know they belonged to each other."*

"It is the same," I said calmly. *"Because I already decided she was my mate before I knew it to be so. I had given her my heart and I would have given it to no one else. We just need to have her do the same. The gods will arrange our meeting for the right moment."*

"That could be forever," he whined. *"The gods work on their own time; they will forget all about us."* He whimpered, and I laughed at his brattiness.

"We have her in our dreams. Can you not live with that for now, you stubborn mutt?"

He snorted in reply.

"And when we do finally meet, it will be all sweeter, don't you think?"

"I think your full of sap and shit, is what I think," he retorted. *"Stupid fucking romance."*

Finding her would be all too easy. I'm sure if I went to Clara and told her I'd figured it out, wanted to take my mate and claim her, she would let me. Clara was the one that had instilled the idea for Evelyn to find her mate and save herself for him. However, the lingering thoughts of why Clara hadn't told me from the beginning was fueling my decision to wait.

Evelyn had to grow, to become the woman she was meant to be. Playing by the gods time would be best not only for Evelyn, but for me as well. I needed more training to not only be a guard and an Alpha, but to rule a country. I needed more time to prepare myself, even if we were not to take the throne for a long time. I had to learn to delegate and fight amongst the toughest Alphas to prove my worth to My Warrior, even though Evelyn would always have the upper hand when we fought.

She had genetics working for her, and her drive to be toughest. I would not stop training and let my mate be the only one to protect the country. I would want to fight alongside her and fight her battles if she would let me. I had to seize the opportunity to prove my worth to her, to prove to myself I was no longer the weak runt I saw myself as all those years ago.

"Are you finished?" Evelyn waved her hand in front of my face.

Now that I knew my sweet Warrior's name, it would be difficult to hide it from her. In my heart, it had already been imprinted, and it would forever stay.

"Guard? You alright?" She waved her hand again. "I think I broke you. Was it all the sugar? I'll make a roast tomorrow," she teased.

I chuckled, wiping the chocolate from my face with the napkin laying across my lap. "No, you didn't break me, just deep in thought."

"I hope all the good things and no regrets?" she mumbled.

Pulling her chair across the wooden floor, I pulled her into my lap, and she squeaked. Her eyes widened, and she gripped my tunic.

"The only regrets that I have is not making you orgasm again before leaving the bed," I whispered in her ear. Her face flushed scarlet, and I pushed my nose into her neck, rubbing the tip of it across her skin.

She was mine and I wouldn't have her doubt my feelings for her.

"You can't just say those things," she giggled, while my lips replaced the gentle caresses of my nose.

"Why not? Do you not like it?" I whispered huskily in her ear. "You like it when I tell you what to do, don't you? Like crawling onto my lap and rubbing your pussy on my cock?" She bit her lip, her arousal already seeping from her body. My hand trailed up her thigh, feeling the heat of her skin. "You want me to tell you what I want to do tomorrow?" My lips trailed down her chest. Pulling one strap from her dress, I reveled in the sight of her right breast. I caught the dusty pink nipple with my mouth and sucked on it tenderly.

"Guard," she moaned.

I pulled down the other strap. My cock twitched at the sight of her dark tattoo filled with a deep blue crescent moon and colored leaves on her sternum. It was delicately done, a perfect combination of her feisty personality and her grace. I licked beneath her breast, and she gasped. The world rippled like a stone falling into a pond, and her voice grew fuzzy.

"Next time," I cupped her breast in my hand. "I'll give you all the pleasure you want."

Evelyn

Waking with a jolt, I rubbed my head with my palm. The sting of his lips on my nipple lingered, and my body was very attuned to what had just happened. The buzzing of the alarm beside my bed was the enemy, that was for sure. I swung my hand, knocking it from the nightstand, and it crashed to the floor.

Groaning, I rubbed my breast where I swore his lips still lingered. It was like he was still sucking, nipping, and biting his way to my core. My legs rubbed together, and I stared out the window with the setting moon and rising sun. I had a few minutes to get to the training field. Surely, I had enough time for an adventure of my own?

One hand traveled to the sting of my nipple, imagining his lips still sucking and biting it tenderly. My other hand trailed down to my underwear, my fingers parting my lips. Gods, he felt amazing. The size of his cock was enormous, more so than I ever thought it could be. Sure, he was muscular and tall, but the thought of it ever entering my pussy was still scary.

How could a dick like that bring me pleasure when it was so large? I was by no means a small wolf like my sister, I was tall, almost matching the height of the alpha of my dreams. However, I felt so small compared to the beast that lay between his legs. Remembering the heat of his cock sliding so close to my pussy, I inserted a finger inside myself. Rubbing inside, I pulled out, taking the wetness of my pussy and trailing it over my clit. I was unbelievably wet. I didn't have to warm myself up to feel the small flicks of pleasure as my fingers strummed it lightly.

I panted, pinching my nipple, imagining it was his lips. The way he held me against his body, his confidence was sexy as hell. My Guard knew exactly what to do to put me at ease. It was too easy to be around him, too easy to get lost in his embrace. The thickness of his arms, those magnificent caresses of his hands as he gripped my ass and forced me grind my hips onto him as I thought of his teeth grazing my unmarked skin.

What would it feel like? To have him bite me in a dream? A bite was supposed to be euphoric on your mating spot. Would it feel close to the real thing one day?

I moaned, rubbing faster, thinking of his body hovering over me. The weight of his body, pushing me into the mattress as he pressed his cock to my entrance. "Guard," I moaned again. If I ever figured out his real name, I would say it like a prayer, begging him to take me, to make me his in the dream.

Taking a second finger, I thrust it inside, my palm still rubbing my engorged clit. It throbbed as the wetness pooled against my hand. With one final forceful thrust, I came apart in the bed with a gentle cry.

I panted, but the banging on the door had me pull the sheets over my body again. "W-what?!" I squeaked. The banging continued until Joshua's worried voice was heard on the other side.

"Princess Evelyn, are you alright?"

That fucker ruined my post-orgasm haze.

"What?!" I snapped. "I'm fine, just stubbed my toe!" I lied. "What do you want?"

"I'm here to collect you to go to the training fields. You were five minutes late. Just making sure are alright." His voice softened, and I instantly felt like a dick. I had been hard on Joshua for months, even if he was being a creep. He was following my dad's orders, which were to keep me and my sister safe at all times. We'd known each other a long time, and even if I saw him as a friend, the protectiveness he'd displayed since that dance was becoming overwhelming.

Surely, he wasn't harboring feelings for me when he had his own mate he needed to find.

We all were out of our element, out of the protective walls of the palace, and Joshua had promised my family he would keep us safe. It was a heavy load to bear when my father could kill you with a flick of his claw.

"Um, yeah, thanks, Joshua." I threw the bedsheets off the bed. "I'll get dressed and meet you there." Reaching for my towel on its hanger by the desk chair, I stepped halfway into the bathroom without another thought.

"Are you sure?" His voice wavered. "No one is in there with you, is there? It's out of character for you to be late." I bit my cheek, trying to be nice. Cinder wasn't a fan of Joshua, but he had never touched us or shown any ill-will so far.

He's just doing his job.

"Yeah, I'm fine. Just a bit out of sorts. Meet you down in a moment."

Because I've gotta shower, so no one smells the remnants of my solo romping in the sheets.

Chapter Twenty Five

Evelyn

"Again!" Wesley shouted.

Alpha Wesley joined us in the training fields. The snow that had fallen the day before had melted, leaving a large mud pit and a lot of sweaty, stinky wolves covered in grime. I was dressed in just a sports bra and tight biker shorts. I lunged at two wolves heading right toward me. It wasn't fair to shift into Cinder when I could overpower them so easily in that form. Practicing in my human form was at least a challenge.

A wolf jumped me from behind, the two wolves in front of me scrambled to join the other in a wolf pile. Reaching behind me, I grabbed the wolf, who'd embedded their claws in my neck, by the scruff. Using my claws to get a better grip, I pulled them up and over my head, throwing them onto the two wolves in front of me. Whimpering and scuffling ensued. I joined them in the sludge, slipping face first into the mud. I might be strong, but I had my moments of clumsiness.

"You just aren't very graceful, are you?" My grandmother's statement echoed through me as I jumped to my bare feet and used my claws to grip the hardened earth beneath the top layer of mush. Jumping forward, I

landed on top of one wolf and stuck my claws in his neck enough to subdue him. He howled and Wesley yelled, "He yields!"

Pushing the wolf out of the way, I faced the two that remained. One ran around me, while the other faked left and darted at my side and bit my hip. I yelled in pain, but I quickly pulled on the paw that found my side and pulled it out of its socket. Unlike how My Guard showed me to dislocate and pop my arm back in during a fight, this wolf had no idea how to pop his leg back in.

His front leg hung at the side of his body, as he stumbled away. Slipping in the mud again, I heard the words of my grandmother telling me I was nothing but a clumsy fool.

"A princess should always carry herself gracefully, no matter the environment." I growled in frustration, wrapping my arm around the last wolf's neck and putting it in a headlock. I pushed him into the ground. Hearing a whimper, I waited for Wesley to call the yield, but it never came. Tighter, I held onto the wolf's neck and my mind drifted again.

"Even when fighting, you shouldn't get this dirty, Evelyn," Grandmother chastised. *"You're to look presentable, even in a fight. You should be above your opponents. They are nothing but dogs."* I heaved a heavy breath.

"Do you yield?" I yelled. The mud splashed beneath our feet as we struggled to maintain an upright position. It shook its head, and I rolled on top of the wolf. "Yield!" I yelled at the wolf until my claws lengthened, ready to scratch down its face.

"That's enough!" Wesley stomped over, grabbing my arm. "He's a stubborn fool, who refuses to yield. I have to call it for him."

Wesley helped me stand. My body was caked in mud, and steam rose from our bodies. "This is Hans. Ebony's beta. He's a stubborn fool that isn't allowed to spar unless his Alpha or I are here."

Shifting, Hans stood in front of me. He had a leaner build for a wolf, but he was strong none the less. I admired his determination, but his foolishness at not knowing when to call a fight was comical.

"Aye, just want to prove myself. Plus, tell my pups one day that I almost beat a royal." Hans winked at me, and I shook my head, letting out a laugh. "Any chance I get to have a beautiful princess pin me in the mud will be a day I'll always remember." He crossed his arms over his tanned chest and looked me up and down. He stared at my chest. "The new tattoo suits you."

Putting my hands on my hips, I let him look. It wasn't like he was going to touch, anyway.

"Back away from her!" Joshua stormed up to the small crowd gathering. "You can't look at the princess that way. You are lower than the dirt you fight on."

Wesley raised an eyebrow and tensed.

"Hey, easy," I snapped at Joshua. "I'm a big girl, I can take care of myself!" I put out my hand to Hans, he took it and shook it gladly. "Anytime you want a fight, and only a fight, I'm here. Just next time know when to yield or I may just kill you," I smirked.

"A death that I would brag about amongst the souls of the Underworld." He took my hand to kiss it.

Flirt. Wandering away, I chuckled.

Wesley followed me. "You hesitated. You could have beat them much faster than that. You were thinking of something. What was it?"

Wesley had become the fun uncle, you know, an uncle that was actually older than me. He was wise in the ways of fighting and technique, and his handle on his wolf was astounding. For an alpha, he had a calm demeanor. He was able to control his wolf better than anyone.

"You know how to read me, huh?" I grabbed a towel from the bench. We watched the others spar. Mostly one on one, but Wesley had taught warriors how to fight two and even three on one. Since the kidnapping of his daughter, he wanted his pack to be stronger than ever. Wesley's pack was quickly becoming the largest in both Americas. And it was all for his daughter.

"I'm sure my parents told you about my grandmother." I wiped away the dirt from my face.

He hummed, agreeing, and rested his elbows on his legs.

"I know she isn't here anymore to bother me, but the remnants of her words are still there."

Melody sat across the arena, her notebook in hand. She and Mason stole glances at each other. Each time her face reddened, blushing. Melody was never boy crazy, not in the slightest. She even mentioned she hoped she didn't find her mate for a long time because she wanted to travel around Bergarian. She was going to be a scholar, or some sort of ambassador for the Cerulean Moon Kingdom one day. Her obsession for knowledge outweighed her desire to inherit the Crimson Shadows Pack. Guess the twins would have to take her spot.

Wonder what's going on with her.

"I know the things she said broke me. To make me into something I was not. I can't erase years of verbal abuse once it has been embedded in my memory."

Wesley sat up straight, sighing heavily. "You should talk to Charlotte. She experienced something similar. Not as many years as you endured, but she also had trouble finding her self-worth. She thought I could never want her in that way after the filthy things said to her." He growled. "It took her time and the help of her mate." He wiggled his eyebrows. "She could see her worth. That she was born to be someone amazing, someone special. Without her, I would not be the wolf I am today. She healed my wolf when I didn't know he was struggling from depression. She loves this pack, protects it like everyone was her own flesh and blood." He paused, looking back at the house.

Charlotte spent her time serving others when she was not in a slump over their daughter. She worked on the pack's border security and visited wolves in their homes, making sure they had everything they needed to live a comfortable life. Her sons adored her, and Wesley fell more in love with her each day.

"Charlotte has her demons. She still has thoughts she isn't worthy. When you find your mate, those voices in your head will lessen, you will come to find yourself again slowly—of who you are meant to be." He patted my head. "Just keep those thoughts away when you fight. One slip up and you will find yourself face down in the mud." He chortled.

"Hey!" I pushed his shoulder. "That was an accident."

"Because your head wasn't in the fight," he said in all seriousness. "She isn't here anymore." He waved his hands in front of him. "But she is going to continue to be in here." He pointed at my head. "So, do something about it and become the kick ass princess of Clara and Kane."

"Even if that means I'm a dirty princess, covered in mud, have no desire to be dressed up all the time, and cuss like a sailor?" I snickered, standing up.

"Exactly. Bergarian doesn't need a royal pain in the ass, they need a fighter with passion. You got your parents to thank for those traits." Wesley smiled, putting his arm around my shoulder.

"Now, you and Melody are due for dinner at our house tonight. Leave those guards behind," he ordered, leading me back to the pack house.

Glancing behind me, I saw Melody grab Mason's hand and lead him away into the woods. My intellectual sister now had me wondering what she was really doing with Mason and if her heart was going to get hurt in the long run.

"Ashley, what do you think?" Charlotte asked while she passed an enormous plate of steaks. Mashed potatoes, corn, rolls, and werewine littered the table. Dante, Hunter, and Stephen ate at a smaller table in the kitchen while we ate in the formal dining room. The house was a smaller version of a southern-style plantation home. Decorated with bright white and creams, it suited Charlotte's bright personality and her sweetness.

"Yeah, I think the meatball eyeballs can stay. Just don't make the brain meatloaf. I swear I gagged last year." Ashely was Charlotte's best friend. Also, she was the party planner for the large Halloween party coming up next week. It was the biggest party of the year for the Black Claw Pack. Four other packs were attending, and the dormitories were ready to house the single supernaturals that wanted to attend.

"I've got our costumes ready too." Charlotte clapped her hands excitedly. Her face was still pale, but we took whatever smiles we could get from her. "Wesley, you sure you will dress up?"

Wesley grabbed her hand across the table, squeezing it. "Anything for you, Kitten. Just none of the girly shit."

She laughed, patting his hand. "Hardly think dressing up as the Hocus Pocus characters is girly. Besides, you are Billy the Zombie. That isn't girly at all."

Wesley rolled his eyes, stuffing a large piece of steak into his mouth. I chuckled, watching Melody. She had been quiet all afternoon while we got ready for dinner. Now she continued to look out the window, as if she was looking for something or someone. Then I saw Mason stick his head in the window, waving at her. I scowled, wondering what the hell she was doing. Not once did she say she wanted to wait for her mate, but still, she was sixteen. Well, I guess she would be seventeen in a few days.

"Are you two going to dress up?" Charlotte asked.

I shook my head. "Not really into dressing up," I said honestly. Melody shook her head as well.

"Princess Evie doesn't have to dress up," Hunter pipped up from the kitchen. "She's a princess and too pretty." His voice grew lower as he called me pretty.

"Aww, thanks, Hunter." I shot him a wink. He blushed, turning away to eat his steak.

"Think you have a little admirer." Melody elbowed me in the ribs.

"Seems you do too." I nodded to the window before he darted away.

"What's up with that?" I linked, eating another mouthful of steak.

"N-nothing," she replied. *"Nothing to worry about."*

"Just don't want you getting hurt. I know you haven't decided on saving yourself for you mate, but—"

"I know what I'm doing," Melody snapped.

I jolted in my seat at her harsh reply.

"Listen, I'm sorry." Melody swayed her head. *"I've got feelings for him. That's all. Just a little crush."*

I huffed, dropping the subject. Melody was smart, but as far as romance went, I wasn't so sure.

Wesley cleared his throat, wiping his face. "We need to talk about Joshua."

The table went silent. Hunter and Dante stood from their table and walked into the room with their arms crossed. For a fourteen and a ten-year-old, they sure were menacing looking.

"We think Joshua has an infatuation with you. I know you can handle yourself, but I don't like how he looks at you." Wesley pointed his fork at me. "I can't hide things from your parents. I'll be speaking to them about it."

I waved my hand in dismissal. "He can't do shit. I can kick his ass, no problem. As long as he does his job and doesn't touch me, he will be fine. Otherwise, I'll swipe his balls off."

Charlotte blanched.

"That might not be appropriate for the table," Melody said giggling.

"Sorry, Charlotte," I said.

She shook her head, taking a large gulp of werewine.

Wesley sat back in his chair. "I technically don't have enough evidence to do anything about him, just wanted to make you aware." Wesley's eyes grew dark. "Still gonna talk to your parents, not going to have your father kick my ass."

I nodded, putting another fork full of food in my mouth. Right now, I felt Joshua was the least of my worries. My worries lay where my heart was and where my mind continued to stay—still stuck in the past with my grandmother and in my dreams, my heart falling deeper in love with an Alpha that I had no business being with.

Chapter Twenty Six

Evelyn

His mouth hungrily demanded my lips. His tongue pushing through his own and massaged the inner corners of my mouth. My chest heaved, feeling his hard body pressing me further into the bed. I moaned, his hand tracing down the side of my body and dipping into the curve of my back and down to my ass. He lifted my leg, wrapping it around his back. His cock pushed into my core in a possessive claiming.

My Guard's scent surrounded me. He smelled of deep forest and wet moss. Cinder purred in my head, begging for more of the touches that lit my core on fire.

Breaking from the kiss, we panted, my fingers threading through his now dark ebony hair while he pushed his forehead against mine.

"This will never get old," he breathed. His hips gyrated into my core again, and I gasped at the burn of pleasure.

It was true; I don't think it would ever get old, but there was so much more to explore. His hands had stopped wandering below the waist, always falling short of my core. "Yes, but I need more of you." I nipped at his bottom lip. He growled hungrily, pulling me in for another kiss.

The Halloween Mixer for the Black Claw pack was tomorrow. I had warned him it would be a late night, and I might not even sleep. I promised Wesley I would be on guard, keeping watch and not playing the part of a guest. Wesley frowned at that, wanting me to mingle with the rest of the crowd, but I didn't have it in me. The nagging thoughts in the back of my mind of my mate being out there plagued me. I wasn't hunting for my mate because my dreams had claimed this Alpha.

Cinder felt the same, but her hesitation lingered just as much as mine. Her thoughts went to our Guard every day, but there was a dark shadow hovering over us. Our Guard wasn't our true mate, at least I didn't think he was. He and I could very well have mates waiting for us on either side of the veil of the dream we met in.

Once we found our mate. We had to stop this. It wouldn't be fair.

He ripped my top from my chest, his famished mouth reached for my nipple and sucked at hit hungrily. Arching my back, I forced more of my breast into his mouth, his other hand traveling where he had yet to explore.

His eyes peeked up at me, watching my chest rise and fall. I wiggled my hips as his thick fingers untangled the ties that led down to my pussy. He paused, my groans of appreciation mistaken for protest.

"Keep going," I muttered. "Please."

His lips curved into a smile, his fingers dipping lower into my leathers to meet my pussy.

No one, besides myself, had ever explored this part of me and any hesitation I had vanished. It felt so right, so good, as his fingers lay atop my mound.

"Is this okay?" he hesitated, his fingers rubbing my bare pussy.

"Gods yes!" My eyes rolled into the back of my head as his finger dipped between my folds. I gripped his shoulders tightly as his finger pressed the small bud of pleasure.

My leathers sat on my body, still covering me. For some reason, that comforted me. I wasn't ready to expose all of my body to him.

"Fuck, you smell so good," he growled. "Like cherry blossoms and champagne."

I whimpered, feeling his finger sink lower into my pussy.

"This is the greatest gift." He pushed his finger inside me. I felt the thick intrusion, his finger slid in and out while his palm rubbed my clit. Shocks of electricity ran through my body, Cinder howling inside me while he lingered.

"More, faster," I panted. His calloused fingers pushed deeper, harder. My Guard's other hand rubbed my breast as I shook with a need for release. His lips traced my neck, body hovering over me as he continued his assault. He lazily inserted another finger. I winced at the tightness.

"I'm going to have to stretch you if you are going to take me one day." He hummed appreciatively. "Would you want that? To have my dick inside you?"

I groaned, feeling his hand slow down. My clit throbbed for more of his touch, but he paused.

"I want you to answer me," he commanded. "Do you want my dick inside you?"

I nodded, but his hand remained still.

"Words, Sugar. I enjoy having you answer me. Hearing that you want my dick in your body, to claim it here in this dream. I want to hear your words," he said huskily.

"Yes, I want to feel your dick inside me," I said hurriedly. "Please, don't stop, please!"

"Now, now there is no need to beg," he chuckled darkly, moving his hand up and down. The wetness of my pussy rubbed across his palm, leaving a warm slick feeling on my clit. He was pushing his fingers quicker, faster, and deeper. My pussy fluttered, the inside of my body feeling the rise of my orgasm.

"Warrior, you are sucking me in. Having you around my cock would be fucking amazing," he growled. His body shuddered as he hovered over me.

It was like he was pretending to be fucking me, giving me the perfect visual of his pleasure watching me reach my high.

"Are you going to cum? You look so close," he cooed, his fangs now tickling my neck. "Cum on my fingers, Warrior. Let me taste your sweetness."

I silently screamed. His fingers continued to push in and out of me, milking me of my orgasm. He prolonged it with his heated breath on my neck, his nips and the purr in his chest calming me.

Once I fell, he removed his fingers from my loose leathers, bring his fingers up to his lips. I watched with abated breath as he stuck both fingers into his mouth. He closed his eyes, humming, while he pulled them from his lips.

"Just as I thought." He winked. "You taste just like champagne."

I blushed, covering my face, but he wasn't having that. He removed my hands. As he kissed me, I tasted myself on his lips. While he kissed me, I slid my hand to his hard erection, my fingers pulling at the strings.

"Warrior, you don't have to do that." He reached to pull my hand away, but my hooded eyes told him something different.

"I really want to," I whispered. "If you are okay with it?"

It wasn't like I had never seen a dick before. Being shifters, it was part of the territory, but I had never really seen *his*. We had known each other in the dream since we were young, but he had hidden himself when he shifted, and I gave him the courtesy of closing my eyes.

My heart beat faster at the thought of seeing it, but part of me didn't want to look. It would be the first dick I'd seen up close, that I'd touched and held in my hand. Well, probably hands. He was large, no doubt about that.

"I want to touch you," I said again. He rolled onto his back. My fingers untangled his leathers. His breath quickened and his abs contracted, feeling my fingers graze the side of his torso.

"You can pull it out," he muttered. "You can see all of me."

I felt guilty about not pulling off my pants earlier.

He grabbed my chin. "Sugar, only do what you're comfortable with. You gave me a wonderful gift already. You are letting me touch you and claim you with my fingers."

Blushing, I looked away and down at his leathers. His shaft begged to be free. No wonder he said it could come out. It was trying to burst from his pants!

I gazed at his face, my hand slowly tracing his v-line and down his pants. It didn't take long to find the beast, and I wrapped my hand around his shaft.

His hips bucked, head rolling back into the pillows. "Fuck, fuck, fuck," he muttered to himself.

"Did I hurt you?" I let go, but his hand gripped mine and pushed it back down.

"No, feels so good, do it again," he gritted his teeth.

My hand wrapped around him, my fingers almost not touching around his girth.

How the hell was that going to go where it was supposed to?

"What do I do now?" I asked, still unsure. My curiosity grew and my eyes finally caught the size of the beast. It looked angry. The tip was slightly purple, and as I moved my hand up and down the shaft, the velvet smooth skin with the ridges of veins made my mouth water. My thighs clamped together, trying to rub the quiver in my clit.

"Just what you are doing," he gritted.

His fingers fisted the sheets, and my interest intensified as a pearl-shaped liquid appeared at the tip of his cock. My thumb swiped over it, letting it lubricate my hand as I tugged at his erection. He pulled down his leathers lower, his balls coming into view. They looked heavy, and my other hand itched to cup them, hold them.

My Guard's eyes closed, as he breathed deeply. "So good," he muttered. "So good, just like that."

My lips parted, my tongue darting out. I wanted to taste him, put him into my mouth. My nipples tightened, the cool air from the open window teasing over my skin. My desire grew more as my hand rubbed up and down his shaft.

To take him into my mouth, for him to be at my utter mercy made my pussy flutter. My Guard could show his dominant side, making me cum with just a command of his words. Now I held the power, my hand still stroked his shaft as I straddled his lower legs. My leathers still untied, giving me the flexibility I needed to lower my head, stick out my ass, and take one long lick of the top of his cock.

"Gods!" He yelled. His eyes flew open, as my tongue lapped at the end. "Sugar, you don't..."

His words fell on deaf ears as I wrapped my lips around the head. My hand had a firm grip at the base while the other hand fondled his balls.

Thank gods for erotica novels.

My head bobbed, and he muttered curse after curse while my tongue circled the head and moved back down his shaft. I pushed myself further down, gagging. I wanted more inside me, to feel him touch the back of my throat. Widening it, I pushed further down. His hand grasped at the back of my head, tugging at my hair. My clit thumped along with my racing heart as he pulled me up and down his shaft. It had a hint of a salty taste as it slid down my throat.

His guidance had him cursing, his hand gripping my hair tighter. Fuck, it felt good having him pull me up and down, having me give him what he wanted. "I'm going to cum." He let go of my hair. "Get up." I shook my head and hummed into his cock. Before he could push me away, hot streams of his cum streamed down the back of my throat. His cock throbbed, pushing more and more of the hot liquid as I drank him down.

His roar shook the cabin, his face contorted in pleasure. Red in the face, he panted, waiting for me to arise from his freshly sucked member.

Letting go with a pop, he pulled me to his naked torso, my breasts leaning up against him. "Holy fuck, Sugar, you didn't have to do that."

I giggled, tracing his peck muscles with my finger. "I know I didn't." I paused. "But I really wanted to taste you." I blushed. "I never thought I would want to do that sort of thing."

"And you don't have to do it ever," he commented. "But fuck, that was incredible." he sighed, pulling my chin up to him. He bent down to kiss me, not caring that I'd drank him down like an animal thirsting for water. It was long, savory, and his tongue entered my mouth again.

His body hovered over me, his shaft already hard again. "When do I get to taste you? Like a real taste?"

I blushed, covering my face with my hands.

"No, let me see that pretty face. Come on." He playfully took my hands and raised them above my head, holding them with one large hand. "You can't get shy around me now. You just sucked my dick."

I laughed out loud, as he kissed around my neck.

"I love you, Warrior," he mumbled into my neck.

"I love you, too," I whispered back, trying not to squirm. Because I did, I really loved him. My only issue was, did I love him more than my future mate?

The same thought must have appeared in his head because, he smiled tenderly, his hand coming down to trace my cheek. "But not with your whole heart, huh? Not yet anyway."

I pursed my lips, and he kissed them.

"You may not love with all your heart yet, but you will," he said, determined. "I'll make you want me and only me."

"But your mate—"

He silenced me with another kiss.

"You are my mate," he growled. "And one day you will see it, too."

Chapter Twenty Seven

Eve-

lyn

The pack house was a wreck for days before the big party, decorations thrown over banisters, fabric placed on the floors.

Glitter.

So. Much. Glitter.

It was the biggest party of the year and for good reason. Charlotte and Ashely were miracle workers and transformed the rather plain ballroom of the pack house into a gigantic, haunted mansion. The decorations extended outside onto the pack house steps, into the hallways, and into the now decked out ballroom.

The grand staircase that reminded me of the palace back home was covered with black feathered boas, fake cobwebs, and animatronic rats running up and down the marbled stairs. Violet lights sparkled from the giant black disco ball, keeping the area more lively than scary. DJ Lyel stood between the twin staircases, rotating a disc, and mixing songs for the entire party.

Hordes of wolves were dressed to the nines. Those hunting for their mates had integrated some sort of red color into their outfits to attract their mate. Some held a boutonniere a handkerchief, or even a tie. The women, however, wore overly decorative red dresses, making them the center of attention.

Charlotte and Wesley were indeed dressed up. Wesley was Billy from Hocus Pocus while Charlotte dressed as the witch Sarah Sanderson. Poor little Stephen got the short end of the stick and dressed up as a black cat called Binx. Luckily for Hunter and Dante, they could go dress up as something scary.

The smile on Charlotte's face was forced while her mind still lingered on their missing daughter, but her appearance at the party was appreciated by the pack. Many came to talk to Charlotte, and she offered smiles and hugs. Wesley kept his eyes trained on her, as if she was fragile, but after spending a lot of time with her, I knew she was stronger. Every day she came up with alternative places for us to search for Ember, such as the mission in LA we were leaving for in several days.

"Look at you," Ebony drawled, her arm in the crook of Easton's arm.

I didn't want to dress up but somehow, like magic, an outfit appeared on my bed before the party. Black leather pants with a corset along with a deep black wig with dark purple highlights, an enormous number of clip-on piercings, and an undershirt with tattooed sleeves. I threw my head back and laughed so hard. Melody came in and was all too excited to see me dressed up. She was dressed as Alice from Alice in Wonderland which made her look far too young.

"You look like twins!" Easton laughed. "I better be careful, or I might grab your ass instead." He hooked his thumb at me.

I snorted, shaking my head because we both knew that wouldn't happen. Ebony playfully growled. She had extended her fangs to go with her vampire costume. When she'd entered the room, I did a double take at her red glowing eyes and painted skin. Ebony could totally pass for a brooding vamp.

"I'm missing my tit piercings," I laughed, cupping my boobs. "Those clip-ons hurt too damn much, and I don't want to be uncomfortable all evening."

"That's a shame." Easton rubbed his face in Ebony's chest. "Because Ebony likes a little pain when we play, don't you?" Ebony blushed, putting her face in Easton's shoulder. For a dominant woman, she had a playful submissive side.

The music thrummed, and more and more wolves entered the ballroom. The four visiting packs made the large territory seem smaller. It was a lot of wolves with several alphas that knew Wesley and Charlotte well.

My back straightened, taking in the scene before me. Warriors were stationed throughout the room. Two at each doorway, a team at the top of the stairs and many outside. This place was an official fortress, all thanks to Charlotte and her extra security. Not one room in the pack house was unattended. Cameras catching all corners beside the bedroom and bathrooms. No blind spots in sight.

"Hey, have you seen Mason?" Basim wore his white uniform with a red sash. His hair had grown over the months, so he slicked it back and away from his face with gel. Unmated she-wolves eyed him carefully, some winking and waving.

"Not in a while." I kept my eyes trained on the dance floor. "He shouldn't be that hard to pick out if he's wearing his uniform."

"He isn't wearing it." He side-eyed me.

I raised a brow in question. I may have been dressed up with fake piercings and a wig, but my duty was to help with security. My outfit was flexible enough that I could easily wrestle someone to the ground if needed.

"He requested the night off. Joshua and I are working. However, Alpha Wesley has asked us each to have fun for at least an hour through the night. If that is alright you with you and your sister?"

I waved my hand, not caring. They were always working, always on alert. They needed a break. Besides, I could take care of myself. It was my sister that didn't care to fight.

"I don't care about that. You can take orders from Wesley. Dad trusts him, too."

"Ah, there he is." Basim scowled as he stared across the dance floor.

Melody and Mason talked cozily in the corner. Continually, she looked down at her glass and stroked her finger across the rim.

"I'm not sure what is going on between those two, but his life is at risk if your father finds out." Basim took a sip of his drink and began to walk toward them.

Putting my hand to his chest to stop him, I shook my head. "I'll take care of it. Melody has to learn on her own, but I know she doesn't have the same views on mates as I do."

Basim let out a heavy sigh, clinking the ice in his glass. "I know, neither does Mason. However, Mason is older. She's a princess. He knows she is not his mate and yet he dares to play with fire. It's how he's always been."

I pursed my lips in acknowledgement.

"Enjoying the party?" Joshua scowled, glancing at me and Basim. His grip on the glass tightened, and I cleared my throat.

"It is," I chirped. "Just talking to Basim about Mason over there." I nodded their direction. The atmosphere of thumping music faded, and slow music began, giving the perfect opportunity for Melody to dance with him.

"I don't like it, but what can you do?" Joshua shrugged. "I've warned Mason to stay away, but he swears your sister is alright with it."

"Melody isn't in for a fun time or a quick fuck. She looks for something serious. She still would choose her mate over any relationship. But her heart is full of longing for affection like our parents have, like all those romance stories she craves." My faint smile wobbled, worried about her getting her heart broken. "She may want to be more experienced for her mate. You know a lot of males don't wait for their mates, so her reasoning is, why should she?"

And she was right, women shouldn't have to wait. It should just be a preference. Yet, here I was, determined to give my mate a special gift. "Melody's wolf just has a drive I didn't have at that age. Wolves are all different when it comes to their sexual appetite."

Except for My Guard and me.

"That is true." Joshua tapped his glass with his finger. "She's not wrong. She should fuck who she wants," he said, taking a sip of his drink. Basim gave a look of disbelief, but the stoic look on Joshua's face wasn't budging. "I mean, if you want to wait, that's fine." He waved his glass around. "But what if you don't meet your mate for fifty years? Take your father, for example. He didn't get his mate until he was around a hundred and twenty-five. Of course, he didn't wait, but what if he had? That's a long time to have blue balls." He chuckled.

Dad regretted not waiting for mom, but he thought a beast like him couldn't have a woman as good as her. He continued to show how much she meant to him.

Torin was a tough wolf to get a handle on, and dad just had to let him do his thing some days. As he got older, he figured out a coping mechanism to keep his dick in his pants, but the regret still lingered. Mom, of course, didn't care, she loved dad for who he was no matter what he'd done in the past. He was with her now and mated to her. That's how I learned my desire to wait for my mate. Melody just saw it differently. Too many times, she'd snuck into the ballroom while we were supposed to be sleeping, watching unmated wolves kissing and holding each other.

"That's what a hand is for, you doofus," I snarled back.

Basim spat out his drink, wiping it away with his sleeve. "You got this." Basim patted my shoulder, still dribbling liquid.

"Excuse me?" Joshua barked a laugh. "It isn't the same."

"And how would you know if you've never had sex before?" I shrugged. "You don't know what you are missing if you haven't had a dick planted into some wolf's pussy."

"But the feeling is there," he countered. "Your dick gets hard. Your wolf is wild. If you have a willing participant, then it shouldn't be a problem." He snorted. "Not that I am judging you, Your Highness. I'm just saying holding off isn't practical when you don't know when you'll meet your soul mate. Who says you should live celibate for all those years? There isn't some law dictating that you're supposed to wait. It's a preference."

Huh, something that Melody would say.

Technically, he was right; who is to say you would ever find your soul mate in the first two decades of your life? Dad didn't wait, doesn't make him a bad person. He had trouble controlling his wolf, hell, many people do. When you are with someone that gives you the warm fuzzy shit, then yeah, you will catch the feels. Just like My Guard.

Gods, was I being a total hypocrite? Doing all sorts of delicious things to him while I chastised my sister? She couldn't have dreams like I could to get a release. In reality, I had no urges, only when I thought of My Guard and in the privacy of my bed. In my dreams, I had control of my surroundings. I could create a world where nothing mattered but him and me. But, hell, I could barely control my feelings or my body anymore during our dreams.

I had a way to find release. Melody didn't, except in reality.

Electricity buzzed in the air when My Guard and I were together, but not on our skin. You could find your mates by touch, by smell, by sight. I had none of those things to go by. Could he be my mate?

I wasn't sure. I didn't know. However, I didn't feel like I was cheating on my mate anymore because it was in a dream. My Guard had never "really" touched me.

"Hmm, I guess it is just a preference. I don't judge anyone that decides to do anything sexual before their mate," I said.

"Y-you don't judge?" He raised an eyebrow.

"No, why would I? Just because someone wants to have sex before their soul mate comes along doesn't mean they're a bad person, or I think less of them. I just...personally want to wait." I sipped my glass, feeling uneasy. "I mean, it would have to be a really special person for me to want to do that. To give part of myself to them. Maybe I would, I don't know, other things..." I tried to make myself feel better. Because what if I met My Guard in real life? Would I do those things with him then, even if he wasn't my mate? I wasn't sure I could stay away. "But they would have to be an amazing person. Like, falling in love with them. A deeper connection."

Like with My Guard.

"Your Highness—"

"Evie," I corrected.

"Evie, I know—"

I interrupted him again, rubbing the thick eyeliner around my eye. "I don't know why I'm talking to you about this." I cleared my throat. "That was embarrassing to talk about. Let's forget it."

I started to stomp away, but a warm hand that felt nothing like My Guard gripped my forearm. Turning, I found Joshua with softening eyes. It was the first time I had seen him let down his defenses.

"Evie, there is something I've got to say."

I gulped audibly, and he chuckled, pulling me back into the corner. The wolves still danced. Charlotte was chasing Stephan, and Wesley was having a beer with his beta, Beau.

I was concentrating on everything else but Joshua, not wanting to stare into those puppy eyes he was giving me because I knew I was about to kick him where it hurt. His heart.

There was no denying he liked me, but I could barely stand him as a friend.

"Evie, I'm sure you know I care about you. On a deeper level than just being your guard." His words came out smooth, like he'd rehearsed them a thousand times. There was no tremor in his voice, his eyes full of determination. "And if you ever decided you were done waiting and wanted to have something before you meet your mate, then I want you to know I'm here. I'll wait like a helpless puppy for you to change your mind about having someone to hold you every night until you find your mate." He bit out those last words like they were bitter.

The uneasy feeling about Joshua being around both my sister and me had intensified tenfold. It was time to have him transferred out of this realm and back to where my parents could handle this. I nodded to him, not saying a word as he backed away and returned to his post.

My dry, scratchy throat ached for the punch behind me. Taking the ladle shakily and scooping the sherbert punch into my class, I drank it down. I laid my hands flat on the table until I blinked several times.

"We get him out of here." Cinder pricked her head up. I gripped the tight band t-shirt.

"I agree, maybe before that."

"We can't have him suspect. It would be too quick if we transferred him out tomorrow. After the mission?" I gulped again, not sure what to do. I could kick his ass if he ever attacked, but he wasn't attacking, or touching, forcing. He knows I could kill him if I wanted. I could very well be paranoid, but something wasn't sitting right. There was something...more to this.

Turning to face the crowd again, I caught my sister danced with Mason. She smiled, looking happy, and for once, she didn't have her nose stuck in a notebook. Her eyes met mine, and I gave a small wave. Mason wrapped his arms around her waist, whispering something into her ear.

"Evie," I felt a tug on my shirt. Glancing down, I saw Hunter with his mask hanging around his neck. His little face blushed red, and his hands wrung together nervously.

"What is it, warrior?" I arched an eyebrow, nudging him playfully. He cleared his throat until he spat out the words so quickly, I almost missed it.

"I was wondering, would you dance with me?" His little eyes fluttered, and my heart damn near exploded.

"I would love to," I smiled, grabbing his hand.

He led me out to the dance floor, though I kept an eye on Mason and Melody. He wrapped his arms around my waist, and his face planted straight into my boobs.

Oh hell.

"I won't look," he muttered.

I couldn't help but giggle. As we danced, we floated near Mason and Melody. She waved, her cheeks flushing pink. It was the most smiles I had seen from her since Grandmother had been sent away. Melody snuggled into his chest, and Mason's head turned to me.

"*You break her heart,*" I linked Mason, "*and I'll break your dick.*"

Chapter Twenty Eight

Kit

Evelyn wasn't in the cottage, nor at the swing where I normally found her. Lifting my nose to the air, I had Riddick take in a deep breath to search her. Our world had become vast. It no longer just held the forest where we first found each other, the tree that held the swing, or the cottage she created for us just over a year and a half ago.

It had turned into our own paradise with warm watering holes, snowy mountains, and beautiful jungles. We would normally meet at the cabin and wander in different directions as we talked about our lives, slowly letting small details slip about ourselves. She told me of her sister, brothers, and her mother's and father's funny quirks. Evelyn did an excellent job keeping the important details that might reveal hers and her parents' secrets. I could only smirk at her fun adventures, as I tried to keep a straight face as she told me of her father's possessiveness of her mother. What would she say when I told her I knew everything about her family?

Stepping through the fallen leaves that never seemed to die, I found her sitting on the end of the pier that jutted out into light blue waters where dolphins and mute sirens swam. My bare foot hit the wooden plank, and her head jolted from her longing stare at the water.

"'Bout time you showed up." She waved her hand.

I took my time walking to her, enjoying the view of the setting light source and how it delicately highlighted her best features. Once I approached, I sat beside her, pulling her to my lap and sliding my feet in the water.

"You took a while." She kissed my cheek. I wrapped an arm around her shoulder, letting my fingers play in her hair, as I gazed into her eyes.

"You weren't at the cottage," I whined. "We always walk together when we go exploring, and you left me there all alone."

She snorted, covering her mouth.

"I was late getting to bed. Friend A complained until I finally fell asleep to his whines."

"Oh, and what did he say this time?" she asked, amused.

"Right now, we are in the Dragon Territories, and it's snowing." I pretended to shiver to make her breasts shake. Evelyn knew exactly what I was doing and playfully hit my chest. "He said, and I quote…" I cleared my throat. "It is colder than a witch's tit out here."

Evelyn threw her head back and laughed, her arms wrapping around my neck as she sighed into my shoulder.

"He's too funny. I hope I can meet him one day."

I hummed, kissing her neck. "Maybe we should," I countered.

Evelyn's eyes fluttered nervously, returning her gaze back at the water.

"What is holding you back?" I pulled her chin to me. "Do you still not love me with your whole heart?"

I knew she did. I knew she cared about me more than she let on. She had kept her heart guarded for too long, and I was ready to break down the high palace walls of doubt she had erected around it.

Evelyn grew quiet, shaking her head, getting lost in her own thoughts. The amused twinkle in her eyes was missing.

"Sugar, I didn't mean to push you." I kissed her lips. "I don't enjoy seeing you lie. You are lying to yourself about our relationship. I can see it." I pushed her hair back behind her ear. "I can feel it." I put my hand on her chest. Drops of dew from her tears laid on her lashes. She looked so vulnerable in my arms, so beautiful, so innocent despite her mischievousness. "My Little Warrior."

She dove into my chest, wrapping her arms around me until she straddled me. The hard boards of the pier vanished, and we now lay on an enormous blanket on the lake's shore. I laid back, rubbing my hands up and down her back. Tiny sniffs tickled my neck, and I chuckled. We sat in silence as I rubbed up and down her back.

"My sister got her heart broken yesterday."

My hands stilled, my fingers forming a fist. "What?" I growled.

"She caught him fucking some other she-wolf. My sister is devastated. Even though I told her that it would end in disaster, I still feel for her."

I had heard the stories. Her sister had not promised herself to her mate, instead seeking romance. Many wolves took part in relationships before finding their mates, but it ended in disaster when one found their mate while the other was left to be alone. It was the way things were.

"I'm so sorry she has to go through that." I continued to rub my hand up her back. My other hand traveled up her shirt, feeling her bare skin. She was warm against my skin as I felt her body shudder.

"I don't think it would have hurt her so much if it were his mate. She understood that at least, that there would be a time when one of them would find their mate and it would be a clean cut, you know? Her boyfriend didn't even find his mate, it was just a casual fuck, and that was what hurt her."

I rolled my eyes and ran my hand through my hair. "What did you do?" If I knew my Evelyn well enough, I'm sure his balls were stuffed into the idiotic wolf's mouth.

"Oh, I took care of him." I felt the smile on my chest. "Let's just say he won't be using his good looks to bag another she-wolf in a while. I may have put on silver-laced knuckles to scar him up a bit."

"So bad ass," I chuckled, squeezing her tighter. As much as I wanted to prove my worth to her, that I could protect her when she needed it. Evelyn was so damn strong. That in itself was an enormous turn on.

Birds flew overhead. The deer that came to the waters drank and held up their heads when we made the slightest noise. She sighed, nuzzling into my neck. This was everything I ever wanted—a mate to hold and cherish. But I needed more. The dreams only sated part of Riddick and me. His impatience was insufferable and to be truthful, the months had been long while she grew.

"You gonna talk to me as to why you keep me at arm's length?" I asked.

She shook her head, and my heart broke once more. Rolling her on her back, I pushed up on my forearms to gaze at her face. Her tiny nose was red, her cheeks flushed, and her attempt to keep her mascara running had failed.

"I'm getting jealous. You can make that mascara run so easily when I can barely get you to cry when you orgasm." Trying to lighten the mood, I kissed her salty lips still wet from her tears. Her hands ran up my back, pulling off my tunic and baring my chest. Evelyn took in a breath, eating me with her eyes.

"I want to kiss you, Sugar," I stated.

"Then kiss me," she sighed.

"No," I shook my head. "Down here." I cupped her mound, and her hips thrust upward to feel the friction. Evelyn continued to give me the best blowjobs, sucking, licking, fondling my balls until I spilled my cum into her mouth, but yet she still had not let me see her pussy.

She had become shy. Wearing skirts and no underwear for easy access, for my fingers to rub along her entrance, brush her clit and make her cum over and over into my hand. My Warrior was reluctant and didn't trust me fully. Or perhaps she was afraid I would give her so much pleasure she could never let me go.

I was hoping for the latter.

She had just turned twenty, in a dream world with her dream boyfriend, and she was fucking scared I wouldn't like her slit?

"Warrior, you are not ugly," I reiterated the words from nights ago. "The thought of being able to see you, touch you, lick you." I groaned, grabbing my erection and showing her my desire. "Would give me more pleasure than you realize."

"You won't think it smells weird? Looks weird?"

I shook my head at her trembling voice. I had not done my job as a mate—give her reassurance, comfort her. I had failed. Not tonight. I would no longer give her reason to doubt.

"Sugar, your arousal smells like cherry blossoms and champagne to me. When I lick my fingers after you cum, it makes me want more. I think the problem is that I have not been forceful and demanding enough. I shouldn't given you time to think and let doubts arise in your mind." As I lowered my body closer to her, I growled, nipping at her hip.

"If you truly do not want it, you can stop me." I lifted her skirt, looking at her lacey white thong. My cock hardened, and I pushed it closer to her leg. Feeling the length, she gasped, her fingers tangling into the sheets that covered the sand.

"I want to, I need to," I muttered. My nose went straight to her pussy, smelling her arousal. "Gods, I want it."

Her head leaned back. "Okay," she whispered.

My head perked up in excitement. "Really?" I squeaked and the surrounding air filled with laughter.

"Really?" she covered her face.

"Hey, hey, let me see that gorgeous face." I crawled back up and pulled her hands away. "I want to see you cum." She squeaked, embarrassed. "You look so damn hot when you cum."

"I do?"

"Fuck, yes." Not wanting her to speak anymore, I pressed my lips to hers. My hands traced down her clothes, taking my claws and ripping her shirt open. Her bra was quickly removed and her skirt along with it. My lips trailed down her neck, slowly nipping until I bit down on her nipple. Her fingers trickled through my hair, grazing my scalp with her nails. I forced myself to let go of her hardened nub and slowly trail down to her navel.

The small white piece of cloth that covered her pussy didn't catch my eye like I thought it would. Instead, a decorative tattoo lay across her hip. I paused, lifting my head, letting my finger run across her hipbone.

"Uh, oh," she muttered. Sitting up, her eyes widened, and her sheepish smile made me grin.

"Is this for me?" The delicate, intricate lines were swirled so decoratively I almost missed its wording. I grinned like a damn wolfling and kissed it. "When did you get this?" I asked giddily.

"The same night I got my sternum tattoo."

"That long? And you didn't tell me?!" I barked out a laugh. "I feel so honored you would put this here. But it's on your skin, permanently," I whispered. The words, "His Sugar," made my back straighten a little taller with pride. She would mar her skin with my nickname that no one else called her. The word "his," meant for me, and only me.

As much as she didn't want to admit it, her subconscious had claimed me. I just had to pull that thought deep inside her and let her show it to the world.

"Is this why you've hidden this pussy from me?" I cupped her mound, rubbing my palm against it.

"Partly," she moaned. "I didn't want you to take it too seriously. That you wouldn't hold on to it when we aren't sure—"

"You are mine!" I said sternly. Evelyn's name danced on my lips, but I quickly silenced them as I pulled down her underwear and licked from the bottom of her slit to the top. My cock throbbed harder at her breathy gasp, her hands digging into my hair as I prepared for my meal.

I took my time, lapping her clit with the roughness of my tongue. Her hips wiggled, moving with the same rhythm. Moving my forearm arm, I laid it across her stomach to keep her still. I growled, the vibrations seducing sweet curses from her lips.

Dipping my tongue inside her sweet cavern, I drank her essence.

"Guard!" she cried as I inserted two fingers into her slickness. Her pussy fluttered, clamping down around me.

"You will feel so good around my cock," I growled. I wanted to bury myself in her. Now that I had my tongue in her pussy, I wanted all of her. It had taken her so long to open up to me, to give her most precious part for me to see, to taste, to devour. I knew that my time was short in this world.

She had grown into a beautiful woman. Had completed mission after mission for an Alpha and his Luna that needed her help. She had lived; she had experienced enough, and my patience had grown thin. Riddick had become uncontrollable. Snapping at anyone and anything that moved within a ten-feet radius. My lapels were decorated with medals upon medals from various fights around the realm. I was more than ready to bare myself to her, have her not just in her dreams but in reality.

My fingers thrust forth, pushing harder into her pussy. Her body arched. Her sweet moans of "Guard" would soon be replaced by my name. I growled again.

"Cum, cum on my tongue, Warrior."

My Warrior's silent scream fired pleasure down my spine, my cock rutting into the blanket beneath us. Her essence poured onto my tongue while I sucked on her clit until she came down from the mountain.

Gathering her in my arms, I brought her head to my shoulder. I hovered over her, my lips licking her marking spot. Riddick's heavy breathing, his ultimate desire to mark her, to claim pushed to the forefront of my mind. He had waited too long, and my ability to keep him away wavered. I ground my teeth, forcing Riddick to keep his fangs at bay. We were able to compromise and force our head into her shoulder. We sucked her delicate skin. Evelyn's body was covered in sweet chills, her body shuddering as she finally released her building euphoria. My body tensed, savoring and bathing in the soft mewls of pleasure licking at my ear.

"Guard," she whimpered. I licked at the temporary mating mark on her body. Deep red and purple marks adorned her shoulder. Riddick oozed the scent that was meant only for our mate. She shuddered, and her body relaxed.

"You scented me," she breathed wistfully.

"I did because you're mine," Riddick growled heavily.

Her fingers gripped my back, pulling me closer. She didn't argue, her body laying limp in my arms. Evelyn had guarded her heart too long. I had been patient, but the time was now. I would wait no longer. It was time to move back to the Cerulean Moon Kingdom and ask Clara and Kane for their blessing to take what was destined to be mine.

Chapter Twenty Nine

Evelyn

I yawned, not covering my mouth as I stood behind the sofa in Wesley's office. His arms were crossed behind the desk, staring at Mason—the scum of the earth. Actually, he might just be lower than scum. The decomposing worms and grubs that lay beneath it might be more fitting.

I was awoken at early hours of the morning by Charlotte gently knocking on my door. Her motherly tone and the gentle touch of her hands made me feel like I was back home in the palace. She told me to get dressed and come to Wesley's office. After Wesley had been briefed last night about my indescribable rage and the punishment I had inflicted on Mason, I had gone up to my room and went to sleep, seeking comfort from My Guard.

Melody was hurt so badly when she walked in on Mason, her companion, pounding into a she-wolf late at night. Her wolf reached out to me, begging for me to save Melody from herself as she continued to watch them with no emotion on her face. She had been stunned, watching the wolf she had feelings for defile someone else.

Melody doesn't cry, we just aren't criers, but a tear had escaped her when I finally saw the gross act. Cinder, roaring with anger, took over my body and ripped the she-wolf from his puny dick. Luckily, I had been gifted with such an exceptional set of steel colored brass knuckles by Ebony. I strapped those babies on before I gave him an excellent right hook while Melody left the room.

The she-wolf that rode him did not know the relationship that Melody and Mason had and was pardoned and told to leave the territory last night. Mason, on the other hand, was in deep shit. It was so deep he would not be able to climb out of it. I dragged him into the hallway, growling while I beat him to a bloody pulp, ruining Charlotte's recently replaced carpet.

Oops.

It took three wolves to calm me down, two of them being Ebony and Basim. I was cursing up a storm; Cinder was uncontrollable as she tried to reach for Mason. The poor fucker was screaming, pissing his pants as I clawed the wallpapered halls. Melody had already left, running down the hall in embarrassment, so it was my job as the big sister to kick his ass.

The screaming and rough housing had woken up the entire hallway, bringing in more of an audience. Cinder continued to scream what a disgrace he was and that he would be answering to me.

He was thrown into the pack prison and was going to be dealt with sometime today. Little did I know it was going to be so damn early. My Guard had taken care of me, and for a strange reason, I didn't sleep well like I normally did when I stayed with him in a dream.

I rubbed my neck unconsciously. It was sore, but a delightful sore from his nipping and sucking. When I went to the bathroom to do my morning routine, I was left with a large bruise that covered the entirety of the side of my neck and shoulder. Make-up wasn't something I used often, but I was pretty sure I'd used half a container of the shit trying to cover it up. It was so dark, so red and purple it barely covered it. Wearing a scarf had already raised questions in Ebony's eyes while I stood in formation behind the couch with Mason's battered body in front.

"What the hell happened to you?" Ebony whispered as we watched Wesley continue to breathe heavily.

He was killing Mason in his mind probably sixty times because Wesley saw Melody and me as his own. Melody's broken heart might break more after what was going to happen soon.

"Rough night," I shrugged my shoulders. "Couldn't sleep well." Ebony leaned over to sniff me, and I backed away. Surely My Guard's scent couldn't have leaked through a dream. Then again, a giant hickey on my shoulder and neck certainly had.

How the hell can that happen?

I was in such deep shit trying to hide this thing. Shifting into Cinder would have to happen sooner rather than later to use her healing abilities to make it vanish.

"Yeah, this isn't gonna come off until tomorrow." She huffed, shaking her head. *"It looks like we got in a fight with a vacuum."*

Great.

"Do you have any idea what you have done?" Wesley growled. His hair was a mess. Even Charlotte, who stood by his side, couldn't comfort him. Wesley had a strict "no cheating" policy. In fact, if he had it his way, no wolf in his pack would be allowed to have relationships with anyone until they found their mate, but Charlotte was the voice of reason. Everyone should have agency, their ability to choose.

Unfortunately, since Mason was a Royal Guard, he was held to a higher standard. Guards pledged and vowed to always be truthful to the Royal Family and never withhold secrets. If they broke their vow, they would be put to death immediately.

Now, Mason, a Royal Guard, had broken the heart of a princess. She'd been lied to, cheated on, and not respected. He now gets to deal with the King of the Cerulean Moon Kingdom whose is known to be unforgiving.

Like I said, he was in deep shit.

Mason turned his swollen face. I wanted to laugh, but the atmosphere was far too serious for that.

"You have broken your oath to the Royal Family. You have lied to the second in line to the throne, you have betrayed your teachers from the Alabaster Academy, you have thrown away your life. And for what? To get your dick wet?" Wesley growled. Charlotte cleared her throat, nudging Wesley. He put his arm around her waist and pulled her close.

"I... I didn't mean to," Mason stuttered.

"Oh, did you just trip and fall into her pussy, then?" I snapped.

Ebony chuckled, raising her hand up for a high five. "Classic," she whispered.

"No, I care about Melody. I really do!" He feigned sincerity. "It's just that, the past year and a half, she hasn't really, you know. Done anything," he said sheepishly.

"Meaning what? She wouldn't let you brand her with your tiny dick?" I growled. "Glad she had the sense not to give you something so precious."

"She's wonderful, I just...I needed a release or something. Basim found his mate two months ago. I got jealous he was getting some. My wolf has been wanting Melody, but I didn't want to force her!" he cried out.

"And if you had, I would have ripped you apart slowly," I whispered into his ear. "In fact, I think my warning still stands. I think I get to cut off your dick and feed it to you. And just so you know, those don't grow back," I hissed.

"No, please don't!" He tried to stand up, but Ebony and I grabbed his shoulders, shoving him back down on the couch.

"Ladies." Wesley stood from his chair, buttoning his suit jacket. "The reason I have called you all in this morning is that I have just gotten off a call with Their Majesties about our dilemma. Mason's purple face paled, the crack in his lip still bled. Rounding the desk, Wesley stood in front of Mason. "Dante, why don't you take your mother and see if you can get Melody to eat something? She hasn't eaten since last night."

Charlotte gulped. Dante stood by his mother, grabbing her arm. His face was stoic and stern for a fourteen-year-old. He did what he was told. Opening the door, Basim, who stood on the other side, stepped inside and guarded the door.

"Basim?" Mason questioned. Basim gazed at his friend until he looked downward.

"I'm sorry, Mase." He shook his head. "I can't help you this time. I warned you not to hurt Melody. Being a guard puts you on a higher pedestal for following the laws of our King and Queen. You should have done the respectable thing and broke things off with her. Melody is a smart woman; she knew this wasn't forever. You were to comfort each other until you both found mates."

"I didn't want to let her go," his voice cracked. "I'm a good wolf. I just fell astray. I'll make it up to her, I'll never do it again. Let me make things right, let me apologize!" he pleaded. "Let me at least talk to her!"

"No," I growled. "What would you exactly say to her? Rehash what you've done? How you fucked her? Let me ask you something. Is the wolf from last night the only one you've fucked?"

Ebony's wolf growled beside me while the room went silent.

Mason's parted lips pushed to a thin line, his head swinging in defeat.

The fucker knew what he'd done. He would have done it again, over and over. Whoever his mate was supposed to be will be blessed with another, or maybe he wasn't blessed with a mate at all because of how heartless he truly was.

Wesley's hands balled into fists. He was one of the most levelheaded alphas in both realms, and he was losing it far quicker than I expected. Then again, he saw us like family, like one of his own. If this had happened to his own daughter even without the title of guard, he would have killed the fucker on the spot.

"His Majesty Kane has requested your execution. For treason against the crown, for lying to her highness, and breaking your commitment to a she-wolf. You are therefore stripped of your Royal Guard title and your name erased from the Alabaster Academy's history books. Your family will be notified of your dishonor."

"Fuck, please no." Mason swayed as he stood.

"Alphas, hold him." Wesley commanded.

Ebony grabbed one arm while I grabbed the other. Mason struggled, shrieking for mercy.

"I am giving you mercy," Wesley growled. "I should torture you slowly, make you suffer. In what way do you think you had the right to hurt the princess when she gave you something as precious as her time and energy to comfort one another while you looked for your mates? You are disgrace to your kind."

Wesley placed a and on each side of Mason's head and twisted until his spinal cord snapped and was severed inside his body. When Wesley let go, Mason's head fell backward, hanging at an odd angle. In my arms, I held the body of the wolf that broke my sister, and he would never have the chance to do it again.

"Ebony, Basim, please take the body to the incinerator."

Ebony nodded to me and drug Mason's body by one hand while Basim grabbed the other.

Mason understood when he took this job that he was supposed to protect us. He may or may not have had feelings for my sister, but his dick certainly didn't. Betraying even a companionship bond was highly taboo in Bergarian, not usually punishable by death, but being a guard held certain extra responsibilities. Mason's oaths and vows to hold no secrets to the crown made his death inevitable.

"Come, we must contact your parents." Wesley sighed. He opened the door and led me down the winding hallway to the magical mirror to contact Bergarian. Melody and I used it at least once a month to talk to our parents, except this time, Melody wouldn't be joining us.

I considered Mason a friend. Not one I would confide my secrets to, but someone I had respect for. I thought he was better than that but finding him under some random wolf when he promised my sister a commitment to be each other's emotional support severed all emotional ties to him. To me, he never existed.

I should have killed him.

Cinder huffed in agreement, but this wasn't our territory. Killing was meant for Wesley, and I'm sure dad didn't want blood on my hands just yet.

As we entered the smaller communications room, Cyrene, the most powerful sorceress of the Earth realm, stood, waving her hand for us to approach.

"Cyrene, what are you doing here?" Wesley asked.

Cyrene was powerful. Her coven lived on the pack's territory and helped with tiny jobs such as willing the mirror to work so we could speak to those on the other side, but today, she had arrived to help instead of a lesser member of her coven.

"I just wanted to give Evelyn a hug." Cyrene came toward me and engulfed me. Giggling, she pulled me back by my shoulders and patted my cheek. "I'm gonna miss you," she whispered. Heading out the door, she flicked her finger for the reflection in the mirror. It rippled until my parent's room opened on the other side.

"What the heck is that supposed to mean?" I raised a brow at Wesley.

He shrugged his shoulders. "Sorceresses and witches are strange creatures. Could mean anything." Wesley unbuttoned his fitted suit jacket and sat down on the decorative chair. He glanced at my scarf eyeing it carefully as I fidgeted.

Gods, I'm in trouble.

Sighing, I sat beside him, waiting for my parents to appear, only to see the top of a head with black hair at the bottom of the mirror. "Move over, let me see!" A squeal came from the mohawk.

"Dax?" I chuckled, rubbing at my shoulder. The harsh push of a chair scooted across the marble, and his little face lit up the screen.

"Evie!" Dax screamed, his hands waving in the air.

"Where is Evie? I don't see her! Move over, you ass!" Dimitri yelled.

"Hey, no cursing," I said, holding my laughter. Once Dimitri had his own chair, the two five-year-olds sat happily and began discussing their day. I nodded my head as they both completed each other's sentences as Wesley shifted uncomfortably in his chair.

"Hey, hey..." I held my hands up. "It's great to see you guys, but where are Mom and Dad? I need to talk to them."

Dax and Dimitri snickered and whispered to each other. "They are in the closet looking for 'linens.'"

"I don't know what kind of 'linens' Dad is looking for in Mom's cooter, though," Dax replied.

"Oh my gods, your language is awful!" I cried. "How would you know any of that?"

Wesley's face had gone red, his hand covering his mouth.

"They're almost done. Mom is on her fifth, 'oh, Alpha,' so they will be out any minute." Dimitri sat happily on the chair. "Hey, why are you wearing a scarf? Isn't it spring there?"

I cleared my throat, rubbing my shoulder again. "It's a human thing. Wanted to try it out for...styling reasons."

Dax looked at me warily but was soon distracted by a bug that landed on his nose. Dimitri took the opportunity to slap his brother in the face and laughed hysterically. "Ouchy! What the fuck!" Dax screeched.

"Your mother has her hands full," Wesley chuckled. "Glad that Charlotte is finished."

"Dax! Dimitri! What are you doing?" I heard mom's voice hissing.

They scurried off but not before they yelled back at her. "Did you find your lineeeens, Mom? How about you, Alpha?" Dax and Dimitri spoke to Dad and ran off with Dad's growl not far behind them.

"They need to be training with all that energy." Dad shook his head. Pulling mom into his lap. Dad had messy hair, and an untied tunic, but Mom was prim and proper, like always. I wasn't sure how she did it, but she didn't look like she had come out of the closet.

"Is it done?" Dad asked gruffly.

"It is. The body is being incinerated right now," Wesley replied.

Dad nodded, showing his appreciation, but Mom's smile dropped.

"Is Melody alright?" Mom's soft voice penetrated me.

"She will be fine. She's strong," I said with conviction. "Melody mind-linked me earlier. She's having hot cocoa with Dante."

Mom's face didn't change, but Father's sure did when he spotted the scarf.

"What are you wearing?" Dad's mood was in no-nonsense mode, and I couldn't brush this one off.

"It's a human thing." I waved my hand dismissively. "They wear them all the time around here. I kind of like the fashion."

"Oh yes, I used to wear one," Mom chirped. "Especially when I had to work in the freezer room some days to organize inventory."

"Since when do you care about fashion," Dad growled. "We could barely keep you clothed as a baby nor get you to wear dresses when you were tutored. Why the fuck are you wearing a scarf, Evelyn?"

"What? No princess title?" I jutted out a lip.

"Honey, your father is not in a good mood right now." Mom shuffled in Dad's lap. A tiny curl of his lip could be seen but dropped as quickly as it arrived.

"Take it off," he ordered.

"What? No!" I cried. "It's a special scarf, took me forever to tie it this way."

"Evelyn!" Mom jumped when Dad barked my name, and Wesley gave me a look.

Shit, shit, shit.

Pulling it away with my eyes closed, I prayed to the gods that the hickey had magically disappeared, that the makeup was enough to cover up the bruises, but as Mom, Dad, and even Wesley sat in silence, I knew I was in deep shit.

"Who the fuck touched you?" Dad roared, almost dropping Mom. "Who the hell touched you, Evelyn?!"

Melody had the ovaries to tell Mom and Dad she was seeing Mason. That she wanted companionship, and they respected her decision after many weeks of coaxing. Mom knew we had to make our own decisions, and Melody's was that she wanted to date. I didn't realize the extent of how far she had gone with Mason, but it sounded like she didn't go all the way. Thank the gods.

Now, here I was, a wolf that had made a vow when I was younger to stay pure for my mate, showing up with a giant hickey on my neck.

"The fuck do you think you're doing, Evie?" Dad's eyes glowed, and Torin came to the surface.

"Hey, Papa?" I questioned my dad's wolf.

"You are to return to Bergarian. Take the next flight to the portal. I expect to have you in your room by tomorrow morning," his voice echoed through the mirror. Wesley grabbed the mirror, making sure it didn't topple over.

"We haven't found Ember yet!" I pleaded. "I can't go home now!"

"You and Melody obviously can't take care of yourselves. You will return home, and that's final." Dad's fist banged on the table.

"Kane," Mom whispered, trying to calm him.

"No, baby. This is it. They have been gone too long. They will return to the palace. Evelyn has had enough time away from us. I want my daughters back in the palace where it's safe." Dad pushed away from the table, and Mom sat staring back at me.

"It's for the best, Evie." Mom didn't fight Dad's words. Mom could usually alter a decision, if need be, but the softness in her eyes made me crumble. "We miss you and Melody. It's been hard not having you both here. Plus, the Peace Ball is coming. Wouldn't you like to find your mate? I have a fantastic feeling," she cooed.

Thank gods she didn't question the hickey. She just looked into my eyes, holding her breath so I wouldn't fight her.

I gritted my teeth. The Peace Ball was the anniversary of the Dark War being won. Like all the balls, it was created as a large mating party. I wasn't ready to go back and possibly meet my mate. I had fallen too hard.

My Guard was who I wanted. The one that knew my secrets and knew my body. How could I go back home and possibly find my mate? How could I give up the dreams, give him up? I wasn't ready to leave the dream world. I wanted him more than the mate that was destined for me.

"Pack your things, Honey," Mom soothed. "Wesley, will you see to it they begin their journey?"

"With pleasure, Clara. I'll escort them to the portal."

Chapter Thirty

Evelyn

Since waking up with the hickey on my neck, my life had been in shambles.

We had taken the earliest flight, using Wesley's jet to fly across the country to the portal. Charlotte and the boys cried, wishing we weren't leaving Ebony didn't cry because she wasn't a crier, but she held onto me longer than I ever thought she would. After many promises to keep in touch and to visit soon, Melody and I left the pack we had called home for a year and a half.

Once we told Melody we were heading back home, she stopped crying. A mask of indifference fell on her face, and her back straightened. It reminded me of grandmother how she could shield her emotions and explain that it was "for the greater good of the people" to hide something trivial like this. What had happened to her was far from trivial. She saw Mason as a close friend, someone she could confide in and cuddle up to when she felt sad. I thank the gods she didn't let him take her virginity.

I was a total hypocrite when I thought of Melody doing things with another man. In my dreams, I had succumbed to my desires for My Guard to take me with his mouth. I had thought over and over about the night I finally let him take my throbbing clit between his lips because, for the strangest reason, I'd not seen him since he planted that hickey on my neck.

It had been almost a week that he has been missing from my dreams, and it made me think of the worst. Had he found his mate? Now I knew what he felt like when I made the decision to leave him alone for six months. It was heartbreaking, and the light inside me died slowly each day.

I missed the hell out of him. I missed my friend, my soon to be lover as I thought him to be. I loved him, and I was ready to give him the fullness of my heart. The space between us had only strengthened that notion. The fleeting thoughts of letting him go because of a mate in this reality had vanished. I wanted to reject the mate that was meant for my reality and only live with the alpha of my dreams.

When we arrived home, Joshua stood at the front of the palace in his dress regalia. We'd sent him home after the mission in California. I gave my parents the excuse that I didn't need him there, that we were well protected, and he needed to be here for Mom when she traveled the kingdom. They didn't question me, taking my word for it. But seeing him back within the same palace walls brought unceasing feelings of dread to have to deal with him all over again. I had hoped to stay longer in the Black Claw pack and have him forget about me, but that was not the case.

His eyes wandered over me when I arrived. His smile, meant for warmth and friendship, filled me with dread. Joshua wanted something I could not give him; and when I was cornered in the hallway, I gave him the rejection and officially pushed him away.

With Joshua's sorrowful eyes and slump of his shoulders, I called it a win. He wouldn't pursue me further. He had stayed away after that confrontation, only doing the duties a typical Royal Guard would pursue, which was to stand silently in the corner just watching. Not that I minded. It was how he was before we had our first dance just two years ago.

Now I stood in the royal throne room in a red, lightly sequined dress that hugged my curves at every angle. The single strapped dress curved around my breasts, accentuating their full perkiness. My eyes had been done in a deep smoky black and sparkles littering the sides of my cheeks.

Any she-wolf would be jealous to have such a dress, but here I was thinking of things I couldn't have and a mate I did not want.

"Evie will never find us here." Dimitri snickered behind the throne.

My eyes lit up for a fraction of a second as I snuck around the decorative chairs. Dax and Dimitri were troublemakers, Dimitri usually being the brains of the operation and Dax being the muscle.

"Gotcha!" I tagged Dax in surprise, and he growled fiercely.

"We are going to get you!" Dimitri called as I ran up the grand staircase.

My feet were bare, my silk dress dragging behind me while I ran down the cream-colored hallway to the royal wings. Mother's door was open. She brushed the curls from her face while she stepped out of the bathroom.

"Evelyn, what are you doing? You should get ready for the dance!" My once perfectly curled hair was now wild, sweat gleaming on my forehead from the run upstairs. Panting, I sat in my mom's make-up chair. "I have a marvelous feeling he will be here tonight." She hummed, taking pins to pull the hair from my face. I grumbled at that, tapping my short, mani-cured finger on the vanity.

"What makes you say that? I smell nothing, my heart isn't racing, Cinder isn't even howling about anything. He isn't here, I'm still too young to find a mate," I grumbled. Most of those statements were lies. My heart was racing, Cinder was pacing, but it was due to the fact that my mom's feelings were usually right, and that thought terrified me. My mate could very well be here.

"Did you wear red when there were balls in Charlotte and Wesley's pack?"

I nodded, fiddling with the makeup brush. "Yeah, but they were differ-ent. They were like real parties, none of the fancy stuff. They had pizza, burgers, all sorts of things. They have a fancy one, the Spring Ball but I went as a guard."

Mom finished my hair, sitting beside me on the bench. "You know, your hair has turned lighter," mom mentioned, stroking the side of my head. "There is more of a gold sheen to it. It reminds me a lot of your—" her voice went silent.

I knew exactly who she meant.

Grandmother.

"She's doing fine." Mom sensed my unease. "I talked to your Pop yesterday. She still has a long way to go, but she is relying on her wolf more." I gave mom a cramped smile and a heavy breath of relief. The silence was broken between us when my two rowdy brothers burst through the doors.

"We found you, Evelyn!" Dax screamed as they both pounced and grabbed my legs. They pretended to gnaw at my ankles, and I giggled.

"Yes, yes, you found me," I huffed while crossing my arms.

Mom threw her head back and laughed. "Working on your tracking skills, I see."

"Mom, we found her in less than five minutes, a record," Dax screamed.

I continued to stare at myself in the mirror, pulling at the fabric. I really didn't want this night to proceed; I didn't want to find him. My gut twisted in knots. Mom, sensing my unease, grabbed pins that held pearls at the end and put them in my hair. Placing perfume on my neck, she sighed, rubbing my shoulders.

"Mom, I can't do it," I whispered.

Mom motioned for the boys to leave the room. Their excitement died when I put my hands to my face. My lip quivered, as I tried to hold back the tears. I thought I went through enough emotional torment with my grandmother, but what I was going through now was worse.

A mate was sacred, a gift from the goddess, and I had decided to reject him to live alone in this life and only care for the wolf in my dreams. It wouldn't be fair to either of them if I kept them both, so my decision stood to keep My Guard with me, to let my reality be my nightmare.

"Honey, what's wrong?" Mom's compact form tried to pull me into her lap. The gesture made me chuckle, and I leaned down uncomfortably to put my head on her shoulder.

"I've fallen in love with someone else," I whispered.

She sighed heavily, her hand running up and down my arm.

"I didn't mean for it to happen. I tried to stay away," I sniffed. "But there is something about him that calls to me. I can't feel the spark when our skin touches, I cannot smell his scent strongly, but my heart declared that he is to be mine."

"Oh, Evie," she soothed, kissing my head.

"If I meet my mate tonight, I will reject him. I can't be mated to someone and still have these feelings." I waited for my mom to reply in anger or beg me to rethink what I was doing. But she didn't, she kissed my shoulder, hugging my muscular arm around her tiny torso.

"Evie, if you are worried your father and I would love you less, we wouldn't."

Alright, was not expecting that.

"This is your life to live, my sweet baby. Your happiness is important to me. I have to say, you are the strongest she-wolf in this palace, not just here." She squeezed my arm. "But in here." She put her hand over my heart. "You follow your heart, follow the pull that guides you to love the wolf that you believe to be yours."

I felt the heat of my father standing behind me. His hand touched the shoulder that had been covered in bruises just days ago, rubbing it tenderly. Not once did he chastise me when I arrived home with Melody. He only hugged us, told us he loved us, and was so happy to have us home. Mother said his mood had considerably lightened since we returned, and for that I was thankful.

"Can I ask who this wolf is? Do we know him?" Mom asked.

I sighed, sniffing again. Dad pulled a handkerchief from his pocket and handed it to me. "Thanks, Dad."

Looking up at him, his face was soft. The hardened lines of the grumpy beast were long gone. He looked youthful, brighter even.

"It will sound crazy." I shook my head.

"Honey, nothing will sound as crazy as when I walked into the small town of Ever Green and found out the whole town was a bunch of were-wolves, and your father was my mate." She laughed. "Try me."

Letting out a shuddering breath I explained how I first met My Guard. How we trained, how we laughed, played, and learned about each other. Never exposing who we were for fear I was some sort of succubus that was trying to eat his soul. Dad growled at that, but mother hushed him quickly. And by the time I turned eighteen and didn't feel the sparks on my birthday, a tear rolled down my cheek. Mom hastily fixed my makeup as I continued, avoiding the physical details except for the giant hickey on my neck.

Couldn't lie about that one.

Once finished, a burden had been lifted from my shoulders. There was no yelling or screaming at me to forget this Alpha. That I was crazy to throw away the life with my mate to just live in my dreams with this possibly imaginary wolf I had created.

Instead, I was greeted with silence.

"You make your own decisions, My Warrior Princess," Dad said as softly as he could. "We love you; we always will. If you feel you cannot love anyone more than this guard, then you go to him."

"I'm not sure how," I whined, wiping my nose with the back of my hand, rather un-princess like. "He has been missing for the last six days, maybe he found his mate!"

Mom shook her head. "He sounds utterly infatuated with you, Evie. I don't think he would give up that easily. Give it tonight, you can even go to bed early and see if you can meet him again. Maybe get his name and see if we can find him?"

I silently agreed, leaning on her shoulder.

"Just please, have some fun for at least a few hours. Melody could use the company. She likes to bottle up her emotions, too. She's had it rough."

I straightened, and mom fixed the makeup on my face once more.

"When you meet your mate tonight, he has to ask my permission," Dad scolded. "Dream world or not, he still abides by my rules." He tapped my head with his fingers.

I laughed while he pulled me from the bench. "Thanks, Daddy." I wrapped my arms around him, nuzzling in his embrace. I could feel his warmth seep through me.

I stepped out of my parents' bedroom and saw that Melody stood on the other side of the doorway. She didn't have her signature notebook. Her natural curls covered the front of her green strapless gown.

"Where is your red dress? This is your first official mating ball?" I raised an eyebrow.

"I don't need a mate," she whispered to me. "Mom, they are asking for our presence at the ball. It's starting." She ignored my question. I linked my arm through Melody's, and her once emotionless mask faded, and she smiled.

"Thanks for kicking what's-his-face's ass," she said pleasantly. "That was an exceptionally sisterly thing to do."

"I try my best," I replied. "Just know I'll probably try to kick your mate's ass too when you meet him. You know, just to be sure he knows his place."

"Not happening anytime soon. Think about it, Dad was old when he met mom, so was Jasper and Taliyah. Think of poor Marcus, he still hasn't found his mate."

"Oh, that's right," I muttered. "How can we forget about him?"

"It's easy to do." Melody walked us to the balcony that overlooked the ballroom. "He never comes around anymore, not since we were little.

Sometimes I think he likes to hide in that pack house and never venture out." Melody grabbed a chocolate strawberry from one of the servants.

"Doesn't need to when he's got she-wolves vying for his attention." I rolled my eyes.

"I don't even remember what he looks like anymore. I think the last time I saw him I was eight, and that was at a distance."

"Ladies, be nice," Mom chastised. "Marcus is going to be here tonight, and you shouldn't believe all those rumors. He's a decorated warrior and has sacrificed much for this kingdom."

Melody and I ducked our heads in embarrassment while we looked over the balcony. We gazed over the seas of red dresses, black tuxes, and the few Alabaster Academy graduate uniforms. They stood out like a sore thumb with those white suits decorated with scarlet sashes.

Dad stepped up to the podium, holding onto Mom's hand. Mom hated public speaking, but Dad might have hated it even more. Fortunately for Mom, Dad would do anything for her. "Welcome to the annual Peace Ball. We hope you enjoy the beverages, food, and dancing. Please help yourselves, and for those of you finding mates tonight, congratulations ahead of time." Dad's hand waved for the music to play, and my parents, sister, and brothers began their descent down the stairs.

Short and to the point. Just like Dad.

Dax and Dimitri had already found their way to the food, sticking their fingers into the individual cakes. Melody hopped down the last step, and I pulled her to the dance floor. She grunted, her dress catching under her feet.

"What are you doing?" she hissed. I pulled her into dancing formation, playing the part of the male.

I bowed, lifting my head slowly, so I was looking up at her. "My lady, will you have this dance with me?" Melody snorted, giggling frantically as she jumped into my arms.

We danced, we twirled. I had told my parents what my intentions were. That I was going to give up the mate the Mood Goddess gave me and give myself to My Guard. My heart felt lighter, knowing they supported me in whatever decision I made. It was far too easy, but maybe they just wanted to see me happy.

I laughed, the surrounding she-wolves looking on in bewilderment that the two princesses would horse around at an event such as this. But I didn't care, we didn't care what anyone else thought. We weren't snobbish princesses; we were just us. The approachable royalty that would carry on our mother and father's legacy of helping the weak.

As I twirled Melody one last time, Cinder howled inside me. "MATE!" she yipped, and the overwhelming smell of evergreen and moss blanketed me. A tall wolf in a white uniform caught my eye across the room. It was the same black ebony hair, but the people gathered around him kept me from seeing his face.

Letting go of Melody's hand, I filtered through the crowd. She stayed behind. A laugh came from the wolf, and my heart fluttered all the more.

"It couldn't be," I muttered to myself.

That was when he stepped forward, moving the bodies that kept his face from me. Once the wolves parted, my eyes gazed from the floor up to his chest. An Alabaster Academy student, decorated with medals and ribbons of honor. His Alpha aura oozed through the room, and Cinder howled once again.

The same stormy eyes I had seen far too often looked back at me with such warmth. His smile broadened, and my heart began to beat again. My hands trembled, and we both ran across the marbled tile, not caring about the onlookers surrounding us.

Chapter Thirty-One

Kit

"Come on, we are going to be late!" I rushed up the steps outside the palace. The approach to the palace was filled with carriages drawn by white horses, nobles from Vermillion, and Pixies flying in. Royal Guards stood in their own white uniforms. I was the most decorated from my class, and a smile brushed across my face as my friends and I approached the front doors. Two guards bowed, letting us pass through.

"So, she's really here, huh?" Leland buttoned the top of his uniform. He had several medals too. I hoped he and Clint would be selected to work inside the palace as well since their time at the Alabaster Academy was complete.

"Yeah, she is." I smirked, excited to finally see my mate in person rather than in a dream.

After tasting my sweet mate's pussy, my wolf couldn't stand it anymore. We had waited and yes, many mates had waited longer to claim those that were there's, but not like I had. I had a taste of her each night, knowing who she was for the longest time. Evelyn was always out of reach, barely able to satisfy my needs. I'd been unable to show her just how much I truly cared for her with my hands, my tongue, and my soon to be growing erection. Once my tongue had lapped the essence of her body and she came in my arms, it was over. I was going to take her.

The next day I made an emergency call with the help of a witch in the Dragon Territory. She was happy to do so, just to get a glimpse of the queen herself. I explained to Clara I knew who Evelyn was, and I had spent the past year and a half keeping the secret from Evelyn. Clara praised me for my patience.

My pride swelled at my queen's praise for allowing Evelyn to mature and grow—to have her fall madly in love with me without the use of a bond. It would only make our bond that much stronger in the end.

Once I explained I could no longer wait, that I had to have her, Clara immediately agreed. Kane was not as thrilled, believing she needed more time, but Clara silenced him quickly. His string of curses made me laugh, but I wasn't afraid of his wrath. He knew all too well the importance of mates and the timing of the gods.

That was when the bright idea of bringing Evelyn home so we could meet at the Peace Ball was created. It would complete the fairy tale that Clara had envisioned for her daughter since the day she learned about us being mates. I should have been angry not knowing, but of course Clara had her reasons.

"Will you finally tell us who she is then? Her name?" Clint ran beside me as I strode into the ballroom. It was our first ball at the palace. Being a hermit, I stayed away from the palace balls and my friends chose to follow my lead. Now they knew why I'd stayed away all those years. That my mate had haunted my dreams, my subconscious recoiled at the thought of meeting other she-wolves for fun. I would much rather stay in a world filled with nothing but her than waste my time with women that I would never having feelings for. Evelyn was the only one I'd ever wanted.

Standing outside the doors, guards lined up along the pathway. Shifters, fae, and vampires continued to filter in as we heard Kane's welcoming announcement and the music start playing. Stopping before the doors, I took a deep gulp. The first yells of claiming filtered out of the ballroom and echoed into the foyer.

"How do I look?" I straightened my lapel again, the decorations gleaming in the candlelight.

Leland snickered, pretending to dust off the invisible dust on my shoulder. "Like a fucking Christmas tree. You glow so beautifully, Guard." He fluttered his lashes while I playfully punched him in the gut.

"It's kinda sad; now we won't be the three musketeers anymore," Clint whined. "I bet my mate isn't even in there."

"Our time will come. Until then, you get to put up with my ass." Leland pushed him back. We all gasped, walking into the brightly lit ballroom. The white marble, along with the gold trimmings and crystal chandelier hanging above the ballroom cast bright lights in all directions. Classical music played while a DJ set up in the corner for the "after party" of the traditional ball. I tugged on my collar, watching the floor, seeking my mate.

Soon we were surrounded by women and other guards welcoming us. We had gained a following among our classmates, eager to not only spar but train with me. With Evelyn's help, I was able to let other wolves into my life, showing them both techniques I learned from Evelyn and new techniques I'd created myself. I had become a teacher, rather than just a hardened shell of a guard.

"You must be Kit," a she-wolf purred. Her hand brushed the shiny metal on my suit. "I've heard so much about you. Do you think you could spare me a dance?" I raised an eyebrow, flattered she would ask, but disappointed it wasn't the woman I was after.

"Thank you for asking, but no. I'm looking for my mate tonight," I replied. Other women sighed, some even fanning themselves.

"That's sweet and all, but what about having some fun for a change? You might not even see her."

"He's taken a vow to only touch his mate," Clint said, feigning sadness. The women again groaned but still did not leave our presence.

A woman in a traditional red dress with an utterly low neckline approached, trying to capture my attention. Her violet eyes fluttered, her manicured finger tapping on the metals. I couldn't understand why they were going after me when my two best friends stood beside me.

"Why stand around waiting for a mate that you may not see and enjoy one of us to give you the thrill you are seeking?" Her long blonde hair was tossed over her shoulder, and her neck was bared as if waiting for someone to bite her. I shivered in disgust, ready to lash out at her for being so forward.

"I've got something that will get them away." Leland nudged me.

"Ladies." He tipped his head. "My friend here says his water park is closed, but you could always slide down my face." He winked.

The women surrounding us giggled, but Miss Violet Eyes scoffed. I, on the other hand, threw my head back in laughter and when I did, the smell of cherry blossoms and champagne hit my nose.

Evelyn was near.

"Excuse me." I went to push through the crowd, finding it more difficult than I thought it would be with the throng of women. But my tall stature allowed me to see over their heads to find the most gorgeous wolf I had ever seen. Could it be possible for someone to be more beautiful than a dream?

I pushed my friends out of the way, watching Evelyn walk toward me. One side of her hair was pinned behind her ears, golden highlights created by the sun of Earth cascaded down her back. Her hands trembled, and her lips parted in awe as she saw me.

I smiled, taking long steps toward her until she leaped into my arms. My suit jacket tightened as I wrapped my body around her. Evelyn's grip grew tight around my neck, pulling at my hair. She breathed heavily; a silent sob wracked her as I held her close.

"So, are you going to reject me now?" I whispered.

"This isn't a dream, right? We aren't dreaming right now, are we???" Evelyn jumped, squeezed my neck, cutting off my air supply. As I choked, she loosened her grip, her nose diving into my shoulder, wetting my suit with her tears.

My hand raked up and down her back while her body trembled. I had been a dick the past week, switching up my days and nights because I wanted her to miss and crave me. Want me. Decide she needed me despite a bond chosen for her. Clara had mind-linked me before the ball began informing me of Evelyn's plan—to reject her mate and only live in the dream world with me.

I soared at those words. She had fallen for me truly, and my heart was about to burst.

"No, we are not dreaming, Evelyn." Her name rolled off my lips like a silent prayer. Her eyes widened, her hands gripping my biceps.

"You know who I am? Wait, of course, you would have seen me up there," she said, trying to reason it out as she pointed to the balcony.

"Oh no, I knew exactly who you were a year and a half ago." I smirked.

Her grip tightened, her head pushing back into my chest. My hand cupped the back of her head, letting my fingers entangle in her hair.

"H-how?" she whispered.

"You make excellent pies, just like your mother."

"No way!" she squealed. "Are you kidding me? That is how you knew? From food?"

I pushed her away, rubbing my stomach. "Oh yes, she made me quite a few pies growing up."

Evelyn's eyes wandered over my face, thoughts racing through her head. "Wait, are you? Are you Kit? Mom's Kit?"

I chuckled, pulling her back into my arms. "Not anymore, I'm your Kit now, Sugar. Now, come here, and let me touch you."

Her face turned red. Reaching for my gloved hand, I pulled it off, ever so slowly, then I took the back of my fingers and brushed her cheeks. Sparks flew down my arm and straight to my dick. Her eyes closed, her face leaning into my touch.

"I should be so mad at you for keeping this secret from me," she said sternly.

"But you won't," I countered. "I told you I was your mate."

She sighed, taking my hand with both of hers.

"I meant what I said. I would have you, take you, and make you mine whether you wanted it or not. It didn't matter. I knew who you were. Are you ready for that? To be mine? Because after tonight you will no longer be an unmated wolf," I growled, pulling back her hair entangled with my fingers.

Her neck bared, I place opened mouth kisses along her neck, tracing her marking spot. It was a damn shame my marks had faded, but soon I would plant a permanent one.

Evelyn moaned. Her body leaned into me, her fingers pulling on my suit. "Yes, more than anything." She sighed, her eyes boring into me.

"Good, now dance with me. I promised your parents I would at least give you one before taking that virgin pussy." My hot breath rolled down her chest and between her breasts.

"Kit," her face flushed. "People can hear you."

"Oh, that reminds me," I chuckled.

"MINE!" I shouted through the ballroom.

Cheers echoed, filling the high ceilings with congratulations and howls of approval. Evelyn glanced behind her, seeing her father and mother in the corner.

Clara rubbed Kane's arm. His jaw was tight, as he held onto Clara. "*One dance, then go claim her,*" Clara's mind-link echoed into my mind. "*I'll take care of her father.*" She looked up at him with such love, but the fury on his face had only strengthened.

Still, I wasn't afraid. He wouldn't keep me from her. No one would.

"Sugar, would you give me this dance?" I let her go, bowing until she stepped forward and put her hands on my shoulders.

"As long as you promise to fuck me later, then yes, I'll dance with you."

I groaned, knowing my cock was going to be hurting for the next five minutes. Pulling her closer, I let her feel my shaft next to her pussy.

"Kit."

I growled lowly in her ear. "Yes, I want you to say my name all night while I take you."

She pressed her lips to my neck, sending fire rushing through my skin. "Everything is so much stronger, the feelings, the touch," she confided in my ear. "I don't think I've ever been this turned on before."

I gripped her waist hard enough to leave bruises. I could smell her. The arousal dripping down her leg. It was potent. I swear to the gods if anyone else smelled it, I would rip them in half.

"Are you wearing underwear?" I growled. My hand traced down her hip to the dress's high slit. With the crowd gathered, dancing with mates or their company for the night, I knew no one would watch. I had claimed her, scented her.

My fingers trailed through the slit of her dress until I touched her bare pussy. "Fuck, Evelyn, what are you doing not wearing anything? Exposing my pussy like that?"

She bit her lip, gripping my shoulders tightly. "So, I could finger fuck myself to sleep, thinking it was you," she confessed.

Dear. Gods.

I cupped her pussy, my body covering my hand where I played with her clit. "This pussy is mine now. You will not play with it unless I am with you," I hissed in her ear. "Every part of you is mine now. I've become a selfish bastard and now that you know I'm yours, I won't let you pleasure yourself any longer. It's my job now," I demanded.

Evelyn whimpered, my finger rubbing her clit. Out of the corner of my eye, I saw Kane had his attention diverted elsewhere. My finger rubbed her folds, her knees buckling.

"Who does this pussy belong to?" I nibbled her ear. Evelyn didn't answer, only leaning into my touch. "Evelyn." I pulled my finger away.

"Nooo," she whimpered.

"Whose pussy is this?" I challenged.

"When did you get so demanding? Where did you learn to say such things?" she quietly argued.

"And when did you become so defiant?" I raised an eyebrow. "I asked you a question."

"Yours, it's your pussy." She bit at her lip.

"Yes, it is, it's mine. And how did I end up this way? Well, let's just say my past year and a half, I have become a demanding bastard that has heard all the wicked ways to please a mate. And believe me, I will please you." Riddick's eyes reflected into hers.

As strong as my mate was physically, she needed to learn to let go. And I, as her mate, would take care of her in all ways, even if she could kick my ass in a sparring ring. Her submissiveness in the bedroom, being able to fully trust me, would be the greatest gift.

Another roar echoed across the room. "MINE!" My hand pulled away from Evelyn's mound when her head perked up to see who the new couple was. She gasped in surprise.

"Melody?" she shrieked. "And Marcus! Oh, my gosh, that's Dad's best friend!"

"Oh shit." I laughed. Kane's face went red with fury.

"Time to go." I pulled Evelyn away from the crowd, her gaze still lingered on Melody, but now wasn't the time. No, the time was for my claiming. I wasn't even sure I could make it to her bedroom. My finger was still wet with her essence. I pulled it up to my nose, smelling her sweet ambrosia.

"Kit! Wait!" Evelyn pulled on my arm, but I immediately threw her over my shoulder. "Gods! What are you doing!" she cried, and I ran up the grand staircase.

"Get her done, Kit!" Leland shouted, his voice reaching over the crowd. I turned around, saluted him, and ran down the darkened royal wing.

Chapter Thirty Two

Evelyn

He carried me down the dimly lit hall. The orbs of light flickered while I listened to the clinking of his decorated lapel. He stopped halfway to my room, his nose flaring, and a deep rumble in his chest shook me.

Oh gods, him smelling my arousal must be too much.

Kit's growls had my thighs tightened, loving the vibrations that shook my body. Gently putting me down, he stepped away. The fire in his eyes tightened my nipples, watching the animalistic hunger in his slow predatory steps. The heat of his stare pushed me back into the wall.

I laid my hand flat on the wall behind me as the ornate chair rail pushed into my lower back. Kit's cock strained against his pants, no doubt enticed by the combination of my shallow breaths and hooded eyes.

Kit.

Kit, the same wolf pup that had wiggled his way into my mother's heart all those years ago. We'd heard stories of the first pup that captured her heart and made her want to be a better Luna for those who were vulnerable.

She would bake pies and cookies around holidays and have them packaged up and sent to the Alabaster Academy.

Not once did I meet the pup, and now I believe that was done purposefully.

"I can't wait another minute," was all his deep voice said while he lowered his lips to mine. My mouth parted, letting the heat of his mouth capture my tongue. First it was slow, tenuous, my body craving more when I wiggled against him.

I had spent my life strengthening my body, to make myself strong and unwavering for any battle I might encounter. My father was the beast of this realm and, being his daughter, I looked up to him. I wanted to be like him—the ferocious beast that protected the realm all those years ago.

Now, I was strong, in the physical sense, anyway. I didn't understand how to pull down the defenses of my heart. I had hidden behind the strength. Fabricated the tough persona so nothing could hurt me or break me.

That was all untrue. My heart could be hurt, and my grandmother had bruised part of it. But My Guard, my Kit, held my heart in the palm of his hand. I had given it to him the first moment I turned eighteen, and I didn't even know it. I had loved him all along.

The decision to let my mind go, to let it float away into the void of doubt, was freeing. I didn't want to be the ruler over my mate, I wanted us to be one, as equals. I wanted to let my burdens be equally carried by the mate that stood before me. I wanted to fully give myself to him, let him take care of me. Not always be the strongest, learn to let go.

And with Kit, I knew I could do that. Let everything go.

Cinder purred in my head, her body rolling onto her back in a sign of submission. She enjoyed that notion, too.

With my hand flicking toward the orb to let its light dim low, Kit's hand slid down my waist and to my hip. Then he ran his hand down my ass and lifted my thigh to wrap around his waist.

"Kit," I moaned.

His other hand cupped my face. His cock pushed into my core. The only fabric now between us was his trousers since the dress slit had been purposefully moved away by his wandering fingers.

"If I had known you were so close to me when you were eighteen, I would have come for you," he murmured against my neck. The open mouth kisses became sucks and nips. "I would have found you, claimed you right then, but somehow the gods had better ideas."

I hissed, feeling his teeth bit into my neck.

"Gods, you look so beautiful, Evelyn." Kit pushed his cock harder into my mound, my body trembling and my high-heeled shoe falling to the floor.

"Did my parents know?" My voice shook.

His finger slipped under my dress's hem along my bare shoulder, allowing my nipple to break free from the prison of fabric containing it. His fangs pierced right above my breast, my head rolled back in delight as I savored the pain and pleasure. I could feel the build of pleasure between my thighs as my hips moved rhythmically against him.

More, I needed more.

"Your mother has known since the day you were born," he mumbled, suckling at my breast.

My fingers tangled in his hair. Soft whimpers echoed down the hallway.

"H-how?" My voice cracked, his finger trailing to my core.

"I think we need to talk about this later. I can't think straight." His hips ground into me further, my breathy gasp causing another bite to my chest.

A throat clearing interrupted us, and my body immediately shut down. Kit was already turned while I covered my body as I pulled up the top of my dress.

"Who the fuck are you?" Kit growled. I clamped my thighs, sticky with arousal, shut, but I could still feel the free flowing of my juices hearing Kit's forceful words. He was, in charge. I didn't have to worry when I was with him, and that turned me on all the more. .

Damn, possessive alpha wolves were hot.

"Warrior," he growled again, and I giggled. His tight ass in his uniform had me licking my lips.

"I'd take a bite out of that." Cinder wagged her tail playfully.

"Ditto. Maybe he could like strip or something like one of those Magic Mike shows? We've got the poster bed for it." I reached out, my hand palming his ass.

Cinder howled inside me. Kit turned his head, an eyebrow arching. Pulling my hand away, I playfully slapped it. "Bad hand, bad."

"I think it is best you leave the hallway, Your Highness." The tone was condescending. I rolled my eyes at the all too familiar voice.

Joshua.

"Sorry, we will be on our way then." I grabbed Kit's hand and pulled, but he didn't budge.

"Did you see her?" Kit growled, stepping away from me to confront Joshua. Kit was larger, but Joshua was broader, his buzzed cut hair and his scowl didn't deter Kit as he stepped up chest to chest with him.

"I asked you a question, guard. How much did you see?" Kit hissed.

"Didn't see much of anything." Joshua shrugged. "Just the sweet smell of Evelyn's arousal flooding down the hall."

"I suggest you learn your place!" Kit growled, his hair rippling down his back. "Or do I need to show you where you belong?" Joshua looked Kit up and down, no doubt assessing the awards decorating his jacket. "I outrank you ten times over," Kit muttered. He pushed his aura more forcefully, letting it leak down the hallway.

Joshua cleared his throat again, feeling the effects of a strong Alpha standing so close.

"I apologize," he stepped away. "Evelyn, I can still take care of him if he is bothering you. He has no right to try to overpower you or make you feel uncomfortable. You said you were waiting for your mate," he spat out the last words.

I held back the head bobbing, finger wagging "oh no you didn't" as Kit growled again.

"She is my fucking mate, you insolent fool. Get out of the royal wing before I drag you out by your dick!" Kit punctuated his threat with a low growl.

I giggled like a damn schoolgirl, holding onto Kit's jacket. It was so fucking hot how territorial he was being. I gripped my thighs together again, trying to hold back the blush decorating my cheeks.

"This true?" Joshua's face softened. I nodded, holding onto Kit's arm.

"Very well, my apologies to you, Your Highness." Joshua bowed and walked down the hallway away from us. The tension in his back radiated as he took the walk of shame back to the party.

Speaking of tension, Kit's didn't seem to go away either, even when my hand rubbed his ass.

"What is your relationship with him?" he asked shortly.

I furrowed my brows in confusion, dropping my hands. "What do you mean by that?" I squealed.

Kit turned, pulling me closer to his body. "He obviously has feelings for you. Knowing your vow to remain pure for me. How close is he as a family guard? A guard is to show no emotion when protecting the royal family, and he obviously was breaking protocol. He acts as if he is your friend, maybe something more."

I tapped my two index fingers together, shifting from foot to foot. My bare feet on the lush carpet was a simple comfort that I shouldn't take for granted. For I knew it was going to be taken away because he was going to haul my ass out of here in a minute and I may never touch the ground ever again.

Males were just like that, all caveman like. Poor Mom was carried around everywhere.

"Remember when I said there was a guard that confessed his feelings for me on Halloween a while ago?"

Kit's glare became impossibly darker as he bore into me.

"Ha, you see. That is the guard that liked me." I pointed down the hallway. "I never told my parents he liked me. He's never touched me or anything. Joshua just gave me creepy vibes, so I just had Mom transfer him out since I didn't need a guard all the time."

Kit sighed, his wolf growling beneath his chest.

Before I knew it, I was thrown over his shoulder and a sharp sting hit my ass. "Owie!! What are you doing?!" Kit raced down the hall, my stomach wanting to heave the small amount of chocolate I had with Melody before our dance.

"We will discuss his transfer out of the palace later," he huffed.

Kits steps slowed, as he took a deep breath, sniffing for my room. He shoved open the double doors into my bedroom and quickly shut them behind us. I had kept this room mostly bare. Just the basic necessities. Unlike Melody, I didn't care to stay cooped up inside my room all day. I craved the outdoors, to run in the forest, to climb the tree that I'd replicated in my dream.

Kit strode over to the dresser. Perfumes, jars filled with makeup, hairpins and the like were swiped to the floor. The loud sounds of glass breaking didn't deter his movements as he grabbed me and set my butt where my things had been moments ago. I squeaked with his abruptness. Kit unbuttoned the first button of his uniform, his tanned neck and thick Adam's apple bobbed free, and I found myself licking my lips.

"How fond are you of this dress?" he continued to unbutton his uniform.

I bobbed my head back and forth. "Not gonna wear it again—" in one swift swipe of his claws, the lower part of the dress was removed, leaving my bare pussy open wide for him to see.

"Perfect," he spread my legs, taking a proper look of what was now his. He had only just seen my pussy in a dream. Now that it was real, I became increasingly shy the longer he looked at it.

"So plump and pretty it is." His tongue took one long lick from bottom to top, and I moaned in happiness.

Kit grabbed my ankles, forcing them on either side of his hips. "Such a flexible little thing, aren't you," he mumbled. "Keep your feet right here." My face turned crimson. In this position, he didn't just get a good look at my pussy but my damn ass!

"I don't think—"

"Hush." He silenced me with a kiss, and I tasted my arousal. I hummed, his body breathing heavily into my chest. "Every part of you is beautiful, Sugar. Every bit of you is mine. Are you ready to submit to me? Let go of all your fear, your hesitation? Let me take care of you?" His cock pushed into my core, rubbing the front of his pants against it. It was too much material, too much clothing between us.

"I've already given you my whole heart. I guess giving you my body can only come naturally," I said breathily.

"Good, I want you to trust me. If you ever feel overwhelmed, don't like what I'm doing, I want you to say 'red' and we stop. Is there anything you don't want me to do to you?" He kissed down my neck, my hips grinding into his cock.

"N-no."

He hummed in delight. "Hmm, we will see. Word still stands. You will say it if I'm too rough?"

"Just because I have a pussy doesn't mean I am one," I countered playfully, pulling his hair.

Seriously, I can take scratches and punches, and he thinks he will hurt me?

"Sugar, don't play. I'm on edge and so close to just fucking you right here on the dresser. Riddick is going insane. He's air humping right now, and it is disgusting to see."

I giggled as Kit's hand trailed down the rest of my dress, ripping it as he went. My breath hitched, feeling the cool air of the open window hit my breasts.

My legs spread wide, Kit discarded the top half of his decorated uniform and buried his nose into my slit. I grabbed his hair, needing something to hold on to while he flicked my clit with his tongue. He wasn't slow in the slightest, feasting on my most intimate body part. His tongue flattened to provide the most surface area for my clit.

My hips gently moved to the rhythm of his licking, his fingers tracing my inner thigh until he slipped one inside my core.

"Kit!" I held onto his hair, pulling at the root.

He groaned, sending vibrations that hit the back of my spine.

"Gods, Kit, what are you doing?"

He hummed again, sticking another finger inside, curling it to the spot that would be my undoing.

"Kit!"

He pulled his face away, thrusting two fingers inside me. "That's it, Sugar, say my name like a fucking prayer. Take my fingers, use them." I panted along with his thrusting, and my hips moved to take them deeper inside me.

"I'm adding another." He pulled his two fingers entirely from my body. "Because if you are going to take this." He shifted his cock in his pants. The enormous outline of his cock looked far bigger than in our dreams. "I will have to stretch you."

Rolling my head back, he pushed in the third finger. I groaned at the tight sting until I was fully stretched. "Good girl, Sugar. Now I'm gonna move. Tell me if it's too much."

"Never, it will never be too much," I cried.

"We'll see," he growled, placing his lips over my clit. While he thrust his fingers inside my core, I cried out when my orgasm climbed. The touches in our dreams were dull compared to what I felt now. I could feel myself soaring into the night, reaching amongst the stars until they exploded before my eyes.

"Cum all over me, yes, Sugar, keep going," he praised. "Let me feel you tremble beneath me. Give me all you got."

The heat of his body was so close to me, his scent encased me in a cocoon of pleasure while he sucked and used the roughness of his tongue to glide over my sensitive nub.

My loud cries echoed through the room as I fell blissfully back to the dresser that had been rocking into the wall. Dents, there had to be dents in the walls by now.

"Kit." I let go of his hair as his face rose from between my legs. His mouth and chin glistened from my cum.

"Fuck, you cum beautifully. Let me clean you up," he muttered, descending back between the folds.

"I can't. I'm jello..."

He raised an eyebrow and my feet, which had been perched on the edge of the dresser. He chuckled, scooping me up in his arms, and laid me on the pale blue duvet covering the four-poster bed. Pushing my legs wide, he licked my inner thighs, cleaning the arousal still seeping out of me.

"That... Wow, oh gods." I threw my arm over my eyes. "So much more intense than in the dream."

His mouth covered my clit again, sucking until he let go with a pop. "Your taste is heightened too. Fuck I'm so hard, Evelyn." He groaned, and a fresh wave of energy filled my body. I wanted him to feel exactly what I had been feeling. Pure and utter bliss.

Sitting up, I pulled on his arm. His trousers still sat on his hips and his cock pushed through the fabric, trying to get free.

"Sugar, wait." He held up his hands, but I had already straddled his legs. I unclipped his belt. The tinkling of the sound sent a new flame to my core. It wanted more. I need more. My claws ripped through the buttons of his trousers, too impatient to peel back his clothing.

"Hey, I still need those!" Kit's hands went to his pants, but my guttural growl warned his hands away. I smiled brightly, ripping them all the way down, along with his underwear, until *it* sprang free.

Fuck, it looked angrier in real life.

Thick veins covered his shaft, and the bulbus head almost looked purple from the blood flowing through it. I reached out, grasping the base, and I licked between his slit, coating my tongue with a pearl of pre-cum. My mate's eyes rolled back into his head, but I pulled away. His neck snapped back, staring in curiosity.

"You watch while I take you in my mouth," I purred.

"Fuck," he sighed heavily, his hand reaching for the back of my head.

Chapter Thirty Three

Evelyn

Kit reached behind my head, tugging at my hair. For a moment, I thought I would be the one in charge, but Kit was taking all the thinking away from me. He was letting me be, letting me get lost in pleasuring him, only him.

He pushed my head lower, his cock reaching the back of my throat. Tenderly, my hands cupped his massive balls. They twitched as I lightly massaged them.

"Evelyn, yes. You feel so fucking good," he hissed.

His praise did not go unnoticed. My core wept with the warmth of his deep voice reverberating in his chest. I sighed happily, absorbing his cock until his fist tightened in my hair, pulling me off.

"Ride my face," he commanded. Even Cinder's ears pricked up in surprise, her head lulling to the side as we replayed his words over in our head. "Sugar, I gave you an order. I expect you to listen."

"But I—"

He sat up so quickly, I missed his calloused arms, shifting my body over his lap, and slapped my ass abruptly.

Holy shit, did he spank me?!

"*Hell yeah, he did,*" Cinder wagged her tail side to side, wiggling her ass like a damn puppy.

"I don't want you thinking anymore. I'm in control in the bedroom," he said firmly. "Isn't that right?" My fists gripped the duvet, my eyes wide not in embarrassment but...arousal? Hell, having him in charge, someone I loved, was sexy as hell. I didn't have to think about my next move like we did when we sparred. I just...followed orders.

Not that I would follow orders for anyone else.

Just him.

"Yes.... Sir?" I questioned. How do I address him? *Hey big alpha daddy?* Cinder shook her head, not liking that name one bit.

"I think calling me Kit will be just fine," he purred, his hand rubbing the sting off my ass. "Or 'he that wields the largest dick in the realm.'"

My mouth hung open until I fell into a fit of giggles.

"Now, straddle my face and put my cock in your mouth," he ordered, all playfulness gone. He pushed his body back into the sheets. My knees took a widened stance around his head. He grabbed my hips, lowering my pussy to his face. "Suck my dick, Little Warrior, we don't have all day," he mocked.

The urge to rub my thighs together was strong but then his tongue lapped my folds. "Kit, gods," I arched my back, my face getting further and further away from his cock.

He paused, slapping my ass with the palm of his hand. "Your mouth isn't on my cock, Sugar."

Oh right.

I licked the tip, concentrating on the task at hand, savoring the rich and salty taste of his cum. I tried to concentrate, sucking him like my life depended on it. My tongue swirled around the head, his mouth humming into my pussy.

"So delicious," he mumbled. My knees faltered, almost slipping in the sheets and falling into his mouth.

"I've got you, Sugar. Don't worry." Grabbing my ass, he pushed it heavier onto his face.

I was choking, taking him deeper to get a rise out of him, he sucked in a breath. The warmth of his breath ran down my thighs.

His balls contracted, my core quivered, pulsing around his tongue.

"Cum on my face, Sugar. Give me what I want!" Kit's command shattered me, his Alpha aura pressing heavily on my body as I fell over and over with pleasure. Feeling my arousal coating his face, he came up for air, growling my name as he shot hot ropes of cum down my throat.

Greedily, I drank him down, sucking him dry while he kneaded my ass like a pup looking for sustenance from their mother.

"Yes, Evelyn, fuck you feel so good." His cock didn't soften, he was getting harder than before. I could feel the ridges of his veins with my fingers, worshiping the cock that was about to grace my pussy. He pulled me away, holding me to his body.

I straddled him, his fingers pushing into my core. I gasped, feeling the sudden abrupt forcefulness of his thick fingers.

"You're ready for me, aren't you?" He grinned lustily.

I nodded, unable to speak. The smirk on his face fell away as he grabbed the back of my head, pulling me into a passionate kiss.

"No pups yet, right?" his eyes sparkled.

I shook my head.

"Good, I need several decades with you before I'm willing to share." He smiled. "Be right back." He left me on the bed, heading to the washroom. Each washroom in the palace contained a tea-type drink that would kill sperm before it left the body. It was the male's job in Bergarian to manage birth control. It had been a surprise to learn that it was considered a woman's job to deal with it on Earth.

I sighed back into the bed, pulling the duvet over my body as I waited. My hand trailed over my breasts, still feeling the heat of his breath, the fire of his touch. My eyes closed for a moment, relishing in my post-orgasm haze, until I saw the curtain move without the help of a gentle breeze.

I kept my eyes to the bathroom door, watching Kit wait for the water from the faucet to heat up to make his sterilization tea. In my peripheral, I watched the delicate movements of the curtain move toward me. The figure's skin was dark, darker than the night with no moon. Then the curtain was fully removed from their body, gently swaying away from the body. The figure now stayed in a crouched position with a dagger in their hand. The gentle sway of cloth, rustling against their skin, barely covered her privates. Yes, it was a her...because I could smell the underlying tone of a female's arousal between her legs.

She had seen what was mine. My mate's cock. She had watched us from the shadows, and I cursed myself for not locking the window. I held back a growl within my chest.

My hands gripped the sheets. I waited for the strike that would inevitably come. I could feel the heat of the silver upon my back. Her steps were silent, but my senses were stronger. How foolish. She thought she could get this close to the daughter of The Beast?

Cinder's claws elongated, gripping the mattress, and our body rolled beneath the sheets before the strike. The female lunged toward the bed, stabbing the mattress, cursing under her breath. She ripped the dagger from my bed, pulling cotton stuffing out along with it. I snarled, now standing completely naked at the head of the bed.

The female gripped her dagger tightly, her eyes widening at my swiftness. I lunged forward, grabbing the wrist that held the dagger, and pushed my naked body into hers. The female landed on her back. Using the inertia from my pounce, I flipped over her and sank my claws into her shoulder, chucking her toward the wall. I gripped the carpet with the claws of my feet and rushed toward her, pinning her against the wall. She grunted, showing long, sharp, thick fangs.

She smelled of feline; I growled, throwing the dagger to the floor. We knocked the table side lamp over, the light illuminating our fight as I wrestled her to the ground. I wasn't expecting for her to fight back once I subdued her, pushing her hands into the carpet. She flung her head forward, bashing me in the nose. I fell away from her, as she reached for my hair, tugging it harshly across the floor.

"The hell!? Neari!?" Kit bolted from the bathroom, his eyes full of rage.

"You know this bitch?" I yelled. "You know this worthless piece of feline?" I gripped her wrist. With a twitch of my body, I could break her grip in an instant, but there was one thing I needed to be sure of.

"We've been on a date," the feline purred. "He promised me things that your worthless body cannot give him."

I raised my eyebrow at Kit. I allowed Neari to feel as if she had the upper hand. She kicked my shin, making me stumble, then pinned me to the wall. Her long claw danced around my throat.

His body shook with rage. "I gave you my intentions; we were practicing for our mates. I laid no hand on you!"

The truth rang true. There was no lie detected. I smirked, thinking what a great game I was about to pursue. It was a common occurrence for males and females to go on dates for "practice." As long as communication was at the forefront, it was not frowned upon.

"You know that is not true," the feline replied. "I get what I want, no one has denied me, yet. You will not be the first."

"Neari," Kit growled. "Let go of my mate."

"She is your mate?" She threw her head back and laughed. "A princess? A worthless princess that cannot defend herself? Spending her time behind the palace walls drinking ambrosia and eating cakes? Wouldn't you prefer a woman who can hold her own?"

This...bitch.

"Evelyn is every bit a warrior. Do you not know her father's name?"

Neari scoffed, picking up the silver blade and touching my neck. Little did she know, such a metal would not harm the body of a half-beast. My lip curled in delight, waiting for her monologue to finish.

"You embarrassed me in front of my pride. For that, you will pay. You will come back with me to my pride. I will take you as my mate, just as my father did to my mother. If you come quietly, I will leave this worthless wolf alive." Kit's eyes peered at me, his face stoic. It was the same stern face I saw the first night I met him all those years ago in my dream.

I winked at him, as his hands fisted at his side.

"No," he shook his head, now directing his attention to Neari. Kit trusted me with all his heart. He knew this animal was no match for my determination and skill.

"No?" she questioned.

Cinder released herself, our body shifting into our half-beast. Fur rippled down my body. Neari lost her grip and fell to the floor. Her eyes filled with resentment, watching me shift. I towered over her, heaving heavy breaths that moved her hair.

"My dad calls me The Warrior Princess, you dumb cunt. Ready to fight this?" I waved my claw down my body. "Ready to see who deserves Kit more?" I smirked.

In a fit of madness, she shifted into her panther. Neari looked like a small kitten, upset over spilled cream. She jumped, trying to latch her fangs onto my neck, but I grabbed her neck in my claws. Her hot breath washed over my body as she dangled above the ground.

I had never killed anyone in all my years of training. I was too young, too naïve to think of the potential consequences of my training. The land had been peaceful since the Dark War, my parents making sure that all territories and kingdoms were allied. Now I would put my training to the test, do what I was trained to do. Protect my kingdom, myself, and most importantly, my mate.

He could handle himself very well, I was sure of it. But this was a symbol of my strength, of our bond. I'd fight a hundred more like her just to prove my love and devotion to him.

Dropping Neari to the ground, she hissed, running to the other side of the room. Her claws scratched the wall tapestries as she tried to climb them to gain an advantage. Fur standing on end, she leapt from the shelf that held the heavy tapestry and jumped into my arms. Her claws grazed my chest.

The adrenaline running through numbed the pain. I wrapped my arms around her torso and squeezed her tightly. Her ribs cracked, her breath hissing from her lungs. Cinder purred in satisfaction.

Taking one clawed hand, I pulled on the top of her maw, the other pulled down on her bottom jaw, ripping it completely from her head. The roar of pain shook the room. Cinder howled in victory as we plunged our claws into her chest and pulled out her still beating heart.

Crimson blood dripped onto the cream-colored carpet. My fur was now matted with the blood of the one who dared to take my mate. The guard, hearing my howls of victory from the other side of the doors, charged in with a blast of energy. Wolves filtered in as I finished the job by smashing her skull to the carpet with my hind foot.

Kit was mine, and this bitch thought she could take him from me. Cinder chuckled. My jaws snapped in warning, my shadow covering the intruders into my bedchambers.

Kit watched me in awe, his lips parted until they drew into a smile. I had protected him, and I would continue to do so until all threats were eliminated.

"Leave," I growled out, my back arching while my hair stood on end.

My bloody paws stepped forward, dripping with the blood of our enemy. Cinder pushed to the surface, ready to take control of the situation. She wanted to murder the guards that stood on the other side of the door. This was my chamber, the chamber I was to be mated in, and now it was tainted. Cinder huffed again in annoyance until Kit placed his warm hand in my claw.

"It's over, Sugar. You did so well." His words soothed me. My giant head lowered to my mate, my body trembling from the adrenaline. He rubbed his face against me. "You're so beautiful, Evelyn."

From the instant I knew the feline had entered, I knew I could overpower her. The question was, how did she find my room? The entire palace was oozing with guards, and she somehow found the one window that led to us.

"Sugar, we are okay now. How about we clean you up and finish what we started?" I lifted my head in confusion. I thought our moment was over when II spilled blood all over the room. Why would he want a female that took control?

Embarrassment shook me. Typically, males wanted to dominate females and show them their strength and possessiveness. I should have let him fight. I did not want him to think of himself as less than.

"Sugar, that was the hottest damn thing I've ever seen. I'm so fucking turned on you went into Alpha mode and kicked her ass." He pulled my claw to his cock. "We are marking each other tonight, there is no doubt about that," he commanded. "Come back to me, Evelyn."

My body's furry appearance disappeared, my soft skin returning to the tanned, muscular body I'd worked so hard for.

"So unbelievably sexy," he purred, releasing his musk onto me again. "Let's find another room. This time, no more interruptions."

Chapter Thirty Four

Kit

"What the fuck happened!?"

The roar could be heard down the decorated hallway of the royal wing. The guards winced, recoiling from the door while I held Evelyn in my arms.

"Kane, let's calm down. We still have guests," Clara's soothing voice tried to reason, but Kane was in a frenzy. Both of his daughters had been claimed, and now an assassination had been attempted. At least he knew of my intentions, but now that his youngest daughter was claimed by his best friend, he was going to be in a pissy mood.

"The hell?!" he exploded, the light orbs shaking in their torches. Guards bared their neck, whispering apologies.

"Hey, Dad," Evelyn chirped. She was still naked, stepping up to her father, who covered his eyes. "Jesus, Princess, you're naked." Looking down at herself, she was covered in blood. Clara's eyes widened, looking past her daughter and in at the bloody massacre.

"What happened!? Evie, are you okay!?" Clara hugged her daughter, not caring if the blood stained her ballgown.

"I'm fine," Evie smiled. "Took care of some panther that tried to lay a claim to my mate."

Kane growled. "Get a blanket on, Evie. We don't need to have the entire kingdom looking at you."

I smirked, pulling her to me, covering her nakedness with my own. My cock rubbed against her thighs and a sweet purr left her chest.

"Kit," Kane growled. "Now is not the time to test me. Get your fucking paws off my daughter in my presence."

Evelyn giggled while Clara draped a blanket around the both of us.

"That isn't what I meant, baby," Kane eased his tone for her.

"Alpha, they are mates. They were trying to seal the deal and got interrupted. You can't tell mates to keep their hands off each other!" She shook her head.

"I damn well will, too. Just wait until I get my hands on Marcus. He's gonna wish he was never born, that bastard. His cock has been everywhere, then he gets mated to my child!" he roared. The vein on the side of his head pulsed, and Evie held in a laugh.

"Enough of that, Kane. Now, can someone tell me how a panther got in here?" Mom sniffed around the room, seeing the squashed skull in the carpet.

"Cheesus, Evie. You certainly made a mess!" Clara sighed, shaking her head.

"Is there a preferred etiquette when fighting against some assassin trying to kill me in my bedroom? I think I might have missed that lesson," Evelyn chided.

"That sounded awful, Evie. I'm sorry. It's just that you fight like your father. You like to make big messes and leave a statement." Her eyes gleamed at Kane, but his vision was focused on the guards in the hallway.

"Find out how the fuck she got in here," he demanded. "I want to know what guards were on duty and how they let this slip up happen. The entire platoon will pay for this in the morning!" Kane continued to yell down the hall, chasing guards and ripping his clothes at the seams.

"Go take one of the guest rooms." Clara raced down the hallway after Kane. "Kane! Do not shift in the hallway right now! We will figure this out!"

Evelyn rubbed her nose in my chest, the blanket still covering us. "Come on," she purred. "We still got something to do."

Keeping the blanket wrapped around us, we fell into the guestroom across the hallway. This one had a small window, and I immediately went to check it. It was closed, and my first instinct was to lock and then barricade the damn thing with the chest of drawers that sat to the right of it.

"Kit," Evelyn said, stepping into the shower, her finger beckoning me to follow. With a skip in my step, I stood in the bathroom. The steam shower was already running, the heat of the room teasing shivers from my skin.

"Kit," she called again with a purr. I stepped around the massive bathroom until I rounded the corner, finding an open shower with three gigantic heads of water cascading down her body. Each drop was a delicious temptation that I wanted to devour.

Her body was already clean from the blood spilt just minutes before. Her mind was not with me. Evelyn had buried her worries about Neari breaking into her room. A fire burned inside her; Cinder was furious someone tried to take us. Me. I found it extremely sexy for a woman to fight for me. Evelyn's power exceeded my own. She was a half-beast and had taken down the daughter of the former alpha of the panther tribe with barely a flick of her wrist.

My cock hardened. Her hands were lathered with soap. "Let me clean you." My mind fogged, concentrating on the hands that had been harsh just moments ago, now gentle as she caressed my body. She hummed. My hands traced her waist, grabbing her ass roughly.

Evelyn might be stronger in the ring, but it would be me that dominated in the bed.

"Turn around," I growled. She had only just begun to massage my cock, but I wasn't cuming in this shower or in her mouth. I wanted my cum to slide into her womb, to feel her slickness around the ridges of my angry head.

Growling again, she turned her body to the wall, pressing her tits into the cold tile, gasping at the feel. I slid my cock between her ass cheeks, my hand slinking around her waist and to her core. "What would you think of me taking your ass one day?" I nipped her ear. "Take you not only in your pussy, but into your forbidden hole?"

The cold tile warmed, her breath coming in at an unsteady rhythm.

"Words, Sugar. Tell me," I commanded.

"Maybe one day, that seems advanced," she squeaked. Her submissiveness shined through, the once tough warrior pulling her walls down for me to control her.

"I agree. We have plenty of time, especially with this pussy I'm about to take." I rubbed her clit three times, then plunged into her core. The heat was evident, her slick easily flowing down my fingers. "So wet, are you ready to take my dick, Sugar?" She reached behind my head, pulling my hair.

I slapped her thigh, causing a breathy moan to leave her lips.

"Yes!" she cried, my nose tracing her neck.

"Let's get you prepped then, huh? I must start all over, since we were so rudely interrupted," I admonished. A second finger entered her, her pussy pulsing around me. Then a third. Pumping it wildly into her pussy, her hips rhythmically followed.

"That's it, my mate, get nice and wet for me," I growled in her ear. "Ride my fingers, yes. Gods, you are so hot, Sugar. I've daydreamed of sinking my cock into your pussy for far too long." My cock rubbed on her ass, seeking my own friction as she thrust onto my fingers with a delectable sigh. Turning her roughly against the wall, my lips descended on hers, taking her moans and making them my own.

Pulling her to my side, I barely wrapped her in a towel to dry her. I stumbled toward the bed, the towel barely covering her body. She laughed and I along with her until we fell in an entangled heap on the bed. I didn't know where our bodies began or ended. Mouths, hands, legs—touching all of her body parts had riled me up until I could take no more. I would spend more time worshiping her later.

Right now, I had to have her.

I had to sink myself into her before something disastrous happened. My mouth left her nipple, her hair sprawled carelessly on the pillow. She looked like a fucking goddess. Her body was covered in my marks, pink, purple, beautiful marks that would only last a day. The one mark I needed to give her was to come.

My cock bobbed as I sat back on my heels, taking in the goddess before me. I smirked at her hip tattoo while I pressed my cock to the outside of your pussy.

"If it's too much, I'll stop," I whispered, leaning over her.

She shook her head. "I'm a big girl. I think I can handle that monster," she quipped, but the swirl of fear still lingered in her eyes.

Not wanting to hurt her, I softened my eyes. "Breathe for me, baby, that's it. You can take it, just relax. Nothing to fear. You can take it. You were made for me, remember?" I slid my cock inside halfway and then with one swift thrust I bottomed out inside her. Her back arched and a silent scream stilled my movements. My body heaved over her chest, waiting for her to come back to me.

"Shh, it's okay, Sugar. All done now. I'm so far inside you." My body shook with anticipation, her legs wrapping around me until her eyes hit me.

"More," she moaned. "Move."

My lips captured hers once more before I slid out of her pussy, only to push in again. Our wolves howled, the fire between our bodies only increasing. Her claws raked my biceps and back, then tangled into my hair.

My hips thrust forward again, pushing the entirety of my cock into her body.

"How do you feel?" I asked with a ragged voice. My ability to hang on much longer before I spilled my seed inside her wavered.

"So"—she panted—"full."

Delighted by her answer, I reached my arms around her lower back, tilting her hips to get my cock in deeper still.

"Kit!! Gods!"

My chest swelled, as the inner walls of her core massaged my cock. Her claws scratched my back, sinking deeper into the skin.

"That's it. Dig your nails into me, Sugar. Mark me, cum on my cock and let everyone know who you belong to." I thrust inside her, feeling her thighs tremble. "Cum on my cock, Sugar. I want to feel your fluids run down my balls."

She fell and I along with her. The slapping of our skin was all I could hear while we roared each other's names. Both of our fangs elongated, and I pierced her skin with my wolf. Riddick howled in victory, our hold becoming impossibly tighter around her body.

The sweet sharp pain in my own neck fueled my orgasm to pull more seed, more pleasure from my body than I ever thought possible. It was so long, so euphoric, I was having an out-of-body experience. Her body went limp, her legs falling from around my body. My cock still lodged inside her, I lifted my head to lick her new mating mark.

My cock stirred again, seeing my mark on her body. My hips moved on their own, my cock gently caressing the walls of her pussy.

"Kit," She said my name again.

I swore she was making up for all the years she had not said my name. I had heard my name more this night than in my entire life. I grinned wildly, seeing her flushed cheeks.

Pulling my cock from her body, she groaned at the loss. My cum leaked from her, coating the sheets below us. "Roll over, Sugar," I growled. Obeying me like the good mate she was, she rolled her body over and raised her knees slightly off the bed.

"Your ass is gorgeous, Sugar." I nipped at it playfully before my cock tickled her lower lips. Sinking into her pussy, I cursed, feeling her pussy in a whole new way. "Fuck Sugar, are you okay?" My hand rubbed up and down her back. Forcing her ass backward, I sank my cock deeper into her body.

"More!" She moaned.

"Shit!" I grabbed her hips and fucked her relentlessly, the elaborate metal frame thumping the wall of the bed. Guttural growls left me. A primal instinct to make her mine in every position possible filled my head. Over a couch, a desk, in the forest. I wanted it all. I craved her, I wanted her and wanted to own every part of her.

Riddick growled ferociously. Grunts and moans intertwined in the room. My dick filling the fluttering walls of her pussy, I grabbed her hair and pulled it roughly.

"Who do you belong to, Evelyn?"

Her hips pushed back with every thrust, filling her body with my cock.

"You, Kit. I belong to you!" she screamed as I hit her sweet spot.

"And I belong to you, Sugar," I roared. "We are each other's, aren't we?"

"Yes!"

"Now be a good little wolf and cum all over your mate's cock." Holding on to the last reserve left in me, I waited until I felt the fluid of her body encase my cock. It was an electric shock that flowed over me effortlessly while I roared her name. Even the gods would know of our mating.

Evelyn crashed into the sheets, our bodies dripping with sweat. Laying at her side, I kept my dick inside her, holding her, spooning her. Draping her leg atop of mine, I reached my hand between her breasts and gently cupped her neck possessively.

"Mine," I muttered into her neck, kissing it sleepily.

"Mine," she whispered back.

Chapter Thirty Five

Evelyn

My back arched, my ass hitting something hard behind me. I stilled because that was not the usual problem that greeted me in the morning. No, usually it was drool, messy, tangled hair, and a snort that wakes me. Yet it wasn't really morning, and I wasn't waking up in reality but back in our dream world.

My eyes opened, seeing the rustic walls of our cottage, his arm over my torso, slinking between my breasts and holding onto my neck softly. The small snores made him look like the same young man I met so many years ago.

We could do the hanky panky, even in our dreams.

While I didn't wake up in my usual tree limb, and he didn't wake up in the middle of the forest, we were both now laying in the comfortable bed we had created. We didn't have to look for each other or find our usual spot.

I sighed deeply, feeling the thrumming of his heart behind me. My breath caught every time he mumbled my name in his sleep. I gently moved his gripped hand from my neck and slipped past him, putting a pillow in my place. He frowned but continued to slumber.

His rock-hard cock could be seen in the outline of the sheets, and my mind teamed with ideas.

"Oh, you should lick it," Cinder purred. *"Have him wake up to a mind-blowing blow job."* I shook my head, trying to keep quiet.

"You are such a perv, Cinder."

"Don't tell me you weren't thinking it, too?" She side-eyed me.

Gently pulling the sheet from his body, ready to take in a hungry, taste worthy look, his hand snapped around my wrist, pulling me to the bed. I giggled while he hovered on top of me, his devilish smirk beaming with mischief.

"And what do you think you're doing there, mate?" His nose ran up my neck, and chills erupted down my spine.

"Just a peek?" I breathed softly.

His open mouth kisses traced my shoulders. Once he reached my marking spot, I let out a moan so loud he chuckled into my skin.

"You may be the Alpha on the battlefield, but I am the Alpha in bed."

My legs squeezed together, rubbing incessantly while his lips worshiped my breasts. He nipped, sucking on the pink nipple as I grabbed his hair, giving it a gentle tug. He released, going back to my neck and sucking hard, leaving nothing but markings all over my body. I paused, my hand stopped pulling his hair, and my breathing shallowed.

Sensing my mood change, he lifted his head, pecking at my lips, and rubbed his nose against mine. "You are thinking awfully hard there, Sugar."

I opened my mouth several times to reply, but nothing escaped my lips.

"Keep that up, Evelyn, and I'm gonna put something in that mouth."

My eyes widened, and I covered my mouth with my trembling hands.

How scandalous was he? Mr. No Emotions, and here he was telling me where he was going to stuff his cock.

"Alright, just one question." I raised my finger shakily.

His head bent down, taking my finger into his mouth, and sucked it tenderly, releasing it with a pop. "Ask me," he commanded.

"Well, I can't very well bloody concentrate when you are sucking on me like that!" I squealed, trying to wiggle away from him. His body was too close, and my mind was wandering further away from my question.

Pulling me back into his arms, his cock straining against my thigh, he stilled and petted my hair tenderly. "Alright, I'll stop. Now ask me so we can get back to dream fucking."

My pussy quivered.

"Okay," I breathed. "So, did you know that leaving a massive hickey on my neck a week ago would lead my father to bring me home? Did you plan all of this, our meeting, your claiming me at the ball?"

He cocked his head in confusion. "What?" he shook his head. "What are you talking about?"

"The hickey that was covering the entirety of my neck and shoulder!" I exclaimed. "Did you know I would wake up with that mark on my body?"

He blinked.

"I woke up the next day," I explained. "It was all over me. Then, it was gone in like thirty-six hours, but it was enough time for my dad to throw a huge fit when I talked to him through the mirror! He demanded I come home, but once I got home, he wasn't mad anymore. He didn't even mention the hickey and acted like nothing had happened!"

Kit rubbed his chin, his dark hair falling into his eyes. His hand stroked my naked body, running his finger around my nipple. It instantly hardened, and my panting quickened.

"I didn't know that the hickey would show up." His lips quirked into a smile. "So that is why he gave me the evil eye when I walked into the ballroom."

"What? So, you didn't know?"

He laughed. "No, I didn't. But I had talked to your parents right after our dream, right after I ate that sweet cunt of yours." I blushed. "I got a hold of them as quick as I could. Told them you were my mate, said you were mine, and I wanted you sooner rather than later. That I had waited far too long over the past year and a half. I had to have you." His lips gently kissed mine.

"That was when your mother said she would bring you home. I guess your father, in a fit of rage, saw the hickey on your neck and yelled at you instead. Giving them the perfect reason to bring you home without questioning it." Kit's finger trailed over my hip to my tattoo, smiling as he traced the wording. "They were to keep it a secret, by my request. I'm glad your father kept that secret because I think I found our meeting rather memorable, don't you?"

"W-why would you do that?" I backed away. "You knew all along? My parents did, too? That's why mom kept pushing me to get all dressed up?"

Kit's eyes softened, dragging me back under him. "Listen here." His nose ran up my neck, and my anger dissipated. "I needed you to love me without a bond, Evelyn. I've loved you, even as a child. Not in a creepy way." He chuckled. "You helped me grow into the wolf I am now. It was your turn to grow, to find yourself. You had to fall in love with me without a bond. Find who you are without your grandmother. It only made us that much stronger in the end, don't you think?"

There had been one other couple in the Bergarian realm that had fallen in love before sealing a bond. Their love and bond were so strong, it was envied by many mated couples.

Kit kissed me tenderly. As much as I wanted to be angry, being the only one not knowing, I couldn't be. Not when he wanted our bond to be just as strong as the couple that had become famous for it.

I reached up, brushing his cheek with my thumb. Kit may be stoic, stern, and unreadable to others, but to me, he was an open book. He'd thought of my needs before claiming me as his. Cinder purred in my chest. Feeling the vibrations seep into him, he closed his eyes, as I brushed my fingers across his cheeks.

"You're so beautiful," I whispered.

He grinned, gently shaking his head. "I'm supposed to be sexy. Don't think you can call an Alpha wolf beautiful," he joked.

I smiled back at him, running my fingers over the stubble of his beard. "No, you are. For the longest time, I thought of you as the most beautiful wolf I had ever seen. Even when I was just ten years old."

He chuckled, putting his full weight on me. "Is that so?" His nose traced my neck again, sucking on my neck. "Wonder if I could cover your entire body with my marks so no one would dare come near you. Would they all show up in reality?"

"Not sure if my dad would appreciate that," I murmured, leaning into his touch.

"Well, you're mine now. Not much else he can do about it."

"Listen, my dad is grumpy." I waggled my finger at him. "But he is going through a lot. He lost two daughters in one day, and the other one he wasn't expecting."

Kit shrugged his shoulders, not caring. He grabbed my hips, pulling them up to his face. My upper back was on the sheets, my head buried into the pillow behind me. He was holding my hips like they were a large slice of watermelon, my legs thrown over his shoulders.

"Now, if you excuse me." He winked. "I'm going to eat my breakfast." His cock was pressed into my back, my hips held in his large hands as his mouth descended onto my pussy. One lick had me moaning so loud, he smiled into my lips. Gentle hums thrummed through my clit as he licked each fold and teased me.

"Don't play," I panted.

His tongue was everywhere but where I wanted it. His hands kneaded my hips and my ass as he held me above the bed. Kit was holding me at such an angle he could look down into my eyes as he ate me, licked me, devoured me.

I don't think I ever read anything like this in my romance novels.

My hips rolled, feeling him finally latch onto my clit with his teeth. The sweet pain mixed with his gentle licking and pushed me over the edge faster than I had ever thought possible. He smiled, satisfied, gently lowering my body to the bed.

He laid beside me, pulling me on top of him. "Fuck, your pussy is so warm." My pussy rubbed against his cock. "I need you, Evelyn." He gripped my hips, my arousal still shining on his chin.

"Fuck, take me." Feeling bold, I lifted my hips, grabbing his cock with my hand. His shaft, covered in thick veins and an angry head, probed my entrance. I braced for the thickness of his rod as it slowly sank into me until he was completely sheathed.

"Again, baby. Pull me out of your body again."

My body thrummed with happiness, glad that I didn't have to make the decisions to take control. I could just...be.

"That's it, Sugar. Fuck." He pushed his hips up, capturing my pussy again. "Now, I want you to lean back so I can watch your pussy take me," he rasped. My nipples tightened as my body slowly lowered. "Fuck, such a wonderful mate I have. Look at you, taking my cock so beautifully."

"Kit," I whined, running my pussy up and down his shaft.

"Keep going, you are doing so good. Let's go faster, yeah?" His hands gripped my hips, helping me slide up and down his cock. "That's it, gods, look at your breasts." Kit sat up, latching onto one while I continued to bounce.

"Fuck, fuck," he gripped my hips, pulling me up and down again. "I'm gonna cum, Sugar. Are you close?"

Hell, I'm always close with him.

"Yes!" I gripped his shoulders, sinking my claws into him.

"That's it, baby, a little more." His cum shot inside me, giving the relief that my tight pussy needed. My back arched, still pumping my core to milk him of his seed. It cooled the fire that we'd ignited. My breasts felt heavy, his hand gripping them tightly, rubbing his face against them.

"So fucking pretty. My mate is everything," he purred.

I fell on top of him. He kept his dick inside me. Which, I believe, was his favorite thing. His fingers trailed up and down my back as we lay in our dream.

We no longer had to be apart. Neither in the dream nor in the real world.

Chapter Thirty Six

Evelyn

Water cascaded down my back. Kit's hand firmly gripped my hair while I knelt before him. He was breathing heavily. The steam continued to rise in the shower while I passionately sucked on his enlarged cock. I hummed, his string of curses filling the shower.

"Touch yourself, Sugar. Let me see that hand wander between your legs," he rasped. He leaned firmly against the wall, holding on to my hair like a lifeline.

I felt a nudge in my link, and I groaned internally. Kit was in a state of bliss. His head rolled back against the cold wall, the water blasting into his chest. Not a chance I was letting go. The nudge came in harder, the urgency clear.

"*What?*" I linked, licking his tip.

"*Evie? It's been a week, I need you to come out of your room,*" Mom said quickly. "*We have things to discuss.*"

"*Mom,*" I whined, plunging my mouth back onto his shaft. Hitting the back of my throat, I gagged, my mate giving a guttural growl of approval.

"I wouldn't disturb you if it wasn't important. I know finding your mate is...well, important." Her nervousness leaked through our family bond, and I had the urge to stop to have a proper discussion.

Almost.

"Give us fifteen." I cut the link before mom could figure out what was happening, and my throat closed tight.

"Fuuuuck, Evie!" he hissed, spilling his cum down my throat. Panting, pulling me to his body, he kissed the lips that still had remnants of his essence.

"Turn around, my turn," he rasped, but I put my hand to his chest.

"Mom asked if we could come out of our room. Seems urgent." I grabbed the soap and washed his body.

"Can't keep the queen waiting, can we?" he purred, wrapping his arms around my waist. "I wonder what it could be."

"Probably Dad having an aneurism over Melody, or maybe he's over it and now wants to bite into you," I joked.

"Ah, no," he said confidently. "I asked permission first. I get a free pass at the whole 'I'm going to kick your ass if you hurt my daughter.' Besides, I'm your mom's favorite. I'm like family."

"Cocky much?" I laughed, stepping out of the shower.

"What the ever-living FUCK!?" Kit roared.

Mom stared at Kit in shock. Dad gripped Mom's shoulders to help her sit down.

This was Kit's first time being in the family office. It was situated in the family wing and was where we held our family meetings about important issues or just talked as a family without having the guards hovering over us. It used to be filled with our immediate family and Grandmother and Pop, but now it just held the twins, my parents, Kit and me. Melody was in the library, trying to sort out this mess.

Heavy bags darkened Dad's eyes. He clenched his fists and buried his nose in Mom's shoulder. His tatted chest rose and fell quicker by the minute and if we weren't careful, he was going to explode too.

I gulped, not fully believing what I'd just heard.

Joshua, the Royal Guard that had worked alongside the family since after the Dark War, had declared Kit as unfit to be my mate. Word had spread that I had killed the panther shifter that snuck into my bedchambers and that Kit hadn't helped in the slightest. That he just watched me take down the panther myself, but he and I both knew I could handle it. Neari was barely an Alpha panther, with no training and skills to overpower me. Kit knew it would bring a new high to me, to show my strength to him, that I could protect him too.

Joshua did not see it that way. In fact, his argument had spread like wildfire throughout the kingdom while we romped in a bedroom for a week. Joshua had gone to the library, pulling old scrolls, and looked for a way to break our bond. When he found nothing, he did something so vile it made the bile in my throat rise against my throat.

He found an old law, one that had not been enacted for thousands of years. He wanted to prove that Kit was not enough of a wolf to protect me, that I would need two wolves to make sure I was always safe since I was the next in line to the throne.

Like all royals, our blood was so powerful we could have more than one mate if we so desired. It was a practice used thousands of years ago but was now frowned upon. According to the law, I had no choice but to take Joshua as a mate for the sake of the kingdom.

"I don't share!" Kit growled. "Evelyn is mine, and I am hers. That is all that is needed by the goddess. I did not act; I did not fight against her attacker because Evelyn is strong in her own right! It would have been an insult to her if I stole her battle."

Dad only nodded, agreeing with Kit. "You're right. Evie would have been sore at you. However, Joshua has declared this in front of hundreds of wolves using an old law and using it for his advantage. It's called, 'The Challenge.'"

"Challenge?" I asked. "What sort of challenge?"

Melody wandered in, Marcus trailing closely behind her. Dad growled, stood up, and yielded his seat beside mom to Melody. Marcus smirked, standing behind Melody.

"I looked deep into the archives. This law is old and hard to read because of the dialect, but in layman's terms, if a wolf can give good reason why a shifter mated to the royal is 'unfit,' they can challenge them. It usually ends in death because this would be done before the bond marking. However, there is a subclause that if the couple is already marked, then it will be a fight until the true mate yields. If the true mate yields, then the royal will end up with two mates." Melody rolled up the parchment.

"Never, I'll fight the bastard. Who does he think he is? I'm a fucking Alpha now," Kit growled. My thighs tightened together watching him pace the room back and forth. "Where is he? Could he not say this to our faces?"

Damn, he's hot.

Mom sighed, her hand reaching for Dad. He was glowering at Marcus, who eyed him playfully. Marcus then put his hand on Melody's shoulder, and Dad lost it. He pounced on the couch and pushed Marcus to the ground. Dad's roars filled the room while mom screamed for him to stop.

"Yeah, Dad! Kick his ass!" Dax screamed.

"Let me try, let me help!" Dimitri piled on top of Dad while his fists crunched into Marcus's face.

"Kane! That is enough! Stop!" Mom shouted. Melody stood up from the couch, clenching the parchment. I grabbed her, pulling her away from the fight, pushing her to sit on the couch. Kit jumped over the sofa to help Mom, pulling Dad away from Marcus, who laid on the floor. Dad had straightened his back, rubbing the blood off his cheek, then spat in Marcus's face.

"You will never be good enough for her," Dad pointed at Marcus. "Not my baby. You won't touch her."

Marcus shook his head, his face healing.

"Enough!" Mom yelled. Everyone stilled as her aura leaked through the entire room. It was stifling, more so to Dad, who fell to the sofa.

"Kane." She pointed to him. He whimpered, hearing his name being used. "You will not hit Marcus in my presence. We are not here to discuss their bond. Kit has a fight to prepare for, and this is not helping. Stop ignoring your son-in-law, and you take him out to practice."

"Baby," he purred.

"No, don't you baby me!" she cried out. "The fight is tomorrow, Kit."

My eyes widened.

I jumped up from the couch. "What, that isn't enough time! I still think we should break the law. I mean, you are Queen, Mom! Can't you just say, 'forget it!'?"

"Doesn't work that way." Mom shook her head. "Joshua has made a spectacle of it. It has to be done. Kit is obviously stronger, so I'm not sure why he would dare to challenge him. That is why I need your father to go over some moves with him. Make sure he's ready for anything."

"Can I just kill him?" Dad growled. "That seems to be the better option."

"Just because we are royalty doesn't mean we are dictators, Kane. We have our kingdom to worry about. If we broke this one law, the people would think we can break any law for the betterment of our family." Mom rubbed her temples. "After the fight is over, I will see if we can abolish this law, so this doesn't happen again."

"Baby," Kane stood up from the couch to hold her.

"No!" She pointed her finger. "You are being punished."

Dad's eyes softened, looking down at the floor.

"Aw, Dad, you did a great job. Look, Marcus is taking forever to heal!" Dax said, pulling Dad's arm.

"Wish you could have got him in the nuts, right, Melody?" Dimitri added.

Melody swayed her head, silently laughing.

"You don't have to do this." I pulled on Kit's arm. "I can go kill him while he sleeps."

Kit chuckled, sitting back on the couch with me. "Sugar, you have proven to me time and time again you can take care of yourself. You are powerful, brave, everything a royal woman like yourself can be. Now, with this challenge, I see it as a good thing. I will prove to the entire kingdom I can take care of you. That I will protect you if for some wild reason, you cannot take care of yourself." Kit rubbed away the tear on my cheek.

"I don't think you should have to prove your worth. You are already everything I wanted. A worthy wolf," I muttered. "You grew up as a war-rior wolf and look where you are now? All those years working so hard, training, getting accepted into the Academy. Hell, you even showed me a few things." I chuckled.

Kit rubbed my leg. "Sugar, this will be fine. I promise you; this will be a piece of cake."

Melody bit her lip, squeezing the parchment in her hands, opening and closing it.

"Melody?" I reached for her hand, so she'd sit beside me. This time, Marcus stood on the other side of the room, watching her with possessive eyes. "I'm sorry I haven't been around," I whispered.

Giving a cramped smile, she leaned her head on my shoulder.

"It's alright, I've been trying to find a way out of this for both of you. It has been a pleasant distraction," she whispered.

"Do you not want him to be your mate?" I asked through our link.

"I'm not sure. Dad seems to think he is just another horny wolf. But what am I to do when he is my destined mate?" Her wolf howled lowly inside her.

"You do what you think is right, Melody. Follow your heart. The goddess paired you with him. Maybe there is more to him than meets the eye?"

She nodded sadly, gripping the parchment once more.

"I'm going to go do some more research. See if I can find anything." Hugging me, she slowly stood and nodded for Marcus to follow. Dad snarled, but Marcus kept his distance from Melody, but there was an unspoken glare from Marcus to Dad that he would follow his mate to the ends of the earth.

Chapter Thirty Seven

Evelyn

The thrumming of music pulsed over the royal stand. The once ragged, well-worn sparring ring had been transformed into an elaborate arena filled with bleachers, seats, and an overly decorated viewing box for my family.

I wrung my hands, bouncing my leg up and down as the stands filled.

"Evie, everything is going to be fine." Mom grabbed my hand, petting it softly with the pad of her thumb. "This is Kit we're talking about here. There is no way he will not win this fight."

I cursed under my breath, receiving a scowl from Mom. "I can't help but feel like there is something up Joshua's sleeve." I banged my fist on my leg. "He was cowering at the sight of Kit just a week ago. Joshua's wolf told him to back down, and he did. Then he has the balls to announce this challenge without even speaking to us?" My growl echoed through the stand. The servants that were bringing our lunch backed away with their trays, the cups clinking against the metal.

"Calm." My mother's aura of calming, gifted by Charis, swept over me, causing my breath to let out slowly. "He did it the cowardly way. That is why he has been released as a Royal Guard."

My eyes widened, and my hand tightened around Mom's.

"He showed crudeness, even announcing the challenge to the township nearest to the Crimson Shadows's pack. August was the one who sent word about his announcement, and your father swiftly stripped him of his title when he returned to the palace. He is no longer welcome in our presence. He has turned many against Kit because the wolves do not know your mate because of his time in the Academy. However, I have made arrangements to have the entire school here to cheer him on." She nodded to the stands.

I smirked, watching the white uniformed guards filling the arena. The Academy was prestigious and highly valuable in the kingdom, shaping and molding shifters that otherwise would have just been warriors, their true potential wasted. Having them here would show the shifters that didn't know my mate, that he was an honorable wolf.

My gaze wandered to the stairway. Marcus followed close behind Melody, growling at any male that came too close to her. I smiled, thinking that in time, their match would prevail.

"Mom, Kit told me you knew when I was a baby that I would be mated to him." My mom hummed in agreement, sitting back on the single throne that sat on the platform. Dad had refused to have Mom have her own throne. Once Dad arrived, they would share it and she would sit on his lap promptly cradling her.

"How did you know exactly?"

Mom flicked her fingers over the arm of the chair, probably hunting her memories.

"It was a feeling. A warm, glorious feeling, and I swore I saw a golden glow as Kit held you in his arms." Mom leaned her head in her hand. "The gods put people in our lives, and somehow, we latch onto those once strangers and make them our own. Kit was the wolf that I was destined to meet. He was one of many pups that liked to hang around with me in the kitchen all those years ago, but it was Kit that always shined in my heart. Little did I know that by taking him under my wing, helping the little runt that had no confidence, I would start him on the journey to where he is today—a strong Alpha and worthy enough to have my daughter as a mate."

My eyes filled with tears, but I dared not let them fall. Not here, not in front of all these shifters. "What about Melody? Did you know anything about her?" Melody and Marcus were walking up the stairs on one side of the platform while dad came up the other.

"Out of all of my children, Marcus didn't hold Melody as a baby. I didn't get as strong of feeling like I did with you and Kit, but there was something there I couldn't put my finger on when they were in the same room. I think Marcus felt something too but denied it." Mom's voice saddened.

"Something happened to him during the war, so many years ago, Evie. He isn't the same wolf, and I had feared he would have done something drastic in time." Melody stepped onto the platform and sat beside me, along with Marcus, who took her hand in his. She still had parchments in one hand, skimming through the ornate, hard-to-decipher cursive.

"*Melody may not realize it, but she has saved Marcus's life. The personality I came to love from him so many years ago is resurfacing, and the light in his eyes has returned,*" Mom linked.

Dad growled, causing me to jump. Marcus stood, putting his arm over his chest, and bowed. The smirk he held was full of mischief, but Dad was still in a foul mood. Dad was as quick to get angry as he was to forgive once he beat the shit out of you, but with Marcus, he did not radiate that. We were going to be in for a long ride with Marcus and Melody's courtship. More so with Dad being upset with his best friend being destined for his daughter. I think Melody may pull through just fine on her own.

"*Sugar?*" Kit linked me. His confidence radiated through our bond, and I sighed in relief. "*You're worried?*" He chuckled. "*I thought you would think*

*better of me. I prove my worth to you and your family, and your wolf is
shaking."*

Cinder was shaking, but not in fear he would fail. Fear that something
was up Joshua's paw. He was a strong guard, graduating from the Alabaster
Academy same as Kit, but he was no match for my mate.

Then why challenge?

"Everything will be fine," he said soothingly. The crowd roared, specifically in the Alabaster section of the crowd. The howls of cheers, laughter,
and congratulations weaved through the thickness of the torment surrounding me.

He will win, I know it.

Kit stood in front of our box, naked as the day he was born. He turned,
showing no hidden weapons and no magical aid to help him win the fight.
His hands cupped his privates, and I couldn't help but blush.

Kit's announcer, who stood to the right of our platform, began his spiel
of Kit's awards and accomplishments. The Alabaster Academy roared their
pride, banging on the wooded bleachers.

"The gods have smiled sweetly on the Alabaster graduate who graduated
to Alpha just a year ago, giving Evelyn, the crown princess, next in line to
the throne, a worthy mate." Shifters that had yet to choose sides awed at the
statement. I stood up, leaning over the railing, smiling sweetly and waving
like a proper princess should.

Another announcer joined our platform to introduce Joshua. I sneered
at him as I sat, but I couldn't do anything real to him because he was only
doing his job. He shied away, clearing his throat, and announced all of
Joshua's achievements. Royal guard for so many years, blah blah. I waved
my hand around like I was bored, yawning until Mom smacked me to shut
up and sit down.

"And the reason for this challenge by Joshua," the announcer drawled.
"Princess Evelyn was in her chambers with Alpha Kit when an assassin
came into the room and attempted to murder the princesses. Kit did not

lift a finger, and watched the entire ordeal, leaving the princess to defend herself."

I growled, standing from my seat. "Lies!" I yelled again. "I wanted to kick her ass! I will kill as I please!" The audience cowered, my wolf thundering inside me. Mom grabbed my dress and pulled me back to sitting.

"Easy there," she whispered. "You still must control yourself."

Dad, seething, ignored Mom's advice.

Joshua entered the arena like he was a damn hero. Coming in naked as well, waving to the parts of the crowd that felt like I was wronged by Kit. My fists tightened, reveling at what evil things I could do to him.

Cut off his nut sack and hang it on a spear for the birds to eat.

"Ew," Cinder scowled. *"That means you have to actually touch his nuts."*

Oh, right.

Then it clicked. "How did he know I fought off the assassin myself?" I whispered to Mom. Her sloppy clap paused, her eyes flickering with confusion.

"You don't think he was spying on us, do you??" I asked. My anger rose. "And why would he... Oh gods!" I squealed, shaking the announcer from his thoughts. "Do you think he let in Neari!? Told her where to go? What window to crawl in!?"

Dad's eyes turned red, clutching mom roughly.

"I wish you had mind-linked me instead of saying that out loud," she muttered.

"JOSHUA!" Dad roared into the rink. Joshua cowered, stepping back until he stumbled into the sand.

"Kane!" Mom hissed in his ear. "We have no proof, and we still have to uphold the challenge. If we don't, our people will think we are just favoring Kit! It has to continue. You can kill him later!"

Dad's stance held firm, the entire audience staring at our box in horror.

We couldn't call off the fight. The only way we would know if he'd planned the event was by Joshua's own words. Sure, we can detect lies, but even that wasn't enough to hold up in court. We had no actual proof of what he had done.

Keeping my mind link open during my conversation with mom, Kit's fire lit a new. He was no longer playful, sending me images of our week in bed together. Now he radiated pure anger and hate. It crushed my heart to know he could find this much rage.

"I'm going to kill you," Kit whispered so low I barely heard. "You will face my wrath for looking at what is mine, and for dishonoring yourself, you worthless piece of shit."

My core clenched.

Damn, that was hot.

Joshua stood, shaking the sand from his body. "Can't do that," he tsked. "This is a yielding match, no killing," he said smugly.

"Actually!" Melody stood, who had been quietly reading. "It says here that in The Worthiness Challenge, if the challenged is mated to said royalty, they cannot be killed because of their completed bond to the royal. It does not say that the challenger cannot be killed." Melody then sat down, and Marcus whispered something dirty in her ear.

Gonna pretend I didn't hear that.

Joshua gritted his teeth while Kit smiled in victory. The two naked men faced each other, and Joshua's angered faded. "Well, dear Princess," Joshua smiled sweetly at Melody. "I hope you understand there is a subclause to the challenge." Joshua whistled with his fingers between his lips and three more naked shifters entered the arena.

"Callahan?" Kit scoffed. "The fuck are he and his goons doing here?" He spat into the dirt.

Joshua chuckled while the rest of us on the stand threw questioning glances at each other. "That parchment also says that anyone willing to challenge for the right to mate with a royal because of the incompetence of their fated mate may fight for the royal's hand. It is to be one fight by the challengers, and we are here to give you—" Joshua stepped closer to Kit, chest to chest. "That. One. Fight."

"Four against one! No way!" I yelled.

Alabaster Academy students were stronger than typical warriors, and I could feel another alpha in the area radiating from the group. One that had just upped their skill level to that of Alpha. These guards were stronger than any warrior and could even be compared to a weaker alpha. It wouldn't be fair or right.

"There must be something else! This can't happen!" I panicked.

Darkness closed around me, my body shaking with fear. I knew my mate wouldn't be killed, but the thought of having to have four more mates disgusted me. It would be considered rape. I didn't want it, and yet this stupid law from thousands of years ago was hanging over my head.

"Melody?" I begged. I got on my knees, putting my head in her lap. "Please tell me it isn't true!"

Melody continued to flip through pages and pages of documents.

"Evie..." she whispered. "I can't find anything to argue his claims."

"Mom?" I whispered. "Can I fight with Kit, defend his honor?"

She shook her head. Dad's body shook in rage.

"*They won't have you, My Warrior Princess,*" Dad huffed through the link. "*I'll take down the entire kingdom for you.*"

His words did not calm me, because I wouldn't let him ruin the kingdom that my mom had spent so many years rebuilding. My mom shook in Dad's lap. Her hand gripping my arm.

"*Evie,*" Kit called calmly. He stood below us, his eyes beckoning me to look at him. "*Everything is going to be alright, Sugar. I promise.*"

I shook my head, my hands curling around the railing, breaking the wood to splinters.

"*You will not be theirs,*" he promised through the link. "*I don't fucking share, Sugar, you know this.*"

I let the stray tear fall. Landing on Kit, it kissed his forehead. The crowd was deafeningly quiet. Not even the babies in their mother's arms made a sound.

"We will win this," he said. *"Let me prove to your people that I am a capable mate to you."*

"But you are," I whispered. *"More than capable."*

He chuckled. *"Then let me show that to the world, Sugar. Let me show you what I can do."*

Chapter Thirty Eight

Kit

My mate exhaled, her body going limp. Her mother and father hovered over her as she sat down. Keeping my poise was far more difficult than I could have ever imagined. My fists clenched and released so many times, my claws piercing the skin. Soon, I would be feeling my blood drip down my body not because of self-infliction, but because I would face four wolves that had been trained to be deadly.

Joshua stood behind me, his arms crossed, thinking he had won. Callahan, who I never thought to be a problem, had just raised his wolf to Alpha status, no doubt thanks to the rigorous training he worked so hard for while he and his friends traveled all over Bergarian with me.

I was the one with the awards, the medals, the honor badges that shone brightly on my uniform, not him. He never fought with the Alphas, but he certainly trained with others around him. He fought with his comrades, his classmates, but never to anyone he knew he would lose to.

Against Joshua's pride and Callahan's false sense of security, now that his wolf has gained Alpha status, I may have the upper hand.

"Present!" one of the announcer's voices resounded through the arena.

"*You got this*," Leland snarled through our link.

Now that I had gained Alpha status, not having my own pack, Leland and Clint had automatically become my family. We banded together, protected each other. They may never be as strong as me, have the ultimate drive like I did, but we were a family in our own right.

My biological family was hidden somewhere within the crowd. I could feel them nudging me with words of silent encouragement to face the battle with all my strength. We had been separated for years while I trained, but there was never a time where I did not feel loved. They wrote to me, sent me gifts. My mother and father were proud of me, but they also knew that I did not need the distraction.

The only wolf I fought for today was my mate. My Warrior who was discouraged, not just at me failing, but at having to share herself with wolves that didn't deserve to be in her presence.

Melody continued to skim documents upon documents, not giving her mate any attention, trying to save her sister. I should not be upset or angry that they felt I couldn't complete this mission, because part of me felt I would fail. One slip, one misstep would be my last because if they caught my throat, one claw, one swipe could mean an automatic yield and I would fail. I may be strong, but I was not prideful. I was humble enough to know that there were others that could overpower me.

Joshua, Callahan, and the two other wolves stood back. They shook their bodies, ruffling their skin until the fur escaped from inside their bodies. Joshua rose from the sand, his grey wolf getting his bearings of the terrain.

My wolf's deep ebony hair flowed flawlessly over my body. My maw elongated, my fangs extending longer than they ever had before. Growls, snarls, and snaps came from the four wolves in front of me. There was no going back. For my mate and for myself, I would defend our honor.

Joshua leaped first, taking a bite out of my shoulder. Riddick, howling not in pain but in anger as adrenaline coursed through our veins, snapped back and latched onto his paw. The snapping of his paw placed a grin on my maw until the next two wolves jumped on my back.

Riddick, feeling a surge of energy, used the sand, spreading our paws to get a firm grip and jumped upward to shake the claws and teeth from my hide. My mouth, covered in Joshua's blood, was licked by my wolf, tasting the blood of our enemy.

Callahan continued to circle us, looking for the perfect opening. He was the wolf that I would need to look out for. His tactics, learned fighting his friends, classmates, and the other wolves who dared spar with him, were sneaky and vile. Callahan would watch wolves spar before he would ask for a challenge, that way he would have the upper hand.

A yellow wolf took the low ground, crawling through the sand, while the other pulled on my tail. Instead of snapping my head at the tail grabber, my teeth sunk into the neck of the yellow wolf. It whimpered, as I buried my teeth into its neck. My grip tightened, ready to snap the wolf's neck.

A yip and a head tilt in submission caused me falter.

Kane's voice boomed over the crowd, "Kill the bastard, Kit. Make him suffer!"

There was no rule saying that the challenger could yield, that they could step away from the fight. Melody's words heated my ears, and I jerked the trachea in one snap.

The cries faded. Riddick, not taking a second to revel in our victory, yanked our tail, the tip breaking, and sent the silver wolf rolling in the sand.

Joshua, who had healed his paw, was already stalking me from behind. Callahan nudging him to proceed. I scoffed, setting in a defensive position. Alphas do not take a defensive position often, but I was in the weaker spot for this fight. Three against one, and the silver wolf was next, so I could deal with the two ringleaders.

Joshua snapped at Callahan. The two wolves were almost equally matched. Joshua might not be an Alpha wolf, but he was damn near close.

The silver wolf came at me from the side, thinking my attention was on the two stronger wolves. My peripheral worked its magic, and I turned my head at the last minute to snap my jaws on the outer part of his maw. As I pulled away, it tore the skin, leaving gashes in his lips and nostrils.

Whimpering, the silver wolf backed away. Normally, I would stalk them and make them fear death, but with two arrogant wolves behind me, my time was short. I backed him into the wall, feeling the heat from Joshua and Callahan behind me.

"Rip off his balls!" Evelyn shouted. "Make him pay for challenging you!"

"Kill him." Kane's emotionless tone chilled the crowd into silence. Before my fangs could sink into the silver wolf's neck, Callahan jumped from behind, the tri-colored wolf sinking his jaws into my shoulder.

Riddick didn't falter; he didn't feel the pain. Instead, a surge of adrenaline had me fighting the sand, paws sinking deeper, and my teeth sunk into the back of the silver wolf's neck. My head shook, breaking the bones with my jaws until movement ceased from the mutt. Blood pooled in my mouth. The deeper Callahan's bite sunk into me, the more mine sunk into the wolf dying in front of me.

It wasn't a swift death. The silver wolf's gurgles filled the void inside my mind that had filtered out all the sounds of the crowd—my mate, my king and queen. Nothingness reached the four corners until Joshua grabbed my hind leg.

Callahan hovered over my back, his weight pushing me further into the sand as his jaws met my shoulder. Joshua took this opportunity to grab my hind-leg and pull it from the hip socket. As my body was pulled in different directions, Riddick howled in frustration at the limited movement available to us.

Hopelessness.

I couldn't move. I couldn't stand to push the weight of the two wolves above me. Riddick jerked and twisted his body, but Callahan's teeth had embedded into the bone.

"Fuck, fuck, fuck," I chanted.

"Get up, Kit! Guard, you better get up!" Out of the corner of my eye, Evelyn cried out into the arena. Her face was red, fur sprouting on her arms. She grew taller as her half-beast form emerged, until her mother wrapped her arms around her, forcing her to calm. Evelyn's voice cracked, her fists hitting the railing. "Get off him!" she screamed. Her shift returning her to her tanned skin.

One of my legs was firmly dislocated. Joshua worked on the other side to render me helpless. At least I knew I could relocate my leg faster than the average wolf, but it would still take a moment with Callahan on my shoulder.

Callahan's grip loosened, his heavy panting ringing in my ears. His maw traveled lower until all movements around me ceased. The crowd's waving hands, the roars and screams, everything vanished except the sound of the wind until it to disappeared, leaving only crunching, annoying crunching. A chuckle and a dropped popcorn kernel landed just below my head.

"Oh fuck, didn't mean to drop that," a gravelly voice said. Ares lowered his hand, his foot wrapped with a leather sandal caught my eye. Looking upwards, I couldn't his face because of the glare of the sun. His form was taller than any wolf or dragon I had ever known. His chest was bare, except for the leather strap crossing over his body. His lower half was covered in a leather skirt with pleated metal.

"It's not a skirt, it's like a kilt. You know, like the Scots do?" He threw more food into his mouth as he rounded the wolves that were stuck to my body.

"Damn, you got yourself into a predicament, didn't you?" He crunched on his popcorn again.

"How the hell did he hear me?" I asked Riddick, who was too stunned to speak.

"Ares, God of War, nice to meet you." He stuck out his hand. My body didn't move, because, well, the two wolves were weighing me down. "Oh, right, guess you can't really do shit while you're under there." He took his hand and pushed off Callahan and Joshua just enough so I could get away from their hold. At first, my body fell, until I pulled my leg back in its proper place.

"Better, eh?" He shook his hands to rid himself of the butter and salt and stood proudly.

Shit, he was big.

"May I ask why you are here? Not that I am not grateful. But this is... I just never thought I would...be in the presence of you. Do I bow?" I lowered my head to the ground, and a boisterous laugh shook the ground.

"Fuck no, get up." He waved his hand. "Now if it were Zeus, yeah, kissing his feet would probably get him off, but not me. I'm all about the fight, and you, Sir, are giving a fight I've longed to see."

I tilted my head in confusion, and he just laughed.

"Four against one for a woman and your honor?" He glanced at Evelyn. Her dress was torn from almost shifting, and her eyes were filled with worry. "Pretty heavy shit."

I sighed, sitting on my hindquarters.

"Am I going to die? Or am I going to fail? Is that why you are here? Stopping the fight?" Ares shook his head, pulling out another bag of popcorn from behind his back. Taking a handful, he stuffed it in his mouth.

"Nah, not after what I gift you, you won't." He crunched on his popcorn loudly. "You're going to be king in a few hundred years. And you wanted to prove yourself to a stubborn ass warrior princess and to the entire kingdom that you could protect her, right? Even though we both know very well, she can take care of herself. I figured I'd help."

"I don't want you to win the fight for me. I want to prove myself," I said respectfully. "I want her family, for her, and the kingdom to know I can do it on my own."

Ares smirked, shoving more popcorn into his mouth.

"And you will." He walked away and made a dramatic jump, landing on the first row of bleachers beside a group of wolves. "Now get back into position where you were." He waved his hand like a mother telling a pup to go to school. "Go on!"

The wolves were strategically placed over my body again by an unfamiliar force.

"Hey Kit," Ares yelled. "Being pure of heart makes the best warrior." He leaned back into the bleacher. "That was what Clara saw in you all those years ago. Don't lose that." I nodded in understanding until the roar of the crowd washed over me again.

Callahan bit into the back of my neck. Feeling the scraping of bone, I knew it was close. I would have to yield before he reached my throat. That was until I felt a rush of energy flow through me. It wasn't adrenaline; it wasn't fear. A whole new feeling of sweltering heat slid through my body.

The pain disappeared as my body heated to unbearable temperatures. Riddick howled. Together, we pushed away the two wolves that had hovered over me. Evelyn screamed in excitement, and gasps thundered through the crowd.

"Holy shit," Kane whispered.

"*What the hell?*" Leland and Clint both said.

"Yeah, boy, here it comes!" Ares joked from the stands, throwing popcorn into the arena. "Here comes the real show, bitches!"

Chapter Thirty Nine

Evelyn

"What. The. Fuck?" I gripped my seat.

"Yeah, what she said," Mom said as her mouth hung open. Dad stood from their royal seat, a grin that would be seen as absolutely terrifying to anyone that saw it up close plastered on his face. His fangs had lowered, and his eyes gleamed as Torin growled playfully.

"This is unexpected. I never felt this gift in his wolf," he chuckled. "This certainly puts a spin on things."

"What gift?" Mom asked. Her eyes were locked on Joshua and Callahan. They backed away slowly as Kit's body broke into pieces, doubling in size.

"The gods have gifted him with a half-form, just like us," Dad laughed. "Those fuckers are getting it now." Dad gripped Mom tightly, leaning over the railing to get a better view.

"How can that be? How can he have a half-beast?" I wondered.

Kit hunched over, black fur encasing his body. Almost the perfect likeness of dad, he had long arms, claws that were easily six inches. His back hunched over as he stood on his hind legs. His back arched backward, and he let out the loudest howl for all to hear. The crowd put their hands over their ears, hearing his battle cry as the last patches of his hide were covered in thick fur.

"He's magnificent," I whispered. "I don't understand how he can do that. He isn't royal." I shook my head.

"But he is mated to one," Melody spoke. "Dad was never a royal, nor were any in his line. The gods knew Mom would be too pure of heart to contain a beast such as that." She pointed. "So instead, they gifted her mate with the half-beast. Just as Pop was gifted with his half-beast all those years ago. You would have remembered that if you would have stayed awake in our genealogy class."

I rolled my eyes, no longer caring. Because now, the two wolves that dared to fight against Kit were going to be brutally killed. Half-beasts had the strength of ten wolves easily, and with Kit's skill on the field, there was no doubt left.

Kit spared no time after his mighty roar and launched his attack. His arms are so long, he easily swiped Callahan's wolf into the side of the arena's wall. He whimpered, falling back into the sand. Kit licked his long maw, his tongue as black as the rest of him.

Joshua lunged, trying to embed his fangs into Kit's torso, but he grabbed Joshua by the neck in his massive hand. Joshua wiggled, trying to free himself, but with one squeeze of his hand, Joshua went limp.

"*So damn hot,*" Cinder purred, wagging her tail. "*Think he could choke us, too? You know, just a little?*"

"*Pervy wolf,*" I muttered.

Dropping the corpse onto the sand, Kit did one better and slit him open with one sharp claw from neck to navel. He ripped into his body, hurling his insides onto the sand.

Callahan whimpered, keeping his tail between his legs, and headed to the far end of the arena where he had first emerged. Kit growled, watching him try to leave.

"Don't let him leave," Dad yelled. "He will face the wrath of challenging a Moon Goddess blessed mating!" Dad sat back down in his seat, holding Mom close to him. "It's over now. Our daughter is safe."

Mom relaxed, but I was too far gone with excitement, watching Kit prove himself to us all. He stalked over to Callahan, taking slow and precise steps, prolonging the inevitable. Callahan darted, trying to go around Kit, but instead, Kit took his long arm and wrapped it around Callahan's torso. Squeezing, Kit reveled in the sound of Callahan's ribs popping.

"This is so good! Glad I thought of it."

I paused at the loud crunching, finding a very well-built man in a skirt munching on popcorn like this was just a theatrical moment.

"And it isn't a skirt, it's a kilt." He rolled his eyes, throwing more popcorn in his mouth.

Who the fuck is this and how did he get here?

The strength he radiated, the golden glow around his body, forced me to step back. I glanced to my family. They took no notice of the large being sitting in Melody's vacant chair since she was sitting in Marcus's lap now. My family was watching Kit about to destroy the last challenger. "Yeah, they can't see me. Just thought I'd say 'hi.' So, what's up? I'm Ares. You are pretty hot. I can see why he wouldn't want to share you."

What?

"Come on, Princess, know when to take a joke." He elbowed me. "Kit's got the gift now, so you are evenly matched. If you don't watch it, he might beat you in a fight now, though. So don't get cocky."

I could not speak, watching Ares, the God of War, chat with me as if we were friends.

"Well, that was a good fight."

The roar of the crowd heightened and the popcorn that littered the floor below me was all that remained of the god. Now I stood alone, my family behind me, standing in applause.

Oh my gods, this day could not get any more stressful.

Callahan's head was nothing but a crushed skull and brains in the sand. My heartbeat quickened, my hand covering my heart to keep it from falling out of my chest.

"*It's over, Sugar,*" Kit linked. "*It's all over.*"

Without thinking, I leapt over the balcony box. My torn dress barely stayed over my shoulder as I ran across the sandy arena. Once I reached Kit, I swung my arms around his neck, feeling the warmth of his fur against my face.

"It's over," he said again. His half-beast now giving him the ability to talk. "And to think you doubted me."

"I didn't doubt you," I muttered.

He hummed in response. "You will get punished for that lie, Sugar." Cinder yipped in reply, hearing the rumbling of Kit's chest. "Now, what do you say we give them a show? Two half-beasts on the field?"

I smiled, nodding my head against his chest.

My once beautiful purple gown that Mom made me wear ripped into thousands of pieces as my fur burst through my body. Mom only laughed at my ridiculous display of distaste as I threw it away until my auburn-colored half-beast stood in front of Kit.

"*I don't think we have had a couple on record where both mates possessed the half-beast form,*" Melody mentioned in the mind-link. "*I hope that doesn't mean trouble ahead.*"

"*No, I don't think so,*" Mom said while she lifted Dimitri in her arms, and Dad held Dax. "*I think it's a show of blessings that are about to come.*"

"Let this be a lesson to you all," Dad warned the crowd. "This law is now abolished. As long as the Moon Goddess deems a mate worthy of a royal, it shall not be questioned." The crowd roared in agreement. Kit took my hand. "Now leave my daughter alone, and get out of here," Dad growled.

He was certainly one for words.

Kit pulled me to the other end of the arena. Children gathered to look in awe at our forms, yet they still gave us ample space. I waved but pulling off a smile with this maw was almost impossible. In fact, it looked downright scary, but not to the little pup that forced her way through the crowd. She walked straight up to me, pulling on the fur of my leg.

Crouching so I could look eye to eye with the little girl, I stumbled in shock when she threw her arms around me. Her little nose rubbed into my neck.

"I wanna be just like you! A warrior princess!" she whispered.

I never thought I would hear any child or wolf, for that matter, say they'd want to be like me. I was supposed to be the proper princess. Sit in the palace all day, sipping on tea and biscuits. According to my grandmother, I was anything but a princess.

"Really?" I purred.

"Really, I want to be the best warrior in my pack." She grinned.

"And I'm sure you will get there," Kit said, lowering himself to meet the girl's eyes. "Hello, Lyra. You've never met me before." He held out his claw, and the girl grabbed it firmly. "I'm Kit, your older brother."

I gasped. The little girl cocked her head in confusion.

"Kit, we are so proud of you," said a woman. She had the same sandy blonde hair Kit used to have, as well as a bright smile. She gripped her mate's hand tightly. "And a pleasure to meet you, Your Highness." She bowed with a hand over her heart. "I'm Elizabeth, Kit's mother, and this is Jay, Kit's father." We all had knelt to the ground, trying to stay at eye level with the little girl to keep her in the conversation.

"Please, call me Evie. We are family now. And it is very nice to meet you." I reached for their hands, and they took my enormous paw in theirs.

"A half-beast in the family. Who would have thought my timid little pup would be where he is today?" Elizabeth beamed, rubbing her other hand on his furred cheek.

"You mean he really is my brother?" The little pup jumped in excitement.

"He is," Jay replied. "And with blood like ours, you can be a warrior princess."

"Yes!!" she squealed, letting go of me and jumping into Kit's arms. He purred deep in his chest, rubbing his head over hers lovingly.

I couldn't imagine leaving my family for all the years that Kit had, but I was glad he had. He had become the perfect mate for me. Now, seeing him with a child made me wonder how he would be as a father.

That wouldn't be for a very long time, however.

We said our goodbyes with promises to have dinner the following day. Now that Kit had officially graduated from the academy, he would not only become my mother's guard, a dream he'd had for many years, but also would be able to spend time with his family and especially his mate.

I pulled Kit's hand through the crowd that made way for us. Our speed picked up, running by the throngs of shifters. Our long legs carried us to the forest that we had wanted to run together in for so long. Since finding each other, we had yet to release our animals so they could bond with one another.

"Race ya!" I looked over my shoulder as I lunged over the ravine. Playfully growling, he steadied himself on the wet soil.

"Since when did you like to be the prey?" he called out while I swung from a nearby branch.

"Since you became the hunter," I growled back. Laughing, we shot deeper into the woods, where I would lead him to my favorite tree, the one that he thought existed only in a dream.

Chapter Thirty Forty

Kit

A roar ripped through me, enticing my mate to laugh and run deeper into the thick forest. The forest that surrounded the palace had taken years to regrow after the war, even with the help of the elves and the dragon Horus from the Golden Light Kingdom. Since the animals have returned and repopulated, it was teaming with life.

Not now, however.

Two predators brushed through the leaves and branches of the trees. We trampled the underbrush with our mighty paws as we jumped over stumps of vegetation once destroyed by the war, making way for the hunter to seek his prey.

Riddick licked his lips, his nose thrusting into the air when we no longer smelled our mate. I could no longer smell her lush fur or her pheromones leaking from her half-beast body. My person stilled, standing under the largest tree in the forest. Its roots were large, requiring care to step over. The wind nuzzled the branches, and I still further, taking deeper breaths of the clean air.

I mumbled, cursing myself for letting her get away. My newest form had made me prideful, and I was fucking pissed. I would never live this down.

I shifted, not smelling her in the area. I took my time walking around the tree. She was close. I could feel her through the bond, but I wasn't exactly sure where. At the moment I looked up, she jumped from a limb and screamed a battle cry that sent the birds flying into the sky.

She landed on me with a thump, tumbling us both to the ground. Her naked body sprawled against mine, and my arms wrapped around her tightly.

"Hmm, this scene looks familiar!" She patted her lip. "We just need to go find some mud to roll in, and we could recreate one of our dreams almost perfectly."

Growling playfully, I rolled her onto her back, taking control of her body. The leaves above us fell in perfect tandem. Her hair laid elegantly on the forest floor.

Evelyn pushed back my hair from my sweaty forehead, as I leaned into her.

"Do you know where we are?" she asked.

I continued looking into her eyes, my hands roaming the sides of her body until I pushed up her arms above her head. "Does it matter?" I smirked, kissing her neck.

"Yeah, kinda?" She moaned sweetly, her back arching into my body. "Look," she ordered.

My lips lingered on her neck until I pulled my head away. The scene before us was becoming clearer. The foliage was thick and green and the softness of the roots that stretched beneath the soil recognizable.

Rubbing a nearby root, I remembered this feeling from within our dreams. "Sissiel Fern tree?" I pulled away from Evelyn's body, looking straight above me. It was the same thick branch where we had spent many nights holding each other under the stars. The soft bark gave us refuge as we laid on its branches.

"Is this—"

She nodded. "It's our tree, Kit. The same tree that comes with us when we sleep."

I let out a breath, standing and pulling Evelyn with me. We rounded the tree, finding the same knots we used to climb and found our branch for refuge. It was so large and flat we could both sit or lay on it like a bed. I sighed, pulling Evelyn into my embrace.

"You know, this was the same tree where I slept when I had my first dream of you," she whispered. "I have always felt like it has some sort of magic inside it. That it somehow led me to you and that magic followed me wherever I went since I caught you in my dreams." She chuckled.

"There were many times I would come to this tree after dealing with Grandmother. Just hide in its branches because she could never find me here." My fingers ran through her hair as she explained. "I wasn't sure it was because her wolf was out of practice at searching through the bond to find me, or the tree had magical powers that kept her away. I believed the latter, since believing in magic sounded so much better."

"This will always be our special place, Evelyn." I rubbed my thumb over her cheek. "Our place to get away. A dream within the real world." A stream flowed close by, reminding me of how we often went swimming. But I didn't care to relieve my aching muscles with the cool water. I only wanted her.

Evelyn's body straightened, her body pressing to my chest. "We should build our cottage. Like a real one!" Her eyes lit up. "Right there, underneath this tree. We can live there, and we won't have to live in the palace until we have to!" Her excitement rose as did mine. Having time with her, in reality, at the end of the day after our daily duties, sounded more than refreshing.

No servants, no scowling father who would always have a problem with me deflowering his daughter over and over.

"We'll need to have our swing, too." I raised an eyebrow. "The same exact one. With one plank and flowering vines cascading down it." I laughed, pulling her close.

"Exactly, we should! It will be amazing! Don't think the flowers would survive the winter here, though. This isn't exactly a dream where I can manipulate it," she said sourly.

"This life certainly has become a dream," I replied. "I never thought I would actually hold you in my arms. Here in the now. Our dreams have become a reality, Sugar, and don't you forget it. I don't have to close my eyes and wish for my dreams to take over, because now reality is better than a dream."

She smiled broadly, holding me close. We sat in silence for at least an hour, watching the birds return to the tree and watch us, blissfully unaware of how much their home had become ours.

"We can go to the palace every morning together to help Mom and Dad. Then come back here and sleep in the forest. I'd much rather be out here than stuck inside the icy walls of the palace."

Of course, she would want it more. She was wild, free. She would no longer feel like she was suffocating in a palace where bad memories haunted her. Not until she and her grandmother had reconciled. I had hoped that our reign wouldn't be for a long while, so I could be the selfish bastard and keep her to myself.

"Whatever you want, I will provide for you," I said confidently. With my new half-beast form, I would ensure that. She could take care of herself in many ways, and now I could truly protect her if I needed to. I could keep her, her family, as well as her kingdom safe if she could not. When she bears our pups, it will become especially useful since she cannot shift while a pup is in her womb.

"Provide me with anything?" The twinkle in her eye had me smiling. Evelyn knew I would provide her with anything and everything.

"Yes," I purred. "Anything." I slipped lower, my mouth now even with her breast as I suckled one.

"Mmm, just like that," she gasped as I bit down hard on the now-tightened nub.

Licking away the pain, I hovered over her body, taking in the other side of her breast.

"If you are waiting to warm me up, I don't think you need to," she chuckled, her nails raking down my back.

The sharp sting and the cool breeze sent chills up my spine. My cock hardened, feeling the warmth between her legs. Riddick took a deep breath, filling our nostrils with her arousal. "Fuck, you smell good, Sugar." My cock rubbed up and down her slit, my mouth still not finished with tasting her skin.

Her warmth radiated through my lips, my tongue begging for more of her taste. "I very well know you don't need warming up," I replied. Taking my lips, I trailed back up her breast, to her neck, biting into her skin. Wrapping my hand around her neck, I squeezed gently, my hips pushing the tip of my cock into her slit.

"Kit!" Her nails raked down my back.

"Your pussy is soaked. I can feel it, smell it in the air. I know you are more than ready to take this cock, Sugar." She sighed delightedly, pushing her hips toward me. "But," I tsked, her movements ceasing, a look of confusion transpiring on her face. "You didn't fully trust that I would keep those vile wolves away from you, did you?"

"I—" she stuttered. "I never said that! I never believed—"

"You were still worried," I said. "It's alright to be worried, Sugar. I was too. It was...certainly a lot. I just need a good reason to edge you." I smiled wickedly.

"Do-do what!?" She shrieked.

"Shh. I'll take care of you when I'm ready." My lips smashed into hers. Fingers trailed down her hips in soft caresses until I parted the delicate petals that hid her pollen. "I want you to relax. I want you to let go of all of today's stress and let me take care of you." I inserted two of my thick fingers, feeling the flutter of her walls constrict around me.

"But you just fought. I should take care of you," she begged. Her body tensed while I curled my fingers inside her. "Beg for your forgiveness for being so worried." My other hand wrapped around her throat again, tugging it softly. With hooded eyes, her eyes bore into me, and I felt the heat of her gaze.

"You will beg," I playfully said, "but it won't be for forgiveness."

Evelyn arched her back, her walls sucking in my fingers until I pulled them away. "What! No, what did you do?"

Biting my lip, my fang nearly piercing the skin, I chuckled. "Like I said, you are being punished." I touched every inch of her as I fell to my knees. I was thankful for the soft bark of the tree because I knew I was going to be on my knees a long while.

I parted her opening with my tongue, slipping my half-beast's tongue in and out of her body. The thickness of my tongue tugging at her clit.

"Gods! Please, Kit, please!"

I chuckled, enjoying her cries. My mate thought I deserved special treatment, but this was my own special treat. I wanted to make her feel things she had yet to feel, even with a week in bed. I would bring her to new heights. It only made my cock that much harder and ready to sink into her weeping core.

After the fourth time pulling away just before she would orgasm, she had lost all her resolve. Her eyes brimmed tears, as they fell down her pink cheeks. "Please, I can't!" She shook her head. Her hair tangled in the leaves that gave her nature's own pillow. "Please," she breathed again, her hands cupping her breasts.

I hummed, not giving her an answer as I dove in deeper still. My fingers were now playing a crucial role in the battle of pleasure and punishment.

Evelyn was my mate, my love, and even now that I possessed the power of a half-beast, I did not see her as my equal because of this new power.

It was my fierce love for her that made us equal. When she worries, succumbing to the dark thoughts she keeps hidden inside, it is my duty to calm her. Through speech, touch, through pleasure and our bond, I would comfort her and calm the storms she hides from the rest of our world.

My lips parted from her clit, my fingers continuing to thrust deep inside her. "Tell me how good you feel, Sugar." She screamed my name, and I chuckled, taking one swift lick again.

"Say my name when you cum, gorgeous. Release your tension!" I growled.

Her legs shook, a silent scream leaving her lips, tipping her over the edge of oblivion. After the beautiful gasp that left her lips, her legs fell to the sides. Then I devoured her again.

I hummed, my mouth still glistening with her pleasure, and licked her lower lips. She tensed, feeling my tongue wipe away the excess wetness from her body. Kissing up her body, I parted her lips with the tip of my cock, coating it with her essence so I could slide it past her lips gently.

"Kit," she moaned, her eyes filled with tears. Her body was like putty in my hands.

I grabbed one leg, wrapping it around my hip. "That's it, Sugar, take me. Take this cock, let me in. Fuck, you're tight even with your slick coating me. Squeeze me, that's it." My voice shook as I tried to keep my composure in check. I would not cum now, not when I needed to get another orgasm out of her.

I slowly pumped my cock inside her. The angle at which I thrust into her, rubbing her walls in new and tantalizing ways made her whimper.

"Kit, more..." she begged. I tried to keep a slow and steady pace, but I was losing patience I wanted to take her and let my seed coat her womb.

"Let me feel you for a bit, hmm? Let me feel your pussy milk me. I promise you will get to cum again real soon." I groaned, pushing in deeper.

"I can't—" she cried out. "I can't cum again, it's...too much!"

"You can Sugar, show me what a big powerful Alpha you are." I bucked my hips, as she rolled her hips to find a more tantalizing angle. "That's it, Baby. Let me watch myself sink into your cunt."

"The things you say drive me crazy." She gripped my forearm while my thumb reached lower and rubbed her clit.

"Good, it's supposed to." I thrust roughly. I'd pushed her body to the trunk of the tree. With an arm over her head, she pushed against the trunk, so I didn't bury her head in the soft bark.

"Harder," she panted.

I pulled my cock out of her body, and she whimpered.

"Roll over, I'm fucking you from behind, Sugar." She quickly obeyed; my cock slipped into her slit.

She gripped the tree while I pounded inside her. My cock twitched as the new sensations washed over me. Her pussy clamped down as she met my thrusts. I didn't think I could delve any deeper.

"Taking it so well, Sugar." I pulled her hair, her eyes looking up at me. "So flexible, gods, you're beautiful. I'm going to cum, are you ready to cum with me?"

"Please!" she cried. "I can't hold—"

"Now!" I growled, releasing hot ropes of steaming cum into her womb. My body shook, the tingle at the base of my spine pushing my cock deeper into her pussy. "Fuck!" I cursed, gripping her. "So fucking pretty when you cum."

Her whimpers, her sighs of relief had given me a satisfaction I would never tire of. Pulling my cock from her body, I kept her on her knees, gently resting my hand on her lower back. Sliding back slowly, I watched my cum drip from her slit.

It was a fucking beautiful sight. My wolf purred, satisfied with our work. We pulled our mate into our arms as we laid across the limb. It was the perfect width, the flatness working as a natural bed. I pulled her close into my arms, her breasts resting on my chest, my lips grazing her forehead.

"You alright, Sugar?"

She hummed as I played with her hair. As the sweat from her orgasms mingled with mine, I smiled again.

"I feel free." She nuzzled into me. "Like I have nothing to worry about."

"Good, that is how it should be," I replied. "You have me now. I will take care of you, but still let you be the wild wolf you are."

She giggled, wrapping her arm around me. "Not that I would ever let you tame me, anyway."

I raised an eyebrow, gripping her ass.

"Just in bed then," I countered.

"Right, just in bed." Evelyn pulled away, her hand rubbing against the stubble of my cheek. "I love you, Kit." Her fingers rose and touched my lips. It was far more intimate than anything we had done. The love in her eyes, the gentle touches to my skin. She handled me like I could break, and that made my wolf purr with happiness.

"I love you, too, Evelyn. Both in our dreams and reality."

Chapter Forty One

Evelyn

"I wish Pop could be here." Melody exhaled as she braided one side of my head in tiny little corn rows. In between each braid, an ivory ribbon weaved in and out of my now lightened hair. On the other side, mom was curling big, loose waves and repositioning the small crown of baby's breath flowers on my head.

"Me too, but he is where he is needed. They will be back when the time is right, and they will see how beautifully you two girls grew up." Mom, being the sentimental one, let a tear fall.

"Mom, you'll ruin your makeup," Melody joked, taking her ivory hand-kerchief and dabbing Mom's eye.

"I know I will, and I know I will do the same when your time comes, too." She sniffed.

"Don't know how long that will be, Mom," she whispered.

For three weeks, Melody and Marcus had been at odds, partly because of stress and Marcus's past. Dad said it was time for Melody to take over the Crimson Shadows pack. Eighteen was the age of rightful passage to your inheritance if your father or mother deemed you worthy. Since Dad was technically the true reining Alpha and Marcus was just a substitute. Melody's time had come, even if she disliked the idea. It had been many generations since the Crimson Shadows had such a young Alpha, but it was Melody's job now, and I knew she was more than capable.

Melody was the second born, and Dad's blood line had to be carried on to hold the Crimson Shadows. Marcus was Dad's beta and just a place-holder until the second child was of age, and now with all Marcus's time being spent with Melody, he'd been neglecting those duties. But now, he was being pushed to Beta once again—this time as Melody's Beta.

Melody thought she had more time. Hell, we all did. Dad hadn't men-tioned it much because of Melody's strong distaste for the title. Melody was shy and didn't like to fight. She was more of a silent watcher, the bringer of good ideas and wisdom. She preferred exploring the scientific side of things rather than to fight them out. It had already been discussed that the twins would take Melody's spot when the time was right. That was the only way she would take the title from Marcus.

"Marcus is a good wolf, you will see." Mom finished curling the backside of my head.

Melody kept her lips pressed together. She held back from arguing with Mom, there was no point really. Mom was always right, even if we didn't want to admit it. But the feelings Melody had about Marcus were compli-cated. Who knew how long their courting would last?

The shorter the better for Marcus's sake. Marcus has already been beaten up four times for even looking at Melody with heated eyes in Dad's pres-ence. Luckily for Kit, he knew how to refrain from heated glances and just sent me nasty images through our mind-link.

Mom asked my opinion of how I wanted my mating ceremony to go, and with royalty, it was supposed to be an enormous affair. Of course, being the rogue princess and not wanting to do anything normal, I begged for a small family and friends affair. With Grandmother being gone, it was a reasonable request with Mom because she wanted us to see us happy and not be bogged down by royal affairs.

Finally, some peace.

"Evieeee!" Dax ran into the dressing room, falling onto my lap.

"Dax, stop! You'll wrinkle the dress!" Mom fussed.

"Doesn't matter!" Dimitri strode in and grabbed mom's hand. "Evie will just mess it up anyway when she runs into the woods later. Right?"

I chucked, holding my hand out to grab Dimitri's hand. Squeezing it tight, I winked. "You know it."

"Are my beautiful girls ready?" Dad had been sitting in the room's corner, keeping us within sight. Marcus had been pushed out of the room. His presence was always a constant with Melody. It was almost stalker-like, but then again, some wolves could be like that. Luckily, I could take care of my own business, and Kit knew when I needed him and when I was alright.

Marcus may not have figured it out, but Melody could protect herself when she wanted. Just because she didn't have a half-beast didn't mean she was defenseless. She just took care of her battles in her own way.

"Yes, we're ready!" Mom bounced on the balls of her feet, wrapping her arms around Dad.

She was wearing a pale yellow dress, as did Melody, who matched her. Fall had begun around the kingdom; the leaves were turning far quicker than I had remembered for this time of year, but then again, the seasons were never constant around here.

Mom smiled, touching my cheek. "We will meet you outside, alright? Don't be too late coming down. I'm sure Kit is ready to see you walk down the aisle."

I rubbed my hands together to warm them. Suddenly, I felt cold and out of place. I hated being the spectacle of the evening. I didn't like eyes on me. I was grateful for the small ceremony, but in exchange, I'd promised Mom I would have a large coronation many, many years down the road.

A harsh knock at the door broke our gazes from each other. "May I escort my mate to her seat?" Marcus's enormous dress shoes clicked on the marble. Uncertainty and longing filled Melody's gaze. I knew she wanted him. She had wanted a mate before I even wanted one. Then Mason happened, and she told me on the flight back she hoped she never met hers because men were too fickle. Of course, the gods had a funny way of working things out. After finding out about his past and Marcus's reputation among the pack, her mood had soured.

"Sure," she muttered, glancing back at me like I could save her.

"*Go,*" I said softly through our link. "*Give him a chance.*" Would I have been angry finding out he was a man-whore for so many years? I can't say for sure, but as long as my mate only had eyes for me now, I could very well see myself crumbling. It would only be a matter of time before Melody decided what she wanted. A bond was too strong.

Then again, it didn't help that Dad was as angry as a pixie in fly paper about his now ex-best friend being chosen by the goddess.

Dad squeezed my shoulder, leaving me alone. The windows were open wide, letting the tulle like curtains dance across the carpet near the bed. Sitting up straight, I walked to the large bay windows, taking in the scene below me. The garden behind the palace had been transformed into a small paradise. Orange, yellow, red, and brown leaves littered the chairs. The archway had been created with brown vines with hints of ivory and gold fabric woven between the branches. Pixies, daring to sneak in so they could watch the rare event, knocked beautiful leaves from the trees.

I laughed, watching Dax and Dimitri running up and down the aisle with sticks, banging on the back of each chair. Melody and Marcus sat with each other on one side of the aisle while my father glared at Marcus from afar. Mom clung to his hand, whispering something into his ear.

"Wow," someone breathed.

My face lit up, turning away from the window to see my mate standing in the doorway. "It's considered back luck to see your mate before the mating ceremony," I chided.

"Well, I have certainly seen all of you for quite some time, Sugar." Kit strode over to me. His pristine, white uniform didn't have a speck of dirt or debris on it. His medals shined brightly, and his red sash matched the red one wrapped around my dress to match our autumn theme.

"You look gorgeous." His lips grazed my cheek. "I don't think I could get any happier."

My fingers grazed the collar of his uniform, gently tracing down the front. I couldn't get over how lucky I was, to know my mate for so long before we were finally together. I took my hand and cupped his erection, giving it a gentle squeeze. "I think I know something that could make you happier," I purred.

With his arm wrapped around my waist, he pushed it deep into my mound. "Is that so?"

I bit my lip playfully as pools of desire floated in his eyes. "Yes, it is."

"Evie, we are expected to be downstairs in ten minutes." He glanced at his pocket watch.

"Oh, you think you can go that long?" I giggled, and he pushed me onto the bed. My hair flew across the covers, his erection pressing into me again. I groaned, the weight of his body surrounding me with his scent.

"You know damn well I can go longer, Warrior," he growled.

"Prove it," I dared, nipping his nose with my teeth.

"You are so bad," Cinder purred.

Standing up, he untied his sash and the ties of his uniform, letting his pants hit the floor. Already, cum dripped from the head, the hardness of his cock beckoning me. I licked my lips, falling to the floor on my knees.

"Suck and you'll see," he dared.

The two high slits to my dress parted way, baring my naked thighs. I gripped the base of his cock, and my thick lashes fluttered upward to take in his passionate gaze.

"And, just so you know," I whispered. "I'm not wearing any panties." I smiled, and a mouth full of beautiful curse words fell from his mouth. My red lips stained his cock, sucking him inside of me. His hand gripped the bedpost.

"Damnit, what are you doing?" He bent over, trying not to grab my hair. His knees bent and the back of my throat opened wider. Feeling the heat, the beautiful ridges of veins that massaged the walls of my mouth made me moan with eagerness. His cock twitched, and internally I praised myself.

"No more!" he pulled me up, throwing me on the bed. Taking the long piece of fabric that covered the front part of my body he threw it over, baring my pussy to him. The gold chain garter on my right thigh jingled along with his medals while our bodies shifted more comfortably. "Naughty thing, not wearing anything underneath. Why would you do that?" He slapped my pussy.

Kit kicked off his pants, leaving the top part of his uniform on. He gripped my hips roughly, rolling me over so my ass was facing him. He lifted the back of my dress, the long train thrown to the side. His cock nudged my core and thrust deep and hard into me.

"Kit!" I pushed my hips backward, his hard thrusts rougher than I had ever felt. His growls and grunts came in rhythmic beats as he pounded me.

"Eight minutes. I have two minutes left," he panted. "That's enough to make you come, isn't it?" His heated breath brushed across my neck, his thrusts forcing himself deeper. I groaned, widening my legs to give him plenty of room. "That's it, Sugar, let me see all of you."

Those. Words.

His eyes darted away from me, my body shaking with the need to fall over the edge.

"Can I come?" I begged.

A growl erupted from him, his claws raking down the duvet beside my head.

"Cum, mate. Cum with me now!" We roared each other's names, the stars brightening behind my eyes as we fell down. Our once wrinkle free clothing was covered in sweat and now my inner thighs were covered in his cum.

"You are going to wear this." He pulled his cock out of me. I whined at the loss, but his fingers immediately pushed themselves inside me again. "My smell is going to be all over you," he purred and drug it up to my stomach. "Might piss your dad off, but it's too much of a turn on to not to do this," he chuckled.

"You are so bad," I muttered, half laughing. "I like it."

Luckily, our clothes didn't come out as wrinkled as I thought. The sun was still setting, so we didn't lose the low light my mom had envisioned for my walk down the aisle. We had many mind-links asking where we were, mainly from Dad. Mom argued with him until she found an outdoor closet to appease him in for a few minutes until we could present ourselves more appropriately.

Dad had reached his every four-hours "teatime," as mom liked to call it, and I had never felt sicker in my life, learning what their tea-times actually meant.

Close friends and family were the only ones in attendance, thankfully. Ebony and Easton made the trip all the way from Earth. Ebony had officially graduated from Jack's rigorous Alpha training program of Earth. Her new pack would be called the Grimfur Prowler Pack and would reside on the opposite side of the country from where she trained. Unfortunately, Wesley and Charlotte could not attend, still hoping Ember would make it home. Their bond had not broken with her. She was alive, and it tore into Charlotte every day that she wasn't with them. Charlotte said she could feel pangs of from her daughter through the bond. Whether it be physical or mental, she wasn't sure, but it was enough to cause her to cycle in and out of depression.

Melody had planned for a special task force of trained guards from the academy to help search across Bergarian, hoping to find her somewhere in this realm. Leland and Clint, who had become very close to the royal family, were put in charge.

Dad held onto one of my arms while Mom held the other. We smiled, trickling down the aisle and greeting our closest friends. Some were from the Crimson Shadows pack and various friends Mom and Dad had made through the years, such as August the gamma and his mate. Creed and Odessa made a very rare appearance but stood in the back so they could make a quick return to their nest. Sebastian, Christine, along with their son Killian, and Tayliah and Jasper with Cassius all watched from the audience. Killian and Cassius were looking rather brooding, but that was just how they were.

Of course, Kit's entire family, which included his eight brothers and one sister, was in attendance. Lyra, who'd become the official flower girl, held the basket tightly, waiting for us to step out onto the path.

Osirus, Melina, and their two five-year-old twins, an important family from the Golden Light Kingdom, attended. Their children were Thicket, a fae, and Pandora, a siren that wore a unique necklace around her neck that allowed her to be out of the water for extended periods of time. If you sniffed just right, you could tell that Melina was pregnant yet again and who knew what supernatural would be released from her body this time.

The gods had been gracious in letting interspecies pairings mix their souls together and allowed the baby in the womb to ultimately decide who they were to become.

Dad's nostrils flared, my smile widening as I saw Melina gently waving toward us. "Could Kit not keep his hands off you until after the ceremony?" Dad growled, rubbing his nose.

Whoops.

"Sorry, Dad, I am part you, you know. I sometimes have an insatiable amount of drive—"

Mom elbowed me in the stomach. "The only thing I will ask of you when you become queen is to know when to keep your mouth shut," she snapped. "I'm just glad you put your lipstick back on." She laughed as they dropped their hands and acted like nothing had even been said.

Well, Dad tried to act like nothing had happened. Instead, he squeezed Kit's hand so tightly his bones and knuckles popped. Kit continued to give a sweet smile as my dad continued to crush his bones.

"It was worth it," Kit linked me.

Cyrene conducted the ceremony as she had for my parents' coronation. She droned on about the importance of mates and how special they are to this world and now on Earth. The usual ceremonial junk. Her words faded away, and the only person I saw was Kit as the leaves gently fell around us, the pixies dropping their golden dust to reap in a quicker autumn. Winter would come soon this year, but the warmth that I felt through Kit's hand only grew stronger.

We'd made it. We'd been friends through our toughest years. We helped each other grow in ways we never would have understood without each other The gods certainly had a sense of humor to help us find each other. I was sure they were laughing the entire time, waiting for us to figure it out, only for Kit to find out first. Then he kept me guessing, making me fall in love with him without the bond. He kept us together despite my hesitations and doubts. He had the true heart of a king—the kind that would help us rule someday.

As cheesy as it sounded, and completely cliché to the point it would make me sick if anyone else said it, I loved him more than the air I breathed, and without him, I would have never found who I was meant to become.

Kit

"Where did you go, Little Warrior?" My link was loud enough to draw her out of the thoughts she'd trapped herself in. Thinking of the future?

Thinking of her family? Everything was on her mind as she walked down that aisle before her father broke my hand with barely a twitch of his fingers.

He was insanely more powerful than me, and my wolf whimpered, feeling my fingers crack. I refused to flinch or show pain, not on this day of happiness. His glare didn't go unnoticed by his mate, who pinched him in the side. He acted as if she'd mortally wounded him.

My lips quirked up, and Clara gave me a wink in reply.

Evelyn looked ravishing, even though her perfectly curled hair now flowed in messy waves down her back. Her flowered crown was missing a few of its flowers, and her braided hair might have shown a hint of wear.

She glimmered in the setting light sources.

Her tanned skin, inherited from her father's side, and the bright eyes filled with delight made my bones break back into place and I no longer felt the mind-numbing pain.

"*Sorry, just thinking.*" She sighed with a smile. Cyrene continued on, her hands producing a powder-like substance that turned into a purple and blue smoke around us.

"*You can't do that anymore, I'm here for you now. You put your worries on me.*" Riddick purred loud enough to make the first rows of the audience chuckle. Even with just inviting close family and friends, it turned out to be more than I originally thought. Clara just couldn't keep her friends away. Including the seamstress that sewed Evelyn's satin gown. The slits up both sides of her legs and the red sash that held the slits in just the right place so her nakedness wouldn't show had my cock tightening in my uniform. It was the perfect tease of a dress—a non-traditional princess gown, which was perfect if she chose to run away after the ceremony.

Which I knew she would.

The seamstress knew Evelyn all too well. Evelyn's rough wear and tear on dresses was well known. The seamstress knew Evelyn would very well ruin the dress if she didn't have ample movement in it.

"It's almost over, then we can relax. Go back to the cabin and spend our time away from everyone."

She nodded, wrapping her fingers around my own.

Clara begged to have three weeks to plan the ceremony that would only last a half hour with a long reception for the invited guests. Evelyn didn't plan any of it, she let her mother do it all. Evie couldn't care less about formalities. Besides, we were too busy getting started on our own fun and Evie being concerned about her sister and her new mate.

During the three weeks, Evie and I planned and built our cabin in the woods. A small tribe of nomadic elves arrived in the territory while we sat daydreaming away from her brooding father and Marcus. Once they realized who we were, they eagerly set up their tents in the nearby trees and coaxed the sissiel tree into creating our cabin from its vines and branches. In just two weeks, they had helped us create our dream cottage and brought it to life. It was a living structure that had taken root into the soil.

The leader of the nomadic group placed his hands upon the tree, believing there was an aura trapped inside, and when the time was right, an unworldly creature of both realms would be born from it. Evie excitedly hugged the tree, stroking it like it was her own little child, while I brooded about what creature might be born and the potential harm to our family.

The elves put our minds at ease, believing it was made of a life source so strong that it had survived the Dark War all on its own, and even the darkness could not penetrate it. Whatever creature came from the tree would be powerful, and its magic would help the forest and all the creatures that lived in it to flourish.

A repetitive tap fell upon my shoulder. We both were broken from our trance and found Cyrene smiling with her black and purple hair swaying with the gentle autumn breeze. "You can kiss your mate now, Kit." She chuckled as the crowd clapped.

As soon as our lips touched, I knew every decision leading up to this moment was the right one. Letting Evelyn mature in the Earth realm, supporting her when she had doubts. She gave me life, a smile, a personality I thought I had lost long ago.

"*Now look who is getting lost,*" she muttered while the roar of applause deafened the forest. The animals that dared to come close now scattered deeper within. I cupped my mate's cheek and leaned in for the formalities of a kiss when she gripped me by my cock and pulled me closer.

My eyes widened, "Now everyone knows you're mine," she growled.

"Evelyn!" Her father roared in the background.

Then My mate slipped her tongue into my mouth and bent me over backward in front everyone.

Epilogue

Under the Moon

Evelyn pulled out another chocolate cream pie from the fridge. Her sister rubbed her hands manically, grabbing the spoon while Evelyn placed it on the table. They didn't even bother trying to slice it up and put it on plates. They were sisters, and they both knew they would eat the entire pie themselves in one sitting.

It was loaded with so much whipped cream, some dropped off the sides of the crust. Melody took her finger and swiped it through the cream and quickly stuck it in her mouth. "How much vanilla do you put in your cream?" she asked curiously. "Your cream has much more flavor than mom's. Not that it's a bad thing, it's just different." She let her finger go with a pop while she dug her spoon into the chocolaty goodness.

"Yeah, well, I added a bit of lemon, you know? Give it a little zing." Evelyn waved her spoon around dramatically. "Got to experiment when you are stuck in the cottage all day and can't do a damn thing while your mate isn't here," Evelyn sighed dramatically.

"You are about to give birth, Evie," Melody scolded. "What do you expect? I'm surprised Grandmother hasn't come around and told you what day the pup was coming." Melody dug into the pie once more, stuffing her mouth.

"She didn't tell our brothers when their mate would go into labor. Grandmother went to that pampering day with their mate and didn't even let on a hint of a smile, and she knew exactly what was going to happen at the end of it. A damn baby." Evelyn rubbed her nose viciously. She had the itches all over her body, constantly scratching at the dry skin the baby had somehow created.

Evelyn and her grandmother had their moments, but her grandmother had learned from her mistakes. The ten years hadn't been exactly enough time for her to rid herself of her sins. Many still knew of her harsh words, and she would have to rebuild her reputation amongst her people. Most of the rumors of what she'd said stayed within the palace and those that had worked with her before felt hurt and betrayed. Since then, Eden had taken it upon herself to work with the servants, getting to know them personally as well as the guards and warriors who protected her.

In time, she had wiggled through some of their hardened hearts, but still had many more years to go before overcoming the one statement that caused such pain.

Pop had stayed by her side for the entire ten years of his mate's punishment. He helped her regain her wolf, strengthen her, and bring her back to the surface. For too long, Eden had repressed her, and her wolf had become weak and frail. Now she shifted daily, running through the forest and becoming one with the nature that she had lost so long ago.

"You're right, she didn't say anything, did she?" Evelyn grunted, feeling the pup kick. "Damn, this bugger is strong." She rubbed her stomach. "Then again, she might be sore at me for waiting so long to have a pup. Who knew our younger brothers would be the first to knock up their mates and have pups so quickly?"

Dax, Dimitri and their mate, Seraphina's, youngest child was already six years old by the time Evelyn had become pregnant. Evelyn and Kit had waited over fifty years to have their first pup because Kit, like he had mentioned before, was a selfish bastard that wanted his mate all to himself. With no impending wars, Bergarian flourished like never before. There was no rush to keep the royal line going, so why not bask in the quiet life they had provided themselves?

Their cottage existed in both their reality and their dream. They loved the safe feeling they had when they stayed in it. Calmness radiated from the tree they'd lived under for so many years, giving them peace and blessings they never could have imagined. Their souls rejuvenated, and their half-beast wolves grew stronger than ever. They had hoped their reign would not come for a long while, even though Evelyn spent time at the palace daily to help her mother work.

Once Evelyn and Melody finished the pie, Evelyn put the tin into the sink and felt a kick to the underside of her large belly. It was so hard it felt like a balloon had popped inside her, and her stomach dropped.

"Shit," she growled, holding onto the sink.

"You're in labor," Melody squeaked. She laid her hand on her sister's lower back and felt the tightening of her stomach.

"No, I'm not." Evelyn waved her hand dismissively. "I've had these pains since last night." Evelyn grabbed a shawl and wrapped it around her body.

Melody stood with her mouth hanging open, her arms flapping at her sides. "I can feel your pain through the bond, you dumb wolf! You are in labor and ignoring Cinder's warning! She's been telling you she is in labor, too!"

Evelyn huffed, sitting on the couch. "I don't feel a head between my legs yet. I think I'm fine."

Before Melody could argue more, Kit burst through the door. His bare chest gleaming with sweat. Kit's tanned skin was brightly colored with red from exertion. Flecks of bark and debris from cutting up a fallen tree in the forest littered his hair.

"Evelyn," he barked.

Her eyes glittered with mischief. "Well, hello to you too, handsome." She winked. Trying to stand, she fell back into the love seat she had claimed since the beginning of her pregnancy. "Anything I can help you with?" She licked her lips and her eyes trailed down the enormous eight pack he was sporting. Something about being pregnant made her hornier. The nights were long, and poor Kit's cock was completely flaccid by morning. Which was a shame because she liked morning wood.

Another pop came from her pelvic region and her body let go of a tiny gush of fluid. "Damn, just looking at you gets me wet." She giggled.

"Ew, Evie, that is just gross. I'm standing right here!" Melody pointed to the ground dramatically.

"You're in my house," Evelyn countered. "I can talk sexy all I want! Fuck!" She rubbed her stomach again and Kit flinched.

"Let's go, Sugar." Kit went to bend over and pick up his mate, until her eyes widened, and she pushed away from him. Kit flinched again, now feeling the full effects of the bond being so close. "Fucking hell, this hurts," he moaned, grabbing his stomach.

"I think the baby is coming," Evelyn muttered.

Kit's eyes went wide.

"No shit, Sherlock." Melody rolled her eyes. "You feel the baby's head, don't you?"

Evelyn nodded slowly, another twitching pain between her legs reminding her she needed to move to a more comfortable position.

"I'll mind link the physicians, but it doesn't look like you are moving. You are having the baby here," Melody announced.

Kit's once angry eyes now softened to worry and pain. "She can't have it here. There isn't anyone to help!" The tree outside shuddered, sending flowers cascading around the cabin.

"Everything is going to be fine," Melody said soothingly, moving Kit to the bed. "Strip the bed and put these towels down. I'll get the first aid kit from my cabin and be right back."

Melody and Marcus had moved into a cabin. It closer to the palace than Kit and Evelyn's but still deep enough into the forest to not be disturbed. Melody wanted to be around when her sister gave birth, pausing Marcus and Melody's constant travel around Bergarian.

Once she returned, Evelyn was on the bed, her knees spread apart and sweat glistening on her brow.

"Mom and dad are on their way. Physicians are coming too, but they won't be here in time." Melody calmly said, pulling instruments from her bag. She touched her sister's knee.

"Can you hold it in?" Kit whispered to Evelyn. He didn't say it to upset her; he just worried that he would be the one helping deliver the baby. For the first time in a long while, he felt helpless. He felt like he was trapped in their dream before they had met in reality and couldn't do anything to soften the pain felt.

"Don't think it works that way," Evelyn calmly said. Despite the pain, her voice was steady. She clenched Kit's hand tightly. Her high tolerance for pain had got her into this mess. If only she had listened to her body. Instead, she was thinking of wicked ways to get knocked up all over again.

"I see a full head of hair," Melody said. "Now, just a gentle push, Evie," she warned. "Don't need you to go she-Hulk on me. This is your pup, not a rocket."

Evelyn laughed, pushing her pup out gently.

Kit held her tightly, trying to give Evelyn comfort. A mighty battle cry left the poor pup's mouth, angry that the warmth of Evelyn's womb was now gone. The flowers outside continued to fall peacefully to the forest floor while Melody wrapped the large pup in her arms.

"I'd say almost ten pounds." Melody laughed. She patted the pup's back and settled them into Kit's arms. Kit, his eyes watering, wept with joy.

"Oh gods," he whispered. Evelyn smiled up at him while he tucked the little pup's head under Evelyn's chin. The baby purred, the cries ceasing once they felt his mother's skin upon them.

"Such a beautiful pup," his voice cracked. "Sugar look what you made."

Evelyn, feeling the emotions tumble through, shook her head. "Takes two to make one, I think," she whispered.

"Sorry to break it up," Melody whispered loudly. "But the entire family is outside and want to know if it is a boy or a girl?"

Clara and Kane were trying to see past the pale white curtains, but they continued to block out the view they wanted to see. Their third grandchild, now second in line to the throne.

"The suspense is killing me!" Clara jumped on the balls of her feet. "I need to know!"

Kane gripped his mate, purring excessively in her ear. "When they are ready," he chuckled at her.

"Am I allowed to go in now?" Dr Talbert, who had tried to deliver Clara's children but was stopped by Kane each time, growled in frustration. "I don't even know why I show up to these births." He ran his hand through his hair. Kane growled, shutting him up.

The crowd grew—extended family, close friends—all stood outside the cabin to greet the newest royal. They all spoke in hushed tones, marveling at the tree that continued to rain flowers and now sparkles of gold dust.

Kit took the baby from Evelyn, letting Melody clean her sister so they could have their alone time once the baby was announced. Kit stood on the front porch holding the baby swaddled in a grey blanket. His eyes twinkled with happiness, holding the baby for all to see.

"Meet our son, Maximus," Kit exclaimed.

Clara jumped up to the porch, getting a better look at her grandson. Kane, his grip firm around his mate's middle, hovered over the tiny child that could easily fit in the palm of his hand. Eden and Elijah stood close by, watching their legacy come into fruition.

Dax, Dimitri and Seraphina's children began climbing the magical tree. Their daughter easily climbing faster than her brother. The tree wrapped a limb around her ankle, dangling her from above.

"That's my new cousin!" she exclaimed.

Suron, their nanny, frantically held out his arms, just in case the mysterious branch dropped the young girl. The crowd of family all laughed with her as they stared lovingly at the innocent baby in Kit's arms.

Once the crowd dispersed, Kit and Evelyn were left alone in their cottage. Evelyn, being the warrior she was, was already healing at a fast rate and would soon be completely healed.

"I don't know if I could go through that again," Kit muttered under his breath. His fingers playing with their son's toes.

"You didn't have to do much." Evelyn kissed his cheek as she finished feeding Maximus. "You just had to hold my hand and tell me it was okay."

Kit shook his head, his head resting on his mate's shoulder. "Fuck, it was scary. I'd rather kick Joshua's ass all over again than see you like that."

"I'd like to see that, too," a deep voice chuckled through the room. A tall gladiator stood in the corner of the room. His chest bared with just a leather strap and skirt around his waist. "Again, it is a kilt, not a damn skirt."

Evelyn snorted, waking Maximus from his sleep. The baby's eyes widened, looking at his mother and then at the God of War. In his hands, he held a tiny baby himself.

"Wanted to see the next in line to the shifter throne," he said. "But I'm on baby duty, so my mate can rest." Ares grumbled, but the sparkle in his eye when he looked down at his baby girl was that of love and affection. He did not mind at all that he was watching over his child.

Ares hovered over the bed, getting a good look at Maximus. "He will be half-beast as well, I see."

Kit smiled, thanking Ares for the information. Otherwise, they would have had to wait years to find out if Maximus carried the gene.

Before Ares could step away, his daughter reached out with her little hand reached out at the same time as Maximus stuck out his arm toward her. Their fingers hooked onto each other's, and Ares's eyebrow arched into confusion. Sitting on the bed, obviously too small for him, he let the babies touch each other.

Warm feelings filled Evelyn as she watched the two interact. "*You don't think?*" Evelyn mind-linked Kit, who was thinking the same thing.

Ares stood from the bed, breaking the contact between the babies. Both stifled a tiny cry but were quickly silenced as each parent nuzzled their faces into their children.

"She is my firstborn," Ares ruffed, holding her tightly to his chest. "I won't let her go so easily."

Ares had picked up on the connection as well, and his rage intensified. Only, he couldn't be angry, because this was the will of the goddess and of his good friend, who had done nothing but bring him happiness by helping him find his own mate. Ares' sighed heavily, kissing his daughter's forehead.

"The goddess will decide when they meet," Ares ordered. "Not a moment sooner." Before Evelyn and Kit could reply, Ares was gone.

"Our life is never boring," Evelyn said, rubbing her cheek against Kit's chest.

"This is true, but I don't think I'd change any of it." Kit placed a kiss on his mate's shoulder.

"You're right, I wouldn't. Not a damn thing."

Kit curled around his mate, who held their son in her arms. Night had fallen, and before they drifted off into the dream world where they still met every night, they whispered their, "I love yous," while their son snored happily, blissfully unaware of his own adventure to come.

If you would be so kind, please leave a loving review to help this small indie author.

Please Subscribe here for upcoming books and news!

More Books

Under the Moon Series

Under the Moon

Clara and Kane's Story

The Alpha's Kitten
Charlotte and Wesley's Story

Finding Love with the Fae King
Osirus and Melina's Story

The Exiled Dragon
Creed and Odessa's Story

Under the Moon: The Dark War
Clara, Kane, Jasper and Taliyah's story

His True Beloved: A Vampire's Second Chance
Sebastian and Christine's Story

Alpha of her Dreams
Evelyn and Kit's Story

The Broken Alpha's Princess
Melody and Marcus' Story

Twinning and Sinning From Mutts to Mates
Dax, Dimitri, and Seraphina's Story

Under the Moon: God Series

Seeking Hades' Ember
Hades and Ember's Story

Lucifer's Redemption
Lucifer and Uriel's Story

Poseidon's Island Flower
Poseidon and Lani's Story

Thanatos' Craving
Thanatos and Juniper's Story
Coming soon!

More to Come

Under the Moon: The Promised Mates of Monktona Wood Orcs

Thorn
Thorn and Ellie's Story

Valpar
Coming Soon

Sugha
Coming Soon

Iron Fang MC Series

Grim
Hawke
Bear
More to Come

Visit authorverafoxx.com
for updates and future books!

Visit authorverafoxx.com for updates and future books!
Be sure to subscribe to get naughty new books to your inbox!
Vera Foxx | Facebook

www.ingramcontent.com/pod-product-compliance
Lightning Source LLC
Chambersburg PA
CBHW070622260626
47161CB00007B/2537